James Oswald is the author  Inspector McLean series of de... new DC Constance Fairchild s... ...OKS, NATURAL CAUSES and TH... ...SOULS were both short-listed for the prestigious CWA Debut Dagger Award. ALL THAT LIVES is the twelfth book in the Inspector McLean series.

James farms Highland cows by day, writes disturbing fiction by night.

of the *Sunday Times* bestselling ... detective mysteries, as well as the ... in this series, James's first two book ... **THE BOOK OF SOULS** ...

JAMES OSWALD

ALL THAT LIVES

WILDFIRE

First published in 2022 by
WILDFIRE
an imprint of HEADLINE PUBLISHING GROUP

First published in paperback in 2022 by
WILDFIRE
an imprint of HEADLINE PUBLISHING GROUP

2

Cataloguing in Publication Data is available from the British Library

ISBN 978 1 4722 7625 4

Typeset in Aldine 401BT by Avon DataSet Ltd, Alcester, Warwickshire

Printed and bound in Great Britain by Clays Ltd, Elcograf S.p.A.

HEADLINE PUBLISHING GROUP
An Hachette UK Company
Carmelite House
50 Victoria Embankment
London EC4Y 0DZ

www.headline.co.uk
www.hachette.co.uk

For Juliet.
Who would have thought we'd make it to twenty books?

1

He stands in the half-dark, shadows all around him. Light from the street lamps bounces off the low cloud, diffusing the gloom into something hellish and wrong. This place stinks of piss and despair, the ground littered with the detritus of broken lives. Time was he would have avoided it like the plague. But now, when the rage is upon him and the sheer helplessness, his guilty feet always seem to bring him here. Same as his guilty hand grips the tiny glass bottle tight. Same as his guilty mind craves the oblivion it will bring. For a while, at least.

He hates drugs, always has. Hates what they do to people, how they change them, turn them mean and selfish. He's seen friends almost kill themselves smoking dope, injecting stuff into their veins, sniffing glue or worse. He's watched the dealers hanging around the school gates and lurking in the seedier pubs. Seen a few of them off, though he knows better than to mess with those kinds of people. He's vowed never to get involved in that kind of thing. And yet here he is.

He can't get the image out of his head. The shock and fear in that young man's eyes as he lay at the bottom of the pit. Why did he not fight? Why did he not climb out? And why did they all do exactly as they were told? Like zombies, like good little drones. They picked up the spades and shovelled the earth even as the young man begged for them to stop.

Held up to the light, the clear glass bottle shows a pale yellow liquid inside, ready to turn to vapour the moment he snaps off the top. Through it, distorted, he sees the graffiti-painted demon's head on the broken wall beyond. It laughs at him, eggs him on just as they egged each other on. All under the watchful eyes of their supervisors. Who can dig the fastest? Who can refill the hole quickest?

Not a hole, but a grave. He knows that now, so why couldn't he see it then? Just an exercise, they said. Team building, training. Brainwashing. Timothy. The young man's name was Timothy. They picked on him as the weakest. Bullied him. Threw him into the deep pit that they'd dug only hours earlier in the day. And then they shovelled that same dry earth on top of him, spade after spade until poor Timothy was covered. The weight of it dragging him deep into the earth. Covering him, pinning him down, filling his mouth and nose, smothering him as he tried in vain to escape.

He shudders so hard at the memory he almost drops the bottle. Perhaps that would be better. Let it go to waste. Get his head straight. Go to the police. Confess. But he knows he will never do that. They would kill him first, just like poor Timothy. And there are more bottles where this one came from, an endless supply.

He hates drugs, but he is trapped by what he has done. What they made him do. He needs the brief respite the hit will give him, even as he knows the ghost of Timothy will haunt him for ever.

He cracks the bottle. Breathes deep.

2

The dopplering sound of a passing fire engine assaulted Detective Sergeant Janie Harrison's ears as she clambered out of the car. Not a great start to the working day. The call had come in as she'd been heading to the canteen for a much-needed coffee, and she had a horrible feeling she was going to regret missing it.

'What's the story, John?' She knew the constable manning the cordon from her own uniform days, standing shoulder to shoulder as they watched the crowd at Meadowbank. She'd escaped this part of the city, and couldn't say she missed it. Not many did, if the lack of onlookers was anything to go by. There wasn't a soul to be seen who wasn't either a police officer or a forensics technician.

'Young lad by the name of Rory Devlin. Body's about forty yards away into the rubble there.' The constable pointed along a marked pathway that ran more or less straight through the derelict remains of an old stone warehouse. Piles of rock, broken up concrete and rusted rebar lay in heaps that looked like someone had once tried to impose some order on the chaos, but if so it had been a long time ago. Scrubby grass poked from every crack in the concrete floor that wasn't covered in broken glass, rubbish bags, discarded needles and used condoms. A few shrubby bushes sprouted single use carrier bag flowers from every branch.

'What is this place?' Janie asked.

'Used to be a lumber yard, about thirty years back. Least that's what my sarge told me.'

'He tell you who found the body?'

'Aye, some kids playin' aboot. Should'a bin in school, ken?'

Janie shrugged, only half taking in the information as she looked around the area beyond the derelict warehouse. The bulk of Arthur's Seat shouldered its way into the low clouds to the south-west, but closer in were drab, low tenements, their windows eyeless sockets on this less favoured area of the city. A few high-rise tower blocks dotted the scene, monuments to the dream of social housing. To the north, she knew, lay the industrial area around Leith Docks, the Firth of Forth and beyond that Fife.

'Crime Scene Manager's set up just inside the wall there, ma'am.'

'Sorry?' Janie dragged her attention back to the case in hand, once again regretting the lack of coffee and the sleepless night that meant she needed it. 'Don't call me ma'am, John. I'm barely a year older than you.'

The constable grinned as he lifted the tape for her to stoop under. 'Aye, Sarge.'

Janie shook her head in mock disgust, then beckoned her companion over. Detective Constable Cass Mitchell was one of the new intake to Police Scotland's Edinburgh Major Investigation Teams. She had the makings of a good detective, as far as Janie was concerned. All she needed was to be a bit more assertive. It didn't help that her tall, slim frame, black skin and short-cropped hair marked her out as something of an oddity among the majority pasty-white inhabitants of the city.

'Come on, Cass. Let's go see what all the fuss is about, eh?'

Mitchell nodded, giving PC John a half-smile as he lifted the tape a little higher for her than he had for Janie. They went straight to the nearest forensic service van, struggled into white paper overalls and paper overshoes that didn't look like they'd last long given the state of the crime scene. Janie signed herself in, handing the clipboard to Mitchell to do the same.

'That way?' She pointed towards the centre of the roofless warehouse, receiving a curt nod from the forensic technician as he took back the clipboard. Another one having a bad morning, then.

A white plastic tent had been set up over a patch of broken concrete and scrubby ground beside what must once have been a substantial internal wall. The approach took them past the part of the building that had survived the best, although that only meant the brickwork rose slightly higher than Janie's head and still had some lime plaster clinging to it like plaque on a rotten tooth. Graffiti covered every exposed surface, layers of it defining the changing years. Janie recognised a few as gang markers, a history of turf warfare in this deprived part of the city. The topmost sigil, and presumably the most recent, was one she'd not seen before though. A stylised devil, with sharp teeth and pointed horns, something like steam or smoke seemed to rise from it as if it had only recently crawled out of hell. Seeing it gave her an involuntary shudder, which didn't bode well for what was inside the tent.

'OK to go in?' she asked of another suited forensic technician standing at the entrance. Like the man with the clipboard, Janie didn't recognise this one. Not that it was easy once they were fully suited up.

'Sure. Pathologist's already in there, mind, so it's a bit of a squeeze.'

'I'll wait, shall I?' DC Mitchell said. Janie looked to her, the forensic technician and then back the way they had come. Not many SOCOs about, for a dead body.

5

'Probably for the best. I'll give you a shout if I need you to look at something. Meantime get all the details about our Mr Devlin. We'll need to speak to his next of kin, sort out positive identification. You know the drill.'

Mitchell nodded once, the relief evident on her face. Not her first dead body, Janie knew, but obviously not something she was eager to see. Right then, best get on with it. She grabbed the edge of the flap closing the tent, pulled it open and stepped inside.

The first thing she noticed was the smell. There had been an all too familiar reek about the derelict warehouse, that mixture of rotting garbage, piss and the charred remains of pallet bonfires. Nothing that had set her internal alarms ringing, anyway. Now, Janie felt the scent tickling her sinuses like the onset of hay fever, and bringing with it an almost citrus tang like those little toilet cakes you sometimes found in urinals. Not that she had a great deal of experience of that sort of thing, thank Christ.

'Detective Sergeant Harrison. What an unexpected delight.'

Distracted by the smell, Janie hadn't immediately noticed the white boiler-suited man standing on the far side of the tent. Not like her to be quite so unobservant, although in fairness Angus Cadwallader blended in with the plastic canvas fairly well. Crouched down like a mother tying her wayward child's shoelace, his assistant, Tracy Sharp, looked around and gave Janie a pained smile. And that was when she finally saw the body.

How she had missed it was beyond her, although a sleepless night and insufficient caffeine might have had something to do with it. He was young, late teens or maybe very early twenties judging by the mottled acne on his face. He wore the standard uniform of all the city's indigent youth, dark jogging pants, expensive but stained and worn trainers, hoodie zipped up tight to his neck. He lay sprawled on his back, legs bent, arms twisted around at improbable angles, but it was his eyes that made Janie glad she'd missed breakfast. Bulging and bloodshot, they stared up in agony.

'Dear God. What happened to him?' She took a step closer, then stopped, turned her attention back to the pathologist. 'Sorry, Dr Cadwallader, Dr Sharp. It's good to see you both.'

'I'll have to admit he had much the same effect on me when I first saw him, and I've had far more experience of cadavers than you, I'd wager. Come.' The pathologist beckoned Janie closer, crouching down as Dr Sharp moved to make room. Janie wasn't sure she wanted to get any nearer the body, but this was the job.

'What happened to him?'

'And that, my dear, is where you differ from your esteemed colleague Tony McLean. He would ask me immediately for a time of death, even though he knows full well I can't give him one. It's his little joke, you see.' Cadwallader's smile faded quickly into something more of a frown. 'Alas, I can't easily answer your question either. He appears to have suffered multiple injuries consistent with a beating. Certainly the way he's lying would suggest as much.'

'I can sense a "but" coming.' Janie looked more closely at the young man's body, twisted and bent like something from a car accident.

'Not so much a "but" as a niggling suspicion all is not as it seems here.'

'You mean he's not been beaten to death and thrown out with the trash?'

Cadwallader tilted his head slightly, the closest the man ever came to a shrug in Janie's experience. 'He's dead, most likely from the injuries we can see here. Both his arms are dislocated at the shoulder, judging by the angle they're lying at. I'd be surprised if he didn't have fractured ribs, possible fractures to his pelvis, legs. Poor lad's a mess.'

'Certainly seems to have been in a great deal of pain.' Janie risked another look at the dead man's agonised face, and then she saw what she'd missed earlier. 'But nobody touched his head. No split lip, no bruised cheeks, no broken nose.' And it wasn't as if his eyes were swollen shut either, quite the opposite.

'I've seen punishment beatings where they've left the victim's face untouched before,' Cadwallader said. 'Usually that's a pimp taking out his anger on a sex worker though.'

'You think he might have been . . . ?' Janie started to ask the question, then shook her head to dismiss it. Yes, the city had its fair share of male sex workers, rent boys and the like, but violence meted out on them tended to focus on the head rather than avoid it. Still, it would be worth having a chat with DCI Dexter, if only on the off chance the whole investigation could be passed over to Vice.

'That's for you to find out, I think.' Cadwallader bent down with much creaking of joints, then pointed his gloved hand at the torso. 'I'm not sure what to make of the state of his clothes, though.'

Janie focused once more on the hoodie, a glimpse of T-shirt at the neck. The sweat pants and those once-expensive trainers. 'They're surprisingly clean.'

'Quite so. You might think that he'd been beaten up elsewhere and then dumped here, but if you have a look underneath.' Cadwallader nodded to his assistant and together they gently rolled the body enough for Janie to get a glimpse. Where the material of the hoodie was clean at the front, the back was both ingrained with the dirt from the derelict warehouse site, and ripped right through to pale skin.

'Could that come from, I don't know, throwing him to the ground?' She looked around the tent, taking in the jumble of detritus on the floor. No obvious difference to the detritus everywhere else.

'Possible, but it seems excessive.'

As they let the body back down again, it groaned like an old man reaching for the floor. Janie almost jumped back in shock, then noticed that strange chemical lemon reek again.

'What is that smell?'

Cadwallader sniffed, leaned in close to the dead man's face and sniffed again. 'I'm not sure. Not yet, at least. It's coming from him though. Possibly something he ate. We'll know better once I've done the post-mortem. I'll prioritise it, since this is most certainly suspicious, and not a little odd.'

Janie grimaced. Odd seemed to be her stock-in-trade these days. The perils of working with Detective Inspector McLean.

'Just as well the boss is on his way then.'

3

It wasn't the most efficient way of getting around the city, but Detective Inspector McLean liked to walk whenever he could. The rhythm of his feet on the pavement helped him think, and the time away from his desk meant fewer distractions. That he still hadn't managed to replace his old Alfa Romeo after it had been stolen and crashed might have had something to do with it too, although this time he had cadged a lift in a squad car most of the way to the crime scene.

He couldn't remember the last time he'd visited this part of the city; a few years at least. The fronts of the tenements still bore the blackened soot from coal fires that had gone out a half-century earlier, and the whole area felt run down. Even so, here and there the signs of encroaching development showed that Edinburgh's demand for housing was as insatiable as ever. How long before the old lumber yard became a modern, and expensive, apartment block? McLean wasn't entirely sure why it hadn't already.

'MacNaughton's Timber. I remember when this place was still trading,' he said to the young uniform constable manning the cordon as he showed his warrant card.

'Been derelict as long as I've known it, sir.'

McLean chose to take that as an innocent response, rather

than a criticism of his advanced years. Ducking under the tape, he headed for the yard entrance, where a cluster of officers and forensic technicians were deep in conversation. By the time he'd signed in, pulled on paper overalls, and followed the marked path to where he was told the body lay, the pathologist and his assistant were both standing outside the small plastic tent, talking to DS Harrison.

'Morning, Tony.' Cadwallader greeted him first. 'I'm afraid young Janie's beaten you to it.'

'Sir.' Harrison ducked her head in that way she had. Not quite a nod, neither a shrug.

'What's the story then?'

'Young man by the name of Rory Devlin. Looks to have been beaten up and dumped. It's . . . He's not a pretty sight.'

McLean looked down at the ground, strewn with rubbish. He could see needles and the odd condom in amongst the empty plastic cider bottles and crushed Special Brew tins. 'Junkie?'

'Hard to say.' The pathologist waved an open hand at the entrance to the tent. 'Maybe best if you look for yourself.'

McLean had known he would have to, but that didn't make it any less unpleasant a task. He pulled back the entrance flap and stepped inside, Cadwallader following behind.

The first thing he noticed was the smell, a sour mixture of rubbish, ordure and, over the top of everything else, a strange chemical citrus tang. It dissipated quickly in the airflow from the opening, becoming little more than a vague memory as McLean concentrated on the body. Harrison had been accurate in her description, the young man's twisted and broken limbs screaming of a painful end. At least there wasn't any blood.

'Most of the damage appears to be to his limbs and torso. If he's been beaten up, then they deliberately avoided his face.' Cadwallader trod a careful path around the corpse until he was at the head, then crouched down. McLean bent forward a little, but felt no need to get any closer than he already had.

'Time of death?' he asked, and saw the twitch of a smile on his old friend's face.

'I'd have thought you'd be more interested in cause,' the pathologist said. 'That'll have to wait for the post-mortem though. Like I said to Janie out there, it looks like a beating gone too far, but there's a few things I need to examine more closely to be sure.'

McLean straightened up, his back creaking with the effort. The dead man certainly looked like he'd been mangled and then thrown out with the trash. Not much consolation for Rory Devlin, but a simple gangland turf war beating gone too far would keep the senior officers and bean counters happy, even if finding out whoever was responsible might prove tricky. Why then did he feel like this was only the beginning of something much more complicated?

'Let me know when you're doing the PM then, Angus.'

'Will do. Should be able to fit him in quite soon.'

'Thanks.' He turned away from the body, pushed open the entrance flap and breathed in the relatively fresh air from outside. 'Guess I'd better go and inform the family then.'

According to the records they'd managed to find so far, Rory Devlin was nineteen years old and lived in a semi-detached bungalow on the northern edge of Restalrig. Not far from where the body had been found, it was nevertheless too far to walk, especially given the threat of rain in the air. Leaving DC Mitchell with the crime scene team, Harrison drove them in the silent electric Nissan pool car that was the butt of many a station joke but surprisingly comfortable nonetheless. They parked across the street and stared out at the unremarkable house for a moment. Neat, quiet, not the best suburb but a far cry from the derelict lumber yard.

'You get any answer from Family Liaison about sending out an officer?' McLean asked as Harrison unclipped her seatbelt and reached for the door handle.

'Aye, they said someone would be here in half an hour, an' that was forty minutes ago.'

McLean shrugged. Everyone was busy, overworked, over-stretched. 'Might as well get started then. Soonest is always best when breaking bad news.'

A girl of maybe sixteen opened the door a few moments after he'd pressed the doorbell, her eyes narrowing in a suspicious glare. That same look he'd seen on countless others down the years; the scowl that said you'd better have a good reason for this unwarranted disturbance.

'I'm looking for Mrs Elizabeth Devlin?' McLean went to pull out his warrant card, but before he had the chance, the girl turned and shouted 'Mum!' loud enough to wake the dead.

'Who're youse?' she asked once she was done with that.

'Detective Inspector McLean. This is my colleague Detective Sergeant Harrison. Would I be right in thinking this is the home of Rory Devlin?'

'What's that waster gone an' done now?' The girl raised her eyes to the heavens, but before she could say any more, an older version of her appeared in the doorway, drying her hands on a dishcloth. She took the two detectives in with a single, sweeping gaze.

'Did you say this was about Rory?' she asked.

'Are you Mrs Devlin?' McLean countered.

'Aye, I'm his mum. What's this . . .' And then the penny dropped. McLean had seen it all too many times before, much like the scathing contempt. The dull realisation that there were two police officers at the door, in the middle of the day, asking about a member of the family. That could never be good news.

'Perhaps we might come in?'

Mrs Devlin opened the door a little wider, almost tripping over her daughter who was standing right behind her.

'Away to your room, Maggie,' she shouted, shooing the girl away with the dishcloth.

'I'm no' a bairn, Mum,' the girl complained.

'Aye, well act your age and do as you're told.'

The girl flounced away, stomped up a narrow set of stairs that must lead to a dormer room at the back of the bungalow. Moments later McLean heard the slam of a door.

'Teenagers.' Mrs Devlin rolled her eyes, then indicated with her free hand for them to follow her. She led them to a compact living room at the back of the house, looking out over a short garden that appeared to open onto parkland. It took McLean a moment to get his bearings, but it must have been Craigentinny Golf Course, which would have added a sizeable chunk to the value of the house.

'Perhaps you'd like to sit down, Mrs Devlin,' McLean said before she could get out the question she no doubt wanted to ask. Worry painted her face in lines, and she was twisting the dishcloth between her hands as if it was a chicken to be killed for the pot. She did as she was told, and McLean sat on the small sofa beside her.

'Your son, Rory. Have you seen him recently?'

'He went out last night, about ten, mebbe? Din't come home, but then that's no' unusual. Why? What's he done?'

'I'm very sorry, Mrs Devlin. There's no easy way to put this. We discovered the body of a young man in some waste ground near Restalrig Road first thing this morning. We have reason to believe he is your son.' McLean nodded at Harrison, who was still standing. She tapped the screen of her phone to bring up the photograph. It showed only the young man's head, and after the pathologist had closed his bulging, bloodshot eyes, but there was still no hiding the fact it was a dead person.

'Is this Rory, Mrs Devlin?' she asked, her voice as sympathetic as McLean had ever heard it. The woman stared at the picture for a moment, reached towards the phone as if to take it. Then her hand withdrew like she'd been stung, and she crammed it into her mouth. Tears glistened in her eyes.

'My . . . My boy.' It came out as a wail of pure anguish. More than enough confirmation for now, although they would have to arrange for a formal identification soon. Something for the Family Liaison Officer to sort out when they finally arrived. McLean scanned the room, his eyes coming to rest on the mantelpiece and a collection of family photographs. Even from where he sat he could see plenty that included a Mr Devlin, and a few of a younger Rory too.

'Is your husband at work?' He pulled out his own phone. 'I can call him for you.'

The words seemed to bring Mrs Devlin back to her senses. She dabbed at her eyes with the dishcloth, took one last look at the image on Harrison's phone and then waved it away before fixing McLean with a glare that could strip paint.

'What happened to him? What did youse do to him?'

'We don't know exactly what happened yet. He was only found a few hours ago. We're working on the theory that he was mugged. Do you know any reason why someone might do that?'

McLean knew he was on thin ice asking. Mrs Devlin had the pale face and rabbit in the headlights stare of someone going into shock. He should really be trying to get in touch with her husband, and maybe he should have waited for the Family Liaison Officer before even knocking on the door. On the other hand, a young man was dead and every minute that passed decreased the likelihood of finding whoever might be responsible for that.

'I . . . I need to call my husband.' McLean's initial offer to do the same had finally worked its way into Mrs Devlin's conscious thoughts. A task she could fixate upon.

'Would you like me to do that?' he asked again. 'I'll need his number.'

A brief pause, and then Mrs Devlin shook her head. 'He'll be driving the bus right now. No phones while you're on shift.'

'He's a bus driver?' McLean slipped his phone away, took out his notepad. 'If you let me know the details, I'll have an officer contact the depot. Given the circumstances, I'm sure they'll arrange a replacement driver and we can get him home as quickly as possible.'

4

McLean settled into the chair behind his desk with a weary sigh and a creak of un-oiled springs. Through the glass wall, he could see across the rooftops towards Arthur's Seat, still shrouded in grey cloud. Summer had been long and hot, the city a sweltering, stinking mess. But recently the wind had taken on an edge, like a mugger after your best coat. The light had that autumn hue to it that meant winter was on its way, and a hard winter at that. Not that there was ever a good time to investigate an unexplained death, but this surely wasn't it.

The initial report into Rory Devlin's sorry end lay on the desk in front of him. Much of the legwork had been done swiftly, a testament to DS Harrison's efficiency. As predicted, the door-to-door interviews had yielded nothing, and that part of town wasn't exactly well covered with CCTV. If someone had beaten up the young man and then dumped him, then it would be up to forensics to provide any clues they could find. McLean didn't hold out any great hopes there. Something else bothered him about the whole thing, though. It didn't sit right, and having had a couple of days to think, he still couldn't put a finger on why.

'Penny for your thoughts?'

He looked up to the open doorway, where Detective Super-intendent Jayne McIntyre stood, one arm leaning against the frame. She'd gone very grey in the past year, no doubt exacerbated by her sudden and unexpected promotion to station chief. Although promotion wasn't really the word for it. More having the responsibility dumped on her shoulders until such time as a replacement could be found for Chief Superintendent Elmwood.

'I doubt they're worth half as much.' He stood up, indicating they both sit at the conference table on the other side of the office. As he poured coffee, McLean told her about his misgivings.

'Drug overdose would be the better option,' he said as McIntyre sipped her coffee. 'Not for the poor lad, of course, but at least it's a simple report to the PF and on to the next job.'

'But you don't think that's what this is.' The detective superintendent didn't even bother with making it a question. How well she knew him.

'My instinct tells me no. I mean, there's drugs involved, for sure. But not your usual kind. Until we know what actually killed him and when, there's not much we can do. I'm waiting to see what Angus comes up with. Can't help thinking this is going to be a difficult one, though.'

Now McIntyre grimaced, and McLean knew that it wasn't at the coffee.

'Well, I've some news you may or may not want to hear, then.'

'Oh yes? Have they finally decided on a new station chief?' He couldn't think of anything else that would warrant this kind of meeting. Not that it wasn't always nice to have a quiet chat.

'In a manner of speaking.'

'That doesn't sound good.'

'Well, it depends on your point of view. They've decided that since I've done such a good job these past few months they're going to make my position official. I get to be a chief super once the paperwork's done, which is nice. Can't say the extra money won't help either, now that Susan's not working.'

McLean recalled McIntyre's partner and her long struggle with cancer. The last time they'd met he'd been impressed with her strength of will, but he knew well enough that could have been a front to hide the pain and exhaustion within. It wasn't as if he was a stranger to such play-acting himself.

'Congratulations. You deserve far more for what you've had to put up with.' He didn't add, 'me, for one thing.'

'Yes, well. Before you break out the celebratory champagne, there's a little catch.'

He'd known there would be. There always was.

'The position is only part time. A job-share, as it were.' McIntyre put considerable venom into the phrase, although whether it was because of the half-hearted promotion or whoever it was she would have to share the position with, McLean wasn't sure. A bit of both, probably. Which begged the obvious question.

'So who gets to share your desk then?'

Even as he asked it, he knew. As if a window had opened into the detective superintendent's mind and he could see her thoughts as clear as day.

'Chief Superintendent Elmwood has been given the all clear by her doctors. She'll be starting again at the beginning of next week.'

'Really? After what happened to her? I thought burns took years to heal.' And never mind the mental scars from being tied up in a makeshift pyre by some lunatic extremist men's rights activist determined to burn her as a witch.

'Well, apparently she's had some experimental new treatment, and I have to say it's worked well. You'd not know what happened to look at her.'

'Experimental? How did she get picked for that?' McLean heard the criticism in his voice as the words came out, and added:

'not that she doesn't deserve it as much as anyone, of course.' Which only made it worse.

'That's all down to Jane Louise Dee,' McIntyre said, and McLean decided maybe his criticism was deserved after all.

'What's she got to do with it?'

'It's her medical research facility that has been working on the therapy, for one thing. And apparently she and Gail had become friends before . . . what happened.' McIntyre's face was a picture of disbelief that must have mirrored McLean's own. 'I know. Surprised me too. It's all academic anyway. She'll be back at work part time on Monday, so you've got a few days yet to get yourself prepared.'

The city mortuary had always been a place of strange refuge for McLean. His grandmother had worked there as senior pathologist for years and had never felt shy about bringing her grandson and ward to work if it was inconvenient to leave him at home. It was probably there that he'd first thought about becoming a police officer, rather than following his grandmother into medicine or his long-dead father into law. Now, as he pushed through the entrance door and was buzzed in by the receptionist without a second glance, he felt some semblance of calm begin to fall.

It probably shouldn't have been a huge surprise that Elmwood was returning to work. The allegation that she might have murdered her former lover had dissolved away like a Forth haar in the sun after she'd become the victim of a savage attack. More surprising, and alarming, was her relationship with Jane Louise Dee. If Elmwood was single-minded in her determination to succeed, it was nothing compared to Dee. The two of them together could mean nothing good. Not for Police Scotland, and certainly not for him.

'Ah, Tony. You got my email then.'

Angus Cadwallader's voice broke through McLean's

meandering thoughts, and for a moment he couldn't quite work out how he'd come to be in the examination theatre.

'Actually, no. Sorry, Angus. I needed to get out of the station, and this seemed like the obvious place to come.'

The central table was occupied by a pasty-white cadaver, partially covered with a sheet to hide its modesty. He recognised the young man from the derelict lumber yard.

'Bad news?' the pathologist asked.

'Unwelcome, for sure. Bad? I couldn't really say.' McLean told his old friend all he had learned from McIntyre earlier. Cadwallader's face turned ever more sombre as the tale unfolded, although he was wise enough to make no comment.

'Was this what you wanted to talk to me about, then?' McLean gestured towards the young man, his face less harrowing now than when he'd seen it first, but alarming nonetheless. Dark pink acne spots and scars flecked his deathly cheeks, making him seem even younger than his actual nineteen years.

'Indeed it was. Interesting and disturbing. We thought maybe he'd been beaten up, you'll recall.'

McLean did, and that still seemed the obvious conclusion. He'd learned over a long career that obvious was often both misleading and wrong.

'Well, I'm beginning to revise my opinion now that I've had a good look at him.' Cadwallader moved around the table so that he was standing opposite McLean, reached down and picked up the young man's arm by the wrist and elbow.

'He has fractures in his arms, and both of his shoulders are dislocated. Those injuries don't match up with the bruising though, at least not well enough.'

'You're suggesting he did this to himself? Some kind of . . . What? Epileptic fit? Is that even possible?'

The pathologist smiled as if McLean were a poor student unexpectedly coming up with the right answer to a trick question.

'Not impossible, Tony. My initial conclusion is he's had a fit so violent it's torn his muscles and tendons, broken bones and then killed him. But this young man has no history of epilepsy. There was this found in his clothing though.' Cadwallader left the examination table and crossed the room to the counter that ran along one wall. A clear plastic evidence bag lay on a tray and he brought both back for McLean to see. A few fragments of thin, medical-grade glass.

'Forensics found the remains of an ampoule on the ground close by him. Manda Parsons has taken it off for analysis to see if we can work out what was in it. I'll send her these pieces and she can see if they fit.'

McLean looked from the bag back down to the twisted body. 'I've never seen poppers do something like that though.'

'Poppers? How quaint.' Cadwallader shook his head slowly. 'No, Tony. This is merely a delivery device. I very much doubt Mr Devlin here was sniffing amyl nitrate.'

'Something new then? But even so.' McLean gestured at the body. 'Could sniffing something really cause this kind of damage?'

'That depends entirely on what the ampoule contained. Hopefully Manda will come up with something, but we'll do a full tox screen on his blood and the contents of his stomach, too. Soon as we've opened him up.' Cadwallader returned the tray and evidence bag to the counter. 'I'm going to have a wee look at his brain too. Get some fluid from that for tests. I know you're not so keen on the saw.'

McLean knew a dismissal when he heard one, and his old friend had the truth of it. He wasn't exactly squeamish, hard to be when his grandmother had been a pathologist for the city for most of her career. More he didn't exactly relish the thought of watching a person being cut up. He was even OK with seeing the results, but not the procedure that led to them.

'Let me know how you get on then, Angus.' He began to turn away, then stopped himself for a moment. 'And thanks. I think. I had a suspicion this case was going to be a headache. Nice to have that confirmed, I guess.'

5

'I think this one's probably beyond my jurisdiction.'

McLean stood at the edge of a deep hole, peering down at a couple of hard-hatted figures as they knelt beside a body that was little more than a skeleton wrapped in the mud. As they both turned and looked up at him, he saw that the subject of their study was lying on its side, knees bent and arms half drawn up to where its chest would have been. He was no expert, but that didn't look like any Christian burial. A quick glance at the old kirk confirmed that the orientation of the grave was all wrong too.

'Tony. What brings you to our little excavation?' Professor Hattie Turner, lecturer in forensic archaeology at the university and occasional consultant to Police Scotland, wiped at her brow with the back of her gloved hand, leaving a dark brown smear in its wake.

'Crime scene a bit east of here. I was there yesterday morning, needed to go back for another look. Thought I'd drop by and see what you two have been up to.' He nodded at the other woman in the trench. 'Em's told me so much about everything you've been finding. Fascinating stuff, and of course I don't have to worry about your bodies.'

'Indeed not,' Professor Turner said. 'Nothing in here's less than a couple of centuries old, I'd say. And this poor dear's been down here a lot longer than that.'

McLean knew most of the story already, thanks to Emma's new-found enthusiasm for forensic archaeology. This particular dig was a last-chance exploration before the extension to the tramline was laid from the city centre down to Leith, after early excavations had discovered the graveyard extended much further past the current boundary and into the road. Forensic archaeology was Professor Turner's area of expertise, although none of the bodies uncovered so far could be treated as suspicious.

'What's the story with this one, then?' He waved a hand at the bones, deeper than the rest of the graves marked around the excavation site now that he thought about it.

'A mystery,' Professor Turner said. 'Middle-aged woman by the look of the skeleton, but she was put here long before they built the kirk. Could be five, seven hundred years ago. More, maybe. And she looks more dumped than buried, too.'

'A murder victim?' McLean couldn't help but ask, even though he knew it was nothing he'd need to worry about. Seventy years was the cut-off for investigating buried human remains, not seven hundred.

'Who knows?' The professor shrugged, absentmindedly rubbed a little more mud onto her forehead. 'We'll get her out and into the lab. Run some carbon dating tests, study the skeleton. But I expect this is one crime that will remain for ever unsolved.'

'Well, I'll leave you to it.' McLean took one last look at the skeleton half consumed by the dark-brown earth, felt a little shudder run through him. As if someone had just walked over his grave, as his grandmother used to say, even though a more enthusiastic atheist you'd have been hard put to find. He was turning away from the trench when Emma's voice stopped him.

'You going to be late in again, Tony?'

It wasn't an unreasonable question, all things considered. He knew he had a habit of letting the job absorb him totally, forgetting about little things like life and home. If someone had to be the voice of his conscience, then he could do far worse than it be Emma Baird.

'Do my best to be home by six,' he said before adding 'I'll pick something up for tea on my way, shall I?' as a peace offering. Whether he'd want to eat after the things he'd seen recently was another question altogether.

The walk from Constitution Street across to Restalrig Road and then down to the old lumber yard was enough to let his mind settle and begin to consider what was going to be a difficult case. McLean had been thrown by McIntyre's news about the chief superintendent returning to work, and Cadwallader's initial post-mortem results had only made things more complicated. If Rory Devlin hadn't been beaten up, then at least they weren't looking at a murder investigation. On the other hand, if he'd overdosed on a new drug, something nobody had seen before, and in such a violent fashion, they would need to trace its source before someone else went the same way. Follow the young man's last movements, speak to his friends, known associates. Piece together a picture of the life cut so horrifically short.

There was no sign of any forensics team by the time he arrived at the derelict yard. A couple of bored constables manned the cordon, but McLean couldn't see much justification in keeping the site protected for long if this was not going to be considered a murder investigation. He doubted they'd have found any useful evidence even if it had been, such was the state of the place.

Walking through the wasteland, he could vaguely remember when it had been a working business, albeit one firmly rooted in much earlier times. As he picked a route around the piles of rubble and waist-height walls, he pictured an open courtyard, stacked high with treated timbers on big metal shelves. There had been two open-fronted buildings, one either side of the yard, and at the back a larger closed warehouse. Had he come here once, looking for some hardwood to mend one of the windows in his Newington tenement flat? McLean stood in what must have been more or less the centre of the site and tried to remember. If he had done, it would have been thirty years ago. Before he joined Lothian and Borders police. Christ, where had the time gone?

There wasn't much to show where the body had lain. Forensics had wasted little time in taking down their white plastic tent and carting it away. Only a couple of numbered flags marked the spot. McLean crouched down where the young man's feet had been, not so much studying the ground as letting his mind wander.

Why had Rory Devlin come in here? Evidence pointed to his taking drugs, but the weather wasn't exactly conducive to doing that outdoors. There were better places to shelter, surely? Then again, you didn't have to look far to see evidence of all manner of drug taking here. Judging by the glistening needles, discarded syringes, tiny squares of foil and other rubbish strewn about, this patch of derelict ground was junky central. Harrison had mentioned the graffiti, and how it mapped the rise and fall of the various gangs that claimed this part of the city. Looking around he could see what she meant.

Standing again, McLean let out a low *oof* of noise, partly at the twinge in his hip, partly because he seemed to be doing that a lot these days. He tried to trace the route through the rubbish that would have brought the young man to this spot. There was a path of sorts, winding past the clumps of broken brickwork, through the remains of a wide door that had once opened onto the sawmill. He followed it, finding himself in what was left of the warehouse itself, the back wall almost intact to a height of maybe two metres. Beyond that, if memory served, lay the old disused railway line. A cycle path for the brave or foolhardy.

Thick cloud hung low overhead, dulling the light as the day faded towards evening. The nights were fast drawing in, but even so he could make out the artistic endeavours of uncounted hundreds of spray can warriors who had graced this ruin. Graffiti covered the entire length of wall still standing, layer upon layer telling of how long it had been since the lumber yard had closed down. At the corners, there were the usual barely literate claims of sexual perversion and infidelity on the part of unknown Keiths, Brendas, Garys and Bobs, the inevitable cock and balls, with or without spurting tip, and a few impotent political cries. Scrawled out in one colour, it was easy to see where the artist had paused for thought, or simply trying to figure out how a word often spoken was actually spelled, by the way the paint spotted and then dripped downwards. So much he could find on any vertical surface away from the city centre, but it was the more skilfully wrought work in the middle of the wall that caught McLean's attention.

His first thought was that it was some kind of stencil, but the more he looked at the line of grinning skull-like heads, the more he could see differences between each one. They were painted in various colours, but all bore the same red-spot eyes, the twin pointed horns, and what looked like a stylised rain cloud above and in front of them. There were no words written, not even the strangely morphed letters that spelled nothing unless you were an inducted member of whichever gang they represented. Only this disconcerting line of grinning devils.

He pulled out his phone, tapped at the screen until he found the camera function, and did his best in the failing light to take pictures. One of the new detective constables could run a search, see if this was some new territorial marker that might shed a light on how Rory Devlin had met his end. It was a long shot, McLean knew. But right now it was all they had.

6

Detective Sergeant Janie Harrison squinted through bleary eyes at the little numbers in the top right corner of her computer screen, trying to reconcile what they were telling her with what she thought the time should be. It was late, well past shift change, and there was still a mountain of work to do. So much for the dream of promotion.

It didn't help that she'd hardly slept a wink these past few days, a combination of new neighbours in the flat below and that time of the month. The first she could deal with by bending a few rules and having a couple of uniform constables knock on the door at an inconvenient moment. The second? Well, give it a while and try not to bite the heads off any of the junior officers.

The dead body in the derelict lumber yard hadn't helped. How she'd ended up being assigned the Rory Devlin case she had no idea. Probably because it had weird written all over it, which meant DI McLean would be involved, and that meant she would be too.

On balance, she didn't mind being his understudy. He was a strange man, for sure, but Janie didn't think she'd ever met someone so utterly unmoved by naked ambition. It helped that he was loaded, of course, but even then he still put in the hours, more than the hours, in pursuit of the truth. And damn the consequences. He could have been a chief super by now, but he just wanted to solve the puzzles. Would she be so dedicated to the job if they offered her the keys to the management level?

Chance would be a fine thing. It wasn't a year yet since she'd made sergeant, and already it was doing her head in. She grabbed the mouse, moved the cursor to the next file, clicked. Her phone rang at exactly the same time, a familiar name on the screen, but the word 'office' appended. Clearly she wasn't the only one working late.

'Hey Manda. What's up?'

'Hi J. You home yet?'

Janie glanced up at the wall behind her computer screen as if checking. 'I wish. See you're in the lab still too. When did we get so boring?'

Parsons let out a low chuckle that sounded almost lascivious once the poor phone signal had compressed and tweaked it. 'Comes in waves, J. Now's a bad time, I know. But give it a week or two and we'll be footloose and fancy-free again.'

'Aye, well. I'll believe it when it happens. You just calling for a chat, or do you want me to pick up something for supper on the way home?'

'Ooh, that sounds like an idea. Quite fancy a pizza if you're passing Benito's. Maybe ask him to go a bit easy on the anchovies this time.' Parsons paused, but Janie had known her flatmate long enough to wait.

'But seriously. I was calling about that wee ampoule the team found. Your dead body in the derelict lumber yard?'

'You manage to get something out of it for analysis? Thought it'd be too clean.' Janie clicked an icon on her screen to bring up the window with the report she'd been editing, her tired eyes making a blur of the tiny print.

'Every contact leaves a trace, remember?'

'Aye, but glass ampoule and something that's designed to vaporise?'

'Oh ye of little faith.' Parsons paused again. 'Though to be fair, it wasn't easy getting anything, and I don't think you're going to like the results much.'

Janie said nothing, only raising an eyebrow to DC Mitchell as she entered the room clearly looking for someone.

'Not going to ask?' Parsons said after a while. 'Suit yourself. I'll put it all in detail in the report, but the bottom line is whatever was in that ampoule is new. Doesn't match up with anything we've seen before. Closest match isn't any kind of recreational drug at all.'

'You're going to tell me what it is though, Manda,' Janie said, as much to let Mitchell know she was on the phone as anything. The young DC loitered just far enough away to make it clear she wasn't trying to listen in on the conversation, honestly.

'Something the Russians cooked up a couple of decades back. Remember that hostage situation, the audience in a theatre? They pumped their special gas into the building to make everyone fall unconscious, kidnappers and victims all the same. Plan was special forces could go in and deal with them once they were under. Only it didn't quite work that way. Half of the victims died.'

'Let me guess. The gas made them spasm like they were having fits?'

'Only a couple. Most of them it just stopped their hearts. The PMs make for fascinating reading. Only injuries were from falling over when they breathed the gas in. Nothing else at all to show what killed them and no residual traces in the bloodstream.'

Janie rubbed at her face with her free hand. She didn't like where this conversation was going, but at least Manda hadn't brought it home with her. Who was she kidding? This was all they'd talk about over pizza and hopefully some wine to dull the edge of another sleepless night.

'Why use something like that as a recreational drug?' she asked, not entirely sure why that was the first question that occurred to her.

'Reckon that's more your department than mine. Details about the incident were pretty well covered up at the time, but things have slipped out since. There's a footnote to the report about interviews with the survivors though. Kidnappers and victims alike. They all reported vivid, almost lucid dreams while they were under. Maybe that's what your poor unfortunate lad was chasing.'

'Rory.' Janie's eyes finally found some focus on the screen, the name popping out almost as if it was in bold type. 'Rory Devlin. He was nineteen.'

'Shit. Poor bastard. Anyhoo, J. I'll get this all typed up and off to you lot. I'll be home in an hour, hour and a half. Better be pizza waiting.'

Before Janie could say anything to that, Parsons had ended the call. She put down her phone and looked up at DC Mitchell.

'You wanted something, Cass?'

The young DC looked as tired as Janie, and it occurred to her that Mitchell should have clocked off already. There wasn't much in the way of overtime going at the moment, although it was always possible DCI Ritchie had sanctioned something.

'Not sure.' She had been leaning against one of the empty desks, and when she pushed herself upright, Janie saw she had been clutching a sheet of paper all the while.

'What is this?' She took the sheet.

'New development near Straiton. I hear they're putting in a thousand houses or something. Only they've found bones. Human. Buried quite deep. Reckon they've been in the ground a long time, but we'll have to get that confirmed.'

Janie glanced across at the window. Night had fallen some time ago, only the orange of the street lamps to see by. If this wasn't a fresh body then there wasn't much they could do about it until the morning. She handed the sheet of paper back, then clicked off her computer.

'Have you run this past DI McLean or DCI Ritchie?' She could see from the look on Mitchell's face that she hadn't.

'OK. I'll have a quick word with the DI. Need to talk to him about Rory Devlin anyway. You should probably go home and get some kip. I've a nasty feeling tomorrow's going to be another long day.'

McLean was tidying up the paperwork on his desk, about to leave, when Janie reached his office. She rapped lightly at the frame of the open door, and he looked up almost guiltily until he saw who it was. He had a weary slump to his shoulders, which she could sympathise with. True enough, he'd been demoted from DCI back down to DI, but he was still the most experienced detective in their Major Investigation Team, so everyone came to him first when they had a problem.

'Hoped I might catch you before you left, sir,' she said. 'I've a couple of things come up that will need dealing with first thing tomorrow.'

McLean tried to hide his sigh, but it was there all the same. 'Rory Devlin?'

'That's one of them, sir. I've had some preliminary results from Manda and, well, it's looking like some new designer drug did for him. At the very least we'll need to try and find out where he got it.'

The detective inspector nodded his agreement, paused for a moment as if considering the news. 'And the other thing?'

'Cass . . . DC Mitchell came to me with this just now.' Janie handed him a sheet of paper. Not so much a case assignment as an advisory from the Control Centre. He scanned it, taking in half of the words at best.

'Executive summary?' he asked with a hopeful, apologetic smile.

'Building site out Straiton way, sir. They uncovered a body when they were digging the foundations for one of the houses. Well, I say body, but it's only bones. Local uniform were called in and they've shut the place down for now.'

McLean nodded slowly, not focusing on the paper or Janie for a while. Then he stared at the glass window wall of his office, black with the night outside.

'Have you spoken to the officers on the scene?'

'Aye, sir. Sergeant Graham's in charge. Out of Loanhead. I don't know him. Says he reckons they're ancient bones, but we'll have to get the pathologist in to confirm that.'

Another long pause while the detective inspector considered his options. Janie couldn't help noticing the odd glint of grey in his hair as the harsh overhead light reflected off it. In that moment he looked so bone weary Janie quite forgot all her own woes. How did he keep coming in to work feeling like that? But then everybody was tired these days. Too much work and not enough officers.

'No point rushing it if Andy Graham reckons they've been in the ground a while. Have him post a couple of constables at the scene to keep folk away, pick it up tomorrow. Whoever they are, they're not going to get any more dead.'

Janie let out a silent sigh of relief. There was the promise of pizza in her not too distant future, and the last thing she wanted was a detour to Straiton.

'I'll get the pathologist lined up for the morning, then. Head out there and oversee it when he arrives. We'll need to speak to the builders either way.'

'Good idea. Maybe take Mitchell with you if you want. She could do with a bit more field work.' McLean closed down the lid of his laptop to put it to sleep, then levered himself out of his chair with a minimum of huffing. 'If it turns out to be ancient remains, we can give Professor Turner a call. See if she wants to have a look.'

Janie nodded, stifled a yawn.

'You should go home, Janie. You look all done in.'

'Aye, sir. I was on my way when that came in.' She pointed at the sheet of paper which the detective inspector still had clasped in one hand. 'Hoped it could wait, but thought I'd check just to be sure.'

McLean looked at it again as if he'd only just noticed it. Janie could see the thoughts playing across his face, and would have bet good money on him driving out to Straiton rather than home, just to have a wee nosey. But then with exaggerated movements he placed it, text side down, in the centre of his desk.

'Time I was getting home myself,' he said. But by the time Janie had wished him good night and left the office, he was still sat at his desk, staring out into the darkness beyond.

7

Rain overnight had freshened the air a little, and a light mist clung to the ground as Janie drove south towards Loanhead. Beside her, DC Mitchell sat silent but attentive, her gaze flicking this way and that as she took in each new detail. It reminded Janie of nothing so much as a cat at a window, looking out onto a garden full of birds.

'You got those directions?' she asked, even though she knew exactly where she was going. The bypass had run through a line of green-belt land circling the city and keeping it contained, but the city's need for housing only ever grew, and developments were beginning to sprout on what had once been farmland, like cinderblock and tarmac mushrooms. The New Straiton development was much like the rest of them, a soulless collection of identikit small houses too far away from any amenities to be anything more than a place to sleep.

'Next right. Site office should be just inside the gates.' DC Mitchell pointed across the road at almost the same time as Janie indicated and made the turning. This early there wasn't much sign of activity beyond a few people wandering around looking like they weren't sure what they were meant to be doing. The site office was a set of six Portakabins stacked three on three with an exterior metal staircase leading up to the first level. Janie parked next to the most expensive and shiny-looking car on site, reasoning that it was most likely the boss's and wouldn't get dented by an errant forklift or something similar. A brand-new Maserati SUV, it was both spectacularly ugly and proof that there was more money in developing housing estates than solving crimes.

'How the other half lives, eh?' Mitchell said as they both walked past the car and climbed the narrow metal stairs to the top level, where the sign screwed to the door read 'site office'.

'Not as nice as the DI's Alfa,' Janie said, then remembered that he didn't have it any more. The last she'd seen he was still tootling around the city in a little electric Renault Zoe, which was the polar opposite of what he had driven before.

Mitchell said nothing as she opened the door and gestured for Janie to go through. Inside was much like any temporary building site office, cluttered, cramped and chaotic. The air had a stale sweat smell to it Janie recognised from having grown up with two brothers. Directly across from the door, a large desk was piled higher with paperwork than even DI McLean's desk back at the station. Somewhere behind the stacks a face peered at them.

'Can I help youse?'

Janie approached, seeing a tiny woman sitting on an office chair, her attention flicking back and forth between her computer screen and the two people who had so rudely interrupted her morning.

'Detective Sergeant Harrison.' She held up her warrant card. 'This is my colleague Detective Constable Mitchell. It's about the body you discovered yesterday.'

The tiny woman made a noise that might have been dismissive or might have been trapped wind. Giving up with her computer, she pushed her chair back and stood up, becoming somewhat shorter in the process. 'Gie's a sec. I'll get Johnny for youse.'

Without further explanation or waiting for an answer, she

bustled to the back of the Portakabin, where a door led to the next section, knocked on it once and then went through. Janie began to follow, but the door closed in her face with a certain finality.

'Charming,' she said.

Mitchell opened her mouth to say something, closed it again as the door swung wide. Janie turned, then had to look up to see the face of the man standing there. Alongside the tiny receptionist, he looked like some kind of improbable fairy tale giant.

'Detective Sergeant.' He held out a hand the size of a large dinner plate. 'Johnny Wendle. You've come about the bones, I hear.'

Despite his enormous size, Wendle's handshake was surprisingly gentle. Janie still wondered whether she might lose her own hand in his grip though. He stared at her a little longer than was necessary before letting go. When she introduced Mitchell, he was equally polite, but the handshake lasted far less time.

'Likely just a formality, but we have to investigate any body. I take it there's nothing on the surveys to suggest there was a kirkyard here?'

Wendle pointed towards the far wall of the Portakabin, where a map of the building site had been pinned up. 'Not according to the records, no. We've looked at maps going back to the nineteenth century. The nearest church is about a mile that way. Off the plan.' He jabbed a sausage thumb over his shoulder in the direction of Loanhead. 'Judging by the depth, and what I saw of the bones, I think whoever it is has been down there a while. Don't think that ground's been dug over in living memory. Just hope it's not some important new archaeological find. We're behind schedule as it is.'

Janie had almost been warming to the man, but his attitude gave her pause. Sure, there was money on the line here, and people's jobs. But a dead body where a dead body shouldn't be was more than just a minor inconvenience. She checked her watch. 'Pathologist should be here soon. He'll have the final say. You want to show us where these bones are?'

The worst of the fog had lifted, but dampness still clung to the ground as Janie followed Johnny Wendle through a warren of houses in various stages of construction. Not being new to the job, she'd brought a change of footwear, a wise move given the abundance of sticky mud everywhere. DC Mitchell would learn her lesson, hopefully. Her patent leather ankle boots offered some protection, but it was going to take her a while to clean them.

The houses closest to the site office were almost complete, at least on the outside. Further away, the roofs disappeared, walls grew lower, until finally there were only the poured concrete foundations and then a series of muddy trenches. A couple of bored-looking uniform constables sat in a squad car close by, and a small area had been cordoned off with tape. Someone had erected a temporary shelter over one corner alongside a drystone wall that marked the edge of the building site. Parked a little way off, Janie recognised the road-grime-and-British-Racing-Green-coloured Jaguar that belonged to the city pathologist, Angus Cadwallader.

'. . . came as something of a shock for poor Davey, the digger driver.'

She focused her attention back on Wendle, suddenly aware that he'd been speaking and she'd not been listening. The developer clearly hadn't noticed, either more interested in the sound of his own voice or simply wanting to move things on as smoothly and swiftly as possible so he could start work again.

'Nothing in any of the other trenches, I take it?' DC Mitchell asked, possibly the first words she'd spoken since they'd left the site office.

'No. Nothing.' Wendle hesitated, then added, 'Well, the odd field drain, of course. And there was an old gas main that should have been on the survey but somehow got missed. Not connected to anything, thank God, but it took a couple of weeks to sort out.'

Janie left them to discuss the vagaries of housing developments. The two constables started to climb out of the squad car as she approached, but a simple wave had them settling back in to what must have been a cushy assignment. She'd speak to them later, once she'd seen what all the fuss was about.

Unlike the stained white plastic of the usual forensics tents, this one was striped in white and red, but it served much the same purpose. It straddled a few metres of foundation trench, and when Janie pulled back the flap, it was pleasantly warm inside. A smell of damp earth hung in the air, and at first she thought she was alone. Then a head popped up from the trench.

'Ah, Detective Sergeant Harrison. A pleasure as always.' Angus Cadwallader clambered up a ladder until his upper torso was clear of the ground, beckoning her over. 'Come see. There's plenty of room and they've shored up the sides for safety.'

Janie approached the edge of the trench with care all the same. Closer up, she could see that it was twice as wide as outside the tent, and the builders had placed boards and bracers to stop the sides from collapsing. It was deeper than she would have thought necessary, even for the larger apartment blocks that formed the centre of the development, but that might have been down to soil conditions. Hadn't she read somewhere that the cost of building a house could vary by tens of thousands of pounds once you turned the soil and found out what lay underneath? Given what she saw at the bottom of the trench, that might well be the case here. No wonder Wendle was so anxious.

The bones were shockingly white against the darkest brown of the damp soil. A leg had been disturbed by the digger, the tibia, fibula and foot bones strewn about a metre away from the rest of the body. Someone had gone to a lot of trouble to expose the top half of the whole skeleton, and to her inexpert eye had done a decent job of it. The body lay on its side, one arm cupped under its head, the other folded around to its chest. Janie was struck immediately by the impression of someone sleeping. She looked up to get her bearings before remembering she was inside the tent.

'Not a proper Christian burial, I take it.'

'I think that's fair to say.' Cadwallader descended the ladder once more, indicating for Janie to follow. 'Orientation of the body is near enough north–south, and she's lying on her side.'

'She?' Janie placed a foot on the soil, feeling it give slightly under her weight. Dr Sharp was already in the pit, kneeling beside the half-exposed skull.

'Best guess from what we can see of the pelvis and other bones.' Cadwallader crouched down awkwardly on the opposite side of the skeleton.

'Don't suppose you can give me a time of death,' Janie said.

The pathologist looked up sharply, smiled at her joke, then shook his head. 'Hard pushed to even say what she died of. I'd like to say it's been more than seventy years and you can treat this as ancient.'

'But you can't.' Janie filled in what she really didn't want to hear.

'I'd say at least thirty years, possibly more. We'll need to get her out of here and back to the mortuary to be sure. See if we can find some DNA or anything else to identify her.'

'So we treat it as a crime scene until we know better.' Janie didn't ask it as a question, and Cadwallader didn't answer. 'Thank you, Angus. I'll get Manda and her team in to go over the area. Let me know when you have any better idea how long those bones have been down there, can you?'

'Of course. Although given the conditions you might be as well calling in the forensic archaeology specialists. If there's anything to be found here, it's going to be underground.'

It wasn't until she stepped out of the red-and-white-striped plastic tent that Janie realised how close it had been down in the trench. Not unpleasant, nor life-threatening; it was more that she felt as if a great weight had been removed from her chest as she breathed in the cool Midlothian morning air. A few paces away, Johnny Wendle was still deep in conversation with a sombre-faced DC Mitchell, his massive hands waving around animatedly as he regaled her with some unlikely tale. For a moment, Janie imagined no time at all had passed out here in the real world while she, Cadwallader and Dr Sharp had been communing with the dead woman in her deep grave. Maybe it hadn't.

'What's the story then, Detective Sergeant?' Wendle asked as he saw her.

'The body's been down there a while, but it's still a crime scene until we can say how long.'

Wendle's face creased with worry. 'What does that mean?'

'Anything over seventy years buried is considered ancient bones, beyond the remit of our investigation. This grave's probably more than thirty years old, but we still have to treat it as suspicious. You've no records of a private burial on these lands, I take it.'

'N-no. Least, I don't think so. That would have shown up on the surveys wouldn't it?' Wendle shook his head as he spoke, no doubt remembering that they'd already found a gas pipe that wasn't supposed to be there.

'Well, I'm afraid we're going to have to keep this cordoned off a while longer.' Janie held up her phone as if it was necessary to explain herself. 'I'm calling in a team of forensic archaeologists to go over the area, see if there's anything else lurking down there. Hopefully we won't knock your schedule off too much. Meantime you might want to go through the title deeds closely, see if there's any mention of private burial on the land.'

'I –' Wendle started to ask a question, then stopped himself. 'Is there not a central register of that kind of thing?'

'Sadly no. Scots law doesn't require it. Would make our lives a lot easier if it did, I can tell you. Do you know who used to own the land maybe thirty, forty years ago?'

Despite his size, Johnny Wendle had a boyish face, and would have been rubbish at poker. Janie could read the emotions parading themselves across his features as he wrestled with some inner conflict. It would come out in time, she was sure, but for now she had better things to do than wait for him to decide which was more important, profit margin or the truth.

'I don't know,' he said eventually, but as he did so he glanced over the drystone wall towards a point in the middle distance. Janie didn't follow his gaze, but she had noticed what he was looking at when they arrived. Perhaps a couple of hundred metres away across scrubby grassland, a clump of mature trees stood guard around a derelict farmhouse. Beyond it, a collection of farm buildings were in slightly better nick.

'Well, maybe ask the people you bought the land from, aye? And have a good rake through the deeds. Would make all of our lives a lot easier if this is recorded somewhere.'

Wendle nodded his head perhaps a little too eagerly. 'Aye, I'll do that right away.'

'Let me know how you get on.' Janie pulled out a business card from her jacket pocket and handed it over. 'Meantime, I'd be grateful if you'd tell the workers to keep away from here for now. We'll be done as soon as we can.'

8

Monday morning, bright and early. McLean sat at his desk, laptop pulled close to him, and squinted at the too-small type of the updated report into the death of Rory Devlin. Both forensics and the post-mortem now confirmed that death had been from a drug overdose, rather than the mugging they had originally assumed it to be. That meant the investigation was downgraded from murder, which would keep the bean counters happy at least. There were just the awkward details about the nature of this new and deadly drug that were giving him concern.

He was half way to reaching for the telephone when he decided it would be better to discuss things face to face with someone. Closing down the laptop, he stood up with a little gasp as his hip twinged in pain, then limped out of his office and down to the CID room on the second floor. Not that it was called CID any more. They were all Major Investigation Teams now. But it had been CID when he'd first joined plain clothes, too many years ago to think about.

'DS Harrison in yet?' McLean asked of the first detective constable he found. One of the new intake, DC Bryant looked up from her desk, one hand innocently straying towards the mouse to close down whatever screen it was she had been looking at. Not work, then.

'Aye, sir. She was away to the canteen to grab a coffee. Anything I can help with?'

He didn't really know Bryant well. She seemed a competent enough detective, fitted in with the rest of the team. And yet for some reason McLean felt a little uncomfortable discussing his concerns with her. Perhaps because they crossed the line between work and personal life. Fortunately for him, the brief moment of awkwardness was broken by the arrival of Harrison, coffee in one hand, bacon roll in the other.

'Looking for me, sir?' she asked as she carefully placed the coffee on the edge of the nearest desk. Not about to relinquish the roll to anyone.

'I was, but anyone would do really. Who's in charge of the evidence store these days?'

'The evidence store?' Harrison echoed him. 'Sergeant Edgehill, I think. Why?'

'I was reading Manda's forensic report into the drug that killed Devlin. Something struck a chord. She said the closest she could find to its chemical signature was something the Russians had cooked up. An airborne instant anaesthetic.'

'That's right, aye.' Harrison looked at her bacon roll with an expression McLean couldn't quite read, then put it down beside the coffee.

'You remember Sergeant Needham? Needy?'

'Not sure I ever met him, but aye. Everyone knows the story. Hard not to when one of your own goes off the rails like that.'

'I don't –' DC Bryant began, then stopped speaking.

'You'll have heard of the Christmas Killer though.' McLean grimaced at the memories. This was why he'd been reluctant to bring the subject up. Bryant's nod was confirmation enough for him to continue.

'John Needham had a mental breakdown when his father died. He'd always been obsessed with that case, but when he went over the edge he started kidnapping and killing women. Not one a year at Christmas like Donald Anderson, but three over the course of a few months. The fourth, his last victim before we caught him, was my partner, Emma Baird. Needy took her from right under our noses. In this station.'

'Oh my God. That's –'

'Old history I'd rather not go over again, Constable. The point is he used something that knocked her unconscious and left her in a coma for the best part of three months. A weaponised aerosol anaesthetic cooked up by the Russians for use in hostage situations. It was in the evidence store, something we'd found when we shut down an organised crime syndicate. One of our rare successes that. Pity it came back to bite us.'

'And you think this drug Manda's analysed is the same?' Harrison asked.

'Could just be a coincidence. Who knows how much of that stuff the Russians made, let alone where any of it is now. The stuff Needy stole should have been destroyed years ago, but I want someone to have a word with Evidence all the same.'

'I'll get right on it, sir.' Harrison stood a little straighter, as if about to rush out the door. McLean held up his hand, then pointed at her coffee and bacon roll.

'Aren't you forgetting something?'

McLean had hoped to sneak back into his office unseen after he'd spoken to Harrison and Bryant, but as luck would have it he arrived on the third floor at exactly the same time as DCI Ritchie stepped out of his open doorway, clearly looking for him.

'Ah, there you are, Tony. Wondered where you'd got to. The chief super's wanting an update on this drug overdose case.'

'Right now?' McLean asked, even though he knew the answer. Ritchie gave him a sympathetic shrug.

'Think she's overcompensating. Hopefully she'll back off

soon enough. Let us get on with our jobs.'

McLean had his doubts, but he followed Ritchie along the corridor and into the chief superintendent's office all the same. Detective Superintendent McIntyre was there already, and Elmwood herself. The chief superintendent stood by her desk, one hand casually resting on the suspiciously paperwork-free surface as if she needed its support but didn't want to admit it.

'Tony. It's good to see you.'

McLean was momentarily stuck for anything to say. He knew the chief superintendent had almost died. He knew also that she had suffered major burns to much of her body. And yet the woman standing in front of him looked scarcely different from the one who had made his life so miserably awkward in the months before a lunatic had tried to burn her at the stake.

'I'm glad to see you recovered,' he said eventually. 'I have to admit, I was surprised when Jayne told me you were coming back to work. After everything that happened.'

Elmwood dipped her head once in acknowledgement, then crossed the room to the comfortable chairs arranged around a low table by the window. She not so much sat as collapsed onto a sofa and waved an arm at the coffee machine. McLean took the hint and poured coffees for everyone.

'I can't deny it's been traumatic, Tony. The treatment was . . .' Elmwood paused as if trying to find the right word. '. . . almost as painful as the burns. But they worked miracles, wouldn't you say?'

An unfair question if ever he heard one. McLean glanced sideways at McIntyre, but she was hiding behind her mug and offering no support. Ritchie had her best poker face on.

'I'd certainly be hard pushed to say you'd been in a bad house fire.' It was the best he could come up with, and to a certain extent it was true. The chief superintendent's face was blemish free, although she was wearing more makeup than he'd noticed her do before the fire. There was something about the lack of animation in her face as she spoke that gave him pause though, and he was fairly certain her platinum blonde hair was an extremely well-made wig.

'Well, you were there.' She smiled with her mouth, but the skin around her eyes stayed smooth and unwrinkled as if she'd had too much Botox. It wasn't until she reached for her coffee mug that he finally saw some small sign of the horrific burns she had suffered. Stretching forward exposed her wrist and a livid mark where the ropes had tied her to the pile of her own broken furniture. Perhaps noticing his gaze, perhaps merely self-conscious, she tugged at the sleeve until it covered up the scar, folded her hands together in her lap like a debutante, coffee untouched.

'Tell me about this case. The young man, Devlin was it?'

Was she really interested, or deflecting? McLean didn't much care either way. 'It's early days. He's overdosed on something, but we don't know what, and neither do our friends at the NCA. The plan is to shake up the local drugs trade and see what falls out that we've not seen before.'

'Is it that important?' Elmwood stared at him with those disconcerting pale-grey eyes, then blinked once. 'I mean, of course it's important, but is it a good use of our meagre resources? One dead drug addict and you've got twenty officers on it. More.'

McLean willed himself to relax, to not take the bait. 'Rory Devlin was only nineteen. He has a sister who's sixteen, mother and father not yet in their forties. They'll all spend the rest of their lives wondering what they did wrong, how they might have stopped this from happening. I'd like to be able to tell them it wasn't their fault.'

He knew the response that explanation would get him, waited until Elmwood began to open her mouth and express her reasonable but heartless opinion, then spoke up before she could get any words out.

'More importantly though, we need to find out where this drug came from, who's selling it. From what the forensics and pathology tell us, it's a potential time bomb waiting to explode. Rory Devlin was the first person to die from using it, but who's to say he'll be the last?'

Elmwood held up her hand, the frown not quite managing to crease the smooth skin of her forehead. This time Ritchie interrupted before the chief superintendent could get her words out.

'He was a junkie, we know. Not worth wasting a lot of police time on. Brought it on himself. But his death was violent and brutal. Once the press get a hold of that we'll have a nightmare on our hands, and if more people die in the same way?' She shook her head. 'Imagine someone doing that in the St James Quarter, or Princes Street Gardens? Somewhere public? We need to be ahead of this, otherwise when the shit hits the fan we're going to get covered in it.'

Elmwood stared at them both, her hands clasped firmly together in her lap, coffee untouched. She waited long seconds, making sure that neither of them were going to interrupt before finally speaking.

'It's been a difficult time, this past year. I might not have been here at the helm, but I've been keeping an eye on things. I know we're as stretched as ever, possibly more so. That's why I've been working hard on a plan to bring more resources to the Major Investigation Teams. I can't go into any details right now, but I think you'll all appreciate the effort once it's revealed.'

McLean glanced at McIntyre, looking for any sign that she knew about this already. He'd known the detective superintendent a long time, so was fairly confident her expression of dubious horror was as genuine as his own. He'd welcome more resources, they all would. But what price would the chief superintendent exact in repayment?

9

'It's not often I have to admit to being spot on with my predictions, Tony. But this is one of those times.'

McLean stood in his habitual place in the central examination theatre in the city mortuary, the other side of the table from his old friend Angus Cadwallader. Unlike most post-mortems, he had no need to worry about the scalpel, the Y incision and slow removal and inspection of organs. The body laid out in front of him was barely much more than bones, a few crumbs of dried earth dusting the stainless steel worktop. It reminded him oddly of the body Emma and Hattie Turner had been digging up down in Leith.

'How so?' He took a step closer, peering at the well-preserved bones and trying to imagine a person who might once have walked and talked and lived.

'I told young Detective Sergeant Harrison that this body was at least thirty years in the ground, maybe more, but not ancient. Of course, it would have made life a lot easier if they were beyond both the reach and interest of the law.'

McLean recalled the progress report DS Harrison had given him before the weekend. Old bones, but not so old it wouldn't be something for the Cold Case Unit to follow up. He'd authorised the forensic archaeologists to survey the scene while the housing developer searched his paperwork for any indication of a private burial. If that didn't turn anything up, then he didn't hold out much hope for any kind of positive identification. 'So how long has this body been in the ground?'

Cadwallader scratched at his temple with a gloved hand, sniffed, his discomfort evident in his every movement. 'From the bones, it's hard to say. That's why I told Janie what I thought out at the scene. There was better preservation of the DNA than I could have hoped for though, so we took a sample and sent it off for analysis. Frankly I'm astonished they processed it so quickly, but apparently they're testing some new machine that can get you results in hours rather than weeks. Imagine that.'

McLean had, many times before. Usually the promised machine didn't work, or was simply too expensive to use for anything but the most urgent of cases. Bones that had been in the ground for decades weren't exactly top priority, but he wasn't going to complain. Unless, of course, the identification brought with it added complications.

'Who is it then?'

Cadwallader paused a moment before answering, as if he was unsure how to break the news.

'According to the results from the shiny new machine, Tony. And unless there's something very wrong with the database, of course. We're looking at the last remains of Miss Emily Worstead, who went missing from St Mungo's Hospice in the summer of 1990.'

Tempted though he was to head up to the second floor, where his Major Investigation Team lived, and find some spare detectives to start setting up an incident room, McLean instead followed his instincts and the steps down to the basement. Tucked in a room at the back of the station that had, depending on who you asked, once been a holding cell for late-Victorian drunks or nothing more sophisticated than an evidence store, the offices of the Cold Case Unit were an ever more frequent refuge from the politics three and four floors up.

Recently retired Detective Sergeant Laird, Grumpy Bob to any who'd worked with him, slouched in his chair, feet on the desk and a report folder draped decorously over his face. McLean had no doubt that the man was capable of identifying approaching footsteps and knew exactly who it was that had entered the room. Otherwise he'd have been swifter at removing the folder from his face and his feet from the desk.

'Kipping on the job, Bob? That's not like you,' McLean said to fill the time while his old friend gathered himself together.

'I'm retired, remember? And it's been a bit slow down here lately. Nothing much coming out of these case reviews.' Grumpy Bob picked up the folder he'd been using as a sleep mask, waved it once and then dropped it back onto his desk.

'Still on the clock though.' McLean shook his head. 'Never mind. I've something more interesting for you. Possibly.'

Grumpy Bob sat a little more upright, leaned forward and clasped his hands together. 'Oh aye?'

'Emily Worstead. Name ring any bells?'

'Worstead, Worstead.' The hands unclasped, one reaching up to scratch at a grey-stubbled cheek. Then he shook his head. 'Give us a clue?'

'Apparently she went missing from a terminal-care hospice in 1990. St Mungo's, over Craiglockhart way.'

'Aye, I know the place. Closed down about fifteen, twenty years back?' Grumpy Bob reached for his keyboard, which had been shoved out of the way to make room for his feet on the desk. He began tapping away with two fingers, occasionally pausing to do something with an ancient mouse. Finally he peered closely at the screen before pulling a pair of grubby spectacles from his breast pocket and sliding them onto his nose.

'Here we go. Emily Gertrude Worstead. Born 1936. Admitted to St Mungo's June 16th, 1989. Untreatable bowel cancer. Disappeared from her room March 13th, 1990. Never seen again.' The detective sergeant mumbled under his breath as he carried on reading from the screen. 'Doctors reckoned she'd only weeks to live, if that. Surprised she could walk at all. There was a search, but nothing came of it.'

'Who was SIO?' McLean asked.

Grumpy Bob tapped a couple of keys, stared at the screen, then let out a little snort that might have been laughter. 'Detective Inspector Charles Duguid. Can't have been long after he got his keys to the executive bathroom.'

McLean glanced over at the other desk in the room, much neater than he remembered it usually being, and unoccupied. 'He not in?'

'Away on a golfing holiday, apparently. I always thought he didn't actually play, just spent all his time at the nineteenth hole.' Grumpy Bob shrugged. Neither of them had got on particularly well with Duguid while he'd been a serving officer, but the detective superintendent had mellowed in his semi-retirement.

'OK. I'm sure we can manage without him. We'll need to review everything in the Emily Worstead case files though, open up a new investigation. Angus is going over the bones as thoroughly as he can, but chances are we won't find anything now. Not after thirty years.'

Grumpy Bob nodded, then peered myopically at his screen again. 'Not much detail here, but it looks like the case files are still in the archives. I'll dig them out and make a start. No doubt Dagwood will be absolutely delighted to have one of his old cases sitting on his desk when he gets back in.'

'Well, don't get too stuck into it yet. I'm away out to the building site to see how the forensic archaeologists are getting on. Depending on what they've found, we might have to escalate this up to Major Investigations.'

'Even though she's been dead thirty years?'

McLean shrugged. 'I don't make the rules, Bob. You know that.'

10

McLean had seen the slow spread of houses south of the city on his infrequent trips beyond the bypass, the gradual encrustation of green fields with concrete, slate and grey harling. Given that it could hardly spread north into the Forth, it wasn't surprising Edinburgh had chosen instead to ooze down the map. Nevertheless it was always a shock to see the countryside he'd bicycled through as a carefree boy swallowed up by row upon row of identikit starter homes.

He'd asked Detective Sergeant Harrison to drive, partly because it gave him time to think and partly because she'd been to the building site before so knew where she was going. She said nothing for the first ten minutes of the journey, but he could tell she wanted to. That she hadn't immediately voiced her thoughts gave him some idea as to what they might have been. Only once they had reached Burdiehouse did she finally break.

'I was surprised to see the chief superintendent back.'

'Because it's not been all that long since she was almost burned at the stake?' McLean asked, not voicing the alternative reason that Elmwood had for a while been a suspect in the murder of a leading lawyer and men's rights activist.

'Well, that as well, aye.'

'The decision was taken way above my pay grade, Janie.

Let's just leave it at that, shall we?'

She wasn't happy, McLean could see that. Fair enough, he wasn't particularly happy either. Elmwood should have been pensioned off. Injuries sustained in the line of duty. A hefty leaving bonus and a nod in the New Year's honours list. All of that was far more than she deserved, but he'd learned long ago there were some injustices you simply had to live with. Having her back at work, even if it was job-shared with McIntyre, made little sense.

'What about the body, then?' Harrison's question was terse, an unwilling change of subject.

'Emily Worstead? I'm not sure, really. We'll need to go over the area where the bones were found, see if there's anything that might give us a clue. It's been over thirty years, though, so I'm not holding out much hope. The Cold Case team can take it from there, and if nothing else, the family get some closure.'

They spent the rest of the journey in silence, although it wasn't long before Harrison was piloting the car into the busy building site. She parked in front of a Portakabin stack site office and was out of the car before McLean even had his seatbelt unbuckled. Maybe he'd misjudged her mood.

By the time he reached the top of the clanging metal stairs, Harrison was already in the office chatting to a secretary sitting behind a desk, and a tall man standing beside it who McLean thought he recognised from somewhere.

'Detective Inspector McLean? This is a surprise.' The tall man approached him, hand held out to shake. 'You probably don't remember me. Johnny Wendle. You interviewed me about that arson attack on Leith Walk.'

McLean struggled for a moment, then another name popped into his head almost unbidden. 'Wendle Stevens, wasn't it? Whatever happened to Stevens?'

'Oh, he's still about. The company's a bit bigger now. He

mostly does the commercial buildings and I'm out here doing my best to improve the city's housing stock.'

That was up for debate, but not right now. There were more important things to be dealing with. 'Sorry we're going to delay you a bit. Did DS Harrison bring you up to speed?'

Wendle nodded his head once. 'Aye, the archaeologists are already here. They went over the ground with some electronic gadgetry. Ground-penetrating radar, I think the professor said it was. They've dug a bigger hole than we'd normally do, but it's nothing we can't fill back in again later. You want to have a look?'

Before McLean could answer, the tall man was out the door. Harrison trailed behind as he hurried to catch up, but then she knew where she was going he presumed. Wendle paused at the steel shed and pulled out a couple of hard hats, handing one to McLean before leading him towards the south edge of the site. He chattered away all the time about his vision for the living experience in this bold new venture, but McLean tuned him out after the first few meaningless sentences. The development was much like so many others he'd seen go up in and around the city over the past forty years or so. Barely indistinguishable houses, seemingly arranged along randomly oriented streets and cul-de-sacs, surrounded a small cluster of four-storey apartment blocks. To his admittedly biased eye, everything looked smaller than might be comfortable for family life, and the gaps between the houses were barely wide enough for a wheelie bin. At least all the roofs seemed to have solar panels, and he caught something about communal heating and each house having a charge point for an electric car.

'And these will be the executive homes. They've already all sold.' Wendle's voice cut through McLean's thoughts. He looked around at half-built walls and piles of materials stacked along the drystone wall that marked the boundary for the whole development. Beyond that was a short stretch of grazing field, and in the middle distance what looked like a derelict farmhouse surrounded by mature trees, and some old sheds. Not much of a view for the executives, and how long before the council decided the rest of the land could be built on?

'Very nice,' he said, with almost no trace of sarcasm discernible in his voice. 'And the body?'

'Ah, yes.' Wendle pointed to what must have been the final plot, and to McLean's mind the most desirable. At least before a dead body had been discovered underneath it. Farthest from the road, and with the field on two sides of its meagre boundary, it would at least offer the owners a decent view of the derelict farmhouse and Hillend artificial ski slope.

As they approached, McLean began to see the size of the excavation work. The standard foundation trench traced the outline of three walls, but the fourth had extended into something the size of a modest swimming pool. A small army of hard-hatted people swarmed like bees around a disturbed hive, and there in the middle the queen bee crouched and studied the earth. She must have been alerted to his arrival, or possessed some strange sixth sense, as she turned and gazed up at him as he reached the edge of the pit.

'Ah, Tony. Thought I might see you here soon enough. Shame though. You've wasted your trip.' Professor Harriet Turner pulled off her hard hat and wiped at her forehead with the back of her hand. She passed the hat to one of the other diggers before negotiating the path of narrow wooden scaffold boards and climbing up the short ladder to ground level. McLean reached out to help her at the last, almost ending up in the pit himself and getting mud all over his own hand as a reward.

'Wasted?' he asked.

'There's nothing down there. Suspected as much when we ran the remote sensors over it, but I can't remember the last time

I dug up an area that size and didn't even find an old ring pull of a coke can, or a bit of rusted barbed wire. We found a couple of mole burrows near the top, but other than that it's good soil until you hit deep clay. Should really be growing food in it, or maybe barley to malt for whisky. Not building houses.'

Beside him, McLean could feel Wendle stiffen at the accusation. 'You've done all you can, I take it?' he asked, hoping for an answer that would defuse the row before it started.

'Pretty much. Those bones were buried in a deep grave. I say bones, but it would likely have been a body then. Angus can tell you more about that. We've found no evidence of clothing, so she was probably naked. We can barely trace the sides of the grave either. It was very neatly done too, and filled back properly. Folk who knew what they were about. If this field was ploughed afterwards, there'd be nothing to show once the crop had been harvested.'

'Fine way to hide a body,' McLean said, but it didn't sit right in his gut. From what he knew, Emily Worstead had been only weeks from death anyway, maybe only days. There'd been no reason to kill her, even less to hide her body.

'Well, that's all they've hidden. We're not going to find anything else down there.' Professor Turner wiped her hands against each other, then on her trousers, before turning her attention to Johnny Wendle. 'Guess that means you can have your building site back. Sorry about the mess.'

It had been nice to get out of the station for a while, but the visit to Straiton had killed the morning and Janie still had a list of things as long as her arm to look into. Was this what it was like, being a detective sergeant? Running around like a blue-arsed fly doing all the things the inspectors and chief inspectors demanded of you while also trying to keep an eye on the constables and make sure they were doing what they were supposed to be doing?

It was bloody exhausting; no wonder she didn't have the energy for much of a social life these days. Still, the boss would be back from the hospital soon and wanted information, so somebody had to dig it up.

The evidence store wasn't as large as it had been when she'd first worked out of this station. Janie wasn't sure if part of the operation had been hived off to the private sector or things had been moved to another lockup somewhere. She'd put money on the former, the way things were going. The mess that Sergeant Needham had left behind had been a perfect opportunity for rationalising the whole operation, anyway.

Security was tighter than it had ever been, too. She had to be buzzed into the basement by one of the team, and she was relieved to see that Constable Strong was on duty. She and Trevor had come through training together, and that shared experience made the favour easier to ask.

'Hey, Janie, how's things? Or should I be calling you Sarge?' he asked as she approached his desk in the corner of a depressingly bare room. Another locked door opposite the one she had entered gave access to the actual store.

'Come off it, Trev. I'm not here giving orders, an' besides, we've known each other how many years now?'

'Aye, well. Best not think about that. So what brings you down into the dungeons? I'm no' fool enough to think it's just for a blether.'

'Always good to catch up, but aye, you're right. I'm here on a mission from the boss.'

'The boss?'

'DI McLean. He's got a hunch about this new drug that's making our lives miserable. Thinks it might have something to do with one of Sergeant Needham's old finds.'

PC Strong groaned at the mention of the name, then sat up a little straighter, pulling the mouse towards him to wake up his computer. 'You any idea what a mess old Needy left this place in?'

'I've heard tell, aye.'

'We're still finding things now, and it's been years. So what're you after then? Can't promise we'll have anything on it, mind.'

'I know, but thanks for trying anyway.' Janie told him about the anaesthetic aerosol the old sergeant had used to knock out his victims.

'Think I remember Sergeant Dundas going on about that. It was some Russian military thing that got into the hands of the mob. Thought it went up in flames with Needham and that old house he lived in.' The constable leaned forward to peer at his screen through narrowed eyes, smacking the mouse up and down on the desk and occasionally jabbing at the keyboard with stubby fingers.

'Ah, no. Here we go. There was a whole box of the stuff and only one canister was missing when they did the audit after . . . Well.' More irritating clacks and taps. 'Here we go. It was scheduled for destruction after the trial was abandoned.'

'Trial?'

'Aye, it was evidence in the Alexei Gereznov trial. Remember that? Only he died in prison while he was still on remand. Well, I say died. Someone shivved him an' he bled out in the showers. No accused, no trial, no need to keep a hold of the evidence, right? So it was sent to . . . Oh, hang on.'

Janie gave up waiting, walked around the desk so she could stand behind PC Strong and peer over his shoulder at the screen. She wasn't particularly familiar with the software the evidence store used, but it was easy enough to follow once you worked out what information was displayed where. There was a case number, a description and even a small thumbnail image of what looked like a cardboard box of small glass bottles. Spaces for a half-dozen, but only five still there. At the bottom of the screen was a small box for additional notes to be input, and that was the line of text that had clearly caught the constable's attention.

'Sample sent to Edinburgh University Department of Chemistry for further analysis. Remaining evidence to MOD facility for controlled disposal. When was that?'

PC Strong's shrug was answer enough, but he clicked the box in the hope it might bring up some more detail. 'Says it was signed out in July 2012. I can check the paper archives, but it might take a while. Might have been shredded, too.'

'No, you're fine, Trev. No' sure if this means anything, but I'll run it past the DI anyways.'

11

Dawn was still more of a threat than a reality as Janie stared out the rain-slicked bus window at the dreary late-autumn city. She'd been up early enough to walk to the station, as she often did. Even if she couldn't cross Jawbone Walk in the middle of the Meadows without looking up into the branches of the Wych Elms just in case there was a dead body up there. That case had been her first in plain clothes, now she thought about it. First time she'd met DI McLean and been drawn into his circle of strange friends and colleagues.

Roadworks diverted the bus away from the main roads on a route through the less well-known parts of Grange. Writer's Block, didn't they call it? On account of the number of bestselling novelists living in the area. Janie had thought it upmarket, but nowhere was safe from the graffiti artists these days, it seemed. Along one sandstone wall some poet had scrawled 'FUCK THE POLIS' in garish yellow letters a metre or more high, and dotted here and there were variations on the same horned devil under a small rain cloud that had dominated the derelict building where they'd found Rory Devlin. No doubt the good people of Grange would be on the phone to their councillor straight away, the offending artwork removed by the end of the day. No such luck in the less prosperous parts of the city.

The insistent vibration of her phone in her pocket interrupted Janie mid-yawn. She didn't recognise the number, but she tapped the screen to accept the call. Any distraction from this endless journey.

'Detective Sergeant Harrison. Can I help you?'

A silence at the end of the line. For a moment Janie thought it might be one of those auto-diallers, a call centre pretending to be in the UK but more likely some city in India. Normally they connected you to a person fairly swiftly once you'd answered, or hung up.

'Hello?' she asked the silence. 'Is there anyone there?'

Still nothing, and Janie was about to hang up, but something stopped her. Whoever was calling, they had Janie's number, which most likely meant it was someone she'd given her card to during an investigation.

'I'm listening, if you want to talk.' She looked up around the half-empty bus. Nobody was paying much attention to anything, least of all her. The nearest person, a young woman wrapped up warm even for this inclement weather, had a massive pair of over-the-ear headphones on, so there was no way she was going to hear anything. Further away, a middle-aged man slumped against the window, his head lolling in sleep. And still the caller had said nothing.

'Look, I'm going to hang up now. Take your time, gather your thoughts, call me back. Or send a text and I'll get –'

'Don't hang up. Please.'

A woman's voice, young. Janie couldn't place the accent from so few words. And then it clicked. A pale-faced girl with unruly hair and a surly attitude, answering the door to a death knock. 'Maggie? Maggie Devlin?'

'I . . . I shouldn't be calling. Shouldnae be talking to the polis.'

Something about the words chimed with Janie's earlier thoughts. She couldn't really blame this young woman for her attitude. It was baked in hard, reinforced by the daily barrage of news and social media, after all.

'Is this about Rory? Because I can assure you we're doing everything we can to find out what happened to him. I'm sorry, Maggie. We can't bring him back. But hopefully we can make sure nobody else suffers the same way.'

'Aye, I ken that. It's just . . . Is there somewhere we can talk, like? No' on the phone, ken?'

Janie glanced at her watch, surprised that Maggie was up so early. But then again her brother had just died and her family was unravelling. Was it really so unusual she couldn't sleep?

'Is there a cafe or anything near you?' she asked. Restalrig wasn't a part of the city she knew well. The bus rumbled on to the next set of traffic lights before Maggie answered.

'There's no' much around here. But there's place up Piershill way I sometimes go to. Think it's called the Bello Caff or something.'

'I know the place. You want to meet there in an hour or so?'

'Really? You can do that? Just drop everthin' and come over?' Maggie's surprise was heart-warming.

'Aye, well. I'll miss the morning briefing, but that's no' such a hardship.' Janie glanced at her watch again. 'Mebbe make it an hour and a half, mind.'

Tucked into a narrow unit between a bookie's and a combined newsagent's and general store, the Bello Caff was either artfully retro or an actual remnant from a different era. Janie had noticed it in passing, more because of its name than anything else. Stepping inside, she found it was more greasy spoon than chain coffee house or artisan boutique. No sign of any young baristas here; when she approached the counter she was greeted with a suspicious scowl by a middle-aged woman wrapped in a stained once-white apron, who directed her to one of the empty tables near the window. Only once Janie had shucked off her coat, hung it over the back of her chair and sat down did the woman approach, a cheap carbon paper flip pad clutched in one hand.

'What you want, hen?'

Janie glanced up at the board screwed to the wall behind the counter. It was a slightly better selection than the canteen back at the station, but not exactly awe-inspiring cuisine. 'Just a coffee for now, please. White, no sugar.'

The woman – Janie couldn't bring herself to use the term waitress – paused a moment then turned and stalked off. She hadn't bothered to write down the order, but then it wasn't exactly hard to remember. The coffee came from a catering-size filter pot that might have been keeping warm since the place opened that morning. It certainly smelled more industrial than she was used to. The door jangled open as the not-waitress was placing it down in front of her, and Janie looked up to see Maggie Devlin hesitate in the entrance.

It had only been a few days since she had first seen the young woman, but Maggie had changed in that short time. The defiance was gone, replaced by something far more fearful. She had dressed to blend in, and her hair was tied up tight and hidden under a black knitted hat, not the sprawling mess Janie remembered. It took Maggie a while to notice her, partly because the not-waitress was obscuring her line of sight, partly because her gaze darted nervously from spot to spot, never resting long enough on anything to register. Finally Janie raised her hand to shoulder height and gave a little wave.

'Over here.' It wasn't a loud shout, but Maggie reacted almost as if she'd been slapped. She stared at Janie, then at the not-waitress, clearly trying to decide whether it was safe in this near-empty cafe or she should turn tail and run. Finally she pulled herself together with visible effort, let the door close and walked across.

'You want anything?' Janie asked, indicating the not-waitress. Maggie's eyes widened for a moment, then she fixated on Janie's coffee mug.

'Aye, a coffee. Thanks.'

The not-waitress huffed her acknowledgement and wandered off. Maggie pulled out a chair, sat down with her coat still on. She was wearing knitted fingerless gloves, Janie noticed. A similar pattern to the hat.

'You knit those yourself?' she asked, nodding at Maggie's hands.

'Aye. I'm no' very good mind.'

'Better than me.' Janie took a sip of her coffee, surprised when it didn't taste of dishwasher fluid. 'Thanks for coming. I know it can't be easy.'

'Why'd you do it?' Maggie asked. 'Why'd you join the polis?'

Janie found herself frowning and tried her best to ease her face into a bland expression. It was as if this young woman could read her mind, or at least see the thoughts that had been bothering her recently.

'Guess it was something to do, aye? No big family tradition or anything. Not like some of the officers I've worked with. Did my Highers, thinking about college, but I didn't fancy getting into that much debt. There was a careers thing at school, some chief superintendent or something gave an inspiring talk, and I thought why not? I didn't think I'd get in when I applied. Didn't think I'd get through the training. Wrong on both counts, as it turns out.'

That got her the ghost of a smile from Maggie, but it didn't last. There was a brief pause while the not-waitress brought another mug of coffee and asked them if they wanted anything else. Janie ordered a couple of muffins just to get rid of her.

'So, Maggie. What was it you wanted to talk to me about? I take it you're not thinking of signing up with Police Scotland.'

A look of utter horror flitted across the young woman's face until she realised it was meant to be a joke. 'Jesus, no. My mam'd skelp me for even thinking it, and my da would never speak to me again.' She paused a moment, hands around her mug as if she needed the warmth more than the caffeine. 'No, it was about Ror. He wasn't all that bad, no' really. Y'ken what big brothers are like?'

Janie did, although hers had become more respectful since she'd moved to plain clothes and been promoted to detective sergeant. She nodded, but said nothing. Let Maggie take her time.

'He changed, though. No' sure, but mebbe a few months back? Just before the summer, aye. He'd always been a bit of a joker, ken? Clowning around and stuff. Never taking anything seriously. Used to drive da up the wall, right enough. But he was doing OK, really. Got himself on some work experience thing in a warehouse up Newhaven way. He was studyin' fer some qualifications too so's he could drive the forklifts an' stuff. An' then he changed. Like that.' Maggie clicked her fingers, earning herself an unfriendly glare from the not-waitress. 'Got kicked off the scheme, started going out all night, coming home stinking of weed. That wasn't Ror. He always hated drugs, said they was for losers. Even got da to quit smoking.'

Janie leaned forward, arms resting on the Formica tabletop, hands either side of her coffee mug. 'But then he started taking them himself. Anything in particular? I mean, was it just the weed? Pills? Something stronger?'

Maggie half shrugged, half winced. 'I don't know. I just know he was always scrounging for money. Sure he pinched some of my jewellery cos I cannae find it anywhere. It's no' valuable, but still.'

'So you think he was feeding a habit, then? Got himself addicted to something?' Janie hesitated as her mind joined up the dots. 'Fell in with a bad crew?'

Maggie took her hands away from her coffee mug and shoved them in her pockets so swiftly Janie worried she might have misread the situation and upset the young woman. Burst of activity over, she sat almost completely motionless, staring at nothing as the seconds ticked by. The door clattered open, and an old man with a walking stick clumped his feet on the mat before shuffling off to a table at the far end of the room. Janie watched him out of the corner of her eye, but all he did was sit, take off his cap and wait expectantly for the not-waitress to come and take his order. Maggie didn't even seem to register his appearance at all, lost in the thoughts that wrote themselves across her young face.

'I went into his room,' she said finally, the words tumbling out as she locked her gaze on Janie. 'Mam's got it in her head it's some kind of shrine or summat. Put everything back exactly how it was after youse lot came in an' searched the place. No' that youse did a good job of that, ken? We're no' supposed to go in there, cannae touch anything. But he nicked my jewellery, aye? An' I know where he used tae hide stuff when he was still a kid.'

Maggie tugged her hands out of her pockets, something clutched in one. Janie knew better than to reach for it.

'Din't find any of my stuff, but I found this. Reckon it's what he was using?'

Now she handed it over, and Janie saw a neatly folded rectangular box of printed cardboard. Yellow and green colours swirled in strange patterns like a migraine corona. An almost familiar pattern began to emerge like one of those dot pictures you have to stare at for a while to see what's hidden within, but Janie had to close her eyes against a headache before whatever it was appeared. Something inside the box shifted about, and she gently prised open the flap, tipped the contents into her hand. Two small glass vials with easy snap-off tops tumbled onto her palm, although the box itself was large enough to hold several more. She slid one back in, then held the other up to the light to reveal a pale yellow liquid.

'D'ye ken what it is?' Maggie asked.

'I've absolutely no idea.' Janie carefully put the vial away, sealed the box and then guddled around in her pockets until she found a clear plastic evidence bag. 'But if you leave this with me, I know someone who might be able to find out.'

12

'Christ on a stick. What happened here?'
McLean ducked under the crime scene tape and followed the marked path through overturned tables and spilled drinks towards the back of the food hall upstairs at the Cameron Toll shopping centre. The call had come in less than half an hour earlier, directed specifically at him. He'd have to find out who in Control had done that, although it was a standing joke in the station that anything remotely weird got pushed his way. Detective Constable Bryant had been first on the scene, apparently having popped into the centre during her lunch break to pick up something from the chemist's. Maybe she was the one who'd requested him rather than a DS. At least now she was doing her best to bring him up to speed.

'Name's Alistair Hamilton, according to the Jobseeker's card in there.' She handed an evidence bag to McLean, a single Yale-type key on a ring with no fob and a faded worn brown leather wallet nestling in the bottom of it. 'Not much else to identify him. Apparently he had some kind of seizure. One of the serving staff's a first aider, did her best. But he was dead before she could even get to him.'

'Any particular reason why you called me in?' he asked, then wished he hadn't as he heard the unintended rebuke in his words. Bryant didn't seem to notice, lifting up another evidence bag for him to see.

'He had this on him. Looks the same as the one Janie – DS Harrison – got from the Devlin girl the other day.'

McLean took the bag, holding it up to the light for a better view. Inside was a small cardboard box printed in fuzzy yellow and green patterns that seemed to move around and change whenever he tried to focus on them. By the weight of it, there were more of the small glass vials inside. As Bryant said, identical to the package Harrison had been given by Rory Devlin's sister. Which meant this was most likely another drug overdose death. Just what they needed.

'The woman who tried to save him, she still here?' McLean handed back the evidence bag. The only people in the food court were uniformed police officers. Everyone else had been cleared out, the whole area cordoned off. Not much good if you'd come in looking for some lunch.

'In the manager's office, sir.' Bryant pointed at a door between the catering units with a security keypad beside it and a sign that read 'Authorised Personnel Only'. 'Asked her to wait until you were ready to speak to her.'

'Thank you . . .' McLean paused, aware in the back of his mind that DC Bryant's first name was Jessica, but also that she either did or didn't like that being shortened to Jess. As ever, he opted for the easy way out, even if it made him sound terribly formal. 'Thank you, Constable. Could you let her know I'll be along to speak to her in a minute. I'd like to have a look at the body first.'

The duty doctor obscured most of his initial view as he approached, but McLean could see straight away that the young man whose death he would have to investigate had not gone peacefully in his sleep. He lay on his back where he'd fallen from his chair, and must have kicked out with enough force to send the table flying. It had knocked over half a dozen more chairs, and nearby tables had toppled like dominoes. The force of it had twisted the man's legs into impossible angles, and the one arm McLean could see was bent back on itself too.

'What the hell happened to him?'

'He's dead, Tony. That's all I'm prepared to tell you.' Dr Buckley stood up from where he'd been kneeling by the young man's side, pulled off his latex gloves and shoved them in his pocket. 'You'll have to wait for that ghoul Cadwallader to come and tell you why.'

McLean had known Dr Buckley a long time, and he knew well enough that it wasn't his job to speculate on cause of death. It never stopped him from asking, much like he always asked the pathologist for a time of death. It was a ritual they went through to ease the tension before he focused on the reason for being there.

'He's on his way, anyway.' The duty doctor checked his watch. 'And I've better things to be doing. You'll get the paper-work as usual.'

McLean thanked him, because that was the polite thing to do, then waited until Dr Buckley was away before turning his attention on the dead man. He could see straight away why DC Bryant had called it in, and specifically why she had asked for him. Apart from the setting, there were remarkable similarities between this body and Rory Devlin's. He was young, although not as young as Devlin. Scrawny, with a messy tangle of light-brown hair, he stared blindly at the ceiling with wide, bloodshot brown eyes. His mouth hung open in a silent scream that re-vealed less than perfect dental hygiene, and the overall impression was of a man who didn't care much about his appearance. He hid his thinness behind layers of clothing, hoodie over sweatshirt over T-shirt, loose-cut jeans that had seen better days, thick socks poking out of the tops of a pair of lace-up walking boots worn down on the outsides of each heel.

Taking a careful step back, McLean scanned the area around the body. He tried to imagine it before the tables had been thrown about. The young man had sat in the corner farthest from the stairs that led up to the food court, a good place to hide away if you wanted some peace and quiet. Had he been meeting someone, or was this a lone visit? A single disposable coffee cup from the nearby cafe lay on its side a few paces away, its contents forming a milky beige puddle on the scuffed linoleum tiles. No sign of any food, but then the dead man didn't look like he ever ate much. Everything was a mess, rubbish kicked about by the rush of people either trying to help him or get out of his way. Just as well they weren't looking for any clean forensic evidence here. On the face of it there was no obvious sign of foul play.

What had happened here? Was this somewhere quiet he could come, drink a coffee and indulge in the narcotic of his choice? It seemed too public, and yet this man, Alistair Hamilton if the name in his wallet was to be believed, appeared to have done just that. He certainly had the drug on him, best leave it to the pathologist to confirm cause of death. Either way, McLean knew what it looked like, and that was very much the same as had happened to Rory Devlin. It was surely only a matter of time before the press noticed that too.

The centre manager's office was tucked away down a narrow corridor, its painted breeze block walls adorned with health and safety notices and motivational posters. The manager himself was a short man with thinning grey hair and a pinched look that McLean first took to be disdain but decided after a few minutes was simply the way his face was built. He introduced himself as Mr Bottomley, no first name offered.

'Is the food court going to be closed for long?' was perhaps not the best opening question, given the circumstances. McLean had heard worse though, and he was more interested in talking to the angry-looking woman sitting in the corner, wearing an apron with the logo of the cafe on it. Presumably the first-aider who had tried unsuccessfully to help Alistair Hamilton.

'The pathologist is on his way, Mr Bottomley. Soon as he's done and they've moved the body, you can have your food court back. You'll maybe want to get the cleaners in before you open it, mind.'

It was hard to tell whether or not that answer was satisfactory, as the manager's face seemed capable of only one expression. His quietly muttered 'Thank you' suggested he wasn't as inconsiderate as he appeared. More likely harassed and overworked, much the same as everybody.

'You wouldn't happen to have CCTV footage of the food court we could look at, would you?' McLean asked. 'It would help us to establish a timeline of events.'

Bottomley stared for a moment, as if the idea were entirely foreign to him, and then it sunk in. 'CCTV. Yes. Of course. I'll go and speak to Bill in security. See what he can dig up for you.'

McLean watched him scurry out, waited until the door was closed and only then turned to the angry woman. 'Thank you for waiting.'

'Not as if I had much choice now, was it?' Her voice was as angry as her face, hostility in every word. So it was going to be like that. Again.

'I'm sorry, Ms . . . ?'

'Braid. Like I telt this young woman here.' She nodded her head once in DC Bryant's direction. 'Shonagh Braid. An' I'd really like to get back to my work, otherwise I'll no' be gettin' paid the day.'

'I understand. And as I said to Mr Bottomley there, we should have the body removed soon. How many customers you have after that's another matter. If it helps, I could have a word with your boss. Explain the situation.'

Baird let out a long sigh, shoulders slumping in defeat. 'I ken y'mean well, but that'd only make it worse. So quicker we get this done the better, aye?'

'Fair enough. I've only a couple of questions anyway. The young lad who died. You served him earlier, right? Cup of coffee?'

'Aye. Paid fer it in cash. There's no' many do these days. It's all tap an' go. I'd have taken him fer a tramp only he was too well dressed. Security downstairs usually moves on the street folk before they can get anywhere near us.'

'Did he say anything? Apart from ordering his coffee?'

'Nah. Folk like him? Don't even say thanks when you hand over their drink.'

'And had you seen him before?'

A shake of the head.

'So you've no idea who he is?'

'Should I? It's no' like I'm his mother or anythin'.'

McLean shrugged. 'Of course not. I'm just trying to establish whether he was a regular or just passing through. Can you tell me what happened after you'd served him? How long was it before he . . . had his fit?'

'No' long, ten minutes mebbe. Thought I saw someone go over to meet him, but I was keeping my eye on a bunch of girls playing hookey. Weren't nobody about when he kicked over the table, mind. Thought there'd been a fight break out or summat. Only when I looked closer I could see he was in trouble. He'd maybe swallowed something an' it'd got stuck, like. Only he was thrashing around that bad he kicked over half the tables. You saw the place?'

McLean nodded, leaving a silence for Braid to fill.

'I couldnae get close tae start with. No way I was gonnae get smacked in the face, not on the shitty wages I get paid. He started to calm down after mebbe a minute? Two? Then he was just spasming like he'd been wired to the mains, ken? An' he was screaming, only it was quiet. Like he couldnae get the scream out. Fair spooked me, an all.'

Braid fell silent, her anger gone as the shock began to set in.

'I'm sorry,' McLean said. 'I know you did all you could. I've one last question, then I'll go and hurry up the medical team.'

Braid sniffed, wiped her nose on the back of her hand, looked at him with narrowed eyes. 'Aye?'

'Did you see him take anything? Drugs, maybe? Pills, something you might inhale?'

The woman's blank expression was answer enough, but she shook her head slowly too. 'No. Once he'd gone from the counter I wasnae payin' him much heed. I didn't get any hint he'd be trouble, ken? Just another customer.'

'Well, thanks for your help anyway, Ms Braid.' McLean shoved his hand into his pocket, pulled out a business card and handed it over. 'If you think of anything, give me a call, aye? And if your boss gives you grief over this?' He shrugged. 'I can have a word, or I can get someone who's not police to have a word.'

13

McLean found the manager, Mr Bottomley, waiting awkwardly in the corridor outside his own office, as if he
hadn't wanted to intrude while the interview was going on. His
face still bore that pained look, the entire world still nothing but
a disappointment to him.

'I have the CCTV footage from the food court, if you'd like to
see it?' His inflection turned the statement into a question, and
McLean couldn't help thinking there was a hope in it that he
wouldn't be wasting any more of the manager's time.

'Thanks. I would.' He turned to Bryant. 'Can you go and see
if the pathologist is here? I'll catch up with you in a minute.'

Bryant nodded, then strode off towards the food court.
McLean followed Mr Bottomley in the opposite direction,
arriving swiftly at another door with a security keypad beside it.
Inside, he found a familiar darkened room, one wall lined with
video screens, another stacked with recording equipment and
other unidentifiable electronic gubbinry. A control desk sat in
the middle of the room, two chairs drawn up to it but only one
occupied.

'Bill? This is the detective inspector I was telling you about.
Can you show him the footage?' Mr Bottomley wrung his hands
like he had touched something sticky as he introduced the

security guard. McLean merely nodded, then pulled the second chair towards him and sat down. Bill looked at him askance, then shrugged and reached for the controls.

'This is the best angle for the coffee shop, here.' He pointed at the central screen on the wall. It took McLean a while to work out the view, and the image wasn't perfect. It was clear enough to show a young man standing at the counter of the coffee shop, handing over change, taking a cup of coffee and walking away.

'Lose him a bit as he crosses the room, but he's on camera nine here.'

The image flickered, changing to a view of the seats and tables as Alistair Hamilton sat down. He popped the lid off his coffee cup and took a sip, leaning back in his chair as he stared around the room. The food court wasn't particularly busy, which McLean found strange. Camera nine only showed one other table occupied, an old couple with their coats still on, a teapot on a tray between them. The young man was off to one side of a fixed image, the fish-eye lens warping the view of him. The low resolution didn't help either, but McLean could still see him take something out of his pocket, although he couldn't see what it was.

He sat there for a while, staring at his hands as the numbers in the corner of the screen counted the passing seconds. Then he looked up, palmed whatever it was, shoved his hand into his pocket as if putting it away while at the same time pushing out a chair with his foot. McLean waited for another person to come into view and sit down, but the scene remained just Hamilton on his own.

'What's going on there?' he asked as the young man appeared to start talking to someone.

'Damned if I know,' the security guard said. 'You can see the other camera angles if you want, but there's nobody there.'

McLean shrugged, watching the silent conversation play out. The image wasn't good enough to see much, certainly not Hamilton's expression, although his body language suggested a mixture of fear and aggression. After a little over a minute and a half on the timer, he leaned as far back in his seat as he could without toppling over, arms waving about in the air and then pushing away at something entirely in his mind. And then he rocked forward, wiped his mouth with the back of his hand, grabbed up the coffee cup and took a long drink. All the while staring in the direction of the stairs leading down to the main concourse as if watching someone walk away.

'That's odd,' McLean said.

'It gets odder. Look.' The security guard jabbed a fat finger at the screen, where Hamilton was sitting almost unnaturally still. He held that pose for perhaps fifteen seconds before pulling something out of his pocket and with hurried, shaky movements held it up to his nose like some kind of inhaler. He'd barely had time to shove whatever it was away again before he exploded in a flurry of uncontrolled action, arms and legs jerking so violently they flung him backwards and flipped the table right over.

'Jesus wept,' the security guard said, which given he must have watched the scene at least once already to have it cued up on the system, accurately described the horror of it. McLean watched as the young man flailed about on his back, kicking over chairs and tables. The old couple managed to get out of the way before their teapot went flying, and then he saw Shonagh Braid hurry up, step in towards Hamilton, back off, and finally go in again as his flailing became more subdued. For once McLean was grateful there was no sound on the CCTV recording.

'I've got footage of him coming in the north entrance. Walked across the car park from Lady Road. He didn't hang about, went straight up to the food court.' Bill tapped a button that froze the image as Shonagh Braid stood up beside an unmoving Alistair

Hamilton. Well, that should make establishing time of death easy enough.

'Can I get a copy?' McLean asked.

'Aye, sure. Gie's a minute and I'll stick it all on a flash drive.'

McLean remembered the days of videotape and hours spent peering at fuzzy images on blurred screens in the tiny video room back at the station. Now the whole city was wired up, images available at the touch of a button if you had the correct authorisation. Or you could ask a helpful security guard.

'Thanks. I'll send a constable to pick it up, if that's OK. I'd better go and see what the pathologist has to say. Then we can get things back to normal round here.'

McLean watched from a position halfway down the stairs as Jo Dalgliesh tried to bluff her way through the cordon. It shouldn't have come as a surprise to him to find his one-time nemesis and recent ally talking to one of the uniformed constables. Quite a crowd had gathered now, a concentration of the otherwise milling throng. Not that any of them could see much going on. By the way the reporter was gesticulating, and the body language of the constable, she wasn't getting what she wanted either.

'You'd better not be trying to corrupt my officers, Dalgliesh.' McLean lifted the cordon tape and ducked under, turning to the officer and adding 'I'll deal with this,' much to the young man's relief.

'Wee birdie telt me there was a dead body up there.' Dalgliesh pointed to the upper floor where it formed a balcony looking out over the masses like a pulpit for the religion of commerce.

'Really? And why would that be of interest to one of the city's finest rakers of muck?'

The reporter feigned indignation, or at least McLean hoped it was feigned. 'You insult me, Tony. If it's important enough for a detective inspector to be called in, then of course I'm interested.

Way I hear it your man there had an unexpected and fatal seizure. Sounds a bit like that poor lad Rory Devlin over in the schemes.'

It was, of course, too much to hope that ongoing investigations wouldn't leak to the press, even ones in their early stages. Even so, McLean was surprised at how swiftly Dalgliesh was on the case with this one, curious to know why she'd singled it out.

'There's something you're not telling me, Jo. How much do you know about Devlin? And how did you find out about this?' He waved a hand in the general direction of the food court. 'The body's hardly cold.'

'So there is a body, aye?' Dalgliesh leaned back and craned her neck as if that might help her catch a glimpse.

'You know the drill. I can't make any comment this early on in the proceedings. If you have information that might help us in our investigation, then I would be very happy to hear it, of course.'

The reporter sighed, shoved her hands in her pockets, then drew them back out again, one clutching the bulky tube of her electronic cigarette. She looked at it mournfully, then away at the southern exit and the car park where she'd be able to turn the thing on. 'I've been hearing a few rumours about a new high the kids are going mad for. Demon's Breath, it's called, apparently. Although some people are calling it Zombo. I also heard a rumour Rory Devlin might have overdosed on some new, unidentified drug. Gave him seizures so bad he broke his own neck. Now that might be an exaggeration, but when I get a wee tip-off about a lad on his own losing it and flipping tables in the food court, complete with a little bit of shaky video footage? Well, that piques my interest, aye?'

Dalgliesh shoved her fake cigarette back in her pocket and pulled out her phone, tapped the screen before holding it up for McLean to see. He didn't really need to watch it, although the angle was slightly different from the CCTV footage. It was in portrait mode, too. Why did people always film that way with their phones?

'Even more interesting is coming here and finding a full police presence already in place, senior pathologist on the scene and my favourite detective inspector attending.'

McLean pinched the bridge of his nose in an attempt to stave off the wave of tiredness that swept over him. The worst-case scenario he'd played out in front of the chief superintendent seemed to be coming good. Or should that be coming bad?

'I can't give you much, Jo. Not without running it past my DCI first, probably the chief super too just in case. Last thing we need is a panic. And you know what the politicians are like if they see a moral football to kick about. Give me time to sort this out, and I'll let you know as much as I can ahead of any press briefing. That sound fair?'

Dalgliesh smiled, something McLean didn't think he would ever get used to. Or trust. Then she drew a tight finger and thumb across in front of her mouth as if zipping it shut.

'Seeing as you asked nicely, I'll sit on it for as long as I can. That video's all over the internet, mind, so I can't promise no one else has seen it.'

McLean glanced at his watch. In all the excitement he'd missed lunch. Again. But it had also only been a few hours since Alistair Hamilton had died. Who had taken that video and posted it to their Twitter or Instagram or whatever the social media of choice was these days? It didn't really matter. This was the way of modern policing, rushing to stay one step ahead of the rolling online news. At the top of the stairs, DC Bryant appeared, searching for him in the crowd. As soon as she had his attention she nodded. Everything they could do up there was done.

'I need to get back to the station,' he said to Dalgliesh, who it appeared had noticed the detective constable's signal too.

'New girl? She's a bit of a looker, eh?'

'Don't, Jo. I'm not in the mood. I'll call you as soon as I've got something you can use, OK? And if you know anything about this Zombo or whatever you called it, don't keep it to yourself, aye?'

'Would I do that, Tony? To you?' Dalgliesh raised both her hands in an expression of mock disbelief, but before he could answer her, she turned and strode away.

14

'Demon's Breath? Zombo? What on earth have you been reading, Tony?'

McLean stopped writing on the whiteboard in the incident room, turned to see DCI Ritchie standing in the open doorway. She looked tired, her face thinner than he'd noticed it before, shoulders a little more slumped. The joys of seniority.

'I think we might have a problem brewing. Another problem, I should say.' He brought her up to speed on recent developments, the horrible similarities between the deaths of Rory Devlin and Alistair Hamilton, the conversation with Dalgliesh. Ritchie's shoulders slumped even further, and eventually she pulled out a chair, almost falling into it.

'What's the plan, then?' she asked.

'First off, we need to put together something for the press. Devlin fell under the radar, but Hamilton's death was public. Bloody ghouls filmed it and posted it on the web.' One of the first things he'd done on returning to the station was set the Social Media team on tracking down the original video and the person who had posted it. Even if they didn't really need to, he wanted to pull them in for a thorough questioning.

'You want me to have a word with Gail about that? Might look best if the senior officer in the city ran the press conference.

Make them think we're taking things seriously.'

'Or they'll think it's more serious than it is, run the story harder than they otherwise might and create the moral panic we'd like to avoid?'

Ritchie let out a heavy sigh. 'We can't win, can we.' It wasn't a question.

'We need to trace Hamilton's last known movements. Still trying to find out if he's got any family in the city so we can have someone ID him. He's a bit of a ghost, really. I'll put Janie Harrison and Jess Bryant onto it.'

'Jessica. She doesn't like it being shortened. Unlike Cass Mitchell, who really hates being called Cassandra. Can't say as I blame her. What were her parents thinking?'

McLean shrugged. 'Fans of Greek mythology, maybe? I'll try to remember that. Still need her to trace Hamilton. And we could do with speaking to some of Rory Devlin's associates too. Spread the net wide enough and, who knows, we might start seeing some overlap between the two.'

'I do admire your optimism, Tony. We're stretched thin enough as it is. Doesn't help that Jo Dexter's poached two of our new DCs and we're still waiting on news about a DI to take over my old position. Remember when this place used to be heaving with officers?'

McLean looked around the near-empty room and had to concede she had a point. He didn't have time to admit it before the door swung open again, a slightly breathless DC Stringer appearing in the entrance. He held his phone in one hand, shook it from side to side.

'Call's just come in. Break-in and assault. Property in Restalrig.'

'Why would –?' Ritchie began to ask, then stopped.

'Aye. It's the Devlin house. Someone broke in and attacked the daughter.'

★ ★ ★

It took longer to get to the dormer bungalow than McLean would have liked, but he wanted to have DS Harrison with him. She was the one who had built up a rapport with Maggie Devlin, after all. By the time they arrived, she'd been taken off to hospital in an ambulance, and they were faced with a pair of irate parents. Or an irate mother at least.

'What's the point of having polis if youse just let killers walk the streets? We're no' even safe in our own homes now.'

Mrs Devlin had channelled her initial shock into anger by the time McLean found her in the kitchen. The house didn't look a lot different to how it had the previous time he'd been there, apart from the half-dozen Scene of Crime techs cluttering up the place, busy dusting for prints and photographing everything. A couple of uniform constables guarded a front door that looked like it had been opened with a police issue Big Red Key. From there, whoever had forced entry had gone straight to Rory's room, either unaware or unconcerned that Maggie was in the house at the time.

'I'm very sorry, Mrs Devlin.' McLean perched on the edge of the sofa, Harrison standing behind him, away from the action. There were two armchairs in the room; Mrs Devlin sat in one, her husband in the other. So far, he'd said nothing, and his general demeanour gave McLean the impression that he was very much second in command here.

'Sorry's all good and well, but what're youse going tae do about it? My poor wee girl in the hospital wi' concussion. She could have been killed. An my boy no' even in his grave yet.'

'It seems that whoever broke in was looking for something your son had. And he knew which room was Rory's too. Have you any idea who of his friends might know that?'

'Is that it? You think my boy mixed wi' the kind of folk who'd kick in your door and beat up a wee girl?'

Mrs Devlin's anger, while understandable, wasn't really helping matters. McLean hadn't spoken to her since delivering the bad news of her son's death over a week ago now. Had anyone updated her about the drugs angle? Maggie knew, of course, but how much did the teenage girl confide in her mother?

'Have you spoken to the Family Liaison Officer recently?' he asked, skirting around the subject in as diplomatic a way as possible.

'That useless wee shite? Nah. I told him we was fine an' tae stop pestering us all the day. Come tell us when youse lot've caught the bastards who beat my wee boy tae death. An' why've you no' done that yet, aye?'

McLean paused. How best to deliver the bad news? Given Mrs Devlin's barely controlled anger and her clear hatred of the police, there probably wasn't any good way. Least worst then.

'You'll not have heard the update on our investigation into Rory's death, I take it.'

'Update?' For the first time since they'd been introduced, Mr Devlin spoke, his whole body suddenly animated as if someone had put fifty pence in the meter. 'You've found who did that to him? Who killed our boy?'

'Actually, we're focusing more on the possibility that he may have had a violent seizure, brought on by exposure to an as yet unidentified narcotic, and all his injuries were self-inflicted.'

In the ensuing silence, McLean could hear the tick of the clock on the mantelpiece, where it sat alongside the photograph of a younger, happier Rory Devlin. The muffled thumps and mutterings of the Crime Scene technicians seemed to almost disappear for a moment, and was it his imagination, or had the temperature in the room dropped?

'You fucking what?' Mrs Devlin's absolute stillness was worse than any violent outburst. McLean had seen enough cold fury in his many years on the job, and this bore all the signs.

'The injuries your son sustained looked very much like those we would normally associate with a vicious beating, and that remains an avenue in our investigation, Mrs Devlin. However, evidence has come to light that opens up an alternative possibility. The break-in here, particularly given that whoever did it went straight to Rory's bedroom, looking for something only there, suggests –'

'Get the fuck out of my house.' Mrs Devlin was on her feet before McLean could react, even though he had been expecting some form of explosion. Her husband shrank away into his armchair as if this was a regular occurrence, both arms coming up to shield his head even though the woman's ire was directed somewhere else for a change.

'Mrs Devlin, I –'

'I said get the fuck out of my house. All of youse. Coming in here wi' your accusations an' lies. What, you going tae arrest me next? My wee boy beaten black an' blue, my girl in the hospital, an youse come in here wi . . .' She swelled with indignant rage, finally lost for words. Some small voice of self-preservation must have been holding her back, but McLean didn't want to risk his unbroken nose on how long that might last. He motioned for Harrison to get the door, not taking his eyes off Mrs Devlin until the exit was secure. She said nothing more, staring daggers at them as they left the room.

Out in the hall, only one Crime Scene tech remained, packing his fingerprint gear into a battered aluminium case. 'Just need comparables from the residents, sir,' he said.

'Maybe later, eh?' McLean waved to the broken front door and the falling darkness outside. 'Think it best if we leave the family alone for now.'

'Well that could have gone better, I suppose.'

McLean sat in the passenger seat of the pool car and watched as the Crime Scene tech van drove away. DS Harrison had kept quiet ever since they'd left the house, which was probably wise of her.

'Really shouldn't have been our job to tell them about the drugs,' she said finally. 'And certainly not like that.'

'Was I that bad?'

'I didn't mean that, sir. I meant the situation, having to break the news there, after they've come home to this.' She waved a hand in the general direction of the house. Its front door still hung slightly askew, no sign of anyone rushing to repair it.

'I know what you meant. Still probably could have handled it better, mind. That's what the training's for, after all.'

In the darkened interior, it was almost impossible to see Harrison's face, so her reaction to that was lost. She reached forward and tapped the button that brought the dashboard to life. McLean hadn't really got used to an engine you started with a button rather than a key, and now these new electric things were even more confusing. He'd learn, of course. He had to. Couldn't keep cadging lifts in squad cars or borrowing Emma's little Renault. And that was just as complicated as this car.

'Back to the station?' Harrison asked.

McLean stared at the dashboard until he found the clock. The detective sergeant's shift had ended, but the way this case was shaping up, overtime wouldn't be a problem.

'Do you know where they took the daughter?'

'Royal Infirmary's closest. You want me to check?'

McLean pulled his seatbelt round and clipped it in place. 'Please. You've got a bit of a rapport with her. Go see if you can speak to her, find out what happened. As much as she remembers, anyway.'

'What about you?' Harrison asked as she pulled out her phone and tapped a speed dial number. McLean didn't have time to answer before she was talking to whoever was on the other end. A swift conversation before she hung up.

'Just as well I didn't drive to the Royal, she's in the Western General and they're keeping her in overnight for observation. Seems strange neither of her parents went with her, don't you think?'

McLean glanced back at the house, dark now except for the light leaking from the broken front door.

'You saw the husband, right?'

'Aye. No' what I was expecting.'

'I don't imagine he's having a great time of it in there right now. It's Mrs Devlin who wears the trousers in that house. She probably doesn't trust him to look after the place if she goes to the hospital, and doesn't want him going without her being there too. They can't go anywhere until the front door's fixed, so she's trapped herself. Probably explains why she's so angry.'

'We could –' Harrison started, then stopped talking. In the darkness, McLean could just about make out her shaking her head.

'Aye, we could offer to put a constable on the door. I would have, too, if she'd given me the opportunity. I think we both know what she would have said to that though, even before I dropped that drugs bombshell on her. I'll have a squad car drive up this street every so often overnight, and if she complains of harassment, well . . .'

Harrison did something with the car's controls, glanced over her shoulder and pulled away from the kerb without much in the way of noise.

'Meant to say earlier. I spoke to Trev . . . PC Strong down in the evidence store. About that stuff Sergeant Needham nicked. Apparently some of it was sent to the chemistry labs at the university for analysis, and the rest was destroyed.'

'Makes sense, I guess.' McLean found himself nodding, even

though in the darkness of the car's interior nobody could see him. 'Have you spoken to the university about the sample they took? Might be worth following up if someone wrote a paper on it.'

'I was going to when I got the call about this. Asked Lofty to look into it.' Harrison eased the car into the traffic on the London Road. At this time of night most of the cars were going the other way, but there was still a bit of a jam at the big Morrisons supermarket, and another at the traffic lights at Jock's Lodge.

'You want me to take you back to the station, sir?' Harrison asked as they waited for the lights to change. 'Before I head over to the Western. Better chance of Maggie Devlin being awake still.'

It wasn't exactly far, across Holyrood Park and up through St Leonard's, but the journey across town from there to the hospital would be twice as long.

'No, drop me off here. I'm meant to be meeting up with Em in an hour or so. The walk'll give me time to think, and maybe build up an appetite.'

15

Janie had never been a big fan of hospitals. There was something about the bright lights, the smells, the manic busyness of them that set her on edge. It was either that or the fear of catching something, irrational though that was. Unlike the detective inspector, she didn't know almost the entire nursing staff by name, either. The middle-aged woman who finally came to speak to her looked tired to the point of collapse, but she had a friendly face, and did her best to be helpful, directing Janie to a quieter part of the main building, where individual rooms were reserved for private patients. A bored constable sat outside one, staring at the screen of his smartphone. He shoved it hastily away and stood to attention as soon as he noticed her.

'I wasn't expecting anyone,' he said, smoothing the creases from his jacket with nervous hands. Janie had met PC Carter a few times before, knew all too well that he had once been, briefly, Detective Inspector Carter. And that he had almost lost his job due to an act of gross misconduct when he'd tried to blame his own incompetence on DI McLean. Somehow he'd managed to survive, busted down to constable and back in uniform, but it had left him with a permanent sense of grievance and a sneering dislike of anyone associated with his old nemesis.

'I wasn't expecting a constable to be keeping guard, so that's both of us disappointed. She awake, do you know?'

Carter shrugged. 'Probably. Doctor went in about five minutes ago and hasn't come out again yet.'

'You got a sign-in sheet then?'

Carter shrugged again. 'Just got told to sit here and keep an eye out, right? Nobody said nothing about signing in.'

Janie shook her head. How the hell Carter had ever made it to plain clothes, let alone passed the Inspector's exams was beyond her. 'Fine,' she said, then knocked quietly on the door and let herself in.

Maggie Devlin had hit the jackpot as far as hospital rooms went. Most people would have ended up on a ward, or been sent home with a handful of painkillers and the advice to call the hospital if they started to feel worse. Someone had decided her plight warranted better treatment than that, and the presence of Constable Carter outside suggested it had most likely been DI McLean. She'd seen him making a couple of calls at the Devlins' house while she was talking to the Scene of Crime technicians; this was probably the result of that.

'Detective Constable Harrison, isn't it?' The woman who stood beside the bed looked even more tired than the nurse who had given Janie directions here, but at least Janie recognised her.

'Dr Wheeler?' She didn't bother to correct her about the rank. 'How is the patient?'

'Sore like some fucker tried tae smash ma heid in wi' a half-brick.' Maggie Devlin's voice sounded weak, but there was no denying the anger in it. Her mother's daughter, it would seem.

'We OK to talk?' Janie asked, not quite sure whether the question should go to the doctor, the patient or both.

'As long as she doesn't overexert herself, a wee chat should be fine.' Dr Wheeler checked her watch, frowned. 'But not too long, mind? I'll be back in half an hour and you'd better not still be here.'

'I won't. Don't worry.' Janie opened the door as the doctor approached, taking perhaps a little too much satisfaction at the sight of PC Carter scrambling to his feet again.

'Give Tony my regards next time you see him, will you? It's been a while.' Dr Wheeler paused once she'd stepped into the corridor, her head at a quizzical angle. 'I guess on balance that's a good thing, right?'

She didn't wait for an answer, merely nodding at Carter before striding off down the corridor in the direction of the next patient. He looked at Janie, a question forming so obviously on his features she could almost see the thought bubble above his head. She didn't have time to explain, so merely shrugged, then closed the door behind her and hoped that half an hour with an angry Maggie Devlin would be enough.

'What was that about Tony? He your boyfriend or somethin'?'

Janie hadn't even finished closing the door before Maggie had asked the question. The young woman's voice was stronger now that she didn't have to play up for the doctor.

'Tony? Gods no. He's my boss. Detective Inspector McLean. You know, the one who came round when we first visited.' She stopped herself from adding that the purpose of that visit had been to tell Maggie her brother was dead.

'Oh aye, him.' Maggie shuffled in her bed, trying to sit herself upright, then cursed under her breath. Clearly her injuries were worse than she was prepared to admit. 'Got a thing for doctors then?'

'Not exactly.' Janie pulled up a chair and sat down. 'More a thing for getting himself injured in the line of duty. She's patched him up a fair few times, so I've heard.'

Maggie settled back into the soft pillows, and for the first time since arriving Janie got a half-decent look at her. For all her bravado, she looked drained, dark circle bruises beginning to form around her eyes. Her hair stuck out in awkward angles from a bandage wrapped around her head, and a small sticking plaster marked the spot on her arm where she'd been on a drip for a while.

'You sure you're OK to talk?'

'Well, I'm no' goin' anywhere am I. No' wi' that cheery wee bugger outside.'

'He's not there to stop you running away, Maggie. If you want to discharge yourself, that's absolutely your right. I'll even sort out someone to drive you home.'

'If he's no' here to stop me, then –' Her eyes went wide as the realisation sank in.

'I don't think you're in any danger. Not here. But there's no harm in being safe.'

'Jesus. An' I thought –' Maggie slumped back against the pillow, then winced in pain.

'You should rest. Get some sleep. I can come back in the morning.' Janie started to get up, but the young woman reached a shaky hand out to stop her.

'No. Stay. Please. I don't much feel like sleeping, an' youse must have come for a reason, aye?'

'I wanted to check you were OK. But I'd also like to ask you about what happened, if you're up for it.'

Maggie closed her eyes, and for a moment Janie wondered if she'd been lying about needing to sleep. Then without opening them again she began to speak.

'I was at home on my own, ken? Mum was at work and Dad, well he and some of the other bus drivers stop in at the pub after their shift's over. No' gettin' drunk like. Mum wouldnae stand fer that. But it's a stressful job drivin' the buses. You should hear the stories he tells.'

Janie said nothing, although having been called out to plenty of violent incidents that had either happened on buses or started there, she knew all too well what the young woman meant.

'I've been off school since Rory . . . y'know. Compassionate leave or somethin' they call it. Reckon it's more to stop me being a distraction to the other students. No' that I'm complainin' like. Gives me time to revise. Exams coming up soon and then I've got to think what I'm goin' tae do next.'

Maggie part opened one eye, staring at Janie through the slit between her eyelids. 'Thought mebbe I might sign up wi' your lot. Just tae see the look on Mum's face. She hates the polis.'

'I'd noticed that. You sure you want to antagonise her that much?'

Maggie closed her eye again, but seemed to have learned not to try and shake her head. 'Probably not. How'd your folks take it? When you signed up?'

'Happy I'd got a job, to be honest. They still can't believe I'm a detective sergeant chasing down leads and solving crimes. Mind you, neither can I sometimes.'

Maggie said nothing for a while, and with her eyes closed it was hard to tell if she was drifting off or not. Janie glanced at her watch. She should maybe have texted Manda to say she was going to be late. Then again, Manda would probably be late too. It wasn't often either of them came home at shift end.

'You gonnae find out who killed my big brother then?'

'We're going to find out who sold him those drugs, aye. We'll do everything we can to make sure whoever made them is stopped, too. I've a feeling they might be behind your unwanted visitor today. They went straight to Rory's room, right?'

Maggie finally opened her eyes. She had her hands on top of the covers, and her fingers started to twitch and flex as if the memory hurt as badly as the damage to her skull.

'Aye, they did. I was in my room, had my headphones on, volume up loud. That's the only way I can think I'd not have noticed the door. First I heard was when the tune stopped.

There's only a thin wall between me an' Rore. That's why I've the headphones, ken? Fair spooked me out when I heard someone in there. Voices muttering, like? I mean, Mum and Dad weren't gonnae be back for ages, and Rore's, well . . .'

'So you went to see who it was?'

'Aye. Only I'd no' got as far as the door before I got smacked on the heid.' The young woman reached up with one hand, but didn't touch the bandage. 'Must've knocked me senseless cos the next thing I ken is Dad kneelin' next to me an' I'm lyin' on the floor.'

Janie watched as Maggie closed her eyes again. What painkillers had they given her? When would Dr Wheeler be back? Head wounds were tricky, she knew; they played havoc with your memory. But if what the young woman was saying was true, then there had been at least two people in the house, possibly more. One turning over the bedroom, the other standing by with a half-brick in case anyone came home unexpectedly.

'You say you heard voices in Rory's room. I don't suppose you remember anything more about that? Was it a conversation, or just one person muttering under their breath?'

'I . . . I couldnae say. It's all a bit of a blur, ken? An' the more I think about it, the more confused it all seems. I'm sorry I cannae be more help.'

'Don't worry about it, Maggie. You've done more than I could have hoped for. You get some rest and I'll go catch some criminals, aye?'

16

McLean wasn't sure when coming to the Thai restaurant had become a regular thing for Emma and him. It was the first place they'd had a meal together, so many years ago he didn't want to think about it. Too much had happened since she'd helped clear his name when he was falsely accused of being on both drugs and the take. Much of it not good at all for her, and yet she stuck around. Stuck by him when anyone else might have thrown up their hands in horror and moved away to another country.

He wasn't the easiest of people to get along with, he knew. And so he'd been trying to make life a little easier for them both. Coming home at a reasonable hour, taking an interest in how she was getting on with her studies, even the occasional weekend away. And once a month, sometimes twice, an evening out on the town and a meal at this same Thai restaurant where it had all, more or less, started.

The walk from Jock's Lodge hadn't taken as long as he'd expected, so he'd arrived early. The place wasn't busy and the maître d' was like an old friend now, ushering him to a table where he could look out the window and wait for Emma's arrival. He might have taken the opportunity to catch up on work texts, set out what needed to be in place for the next day's morning briefing and the ongoing investigation into the mystery that was Demon's Breath. Instead, he placed his phone face down on the table and stared into nothing, letting his thoughts tumble slowly into place until he saw Emma approach along the street. By the time she'd reached the table, he was on his feet to greet her.

'Not like you to be early, Tony. Is something up?' She shrugged off her coat before he could help her with it, draping it over the back of the chair he'd pulled out before giving him a welcome hug. Outside, a haar had begun to waft in off the Firth, its moisture clinging to her hair from her walk down from the university. She smelled of damp and unfulfilled promises.

'Fortunate circumstance,' he said as they both sat down. 'Or unfortunate, depending on your point of view.'

'Oh yes?' Emma cocked her head to one side like a curious kitten.

'I was called out to an incident in Restalrig. Could have gone back to the station afterwards, but DS Harrison had to go to the Western General. She's OK, before you ask. Just checking up on someone. I had her drop me off at Jock's Lodge and walked over.'

'And the unfortunate bit?'

'That'd be the poor young woman Janie's gone to check up on.' McLean gave Emma a brief outline of what had happened, aware both that he shouldn't be telling her about open cases any more and that not talking shop was the only rule of their regular evenings out. His shop, that was. He was happy for Emma to talk at great length about hers. 'So what have you been getting up to today?'

They were briefly interrupted by the maître d', and later by a succession of attentive waiters bringing far more food than they needed. The restaurant grew busier around them, but not unpleasantly so, and there was no pressure for them to rush. For once McLean's phone didn't even buzz the whole time they were eating, chatting about inconsequential things and generally just relaxing in a way they'd not been able to for a long time. And as they stepped out into a night fully dark, with the haar shrinking the city around them, Emma leaned in close, kissed him on the cheek and slipped her arm into his.

'What are the chances of us finding a taxi in this?' She waved her free hand at the thick fog that turned the cars in the street into slow moving points of light.

'Should've booked one while we were still in the restaurant.' McLean pulled out his phone, but Emma waved it away.

'Don't bother. Let's walk a bit. I like it when the city's quiet like this.'

McLean shoved his phone away, happy to acquiesce. Turning it on, even if only to call a taxi, would have meant seeing a screenful of text notifications, the job intruding on this otherwise perfect moment of calm.

'OK. Where would you like to go?'

They were already walking slowly up the hill towards North Bridge and the Old Town. Emma didn't answer for a while, but then she stopped suddenly, forcing McLean to do the same. Even in the strange light of the street lamps muted by the haar, he could see the mischievous glint in her eyes.

'How would you like to see some old bones?'

McLean had never been in the university's department of archaeology before. Somehow he'd imagined it as being a modern building, perhaps concrete and 1960s, so following Emma into the old Medical School off Teviot Place came as a bit of a surprise. The dusty basement room she led him to was not the kind of laboratory he'd been expecting at all, reminding him of nothing so much as the old science lab and classroom at his hated boarding school in the south of England. Three long benches filled the centre of the room, their tops made of thick planks of dark, varnished wood. There were deep Belfast sinks at the ends of each, and stuck in the far corner a fume cupboard that couldn't possibly have passed current safety regulations seemed to have been pressed into service as a place for unwanted things to be left and forgotten. Here and there, a few pieces of more modern technology looked completely out of place.

'So this is where you spend your days now. Very nice,' he said, as he followed Emma along the aisle between two benches. She stopped, turned, looked at him with an expression that was half suspicious, so he hastily added, 'Much better working environment than those horrible sterile labs Manda Parsons has to deal with. I like it.'

'It's great, isn't it?' The suspicion evaporated almost as instantly as it had appeared, replaced by that wide-eyed excitement McLean had missed for so long. Emma smiled and beckoned him onwards towards a workbench that ran the whole length of the back wall. Lit by overhead fluorescent tubes and a pair of anglepoise spotlamps, the skeleton from the pit beneath the old Leith parish kirkyard had been laid out on a clean white sheet in an approximation of its natural human form.

'It looks somehow bigger, out of the ground.'

'She, Tony. This is a woman's skeleton. You can tell by the pelvis, and the features of the skull.' Emma picked it up as she spoke, running a thumb around the orbit of one eye socket. Cleaned of all dirt, the bone was nevertheless stained by its time in the ground, like a fine china cup after too much strong black tea.

'She. Sorry.' McLean studied the bones from a distance, raising a hand to decline Emma's offer of the skull for closer examination. 'So what secrets have you gleaned from her remains so far, then?'

'Where to start.' She held the skull in both hands like a goalkeeper about to kick a football, turned to face the rest of the bones and for a moment appeared to be overwhelmed by the options in front of her. Finally she put the skull back down in its proper place, then picked up a femur, which had a tiny hole drilled into it at the hip end. Judging by the whiteness, that had been done since the body had been dug up.

'There's a sample off for more accurate radio isotope testing, but so far we reckon she must have died some time in the late thirteenth, early fourteenth century, so she's been in the ground a good seven hundred years.'

'Not going to catch her killer then, I guess.'

'Actually, there's no sign that she was killed. At least not violently.' Emma put down the femur and picked up an arm bone this time. McLean reckoned it was more of a prop than to show him anything specific, but it was a joy to see Emma so absorbed and excited by something, so he wasn't going to mention that.

'None at all?' he asked.

'Not even an old fracture, which given her age is quite something. She was probably somewhere between sixty and seventy, which was unusual for those days, especially for a woman. Given her height is above average too, and the state of her bones, we reckon she must have been quite high status.'

'A late-thirteenth-century wealthy Leith woman. I wonder if Rose knew her.' McLean meant it as a joke, but the look on Emma's face suggested he might have missed the mark.

'Actually, that's a good point,' she said as she absentmindedly tapped the bone against her palm.

'She's not that old, Em.'

'What? Oh. No.' Emma laughed. 'That's not what I meant at all. Rose knows more about the history of Edinburgh than anyone. I'd guess she's got more books in that rambling old house of hers all about the wealthy merchants of Leith and their wives than anyone.'

'But why the pit? A wealthy merchant's wife would have a good Christian burial, surely.'

'That's a good point. I wonder –'

A noise at the far side of the room cut off Emma mid-sentence. They both turned to see a dark-uniformed security guard peering at them through thick spectacles, an angry expression on his face that slowly morphed into simple irritation when he saw who had disturbed his nice quiet archaeology department at this late hour.

'Ah, it's you Ms Baird. I heard a noise. Didn't know . . .'

Emma hurriedly put the arm bone back down, and together she and McLean crossed the laboratory to the door.

'Sorry, Albert. I'd have told you we were down here, but I didn't see you when I came in.'

The security guard was old, perhaps in his late sixties. McLean didn't know him, but he put him in mind of one of his more vindictive teachers, a man prone to inventing offences just so that he could inflict cruel and unusual punishment on the pupils under his so-called care. Mr Tavistock would be long dead now, and not much mourned.

'We were just leaving anyway. Should be getting home, really. Long day tomorrow.' He took Emma's hand and led her past the guard. The old man stood silently, watching them go through rheumy eyes, and all the way out of the building McLean couldn't help feeling like he was back at his old school, busted while carrying out some elaborate prank.

'You really should get your eyes tested, Tony. You need some specs or you'll go blind.'

McLean looked up from his seat in the library to see Emma standing in the doorway, a wine glass in her hand. He'd gone straight for the hidden drinks cabinet and a wee dram before bed, but she'd decided on wine and left him to help himself. As she spoke the words he noticed that he'd been holding his phone so close to his face his breath might have misted the screen. Why did the text on these things have to be so small? Only, it wasn't just the phone screen he struggled with these days. Reports were giving him eyestrain, and the paperwork had begun to breed on his desk again. He could claim he was busy interviewing suspects and relatives of victims, checking out crime scenes and witnessing post-mortems. All of that was true, but he was also finding excuses to avoid having to read anything.

'You're right.' He switched off the phone and slipped it into his pocket as he stood up.

'Of course I'm right. Question is, are you going to do something about it or keep on squinting at your phone like a madman?'

'I'll book an appointment with an optician's in the morning. Don't imagine any will be open right now.' He glanced at the old carriage clock on the mantelpiece above the unlit fire. Its face was both large enough to read and showing him it was getting late.

'Fair enough.' Emma sat down on the sofa, shucked off her shoes and drew her feet up under her bum in that manner McLean couldn't imagine was comfortable. 'What's so interesting you have to ruin your eyesight for it anyway?'

'Nothing important. Just a text from Janie Harrison letting me know about the young woman who got banged over the head. She's going to be OK.'

'That's good. You going to catch whoever did it?'

McLean hesitated before answering. Technically they were still in the no talking shop phase, which wouldn't expire until breakfast in the morning. On the other hand, Emma had asked. And he'd not mentioned work or even looked at his phone until a few minutes earlier.

'I hope so. It's a puzzle though.'

'Everything is with you, Tony.' Emma took a sip of her wine, placed the glass carefully on the floor, then rubbed at her temples with the heel of her free hands as if she had a headache.

'You OK, Em?'

'Fine. Just suddenly came over all weary.' She smiled at his concern. 'Don't know why I'm complaining. You're the one working all the hours God gave and then some.'

'I'm trying not to, but you know how it is. Everything's about juggling resources. Trying to do too much with too few detectives. At least your bones are ancient and there's no rush to puzzle them out. It's the other bones we found that are giving me headaches.'

'Other bones?' Emma sat up straight again. She swivelled around and put her feet on the ground so close to her wine glass McLean was sure she'd knock it over.

'Didn't Hattie tell you? They found human bones in a deep pit outside Straiton. Digging foundations for all the new houses going up. Only been in the ground thirty years or so, which makes it very much an open investigation.'

'Thirty years? So you know whose bones they are then.' Emma reached for her wine, drained the last of it and then looked at the empty glass as if it had played some terrible trick on her. McLean had barely touched his whisky, but he took a sip before answering.

'A terminal cancer patient, dying in a hospice, with just days to live. She walked out right under the noses of the nuns running the place and was never seen again. Until a couple of days ago, that is. And now she turns up in a deep pit, lying on her side like she's just been sleeping all this while. Nothing but a skeleton left of her, which put me in mind of your dead Leith merchant's wife. Strange coincidence, wouldn't you say?'

'I know you, Tony McLean. You don't believe in coincidences. Still, I'm too tired and full of Thai food to think about it right now. Going to take myself to bed.'

McLean picked up his glass, the smoky, peaty aroma reaching his nose as he swirled the burnt gold liquid around the bottom of it. 'I won't be long.'

'Can't promise I'll still be awake.' Emma stood up gracefully, stretched like a cat. And then with the quietest little 'oh' she crumpled to the floor.

17

'She's away for a CT scan now, Tony. I'll let you know the results as soon as we have them. Sure you wouldn't be better going home?'

McLean sat on an uncomfortable plastic chair in the waiting area close by Reception in the Western General Hospital. Dr Caroline Wheeler looked tired, but then he couldn't remember a time when she hadn't looked tired. It didn't seem to slow her down.

'And do what? I'd only be fretting. You any idea what could have caused that? She just . . . It was like someone had cut her strings.'

In his mind he could still see it, Emma's legs folding under her, head rolling back as she slumped to the floor. For the briefest of instances, he'd thought she was maybe playing a joke on him, but the crash of her wine glass breaking dispelled that thought. She was unresponsive by the time he reached her, and had remained unconscious ever since.

'There could be any number of reasons.' Dr Wheeler sat down in the chair next to McLean's. 'Has she been under a lot of stress recently? I know your work can be tough sometimes.'

'She quit the forensics. Well, sort of. She's been studying forensic archaeology at the university. Helping out on the digs for the tramline extension. If anything, I'd say she was less stressed than she's been for years.'

Dr Wheeler stared into the middle distance, her gaze not quite focused on the entrance doors. She half glanced at her watch before stopping herself. 'What about any recent symptoms? Has she complained of headaches? Weariness? Maybe burning the midnight oil with her studies?'

'Not that she's told me.' McLean studied his hands, pleased to see that they had finally stopped shaking. 'Mind you, I'm maybe not the best person for paying attention, you know? Sometimes I wonder why Em even puts up with me.'

Dr Wheeler placed a friendly hand on his forearm, her touch gentle. 'You two have a great deal of history, Tony. Emma's been through the wars, and you've stood by her the whole time. That's why she puts up with you, I suspect. Anyway, she's stable and under observation. I know you'll not sleep, so if there are any developments I'll call you straight away. Just go home, OK? Or do I need to call that young DC Harrison in to drag you away?'

'DC Harrison?' McLean's mind took a little while to catch up with the change in conversation. 'Actually she's a detective sergeant now. I forgot she was in here earlier. Maggie Devlin, poor girl. Is she going to be all right?'

'I reckon so. A bit of a concussion, but they didn't fracture her skull. Not for want of trying, judging by the damage to her scalp. We'll send her home tomorrow. Hopefully have some good news about Emma by then too.'

McLean took the hint. 'OK, OK. I'll go home.' He stood up, wincing slightly at the pain in his hip.

'Still bothering you?' Dr Wheeler asked.

'Only when the weather's about to change. It's nothing.'

'Well, take care of yourself, Tony. I've other patients need my attention beside you and Emma, you know?'

★ ★ ★

The kitchen light was still on when McLean let himself in through the back door. He'd followed the ambulance to the hospital in Emma's little electric Renault Zoe, but he couldn't remember much about the drive back. A thousand different worries ran circles around his mind, occasionally overtaking each other but never finding any kind of resolution. It had all happened so suddenly, so utterly unexpectedly. What could have brought on such a total collapse?

Two pairs of yellow eyes gazed up at him from a huddle in front of the Aga as he filled the kettle and slid it onto the hotplate. Mrs McCutcheon's cat had accepted her new companion with remarkable good grace. For her part, Cecily Slater's cat seemed to have settled in as if the house were somewhere she had always lived. Neither of them ate much, no doubt supplementing the dry food diet he provided with rodents and small birds from the garden. He had grown used to them being around; in some indefinable way they made him feel safer. No doubt Madame Rose would smile to hear him say so.

Should he call her? Tell her about Emma? He pulled out his phone, but a quick look at the clock over the door told him it was only a few hours until dawn. Not a time to be phoning people, even if they were as strange as the medium. It wouldn't surprise him if she knew already.

'Going to be a bit of a vigil,' he said to the cats as he dropped a tea bag into a mug and poured boiling water on top. There was an unfinished dram sitting on the table beside his armchair, but the time for whisky was long past. Or not yet here.

Tea made, he took his mug and a half-finished packet of chocolate digestives through to the library. The cats, who had hidden away in the back of the house when the paramedics had been attending to Emma, now followed him, so he spent a few minutes straightening the furniture and cleaning up the last few shards of broken wine glass to avoid cut pads. When he finally sat down, Mrs McCutcheon's cat leapt up into his lap, butting her head against his raised hand in a manner he couldn't ever remember her doing before. After a moment she jumped down to the floor again, and the two of them curled up in front of the unlit fire.

Silence settled over them like some dire portent. The biscuits went uneaten, the tea slowly cooling as McLean stared at nothing and willed his thoughts to settle. He could do little about Emma's situation except wait for the phone to ring, but that didn't mean it wasn't at the forefront of his mind.

It seemed so unfair that this should happen now. They'd had their rocky patches, the relationship almost completely falling apart at one point. But he'd done what he could to change his selfish behaviour, and she in turn had acknowledged his effort with one of her own. So much shared history, that was what Dr Wheeler had said of the two of them, and she wasn't wrong.

No. Don't think about the hospital, the wheeled trolley carrying comatose Emma away to the scanner. Think about the good times, even the most recent. McLean stared at the book-cases, but saw in his mind's eye the laboratory in the basement of the old Medical School building where they'd sneaked in like naughty teenagers just a few hours earlier. Emma's obvious delight in the puzzle that the bones presented was how he wanted to remember her now, even if the way she held the dead woman's skull had awkward shades of am-dram Hamlet about it.

Which brought him to the other puzzle, the bones now lying in storage at the city mortuary. Emily Worstead might only have died three decades ago rather than seven hundred years past, but she had been laid to rest in almost exactly the same way as their mysterious Leith merchant's wife. Em had joked about him not believing in coincidences. That didn't make it any less true. There was no easy rational way to make a connection between the two bodies, and yet he knew instinctively that there must be one.

Perhaps he'd been spending too much time in the company of Madame Rose after all. The old medium would probably spin some yarn about the bodies being sacrificed or something, a protection for the city against the evil forces ranged against it. Only, if that was the case then it wasn't working. You only had to look at the deprivation, the drug dependency that fuelled half the crime in the city or more, to see that. Was it any surprise the likes of Mrs Devlin were so hostile to the police when the tide of lawlessness seemed to be rising all around?

Not that the idea of burying bodies in strategic places was inconceivable, even if any reason for doing it would be clearly bunkum. People believed, after all. It was hard-wired into them. They believed in God and the Devil, in Allah, in the entire pantheon of ancient deities. They believed in fairies and goblins, genies and werewolves and witches and vampires. It didn't matter that none of these things existed, people would still behave as if they did.

How many times had he seen it himself? Things that were hard to explain rationally, or at very least to find a rational reason for? It all made a great deal more sense once you stopped looking for logic behind people's actions.

Which wasn't to say some behaviour didn't have a rational explanation. Two drug deaths in the space of a few short days, horrific though they were, needed no demonic explanation. Drugs were one way of dealing with a world that failed to meet your beliefs and expectations, after all. They were an escape from the crushing mundanity of life. There would always be people who sought that release, and there would always be people looking to profit from that need.

But irrational belief was one thing; holding on to it for the seven centuries between the burial of the rich Leith merchant's wife and Emily Worstead? That was something altogether different. Not possible, when he managed to think through the weariness and worry. Nothing more than idle speculation.

McLean picked up his phone from where it sat beside his mug of cold tea, ready to send a text to DS Harrison in advance of the morning's team meeting. It took a while for the numbers on the screen to register that it was almost five in the morning, longer still to accept that texting colleagues at such an early hour might not be the best way to build team camaraderie. He stared at it until the screen turned itself off, and then continued to stare at nothing for a long time afterwards, motionless, paralysed by anxiety and exhaustion and indecision as the old house creaked and settled around him like dry earth in a grave.

18

'Hey, Tony. Didn't realise you were in already.'

McLean looked up to see DCI Ritchie standing in his open doorway. He had been at his desk since dawn, wading through mounds of paperwork while waiting for a call from the hospital. It had seemed like a good use of his time, but realistically he couldn't have said what the last two reports he'd read had been about.

'Morning, Kirsty. Just thought I'd get on top of some of this before the briefing.' He reached for his empty coffee mug, sure he'd only refilled it a few minutes ago, and saw with a certain dismay that his hand was shaking again.

Ritchie stepped into the office and quietly closed the door. 'Is everything OK? Only you seem a little . . . on edge?'

McLean put the mug back down again, clattering it slightly against the hard wooden surface. Why hadn't he told anyone yet?

'It's Em,' he said, and the whole story tumbled out. There was a certain relief in sharing, but he still pulled his phone out towards the end of it, checking the screen for any incoming text or voicemail message from the hospital. Still nothing, and he didn't know whether that was a relief or a further worry.

'Jesus, Tony. You should have called in. You shouldn't even be here right now.'

He slipped his phone away again, rubbed at his face with both hands, fingers easing the crusty sleep from the corners of his eyes. 'That's the thing though. There's nothing I can do at the hospital except sit there and fret. Caroline – Dr Wheeler – will call me as soon as she has any updates. Until then I'm just getting in the way. Being at home's even worse. Might as well make myself useful here.'

'And you don't think Em's going to want to see a familiar face when she wakes up?'

A hard knot of worry tied itself in his gut at that. He knew full well that one reason he'd allowed Dr Wheeler to talk him into leaving was the horrible thought that maybe Emma wouldn't ever wake up. That's what had happened with his grandmother, after all. She'd slipped into unconsciousness and then faded away, dying eighteen months later without ever waking in between. He wasn't sure he could face the daily trips to the hospital, the hopeless bedside vigil. He'd done that once before, must he really do it again?

'I'll head over to the hospital soon. Just need to get these investigations under control.'

'Don't you think that's what the sergeants should be doing? Janie's busy tracking down Hamilton's next of kin and associates, Sandy Gregg's liaising with the drugs boys about your Demon's Breath or whatever it's called. There's not much either of us can do until they shake something loose, so go be with Emma when she wakes up, OK?'

'And Emily Worstead?' McLean asked. He knew as soon as the words came out that he'd pushed it too far.

'She's been dead over thirty years, for fuck's sake. And anyway that's something for the Cold Case team to deal with. Go, Tony. Or do I have to make it an order?'

There was something in Ritchie's tone that McLean reckoned she'd learned from Detective Superintendent McIntyre. The subtle threat of pulling rank that was so much more effective than actually doing it. He stood up with a weary sigh.

'I'll go, Kirsty. Don't worry, you don't need have a sergeant escort me from the building. You're right, too. I'm being stupid and selfish. Maybe blame a lack of sleep?'

She narrowed her eyes at his bald attempt at raising sympathy, so he backed off quickly and headed for the door. He was reaching for the handle when there was a sharp knock. A startled Chief Superintendent Elmwood stared straight at him when he opened it, far too close for comfort.

'Ah, Tony. Good. I was looking for you.'

'Is it important, ma'am? Only I was just –'

'It is very important, Detective Inspector.' Elmwood cut him off with a withering glare, her gaze shifting past him to where DCI Ritchie stood. Well, Kirsty was only chief inspector; Elmwood had the seniority. And if there was one thing McLean had learned over the years it was that an unpleasant task only becomes more so the longer you put it off. Whatever the chief superintendent wanted, best he find out now.

He turned briefly back to Ritchie, spoke before she could try to come to his rescue and land them both in it. 'I'll do what you suggested, Kirsty. Just need to attend to this first.' Then before Elmwood could step into the room, he gestured up the corridor towards her own office. 'Shall we?'

The chief superintendent's office was the largest on the third floor. McLean remembered when it had been the domain of Detective Superintendent Duguid, before he had retired down to the basement and the Cold Case Unit. It should have been Jayne McIntyre's after that, but there'd been that incident with the journalist and the punch on the nose that had put the brakes on her career progression for a while. By the time she was back in charge of Major Investigations, the best room in the building had been nabbed by the deputy chief constable assigned to the region, and now they had another uniformed officer running things.

Elmwood went straight to her desk, settling herself into an enormous black leather executive chair that made rude little farting noises as her weight displaced air from the cushions. McLean hoped that was what it was, anyway. He was too polite to even raise an eyebrow. On his side of the desk a considerably less luxurious chair had been pulled out from the conference table across the room and Elmwood gestured for him to sit. He'd have preferred to stand, and for this meeting to be over swiftly, whatever it was about. But then he'd have preferred not to have been here at all.

'We didn't really get off to the best of starts here, did we, Tony?'

Preamble, which meant this was going to be a long meeting. McLean crossed his legs and placed his hands gently in his lap, willing himself not to fidget.

'Did we not? I thought everything was going well enough. Until . . .' He left the rest of the sentence unsaid.

'Oh come now. You fought off every attempt I made to bring you into the circle of influence. You were meant to be my right-hand man, Tony. My inside track. But every time I needed you, you weren't there.'

That wasn't how he remembered it. Yes, Elmwood had been interested in him, but not for any work reasons. And she hadn't taken it well when he hadn't responded to her advances, even less so when he had accused her of murdering her former lover. He knew better than to say any of that though. She was still the boss, and the fact that she was still the boss meant she was even more of a survivor than her predecessor, Teflon Steve.

'I'm a detective inspector, ma'am. I run investigations, direct teams of specialists to catch criminals and solve crimes. You read my file before you even started work here, and I've no doubt you've spoken with Jayne McIntyre at length. You know I never sought promotion to DCI in the first place. I was bounced into it by circumstances and I was not very well suited to the job. Being knocked back to DI wasn't a punishment, it was a relief. The last thing I needed was you trying to push me back into that role.'

Actually the last thing he needed was unsolicited sexual advances from a senior officer, but McLean managed to stop himself from saying that. It would only distract her from getting to the point. She glared at him for a moment, but that might have been because he'd called her 'ma'am' rather than Gail.

'You're wasted in admin, it's true. Your methods aren't always orthodox, but you get results. And you have a way of building loyalty in your team that I've not seen in many DIs and certainly no DCIs. But . . .' Elmwood leaned forward, more farting noises accompanying the movement. There were two unopened folders on her desk, and she picked one up, flipped it open with a thumb. 'Policing has changed since you and I both swore an oath to uphold the law, Tony. We're being asked to do more and more with less and less. You can see that every time you go into the CID room downstairs. There's twice as many desks as there are detectives. I'm still waiting for approval to replace Kirsty now she's taken on your old job, and we could really use a few more experienced detective sergeants. But there just isn't the money.'

McLean felt his hands tensing and willed himself to relax. He needed this, whatever this was, to be over as quickly as possible so that he could get to the Western General. He'd not felt his phone vibrate any incoming texts or missed calls since he'd followed the chief superintendent up to her office, but still the urge to take out the handset and check was strong. Should he just come right out and tell Elmwood what was going on? Why he needed this to happen some other time? He opened his mouth to speak, but she held up a hand to stop him.

'I know it's not fair. And I know all the money's being

drained into the Crime Campus and put into more public-facing policing. I know you're left to do your best with too little resources. But the truth of it is there's never going to be enough. We can't win this war, not the way we've fought it in the past. We need help.'

Finally, Elmwood reached forward and pushed the second folder towards him. McLean picked it up, spotting a logo stencilled onto the outside that was vaguely familiar.

'It was your old friend Jane Louise who first floated the idea, while I was still recuperating,' Elmwood said. With her words, McLean's brain made the connection. The logo was a stylised variant of the one used by the Dee Foundation, and seen on plaques all across the city. The foundation ran halfway houses to help young offenders through the difficult transition from institution inmate to upstanding member of society. It ran some of those same institutions, owned care homes for children which it ran on behalf of social services, and at the other end of life catered for the elderly too. All under the beady, watchful eye of Jane Louise Dee. Quite when she had made the switch from evil tech billionaire to saintly philanthropist, McLean wasn't sure. He didn't believe her motives were pure, either. Had he been a betting man he would have laid good odds on her still being very much the devil he had first met, what was it? Five years ago? Eight?

'I . . .' He started, then stopped, unsure exactly how to voice his utter horror at having anything whatsoever to do with whatever was contained within the folder. No good could come of any partnership with Jane Louise Dee, of that he was certain.

'Saifre Industries already provide us with the bulk of our forensic services. You know that, Tony. The Dee Foundation is coming at it from the other direction. Youth clubs, day centres, libraries even. Jane Louise is a modern day Andrew Carnegie.'

McLean put the folder back down on Elmwood's desk,

unopened. 'And what has any of it got to do with the Major Investigation Team? With me?'

The chief superintendent's smile still didn't reach her eyes. The smooth, unmoving skin made her look like some kind of animated waxwork doll. 'You and Jane Louise have a history. She talks about you often. And the work the foundation is doing brings it into contact with exactly the kind of people you bring in every day. The petty criminals, drug addicts feeding a habit, prostitutes. The scum, basically.'

McLean started to protest, but again the chief superintendent waved him silent. Her words had sparked such an instant rage in him, it was all he could do not to stand up and walk out. Consequences be damned. But there was that small, rational, thinking part of him that needed to get to the bottom of this new situation. Prepare for it or find a way to kill it before it could take root and spread. He clenched his fists, pursed his lips and kept quiet.

'We're going to set up a task force to work with the foundation. Call it intel gathering, if you like, although I'd think of it more as the criminal investigation side of community policing. A friendly face to counteract the negative side of your work.'

'And by we, I assume you want me to set up this task force.'

Elmwood gave him another one of those dead doll smiles. 'Exactly.'

McLean stood up swiftly, not giving her a chance to react before he spoke this time. 'Well, I'll be sure to give it some thought, but right now I have somewhere far more important to be.' He nodded once, then strode to the door, pulled it open and stepped out into the corridor. He might have heard Elmwood's voice asking him where he thought he was going, but he couldn't be sure. He'd closed the door behind him before he realised he'd left the folder with the Dee Foundation logo on the chief superintendent's desk.

19

The address they had finally managed to track down for Alistair Hamilton was a tenement block in Newington, not far from the police station. Janie had walked over with DC Bryant, chancing a break in the low clouds and trusting they wouldn't have to dodge showers on the way back.

'I looked at a flat in this street not that long ago. Thought it'd be fine and handy for work.' Bryant peered up at the regimented rows of tall sash windows, the soft red sandstone facade.

'Why'd you not move then?' Janie asked, aware that the detective constable lived in Gilmerton with her parents still.

'Too bloody expensive. This whole city's gone mad, the rentals on flats. Thought a DC's pay would help, but . . .' Bryant didn't elaborate.

'Should get yourself a flatmate. Works out a lot cheaper if you share.'

Bryant merely shrugged. 'Begs the question how a bloke like Hamilton can afford to live somewhere like this.' She pointed to the front door of the tenement they'd been looking for, and Janie had to admit she had a point. Alistair Hamilton had no money in his wallet, wore clothes that some people would have taken to the fabric recyclers long since, looked like he'd not had a square meal in years. And yet his address was somewhere flats sold for well over a quarter of a million. If this really was his address, of course. So far they'd not managed to find out much information about him at all.

'Second floor, wasn't it?' She scanned the buttons on the intercom, looking for but not finding the name Hamilton. It didn't matter, as the door itself had been propped open with a half-brick. They both stepped into a surprisingly clean and odourless entrance, a narrow flagstoned corridor leading to the back and a set of stone stairs that spiralled up to the rooflight high overhead. A hush descended on them as the door closed, cutting off the city beyond so that Janie's sensible boots and Bryant's rather more elegant flat shoes made an echoing noise as they climbed to the second floor. There were two doors, but one clearly advertised itself as the home of a S. Mathieson. It was freshly painted in a deep gloss burgundy, whereas the other door looked like it hadn't seen a paintbrush since the tenement had been built.

'This one, I reckon. You got the key there?' Janie held out a hand and Bryant passed over the clear evidence bag with the single key in it. When she pushed it into the slot it twisted freely and the door cracked open a fraction. She held it like that, listening for any sound from inside.

'Gloves, I think. Don't want to get it in the ear from Manda if we have to call forensics in later.'

Bryant nodded her understanding as she pulled out a pair of white latex gloves and stretched them over her long-fingered hands with delicate ease. Janie struggled a little with her own pair, and then she pushed the door wide for them to enter.

The first thing she noticed was the smell. There was something sickly sweet in the air, like a pot of warm honey. It didn't seem to be coming from anywhere in particular, simply hanging in the still air. The door opened onto a compact hall, with four other doors leading off it. To the rear of the building, there would be a galley kitchen and a bedroom, to the front she could see through into a living room that wasn't a bad size but was overlooked by the tenements across the street. The other door opened onto a tiny shower room with an ancient thunderbox toilet and heavy ceramic basin. The toilet seat was up, a copper-green overflow stain down the back of the bowl, but otherwise the place seemed remarkably clean. Empty, too. There was no furniture in the hall, and nothing visible in the living room.

'You want to check the front, I'll see if there's anything interesting in the back.' Janie pointed Bryant in the direction of the living room, then crossed the narrow hallway to the kitchen. She had been expecting the flat to be untidy, but what she found was quite the opposite. That might have had something to do with the lack of furniture. Had Hamilton been so hard up he'd sold it all? And how could someone with no money save a few coins in his pocket afford to live in this part of town?

The kitchen door was part closed, and when she nudged it with her foot it stuck against something lying on the floor. Squeezing through the gap, Janie found a narrow room with a window overlooking the communal garden and the backs of the tenements in the next street. What she didn't find was much in the way of kitchen cabinets, although they had clearly been there at some point. There was no cooker either, no fridge or microwave. Not even a kettle. Only an old Formica-topped table, shoved up against the wall, and a single toppled chair that had wedged itself against the door. Someone had carefully removed everything else, as if in preparation for remodelling. Reaching out, she flipped the light switch and the bare bulb hanging from an ornate ceiling rose burst into light. So there was electricity, which meant there must have been bills, and someone must have paid them. She switched it off again, and stepped back out into the hall.

The bedroom next door was the same, utterly empty but still with that sweet scent on the air. Janie crossed the bare floorboards to the window and looked out through glass as clear as anything she'd seen in recent years. Suspiciously clear.

'Find anything?' DC Bryant's voice echoed from behind her in the near-empty room.

'Nothing. You?'

The detective constable shook her head. 'For a young man living on his own, it's way more tidy than I'd expected. I mean, the lack of furniture's weird, and that smell . . . But my mum's a neat freak and she'd be impressed with how little dust there is. Even the skirting boards. It's clean.'

'Almost like someone's been in here and stripped out everything of value.' Janie stood up, looked around the room, sniffed that strange scent again. 'Or maybe stripped out any potential evidence and cleaned the place down.'

'How do you mean?'

'Well, look at this place. It's been gutted. Why would anyone do that? Remodelling the kitchen, maybe, but you'd expect a mess while that was being done. This is too clinical.'

'You think we should get forensics to have a look then?' Bryant asked.

'For what, though?' Janie took one last look at the room. 'You know what our budgets are like, and if I ask Manda to look over this place on a hunch, she'll never let me hear the back of it.'

'So Alistair Hamilton remains an enigma?'

'Maybe. Let's have a word with the neighbours, see if anyone knows him. We should dig a bit deeper into the ownership of this flat, too. This smells off, and I don't mean that weird honey scent that's making my eyes water. C'mon. Let's get out of here and into the fresh air. We'll run this past the boss, see what he thinks of it. If he says it's OK, then I'll call my flatmate in to have a better look.'

* * *

Most of the flats in the tenement were empty as the two detectives worked their way from floor to floor and door to door. Or if there was anyone home, they weren't answering. Back on the ground floor, Janie was about to give up and send a couple of uniform constables round once everyone was back from work when she heard the crack of a door opening, and then a voice drifting down from above.

'You lookin' for someone?'

She climbed up the stairs until she could see a face peering down over the bannisters from higher up. 'Police, aye. We were wondering if you knew Alistair Hamilton at all.'

'He's gone, the wee shite. And good riddance to him.'

Janie carried on up the stairs until she reached the second floor, where a short woman with sleep-tousled hair watched her with suspicious eyes. She was wrapped up tight in an overlarge dressing gown, and sported fluffy pink slippers that must have been cosy.

'Detective Sergeant Harrison.' Janie presented her warrant card, but the woman showed little interest in it. 'You'd be Ms Mathieson?' She indicated the open door to the flat opposite Hamilton's.

'Aye. An' I'm tired an' all. Whit's this about?'

'Can you confirm that Alistair Hamilton lived here?'

'That's what I said, din't I? Only he left yesterday, an' made a right racket about it.'

'Yesterday.' Janie nodded as if that made sense. 'You work nights, I take it.'

Mathieson sniffed, then pulled her dressing gown tighter around herself. 'Nah, been off sick wi' the flu. Could've done without all that comin' an' goin' when my head was fit to busting all afternoon. Sounded like they was ripping the place apart, no' jest moving furniture.'

'So Hamilton moved out yesterday. Did you see him, or just hear the noise?'

Mathieson sniffed again, shook her head. Now that she'd mentioned being ill, Janie could see the slight sheen of sweat on her forehead, the puffiness around her eyes and yellow pallor to her skin. 'Saw a van out the window. Couple big men loading stuff. No' Ali though. That skinny he'd break if he tried to lift anything. Spent most've the day in bed wi' a pillow over my head. Gonnae go back to that now if you don't mind.'

'Sorry for disturbing you, Ms Mathieson.' Janie put her hand into her pocket and pulled out a business card. She was about to hand it over, but instead placed it gently on the flat top of the bannister halfway between the two of them. 'That's my details if you think of anything else.'

'What's this all about then?' The woman reached out and took the card. 'He in trouble or something?'

'He's dead, Ms Mathieson. I'd say that's beyond trouble, wouldn't you?'

20

'Y ou seen the detective inspector anywhere, Jay?'
Janie walked towards her desk, spotting the detective
constable staring at his computer screen as she went. She'd sent
DC Bryant down to the canteen in search of some lunch, hoping
to get there herself once she'd offloaded the decision-making
onto DI McLean. What little they'd learned about Alistair
Hamilton so far had her thinking this was something that played
better to his strengths than hers, and if they were going to call in
a forensic team he'd need to OK the cost.

'Not in a while, no. He was in with the chief super for a
while, then he disappeared. Car's gone from the car park, so I
guess he's off on some mad errand. Mind you, the chief super's
in a bit of a mood, too. Heard her shouting at a couple of uniform
sergeants like she was going to explode. Poor sods. No idea what
they'd done, but I'd keep away from the third floor if I were you.'

Janie had been going to see if DCI Ritchie was in her office,
but that was on the third floor, perilously close to the chief
superintendent's. Maybe lunch was the thing after all. Let
everyone calm down a bit. It wasn't as if Alistair Hamilton was
going to get any less dead.

'Oh, there was one thing.' DC Stringer scrabbled around on
his desk before Janie could turn and leave. 'Here. Had a call from

the Western General. Something about Maggie Devlin asking to see you.'

'She still there? I thought they were only keeping her in overnight.'

'I'm just the messenger, boss.' Stringer held out the Post-it, which contained no more information than he had already told her.

'Fancy a trip across town?'

'Would love to, but I'm waiting on a call back from the Jobcentre about your man Hamilton there.' Stringer picked up the handset from the phone on his desk, waved it about a bit, then placed it back down again.

'Oh yes? Not waiting for Cass Mitchell to pass by on some important errand you can help her with?'

Stringer's deadpan face was almost perfect; not a man to play poker with. Janie could see his tell though. He tapped a foot against the floor just the once before getting it under control, and the lightest of flushes spread up his neck.

'I don't know what you could possibly mean, Janie,' he said, the effect slightly ruined by the arrival in the doorway of DC Mitchell herself.

'You looking for me?' she asked, not even glancing in Stringer's direction.

'I wasn't, but if you're at a loose end I've got to go to the Western General, have a chat with Maggie Devlin. Could use some company.'

Mitchell glanced briefly at Stringer now, who had gone back to staring at his computer. Then she turned her full attention on Janie. 'Sure. You want me to sort a pool car?'

A different uniform constable was on guard duty when Janie and DC Mitchell arrived at the private room in the neurology ward, which was something of a relief. PC Carter had that knack of making her feel uneasy, and Janie had no idea how the man would have reacted to Cass Mitchell.

'You OK, Ben?' she asked as the constable struggled to his feet.

'Aye. I was on football duty at the weekend. Tweaked a muscle in my leg. That's why the sergeant put me on this job. How's yourself, Janie. Or should I say "ma'am"?'

'Don't you start. Bad enough in my own station.' Janie waved a hand at the closed door. 'She awake?'

'Aye. Go on in. She's expecting you.'

Janie knocked, then pushed open the door. Maggie Devlin looked up from the bed, her initial suspicion turning into a shy smile. Then her eyes widened as DC Mitchell came into the room too.

'This is my colleague, Detective Constable Cass Mitchell,' Janie said before Devlin could open her mouth. 'You said you wanted to see me?'

'I . . . Yeah.' The young woman kept staring at Mitchell for a while before dragging her gaze back to Janie, a slight blush of embarrassment colouring her cheeks. She still wore a bandage around her head, and her hair didn't appear to have been brushed recently, but she had a much more healthy aura about her than the day before.

'I was thinking. About what you said. 'Bout Rore too. Couldn't sleep much in this place, no' wi' my head like this.' She raised a hand and pointed at herself. 'It's no' easy, ken? Trustin' the polis. Youse lot only ever seem to be around hassling us. Making more trouble, no' stopping it.'

'We're not perfect. I'd be the first to admit it. Clean-up rate for burglaries is pretty rubbish, and don't get me started on sexual assault.' Janie pulled a chair from where it stood under the window, set it down beside the bed and sat in it. Mitchell went to the far end of the room, where there was another chair, and settled herself down out of the way.

'Is your mum on her way?' Janie asked. 'Thought you'd have wanted to be out of here by now.'

'Aye, well. Dad's coming to pick me up, but he had to do his shift first. Can't all of us take time off when we feel like it.' Devlin scratched at the sticking plaster on her arm where the needle had been, then seemed to realise what she was doing and stopped. The young woman was psyching herself up to do something that went against deeply ingrained instinct, Janie knew. She said nothing, giving Devlin the time and trusting DC Mitchell to keep quiet too.

'I knew Rore'd fallen in wi' a bad lot,' Devlin said eventually. 'Had a bit of a barny wi' him about it the day before he . . . The day before youse lot came round. Used to be a laugh a minute wi' him, ken? Oh, I hated it, all his fuckin' aboot an' shit, but he's my big brother so that's allowed, right?'

Janie nodded. Her own brothers could be a pain in the arse at times. Most of the time if she was being honest. But she'd defend them to the death if it came to it.

'He had a job, see? Well, an apprenticeship sort of thing. He was doing fine. Had a bit of cash to spend even after he'd given Mam most of it for dig money. An' then it all went to shit about six months ago.'

'What happened?' Janie asked.

'Never really thought about it. No' until last night when I couldnae sleep. He got chucked off the programme, I remember that. But there'd been wee things before that. He changed, ken? The jokes an' stuff he always used to play on me? They got nastier. No' really funny any more. He hid one of those wee blister packs youse get the pill in, ken? It was empty, so he must've found it in a bin or somethin'. An' he brings it home and hides it. In my bedroom. Where he knows Mam'll find it. Jeez, she hit the roof. Felt like I was only six, the way she shouted at me, calling me every name under the sun. And he was there,

Rore. Standin' in the doorway wi' this look on his puss that I'd never seen before.'

'When was this?' Janie asked. 'After he'd lost his job or before?'

'Oh, before. This was mebbe six months back, more. An' there was other stuff he did. Maybe no' so bad but mean, ken? An' it wasnae like him. Then there was a few times he locked himsel' in his room an' din't come out all day. I mean, no' even to use the lavvy. An' he'd be like he was someone else sometimes. Like I din't even know him.'

'And you think this was drugs?'

'Aye, I'm sure of it. See that packet I gave youse? First time I saw it, there was more of them wee glass things in it. An' he had weed too. I could smell it on him.'

'You any idea where he was getting it from?' Janie knew it was a tricky question to ask. Maggie Devlin might have been helpful so far, but there was a line some people wouldn't cross and giving names to the police was a ways off the wrong side of it. As if she were steeling herself to an unpleasant task, the young woman tilted her head back against the pillows and stared at the ceiling, her hand going unheeded to the sticking plaster on her arm again. When she spoke, she did it to the tiles above her, not looking Janie in the eye.

'Been trying to think about that, but he never brought anyone home after he turned strange, ken. 'Fore that there was a bunch of them he used to hang out wi'. Some school mates, a few from the work. Harry Jacobs was one. Creepy wee shite tried to cop a feel once. An' there was that tall bloke, Simon, I think. Aye, that's right Simon McAllister. There was this girl too. They all called her Mystique, like that blue wifey from the X-Men fillums, but I ken her real name's Stella. Think it's Stella Gordon.'

Janie risked a glance over her shoulder, pleased to see that DC Mitchell was taking discreet notes. When she turned back,

Maggie Devlin had stopped staring at the ceiling and was instead looking directly at her.

'You get all that, then?' She asked with the weary sarcasm of a teenager.

'You've been a great help, Maggie. Really. I know you don't trust us, and I'm sure you've got plenty reason for that. This could help us find out what happened to Rory. Not just how he died but what changed him. If we can stop that from happening to just one other person, it'll be worth it, eh?'

Maggie scratched once more at her arm, ripping the plaster off to reveal a tiny, blood-red scab underneath. She covered it over with her thumb and made a strange 'tch' noise of disapproval before once more staring straight at Janie.

'Jus' don't tell Mam I've spoken to youse, aye? She'd kick me out the house if she found out.'

21

McLean had drunk far too much tea, tried to read several books, even switched on the television when the intermittent rain had become more committed to its task. After storming out of the chief superintendent's office, he'd almost gone straight to the hospital to check on Emma's condition. Two calls in rapid succession, one from Detective Superintendent McIntyre, one from DCI Ritchie, had persuaded him that maybe the best course of action was to go home. At least until Gail Elmwood had calmed down a little. He'd giving up phoning friends to tell them about Emma's condition after the first couple had gone straight to voicemail, sending a few texts to key people instead in the hope that the message would percolate out without him having to deal with it. And all the while he had been willing the handset to light up with more news, while at the same time dreading what that news would be.

The afternoon had faded into evening, fully dark with heavy rainclouds shortening the dusk. Sat alone in the too-quiet library, it was both the rumble in his stomach and the realisation he'd been staring at the secret drinks cabinet hidden behind one of the bookcases that finally force him to move.

Two pairs of eyes looked up at him warily as McLean stepped into the kitchen. The cats had largely ignored him, but the sight of them now reminded him that there was a life beyond his immediate problems. He was going to have to deal with that, too.

'Good thing you two get along,' he said as he retrieved the cat food from the cupboard and filled up their shared bowl. 'Going to be keeping a lot of your own company for a while.'

Neither cat gave him any answer, but that wasn't exactly unusual. They mostly tolerated him, feigning interest or even affection only when the food bowl was empty. They spent more time with Emma, curled up at the opposite end of the sofa to her as she read a book or watched the telly. Had they noticed she wasn't around? They'd disappeared when the ambulance crew had turned up and taken her to hospital.

Shaking his head to dislodge the odd thoughts, McLean went to the fridge in search of something to eat. He was sorely tempted by the bottles of nicely chilled beer, but there was a trip to the other side of the city in his near future so tea would have to do.

He was halfway through fashioning a sandwich out of things that looked suspiciously healthy and vegetable when his phone started to ring. He'd left it on the table, and almost let it go to voicemail before abandoning the jar of mayonnaise and snatching it up instead. He'd barely got his 'hello' out before the voice on the other end of the line was yelling at him.

'My god, Tony. Are you OK? I just got your message. Would have called earlier but I've been in Glasgow the last couple of days, and . . . Oh my god, poor Emma.'

McLean sank into one of the old wooden kitchen chairs, hardly noticing the way it creaked under his weight. 'I'm sorry, Hattie. I should have tried harder to get in touch. Should really have phoned a lot of people by now, but it's just –'

'Don't be so ridiculous, Tony. You've done nothing wrong. Where are you? Are you at home?'

McLean looked around the kitchen, as if he needed re-assurance that he was, indeed, home. 'I am. I'm going to grab a bite to eat then head back to the Western General. That's where Em's . . .'

He tried to get words out, but they wouldn't come. It took him a while to realise that there was a lump in his throat so large he couldn't speak, and the blurring at the edges of his vision was caused by tears.

'You stay right there, Tony McLean. You hear me? I'll be over in half an hour.' And without another word, she hung up.

McLean took the phone from his ear and stared at the screen for a while, trying to steady himself after such a sudden breakdown. Eventually the rattling sound of the kettle broke through his mindless stupor. He got up, made a pot of tea, then returned to making his sandwich. Every so often he would stop, pick up the phone, almost hit the speed dial number for the hospital. Somehow he managed to stop himself each time, but it was a struggle.

The arc of headlights playing across the window and the soft crunch of tyres on gravel heralded the arrival of Professor Turner. Her electric Jaguar made no other sound, but McLean had been sitting in silence, his half-eaten sandwich in front of him, mug of tea slowly going cold. His neck felt stiff as he stood up, threw the uneaten food in the bin and chucked the tea down the sink before going to the back door to greet his self-invited guest.

'You look like shit, Tony,' the professor said before grabbing him into an unexpected hug. Her warmth made him realise how cold he was. And how tired.

'Always the diplomat, Hattie.' Another figure stepped out of the darkness and approached a little more slowly. It had been a while since McLean had seen the professor's wife, Meg. They made an odd couple, the forensic archaeologist and the artist specialising in paintings and sculptures inspired by war crimes. And yet something about them seemed to fit. Perhaps it was the easy familiarity of partners who have been together a long time. McLean couldn't be sure, but found himself glad that she had come along too.

'Why don't you come in. I can put the kettle on,' he said.

'Tea?' Professor Turner managed to make the word sound like the harshest of insults. 'We don't have time for tea. Come on. Grab your coat and Meg'll drive us both to the hospital.'

It was, he had to admit, a very pleasant place to be. Sat in the back of the Jaguar, with Hattie Turner in the front passenger seat and Megan acting as chauffeur, for a short while at least McLean was able to put aside the worries and stress of the day. Neither of the two women pushed him towards idle chat, nor asked awkward questions about Emma, leaving him instead to let his mind wander as the night-time city passed by. Reality reasserted itself as their quiet ride arrived at the Western General.

'You two go in. I'll find somewhere to park and wait for you in main Reception.' Megan pulled in to the kerb a short distance from the front entrance.

'Not coming with us?' McLean meant it as a joke, but something in Megan's glare, reflected in the rear-view mirror, suggested he'd struck a nerve.

'Hattie's a doctor and a professor. They'll let her in anywhere. You're a detective inspector, and every single nurse in that place knows you. Me? I'm just an artist. And besides, hospitals aren't really my thing.'

McLean nodded his understanding, unclipped his seatbelt and climbed out. 'Well thank you for the lift, anyway. Might have to think about getting one of these myself.'

The car pulled away silently into the night. He watched it turn a corner into a side street, then hurried to catch up with the professor, who was already at the door. As Meg had predicted, nobody stopped them to ask what they were doing, although a few of the nurses nodded a greeting at McLean as he passed them in the corridor.

'They really do all know you, Tony,' Professor Turner said as they reached the neurology wing.

'Gran was here for eighteen months. She'd barely been gone a year and then Em was in a coma after . . . well. Let's just say I've spent almost as much time in this hospital as I have at work. Hardly surprising my face is known.'

'He's an old regular is Tony McLean. Not sure what Emma would say about him bringing a date though.'

McLean looked round to see Dr Wheeler emerging from a side door. He caught a glimpse of table, chairs, a counter with a sink and kettle before she pulled it closed and crossed the corridor. He was about to make introductions, but it turned out they were unnecessary.

'Caroline. It's been a while,' Professor Turner said.

'It has indeed, Hattie. Where would it have been? That conference in Brazil, I think. Was that 2005?'

'2007. How the time flies. I see you never took my advice to move into pathology, then.'

'I prefer my patients with a chance of survival.' Dr Wheeler shrugged, then her smile faded to a frown as she turned her attention to McLean. 'I'm sorry, Tony. That was maybe a little insensitive.'

'Is the prognosis that bad?' he asked, only half to lessen the tension. The whole episode was making his head ache. Or was that the result of twenty-four hours without sleep and all the stress he'd been under? Maybe both.

'Why don't we go to one of the consulting rooms.' Dr Wheeler guided them towards another door. 'It's quite late. Don't want to disturb the patients any more than necessary.'

McLean glanced across the wide corridor to the closed doors of the coma ward. Behind them were the patients least likely to be disturbed in the entire hospital, but he kept that to himself.

'The prognosis is tricky,' Dr Wheeler said once they were all tucked away in a narrow room lined with tiny locked cupboard doors whose contents would make a street dealer drool if the labels stuck to them correctly identified what lay behind.

'Tricky how?' McLean asked.

'Tricky in that we're still not entirely sure what's wrong with Emma.'

'I thought she had a stroke.'

'Don't be so silly, Tony,' Professor Turner said. 'You know better than most the term stroke covers a multitude of things. I take it the scans haven't come up with any clear trauma site, then?'

'Nothing obvious, no. It's not a clot or a burst blood vessel, for sure. Emma's scans have always been . . . unusual.' Dr Wheeler gave Professor Turner her full attention. 'You're aware of her history?'

'A little. We've been working together a year now, and you know how us girls like to gossip. She's always been a bit cagey about what happened to her, as I guess you would be. And this one . . .' Professor Turner shook her head once in McLean's direction. '. . . Well, you know what he's like.'

Dr Wheeler almost smiled again, her tiredness dragging it down. 'Well she had a nasty blow to the head some years back, and then she was kept unconscious with some experimental aerosol anaesthetic that played all sorts of havoc with her neural pathways for a while.'

The doctor's words brought a chill to McLean's stomach. The chemical Sergeant Needham had used had been destroyed, hadn't it? That's what Harrison had told him. And yet there was no denying how similar it was to Demon's Breath. Strange that Emma should collapse mysteriously now, just as it was rearing its ugly head again.

'Are you even paying attention, Tony?'

'Sorry, it's just what you said. The anaesthetic. We've encountered it again. Something like it anyway. No way Em's had any contact with it, though.'

Dr Wheeler shook her head like a disappointed parent, even though of the three of them she was almost certainly the youngest. 'Well the bottom line is there's no obvious indication as to why Emma collapsed like she did. The swelling we saw on her brain when she was brought in has reduced now.'

'That's a good thing, right?' McLean looked from Dr Wheeler to Professor Turner and back again, not seeing in either of their expressions the joy and happiness he was hoping for. It was the doctor who answered.

'I hope so. You have to prepare yourself though. Understand that when she wakes up, she may well have problems with memory, speech, maybe even fine motor control. We won't know until she's awake.'

'I can sense a "but" here,' McLean said, knowing what it was even as he didn't want to admit it.

'I'm sorry, Tony. Yes, there's a but. We have to prepare ourselves for the possibility that Emma might not wake up at all.'

22

The new morning found McLean once more at his desk long before any of the day shift officers were likely even out of their beds. He'd managed a few hours' unhappy sleep after Harriet and Meg had dropped him back home, but surrendering himself to oblivion wasn't easy. The sight of Emma, lying motionless in the same ward his grandmother had occupied, had lodged itself so firmly in his mind he could see nothing else when he closed his eyes. In the end, he had risen before dawn, showered, eaten breakfast in front of two utterly disgusted cats, and then driven the Renault Zoe in to the station, knowing full well he risked the wrath of DCI Ritchie. Now he waited impatiently for the rest of the world to wake up so he could start asking it questions.

First in, as he had suspected she would be, was DS Harrison. She tapped gently on the frame of the open door to his office and poked an anxious head in, her expression clearly indicating she was well aware of the situation.

'I heard the news about Em, sir. I'm so sorry. Any updates?'

McLean picked up his phone, the screen showing only icons over a blank background. 'Nothing yet. They're taking things slowly. Best I can do is leave that to the professionals and get on with my job.'

She disagreed, he could tell. But she had the good sense not to argue the point.

'I missed the briefing yesterday. What's on the agenda? Anything I can be doing while I wait?' He nodded at the phone again.

'We've a list of names from Maggie Devlin. Old friends of her brother she thinks might be worth talking to. Was going to split that up between me 'n' Sandy Gregg. Take a DC with us each.'

'Sensible. What about the place where Devlin worked before he went off the rails?'

'Alba Fulfilment Solutions, aye. Big warehouse up Newhaven way. Apparently they run apprenticeships or something like.'

'Perhaps I should go and talk to them, if you're busy already. Who's going out with you on interviews?'

'Sandy's taking Jessica Bryant. I'll take Cass Mitchell.'

'Which leaves me Jay or Lofty.' McLean considered it for all of five seconds. 'Don't think Lofty's going to fit into my car. You want to tell Jay to come find me when he gets in?'

'Aye, sir. I'll do that. Shouldn't be long.' Harrison had stepped into the room, and now she made to leave, before stopping herself. 'Was there anything else you needed, sir?'

Had they drawn straws in the CID room to see who was going to have the unpleasant task of checking in on the detective inspector? Making sure he didn't do anything even more irrational than usual? McLean shook away the stupid thought, but another one popped into the space it left behind.

'There was something, actually. The building site where they dug up Emily Worstead's bones. I've a note from Grumpy Bob about tracking down who owned the land thirty years ago. Seems there's some kind of problem at the Land Registry. See if you can't get Lofty Blane onto it. He's good at that kind of thing.'

'Wouldn't it be quicker just to ask the developer who they

bought it from? Chances are it's the same people. Might even have a copy of the deeds.'

McLean mentally kicked himself. 'You're a genius, Janie. Why didn't I think of that?'

'Because you've other things on your mind? I'll give them a call. Already suggested they check to see if there was a record of private burial. Past time I should be chasing that up.'

'Thanks, but you've enough of on your plate with live investigations. I'll drop the CCU a text, tell them to go ask, if they haven't thought of it themselves already.'

Harrison nodded once, then left. McLean picked up his phone, still utterly failing to bring him news good or bad, and slipped it into his jacket pocket. The detective sergeant was right though. He had other things on his mind that were getting in the way of thinking straight. He'd need to keep an eye on that.

Alba Fulfilment Solutions occupied a large warehouse site in the scrubby wasteland that had been reclaimed from the Firth of Forth between Leith Docks and Newhaven. To the north the tall apartment blocks were silhouetted against an angry grey sky, and swirls of wind brought with them the promise of rain. As they approached the new buildings, McLean saw the remnants of an old warehouse, half demolished, exposed steel rebar rusting in the salty air. Bright yellow weed flowers seemed out of place, still clinging on tenaciously as winter approached. Their colour was matched by the swirling reds and greens and blues of the graffiti covering much of the dereliction. Gang names, strange sigils, professions of love and protestations of infidelity. And every-where, that same oddly stylised devil head he'd seen at the old lumber yard where they'd found Rory Devlin's body.

'Should have brought my coat,' he said as he parked Emma's Renault Zoe alongside a collection of much more expensive executive saloon cars and SUVs. Beside him in the passenger seat, Detective Constable Stringer shrugged.

'Think it'll be an hour or two yet before it gets here. Should be done by then, shouldn't we?'

McLean hoped so, but said nothing more. There was a chill in the air that cut through him, despite his having put on one of his heavier suits that morning. Tiredness had a way of making you cold though, he knew. Without thinking, his hand went to his pocket, searching for his phone and the possibility of news. He stopped himself, smoothing out the material as if that had been his intention all along, while Stringer buzzed the door to Reception.

Inside was much like a million other warehouses across the country and the world. Most of the space presumably taken up by the actual business of the enterprise, the administration side of things had been relegated to a small corner of the building. A smiling receptionist sat at a desk facing the door, the company logo picked out in large letters on the wall behind her.

'Good morning, gentlemen. Would you be from the police?' She didn't wait for an answer before adding, 'If you could just sign in here, I'll get you your badges. Mr Woolley will be with you shortly.'

The receptionist pushed forward a simple A4 sheet registry for them to sign. McLean noted that early though they were, two other visitors had arrived already. A Mr Canterbury and a Ms Llewellyn. Neither name meant anything to him, so he scrawled his underneath before handing the sheet to DC Stringer. By the time they were done, the receptionist had produced two cheap clip-on badges. McLean hadn't even managed to attach his before a door to the rear of the reception area clicked open.

'Detective Inspector McLean?' The woman who appeared was clearly not Mr Woolley, but she looked more like an executive than a secretary. There was something familiar about her, although McLean couldn't have said what. Only a feeling that he had met her before somewhere.

'This is my colleague, Detective Constable Stringer.' He shook the woman's hand as it was offered to him, noting her firm, dry and surprisingly cold grip as he did so. 'Ms . . . ?'

'Llewellyn, but you can call me Susan. Would you like to come through to the conference room? Mr Woolley and Mr Canterbury are waiting.'

'I wasn't aware that we were meeting the whole board,' McLean said as he and Stringer followed Llewellyn through the door she had entered by. The white-painted concrete block walls echoed her reply.

'Oh, we're not the board, no. Mr Canterbury and I are from the Dee Foundation. We run the halfway house that supplies a lot of apprentices to this and other employers in the city. Is there something the matter?'

The final question came because McLean had stopped in his tracks. The nagging feelings he'd been having ever since hearing the name Alba Fulfilment Solutions now coalesced into full understanding. He knew where he'd heard of this place before, and he knew why Ms Llewellyn looked so familiar. He'd not met her or ever visited this warehouse, but he'd seen both mentioned in the glossy promotional literature that had appeared on his desk not long after he'd walked out on the chief superintendent. Printed and distributed by the Dee Foundation and paid for with Mrs Saifre's ill-gotten gains. He'd leafed through it in the wee small hours, then chucked it in the bin.

'I'm sorry.' He pulled himself together. Had he slept properly in the past forty-eight hours the information wouldn't have poleaxed him quite so thoroughly. 'I didn't realise this was part of the Saifre empire.'

Llewellyn looked at him with a confused expression, head

tilted slightly like a dog waiting for a treat. Then she smiled broadly, revealing perfect white teeth that must have cost more than he earned in a month.

'Perhaps if we all go into the conference room, I can explain a bit more.'

The conference room looked more like something you'd find in a comprehensive school than a large company. Whiteboards covered one wall, opposite a line of windows looking out onto the scrubland between the warehouse and the distant apartment blocks. Rather than a central conference table, most of the room was filled with smaller tables arranged in rows, with uncomfortable plastic seats all tucked in underneath them on one side. The far wall was covered in posters, notices and other things McLean couldn't quite make out. Beside the door a table had been laid out with coffee and biscuits. Two men had been sitting at the table nearest the door, but they both stood as Llewellyn led McLean and Stringer inside.

'Colin Woolley, Andy Canterbury.' She made the introductions swiftly. 'Shall we get on with this?'

McLean glanced briefly at the coffee and biscuits, then pulled out a chair and sat down. 'Of course. You know why we're here. Looking into a young man by the name of Rory Devlin.'

'Rory, yes. He was a promising lad when he started.' The man who had been introduced as Colin Woolley sat down a couple of seats away from Andy Canterbury and Ms Llewellyn, and it didn't take an expert in body language to see how uncomfortable he was with the whole situation.

'I take it by that you mean he changed?' McLean asked, then before the man could answer added: 'No, hold that thought. Why don't you tell me what he was employed to do here first.'

Woolley looked briefly at Llewellyn, who gave him a tiny nod. Permission to speak.

'He was here on our apprentice scheme, so pretty much everything.'

'And what exactly do you do here?'

'We're a warehouse and distribution hub. We take delivery in bulk from manufacturers and wholesalers. All manner of goods people sell on the internet. Clothes, toys, fitness equipment, a lot of stuff that comes in plain brown cardboard boxes from China. When an order comes in, we parcel it up and send it out.'

'Do you run the website yourselves?'

'No, no. We offer our services to several online enterprises. You'd be surprised how many seemingly different companies are all actually selling the same product from the same factory and distributed through operations like ours.'

'The illusion of choice,' McLean said. 'A bit like washing powder.'

'Washing powder?' Woolley asked.

'You know how there's ten different brands on offer? They're all essentially the same product, made in the same factory, but pitched at different demographics. Companies have been working their markets like that for centuries. But never mind that, tell me about Rory Devlin. I presume he came to you through the Dee Foundation?' McLean waved an open hand at Llewellyn and Canterbury.

'That's right, aye. We get most of our apprentices through them. They learn about clocking in on time, the ins and outs of warehousing. We run training in basic accounting, filing, office skills.' Woolley gestured to the room. 'And there's also the more manual side of things. Driving forklifts, stacking pallets, picking orders. Some gravitate to the office-based work, others are more suited to physical labour.'

'And what was Rory's leaning?'

Woolley frowned. 'I had high hopes for him. Bright lad. Could turn his hand to anything, really. And the other apprentices liked him. But yes, as you said, he changed, maybe a month or two into the job? Started coming in late, missed a few days entirely. Then when I confronted him about it, he turned quite violent. Called me all manner of names. That's when I called in Susan and Andy, told them he had to go.'

'Does that happen often?' Stringer asked. 'Someone going off the rails like that?'

Woolley seemed surprised by the question, or maybe that it was the detective constable putting it. McLean had suggested Stringer butt in from time to time, of course. It helped to keep an interviewee on their toes, let you know whether or not they had been schooled in what to say before the interview. He'd not been expecting this to be quite such an interrogation, had indeed imagined a quick friendly chat. But the two representatives from the Dee Foundation had changed everything. They looked like legal briefs in a suspect interview, always ready to leap in with a 'no comment' or 'my client does not have to answer that'.

'Sometimes, but no. Not often.' Woolley glanced nervously at Canterbury and Llewellyn again. 'Normally the lads and lassies we get from the Dee Foundation are all very good.'

'I have to say, it's come as a complete surprise to me to find that you're getting your apprentices from them. Almost as much a surprise as finding Rory Devlin associated with the foundation. His parents never told us anything about that, and it's not as if he came up through the care system.'

'The Dee Foundation doesn't limit itself to children in care, Detective Inspector. I thought you knew that.' Llewellyn fixed McLean with a knowing stare. 'We supplement the meagre funding the government provides for these apprenticeships, and, yes, we put a lot of our troubled youngsters through the programme it's true, but we also administer it for any school leaver interested. Rory Devlin came to us through a recommendation from the Jobcentre.'

'So you're a temping agency as well. Seems like the Dee Foundation has quite the influence over the city's youth.' McLean tried to keep the snark out of his voice, but he was tired and might not have been entirely successful. Llewellyn managed to hide her annoyance well.

'Someone has to look after them. It's not as if the state's interested in providing jobs or meaningful training any more. We keep them off the streets, give them skills for life and set them up with jobs where we can. Would that it wasn't necessary, but it is.'

McLean began to respond, got almost as far as opening his mouth to argue, but stopped himself before he said something unwise. He was too tired to trade barbs with this woman, too distracted. And damn her, she had a point. Society had failed, and now Jane Louise Dee was stepping up to shoulder the burden. Was it any wonder the chief superintendent and most of the city's dignitaries worshipped the ground she walked upon? And perhaps that was all she wanted, the adulation of the masses bought with the billions she'd exploited out of them.

'Well, this has been very useful and enlightening.' He stood up, hiding the grimace from the pain in his hip with an unconvincing smile. DC Stringer took the hint, standing swiftly and making his way to the door.

'Thank you for seeing us at such short notice. If we have any further questions, we'll be in touch.'

23

Stella Gordon, aka Mystique, wasn't quite what Janie Harrison had been expecting when DC Mitchell had told her where they'd arranged to speak. Perhaps it was Maggie Devlin's reference to the X-Men character that had primed Janie to expect someone a little more glamorous, if not actually blue. Real life Stella was short and round, with a mass of bleach-blonde hair that defied gravity in the way it rose up from the top of her head before sweeping down past her shoulders and on towards her bum. She wore makeup like war paint, and had talon-length nails painted in alternating gloss black and red, spangled with little gold stars, although given that she worked in a nail salon this last detail was perhaps the least surprising.

'You look like you need a makeover, hen,' was the first thing the woman said. Perhaps she was desperate for business, since the tiny shop was empty. It had about it the air of a place whose front door didn't open often.

'You're Stella, right?' Janie asked, holding up her warrant card. 'Detective Constable Harrison. You spoke on the phone to my colleague, Detective Constable Mitchell, I think.'

She had left the DC locking up the car, but Mitchell took that moment to enter the shop. Stella's eyes widened, her focus shifting from Janie to the door.

'Oh god, it's the Dora Milaje!' she said as Mitchell entered the narrow shop. Janie understood the reference, but pretended not to.

'Wakanda for ever,' Mitchell said with a weary sigh. She didn't cross her arms over her chest though.

'Aye, very funny. But we're here to talk about Rory Devlin, not Chadwick Boseman.' Janie put her card away, turned her attention back on Stella. 'He was a friend of yours, I hear.'

'Rore? Aye, we used to hang out a bit. Might've snogged him a couple times. I'd no' seen him a while mind. Then I heard he'd . . . Well.' Stella looked at the floor for a moment, then back up at the two detectives. 'Here, you want a cuppa? Come on in the back and I'll put the kettle on. Not as if anyone's comin' in here anyways.'

Before Janie could object, she'd turned away from them and set off for a doorway with a bead screen across it. Beyond it, a room not much bigger than a cupboard had been pressed into use as a makeshift storeroom and kitchen. Metal shelves leaned inwards from the walls, stacked with boxes of fake nails and other beauty products Janie couldn't immediately identify and didn't particularly want to.

'Youse lot must get through a lot of tea, aye?' Stella said as she rummaged around in a cupboard until she found a couple of mugs. The roar of the kettle and the tiny size of the room meant she had to shout, which wasn't all that comfortable. At least Mitchell had the good sense to wait out in the shop.

'When was the last time you spoke to Rory?' Janie asked, the last couple of words over-loud as she shouted above a noise that had suddenly stopped.

'I dunno. Week ago, mebbe? No' that we spoke much. Just a wee nod and a hello, aye? He was wi' a couple of blokes. Walking down the street there.' Stella gestured towards the front of the shop. 'First time I'd seen him in ages, but he looked kind of busy, ken? An' he was a prick the time before so I didnae stop for a chat.'

'What about the time before, then? When was that? How was he a prick?'

Stella stirred the teabags around, mashing them with a spoon for a while before answering. 'Couple months? Longer, even. All that stuff wi' the lockdowns, I lost track of the days, ken? You think somethin' happened last week, only when you look in the diary it was a year past.'

Janie bit back the retort she wanted to make. One thing she'd learned from working with DI McLean was that patience was a virtue. Better to let someone come to the point in their own time and their own way than force the issue and either put their backs up or end up leading them. She waited while Stella finished making tea, a heavy dollop of milk in all three mugs and a tablespoon of sugar in one.

'There youse go.' The short woman handed over one unsugared mug to Janie, then looked around for Mitchell, holding out the other mug like a magic police officer lure. 'Where's your baldie friend gone?'

Janie took the mug, passed it through the beads, then she turned back to Stella. 'No' exactly a lot of room in here for us all. You were sayin' about Rory being a prick?'

Stella swallowed hard, grimaced at what must have been sickly sweetness. 'Oh aye, that. It was in here, right enough. He came in wi' a couple of his mates. No' folk I'd seen before, y'ken? They was older'n him. Late twenties, maybe? Dressed tidy, mind. Suits an' all. But they was dicking aboot. Picking stuff off the shelves, puttin' it back in the wrong place, messin' things up. I asked them to stop, an' they just laughed. I mean, proper nasty, cruel laughed. Right in ma face. An' Rory, he was the worst of them. Like he was showin' off tae his new pals. Tryin' tae impress them, ken?'

Harrison risked a sip of her tea while Stella was talking. It wasn't too bad, all things told. 'These two blokes she was with. They the same ones you saw him with last week?'

Stella scrunched up her face as if that was the only way to get her brain to work, then slowly nodded. 'Aye, reckon. I ken what they wanted, mind. They was lookin' fer someplace to clean their drug cash, see? Only, I'm tryin' tae run an honest business here. No way's am I gettin' mixed up in that shite. See what it did for poor Rory after all.'

'What do you make of her, wee Stella back there?'

In the eerily quiet electric pool car, driving away from Mystique's Nail Bar, Janie risked a glance across at DC Mitchell in the passenger seat.

'Seems honest enough, if a little annoying. Think maybe I should grow my hair out though, the Black Panther jokes are starting to wear a bit thin.'

'It suits you like that. You should just ignore all the jokers. They'll give up soon enough.'

'You're probably right. If I let it grow I'll just get called Jackie Brown or some other racist shit.'

Mitchell's tone surprised Janie. She couldn't recall ever having heard her swear, which was almost more unusual than being a black female detective in Edinburgh.

'You know if anyone's giving you grief you can come to me about it, right? I know coppers aren't exactly the most woke bunch, but I need to know if it's getting out of hand.'

'Thanks, Sarge.' Mitchell managed a wry smile that Janie caught out of the corner of her eye. 'And as to your question, the shop didn't come up in the list of premises suspected of being involved in money laundering, so what she says about the blokes trying to muscle in rings true. Reckon they either took Devlin along because he knew Stella, or he was the one who suggested it as a potential hit anyway. We can get Lofty to run financials on her business, see if anything stands out. Reckon she's actually legit though, poor girl.'

'Poor girl?' Janie glanced in the mirror, indicated and turned across the road, earning herself an angry toot of the horn from the car behind even though she hadn't done anything wrong.

'She'll be out of business in a year's my guess. Place like that? Needs to be more central, or in one of the shopping centres. Stuck out here?' Mitchell raised both hands to indicate the grey housing blocks and scabby grassland in between. 'Only reason a place like that exists is to clean dirty money. If she's not willing to cooperate, chances are they'll open another one right next door and run her out of town.'

Janie found herself nodding her head in agreement as she followed the satnav instructions down a grubby street that seemed to go all the way to the sea. 'Gives us a bit more of an insight into what Devlin was involved in, I guess. But not much more than that. I'd been hoping the names Maggie gave us would be a bit more current, you know?'

Mitchell grabbed her notebook from where she had placed it on the dashboard, flicked through to the relevant page. 'Aye, well. Maybe we'll get a bit more luck with McAllister. Assuming he's in.'

24

Simon McAllister lived on the top floor of a three-storey housing block, one of a dozen arranged in some arcane pattern around a small central space. Janie hesitated to describe it as a park, since that implied trees, grass, maybe a few flowerbeds and shrubs, whereas what survived in this bleak, salt-blown outpost was mostly discarded plastic shopping bags and fly-tipped mattresses.

A cold wind whipped in off the Forth as the two detectives stepped out of the car and approached what the sign assured them was the correct building. Unlike the old tenements closer in to the city centre, the flats in these blocks were served by an open walkway running from front to back. Maybe the same architect who had dreamed up the central parkland as a communal recreation space had imagined each individual block being populated with like-minded folk who all greeted each other with friendly smiles every morning. No doubt he'd also assumed the open walkways would foster a sense of shared ownership and a pride that would ensure all the residents kept the place clean and tidy. He'd almost certainly never visited the site.

'Jesus, that wind's a bastard.' Janie pulled up the collar of her jacket as she stepped into the walkway, a gust amplified by the tunnel effect threatening to knock her off her feet. Beside her

Mitchell leaned into it and they both struggled past heaps of uncollected black bags seeping bin juice onto the scratched tile floor until they made it to the relative calm of the stairs. Interesting graffiti accompanied them up to the top floor landing, where they were faced with the conundrum of which door to knock on, given that none of them had any nameplate beside them.

'What was the address again?'

'2Fl2 Begbie House,' Mitchell read out from her notebook. They both looked at the three available doors, still none the wiser.

'Might as well try the middle one then?' Janie studied the peeling paint surface. Perhaps there had been a number on it once, but now it was mostly undercoat and bare wood veneer, a tiny glass peephole at head height. She reached out and knocked hard, the sound echoing hollow on the cheap material. It was difficult to hear much over the whistle of the wind through the walkway two floors down, but she thought she might have heard a light thump, perhaps even the sound of footsteps across a bare floor.

'Who is it?' A gruff voice through the unopened door.

'Simon McAllister?' Janie asked.

'Who wants tae know?'

Janie pulled out her warrant card and held it up to the peephole. 'Detective Sergeant Harrison, Detective Constable Mitchell. We wanted to have a word with you about Rory Devlin.'

'Youse got a warrant, aye?'

So it was going to be like that. 'No, Mr McAllister. We're not here to arrest you or to search your flat. We want to talk to you about your old pal Rory. Rory Devlin. You know he's dead, right? Drug overdose?'

A silence of sorts followed Janie's words, underscored by the wind and a splatter of rain thrown against the landing windows.

She waited as patiently as she could manage, and finally the door opened to reveal a tall, thin man. His greasy brown hair hung in tangles past his ears, and his scraggly stubble-beard couldn't manage to hide his hollow cheeks. He stared at them from sunken eyes, one hand scratching at the crook of his elbow with skinny fingers black under the nails.

'Thought they said he was beaten up,' he said.

'No. He wasn't beaten up. He overdosed on something called Demon's Breath. You heard of it?'

Janie wasn't expecting any quick and simple answer, more looking for what reaction McAllister had to the drug's name. His face barely moved anyway, but there might have been the slightest tick. A tiny flicker of recognition. Or it might simply be that the man was coming down off an epic high and they'd get nothing of use from him whatsoever.

'Dunno. Might've heard somethin'. No' interested in that any more. I'm clean, right?'

From the look of him, Janie very much doubted that. 'You in a programme then, or just going cold turkey by yourself?'

'Inna programme int I. Them Dee Foundation do-gooders. Fixed me up wi' this place, an' there's regular meetings an' check-ups an' stuff.' McAllister scratched at his elbow again, his otherwise pale skin bruised and dark where he'd worked away at it.

'You going to let us in then, Simon?' Janie hoped that now they'd got him talking McAllister would be a bit more compliant, but he stood resolutely in the doorway.

'Look, it's either we talk to you here or we ask you to come to the station. We don't have to go inside, it's true. Can't make you let us in. But we still need to talk about Rory.'

Mention of the station seemed to finally penetrate. An even more haunted look fell over the tall man's face, and he hunched in on himself in that way she'd seen Lofty Blane do when he was trying to make himself less noticeable. Finally he made up his mind, stepped to one side and opened the door for them to enter.

On balance, Janie wished she'd decided to carry out the interview on the landing. The more time she spent in McAllister's presence, the more she was inclined to believe his claim to be going straight, or at least trying. But coming off whatever drugs he'd been addicted to hadn't made him any more tidy. The flat was little more than a bedsit, and a small one at that. It had been furnished for a single occupant with no friends, which meant either sitting on the one armchair with its dubious stains or the edge of the unmade bed, also with dubious stains. Janie opted to stand, and Mitchell hung back by the door, one hand held up to her face at the smell, which suggested she'd not grown up with a couple of older brothers. At least McAllister hadn't offered to make them both tea.

'How long have you known Rory Devlin, Simon?' Janie asked once McAllister had moved a few discarded items of clothing to a pile under the window in a half-hearted attempt to tidy. He sat down on the edge of the bed before answering.

'Rore 'n' me. We go way back. Knew each other in primary school, aye?' His face darkened at some unwanted memory. 'Only it all went a bit shit when I was eleven, ken?'

Janie had seen the records. Or at least those of them that weren't still sealed. 'So you lost touch for a while. When did you get back together?'

'I dunno. A year maybe? Eighteen months? Lose track of time, y'ken?' McAllister's hand went back to the crook of his elbow, but he stopped himself this time, shoving both hands between his thighs to stop them doing unwanted things.

'Was he using, when you first caught up with him?'

McAllister looked puzzled for a moment, as if he couldn't

understand who Janie was talking about. 'Rory? Fuck no. He wasnae interested in that. Tried to get me to quit, only it's no' easy, ken?'

'That was before the Dee Foundation programme, I take it?'

'Aye. I've only been on that a few months. Still, keeping clean, right? One day at a time.'

'So when you got back in touch with Rory he was clean, but you were using?'

'Aye. Reckon so.'

'And when did he start taking drugs himself?'

Again that look of confusion passed over McAllister's face, and this time he shook his head slowly. 'Rore never took drugs, man. That wasnae his thing. He was the one got me onna programme wi' the Dee Foundation. Got me intae this wee place. 'Fore that I was crashing out in squats, sleeping rough sometimes. I was messed up and Rore helped me.'

That didn't sound like the young man whose body they had found in a derelict lumber yard not all that far away from this soulless housing estate, but Janie kept that to herself.

'When was the last time you saw him? Saw Rory?'

McAllister went very still, head drooped low, hands still wedged between his legs. One foot juddered slightly as if he was fighting to stop it from tapping to a rhythm only he could hear. Janie gave him the time he needed.

'He helped me move in here. I remember that,' McAllister said eventually. 'An' he came round a couple times wi' food an' that. Some old clothes his da was going tae chuck oot or somethin'. I'd nothin' to my name till the benefits came in. But there's gaps, y'ken? My memory. I . . .' He stopped talking.

'And you don't remember Rory ever doing any kind of drugs? Not a little weed? Some pills maybe?'

'No way, man. No' Rore. He'd more likely join youse lot than do that.'

Janie stopped herself from repeating what she'd said earlier, that Rory Devlin had died from an overdose. Simon McAllister wasn't in a good place to hear that kind of news, she could see now. He quite probably had managed to clean himself up, but he was still on the edge mentally. She knew well enough that the slightest thing might tip him back over.

'You have a mentor as part of your programme?' she asked instead. McAllister looked up at her so swiftly it was as if he'd been poked.

'What . . . ? Aye. I've weekly meetings, but there's a number I can call any time. They send someone over to talk. Or I can check into their place, y'ken. Like rehab, only there's no celebrities in there, just washed-up junkies like me.'

'You want to give me that number, I can call them. Seems like you could use a little help right now.'

Rain splattered the windshield as Janie drove back south towards the city centre. She could hear it clattering on the roof of the car too, in the absence of any engine noise.

'Why do I get the feeling this morning's been a bit of a waste of time?' she asked nobody in particular, although DC Mitchell was the only person who could hear the question.

'You think it has?'

'Maybe not completely. I'll be interested to hear what Sandy Gregg's found out from Harry Jacobs. And how the boss got on at Devlin's work. So far all we've learned is he used to be nice but turned into a bit of a wee shite a few months back.'

'That's something, isn't it? Gives us a timescale to work with, at least.'

'Aye, I guess. I just thought maybe the names Maggie gave us would be folk Devlin was running around with right before he died. Too much to hope she'd know who his dealer was.'

'Reckon McAllister might know. Even if he doesn't know he

knows. Could be worth having another chat with him when he's a bit more stable.'

'Aye, I'd like a chance to get a bit more out of him, but we'll have to tread carefully there.' Janie had called the number McAllister had given her, spoken briefly to a lady called Allie from the rehabilitation programme. It hadn't taken long for her to start blaming the police, and Janie in particular, for threatening the good progress her client had been making. She'd promised to be there in ten minutes, so they'd left McAllister to wait for her.

'What's with the Dee Foundation anyway?' Mitchell asked, almost out of nowhere. 'They seem to be everywhere these days. Social services, care homes, they even run Bestingfield loony bin. And now they're doing drug rehab programmes? If it wasn't all good stuff, it'd be creepy.'

'You sound like you've been talking to the boss.' Janie negotiated the roundabout at the top of Leith Walk, then slammed on the brakes as the traffic ground to a halt. Up ahead, the shiny bronze spike of the hotel at the centre of the new St James Quarter development rose into the sky like the artistic leavings of some monstrously large metal dog.

'The boss?' Mitchell asked. 'Oh, DI McLean. Yeah, I'd heard he's not a big fan.'

'You ever met her? Jane Louise Dee?' Janie indicated to turn left, then remembered that the road priorities had been changed and she couldn't. Idiot.

'Christ no. Think I move in those kinds of circles? She's like richer than Bill Gates or something, isn't she?'

'Local girl done good, aye. If you believe the stuff on her Wikipedia page anyways. She seems to have a thing for McLean though. Not sure what it is, but she's after him like a drunk lass at a stag do. And you know how strait-laced he is.'

'But isn't she like old enough to be his mum or something? Thought I read she was born in the forties?'

'Aye, but you wouldn't know it to look at her. I'm no' the best judge, but if I didn't know otherwise I'd put her at mid-thirties tops. I guess when you're that rich you can pay for the best treatment.'

'Bathing in asses' milk.'

Something about the way Mitchell said the words made Janie snort with laughter, and it took most of the necessary diversion around St Andrew Square for her to get a grip on herself.

25

Somehow he made it through the day without collapsing under the strain. It helped that Chief Superintendent Elmwood was away at Gartcosh and had taken DCI Ritchie with her. Still, news had got out, and whenever McLean ventured from his office to speak to the rest of the Major Investigation Team, he couldn't help noticing the looks everyone gave him. Sympathy, mostly. A bit of incredulity too. And a few outright hostile glares as if to say how dare he show them up by coming to work regardless of his personal tragedy. Mostly he'd kept to his office, dealing with the team on a one-to-one basis as they reported back their findings. Lots of small snippets of information that really only served to emphasise how little they actually knew. Such was the lot of a detective.

He finally shut down his laptop, switched off the big light and closed his office door when the day shift ended, much earlier than his normal leaving time. McLean had been intending to drive straight from the station to the Western General, even though there had been no updates from Dr Wheeler or Nurse Robertson all day, and his one attempted contact had been politely rebuffed. Some kind of traffic snarl-up in the city centre had him taking a diversion east towards Jock's Lodge, and by the time he'd cut back along the London Road towards

Leith Walk, he'd changed his mind.

There was an empty parking space directly outside Madame Rose's house, as there always seemed to be whenever he visited the old medium, regardless of whether she knew he was coming or not. Then again, she was a fortune teller, so perhaps it wasn't surprising when she opened the door scant seconds after he had pulled the brass knob and heard the clang of the bell inside. He hadn't known he was coming here, but apparently she had.

'Tony. I was so hoping you'd come and visit. I heard the news about poor Emma. I'm so very sorry.'

For a moment he was unable to speak, mind racing at the medium's words. He felt his stomach lurch at the thought that she had heard something he hadn't. Was Emma worse? Was she dead? He reached for his phone to check for texts, knowing that something like that would have been a call, knowing the thought was stupid, but unable to dismiss it all the same.

'Harriet Turner told me.' Rose reached out a hand. At her touch, the tension ebbed away, logic overpowering emotion. 'I could take offence at you for not telling me yourself, but I know you'll have had far more important things on your mind.'

'Professor Turner?' McLean found his voice, absent since Madame Rose had opened the door. 'When was this?'

'Never mind that, Tony. Come on in and I'll put the kettle on. You look like a man who's not slept in weeks.'

Questions still queueing up in his head, McLean nevertheless did as he was told. Through in the kitchen he checked the chairs tucked under the table for cats before pulling one out. When he sat down it was as if he'd been standing for hours, even though he had spent most of the day in car seats or office chairs.

'It must have been such a terrible shock. So sudden and unexpected.' Rose spoke over her shoulder as she set about making tea. The trained detective in McLean couldn't help him noticing that the tray with the teapot, china cups, jug of milk and plate of biscuits had been waiting on the counter when he'd entered the room, the kettle already on the stovetop. Maybe the medium always had things ready for unexpected visitors. How better to maintain an air of mysticism, after all?

'That's one way of putting it, I guess. The doctor reckons she had a stroke, but it was like someone had cut her strings. She dropped like a stone.' He saw it in his mind again, heard the crash of the wine glass breaking on the wooden floorboards.

'She's strong, Tony. She's survived worse than this.'

McLean rubbed at his face, more tired than he could ever remember being. Would it be socially unacceptable to lie his head down on Madame Rose's kitchen table and sleep? Probably. And he needed to get to the hospital even if there was no change.

'I guess seeing her there. Unconscious, hooked up to machines, sunk into those great big pillows they have, just like my gran . . .'

'You're being maudlin, Tony. It's not the same. People go in and out of that ward on a regular basis. Not everyone suffers the cruel fate poor old Esther met there.' Madame Rose placed a cup of tea in front of him, then put the plate of biscuits down beside it. 'And I know you don't necessarily believe the things I say, not entirely at least, but your grandmother had gone before she even arrived at the hospital. She was never coming back. I can't say the same about Emma.'

Was Rose simply being kind? McLean didn't know. His critical faculties were suffering from the same lack of sleep as the rest of him. And yet the thought of going home, of climbing into his cold bed and staring at the darkness, held no appeal. Better to catch some uncomfortable rest in a plastic chair in the hospital waiting area. He took a sip of tea, noting both that it was at the perfect temperature for drinking and that he was parched. Whatever blend it was, it soothed away more than just the dryness in his throat, clearing his mind enough to recall an earlier question the medium had left unanswered.

'You said Professor Turner told you the news. To be honest I didn't even know you two had met.'

'Oh, I've known Harriet Fairweather a long time. Surprised me that she took her wife's surname when they got married, to be honest. But then there was that nastiness with her old professor so maybe the anonymity helps. I think she first came to me when she was a student. Looking for an obscure book on Middle Eastern mythology that had been out of print for the best part of a century.'

'Did she find it?'

'Of course. Took me a little while to track one down, but finding things like that is what I do, Tony.' Madame Rose topped up his teacup from the elegant china pot, adding just the right amount of milk to bring it back to the same perfect colour.

'So why was she visiting you this time? Another rare book? Or had she realised I'd probably not tell anyone about Em, and took it on herself to do so?'

Madame Rose stared at him through eyes slightly narrowed. 'Always the questions. No, Harriet wasn't here about Emma, although I'm grateful to have been told. She came to see me because I asked her to. I needed to talk to her about the bones they dug up across the way.'

'The bones? Oh, in the old Leith kirkyard?' McLean recalled his meeting with the professor and Emma when they were both still at the bottom of the excavation pit, and later Emma showing him the skeleton laid out in the university's forensic archaeology lab. They'd joked about Rose probably knowing more about it than anyone, and then of course Emma had never had the chance to follow that up.

'It really would have been better if she'd been left where she was.' Rose held his gaze for uncomfortably long moments, peering over the top of half-moon spectacles McLean couldn't remember her having put on. 'She was down there for a reason, you know. All of them are.'

'All of them?'

'Really, Tony? I thought you were supposed to be a detective.'

'I am, Rose. But I'm also tired. Physically tired, mentally drained and frankly fed up with all this mystic nonsense. I don't think you mean the bodies buried in the kirkyard in proper Christian graves, so what other bones have we . . . Oh.'

'See? That wasn't so hard to think through now, was it?'

McLean lifted his cup, only to find the tea all finished. Someone had polished off the last of the biscuits too. Had that been him?

'Your body in the kirkyard is over seven hundred years old. That's beyond the scope of any investigation other than what Professor Turner's doing already. But Emily Worstead? She disappeared in living memory. Her death is being treated as suspicious. And you're telling me you knew about it? Knew her whereabouts all this time?'

'She wasn't killed, Tony. She died of cancer, as the doctors knew she would. She merely chose to face that death on her own terms, and to put it to good use. Same with Izabell and a fair few others I'll not mention, since I can see it's going to trouble you unduly.'

'Izabell?' McLean knew he sounded like a poor echo, but nothing Madame Rose said made sense. More so than usual.

'Izabell Kerr. The bones at Leith kirkyard are hers. I was there when she gave herself to the earth.'

He knew he should probably have driven straight home from Madame Rose's, fed the cats, crawled into bed and tried to get some sleep. In truth, he should probably have left Emma's Renault Zoe parked outside the medium's house and taken a taxi home. He'd done the advanced driver training and been on more refresher courses than he cared to think about; he knew driving tired was just as dangerous as driving drunk. And yet McLean couldn't help himself from navigating a path across the north of the city from Leith Walk to the Western General Hospital. There had been no calls or texts to update him on any progress or lack of it, which strongly suggested no change. But after his strange conversation, Rose's talk of willing sacrifice and giving oneself to the earth, he needed to see Emma. He needed to sit beside her, take her hand and tell her it was going to be OK. Even if he wasn't sure that it ever would be.

He didn't recognise the young nurse who eyed him suspiciously as he approached the administration desk, but McLean's reputation must have preceded him, as she acquiesced once he introduced himself.

'Dr Wheeler said you might show up. She said to tell you she'll call in the morning and that nothing's changed from the last time you were here.'

'Has Em . . . Ms Baird been taken off the medication that was keeping her under?'

'It's a little more complicated than that. We expect it to be at least forty-eight hours before there are any signs of change. Could be longer than that before she regains consciousness.'

McLean could hear the unsaid 'if she does' in the nurse's words. He had to cling to that hope though. Forty-eight hours. Could he wait that long? He knew that he could, not as if he had any choice. But it was going to be an exquisite kind of torture. 'Can I see her?'

The expression on the nurse's face suggested that she'd been told he'd ask that. Poor woman, bad enough she'd pulled the night shift, but to have to deal with him too. She nodded assent. 'Don't stay too long though. I could get in trouble. Visiting time was over hours ago.'

McLean thanked her, then turned away before she could change her mind. The lighting in the ward was subdued, but not completely dark. For a moment he was tempted to take the fire extinguisher from the wall and use it to prop open the door, like he had always done when visiting his grandmother. Emma's wasn't the only bed occupied though, and he didn't much want to disturb the other patients. Even if they were unconscious.

He found a chair, carefully set it down so that he didn't mess up any of the tubes and wires that connected Emma to the quietly humming machines arranged around her bed. She lay perfectly still, and he was overwhelmed by a horrible sense of déjà vu again. Harder than the last time time he'd seen her. When he took her hand, it was cool to the touch, pliable, no feeling of pressure from the fingers at all. No evidence that she had registered his presence. Where was she right now? What had become of the bright spark? What had she done to deserve this?

Surrounded by people who weren't really there, McLean leaned forward in his uncomfortable chair, pressed Emma's unresponsive hand to his forehead, and wept.

26

The text was waiting for him when he woke too early the next morning, evidence that McLean wasn't the only one who had trouble sleeping. He'd left the hospital after less than an hour, but that had been enough time for him to work through the sense of utter helplessness and begin to think straight again. The cats had greeted his late arrival home with disgust, mostly because he'd not filled their food bowl before leaving. A couple of slices of toast, dripping with butter and Marmite had been all the food he could face. Then he'd taken himself to bed, where he'd drifted in and out of uneasy sleep.

And now it was a new day, with new demands. Fresh from the shower, he tapped the screen of his phone and stared at the message again.

Meeting in my office. 8.00 AM sharp. Be there. No excuses.

It wasn't signed, but the number told him it was from the chief superintendent. She'd sent it at four in the morning, apparently, so most likely while she'd been at home. Where was she living now? As he went downstairs and set about making himself breakfast, it occurred to McLean that he didn't know. The house she had been renting was a burned-out shell, awaiting whichever brave property developer thought they could turn a profit on rebuilding it, historical listing or not. Elmwood had to be living somewhere, but McLean found he didn't really care where.

Making sure the cats had plenty to eat, he left the house early enough to be across the city ahead of the worst of the traffic, and at his desk before the clock hit seven. He spent the hour dealing with paperwork and reading through the progress reports from Detective Sergeants Harrison and Gregg. Disappointingly little of substance, but at least the press hadn't yet started hounding them about the two drug deaths. Sooner rather than later someone other than Jo Dalgliesh would make the connection between them though. Then all bets were off.

'Go right in,' Elmwood's secretary said to him as McLean approached her desk on the dot of eight. Something about the woman's expression warned him that this was probably not going to be much fun. Another slap on the wrist for walking out on the chief superintendent, no doubt. Maybe in front of the Deputy Chief Constable or whichever top brass was in Edinburgh today. He'd not noticed any posh cars in the car park, but then he'd arrived well before most senior officers had even left home. He tapped gently on the door, opened it and stepped inside.

'Ah, Tony. Good. I like a man who's punctual.' Elmwood sat in the corner of her unnecessarily large office given over to comfortable chairs, a small sofa and a coffee machine. She didn't stand, McLean noticed, although most of his attention was taken up by the other person sitting beside her. Not the DCC, not even the chief constable himself. This was someone he'd rather have seen locked up in the cells three floors down than hob-nobbing with the high heidyins.

'Tony, it's so good to see you. Been an age. If I didn't know better I'd think you were deliberately avoiding me.'

Unlike the chief superintendent, Mrs Saifre did stand up. She moved like a cat as she crossed the room to where McLean still stood by the door. Not a house cat, but something altogether more feral. For a moment, he thought she was going to try to embrace him, but at the last moment she simply held out an elegant hand to be shaken.

'Mrs Saifre. This is a surprise.' McLean found her touch repellent, her skin too warm, too dry, her grip more mechanical than lifelike.

'Oh Tony. You and your "Mrs Saifre". I stopped being her when my husband died, and that was a very long time ago. Everyone calls me Jane Louise Dee now. Or just Jane Louise if they know me well enough.'

'Is there a reason you're here?' McLean asked. He could think of several, and wanted nothing to do with any of them.

'Jane Louise is here on my invitation.' The chief superintendent remained seated, her legs crossed awkwardly, hands folded together in her lap. The full mug of coffee on the table in front of her had a scum on top of it from where it had cooled, untouched. McLean was struck by the thought that maybe Elmwood was a lot less mobile than she had led everyone to believe. He'd seen how tired walking made her, and the effort she put into hiding her pain. Her burns might have healed almost without scar, but under that flawless skin all was not well.

'This would be about the Dee Foundation and your mad idea for Major Investigations to collaborate with you, I take it.'

'You make it sound like I'm trying to take away your job, Tony.' Mrs Saifre slid one arm inside his as if he were leading her onto the dance floor. 'Come, sit. I'll get you some coffee and we can talk like adults.'

She steered him to the sofa, but McLean extracted himself from her hold and took the armchair instead. 'No coffee, thank you. I've a lot to get on with and I should really be briefing the team about the day's work now.'

'And of course there's poor Emma to worry about,' Mrs Saifre said. 'I was so very sorry to hear the news. Is she any better?'

'She's in the best hands. Now, can we get down to the real business of this meeting please?'

The chief superintendent scowled at him, her eyes blazing a promise of some unpleasant punishment in the near future. As if being here, in this room, with these two women wasn't punishment enough. Mrs Saifre was clearly the one in charge here, though, which set McLean's alarm bells ringing even louder than before. She sat on the sofa with all the elegance of a finishing school girl, smoothing the folds of her dress before she fixed him with that snake-like stare.

'I think it would be fair to say that the police haven't exactly covered themselves in glory of late, wouldn't you say, Tony?'

McLean ignored the question, leaving the silence for her to get to the point.

'I know it's been a difficult few years, and the pandemic didn't help. All that conflicting information from the politicians and the poor boys in blue left to be the public face of it all. Coming down hard on one group one week, giving another an easy ride the next. Protecting statues while innocent people are getting robbed at knifepoint and drug use is at an all-time high.'

'None of this has any bearing on my team though, does it? We're called plain clothes for a reason, you know.'

Mrs Saifre shook her head slowly. 'Tony, Tony, Tony. You're missing the point here. Policing has to be by consent, and a large part of the population no longer feels inclined to give it. Don't tell me you haven't noticed the hostility, even in your suit and tie.'

'Jane Louise is right,' the chief superintendent said. 'I've heard it from other detectives in Specialist Crime, too. Even your charm isn't enough sometimes.'

'Investigation isn't all about charm, ma'am. More often it's about asking questions people don't want to answer. It's about putting people's backs up and seeing where that leads. I'll agree that the image of the bobby on the beat's been a bit tarnished in recent years, but I'm not entirely sure that's 'my problem.'

Elmwood finally unclasped her hands, the tremors in her movements almost imperceptible as she brought them up to her face in a gesture that looked like mock prayer before opening her arms wide to encompass him and Mrs Saifre both. 'Nevertheless, the public–private partnership is where we're headed. It's the best way to manage our ever-dwindling budgets, for one thing. And by working closely with the Dee Foundation, we gain the benefit of the goodwill that organisation has built up over many years working with the less well off in the city.'

Slick, well rehearsed, almost tutored. McLean still couldn't work out what Mrs Saifre's angle was, but there was no denying she had her claws deep in the chief superintendent. Elmwood was committed to carrying this through, no matter how much he might object. He would rather resign than work with Mrs Saifre, but he was too tired to fight this battle head on. Not with everything else already on his plate. Perhaps it was time for a different approach.

'OK, then. How exactly do you propose we go about this?'

An hour after first walking in to the chief superintendent's office, McLean stepped back into his own room and collapsed into his chair. He'd barely had time to settle before his computer pinged the arrival of several emails that he knew would be more information about the proposed new close working with the Dee Foundation. Project Tantalus, the chief superintendent had called it, without a whiff of irony. Elmwood had promised to send him everything before he'd finally been able to escape from the room and the unease that being in the presence of Mrs Saifre always brought over him.

He'd almost gone straight from the meeting and down to the locker rooms for a shower. Like most plain-clothes officers, he'd learned long ago to keep a change of clothes in the station; you never knew when a suspect might throw up over you during an interview, or worse. A shower wouldn't wash away the grubbiness he felt deep inside, though. It would take more than anti-dandruff shampoo to clean the stain on his soul.

'Heard you got yourself summoned in front of the head-mistress. What'd you do wrong this time, Tony?'

McLean glanced up at the door to see DCI Ritchie standing there. His first thought was to rant at her about the new direction Major Investigations were being pushed in, but then the full import of her question sunk in.

'You didn't know about it?' She must have known about it. Even if she hadn't been there for the meeting. But then Detective Superintendent McIntyre hadn't been invited, or Detective Chief Inspector Jo Dexter for that matter. None of the senior plain-clothes officers had. Just him, Elmwood and Mrs bloody Saifre.

'Our chief superintendent thinks it's a great idea to partner us up with the private sector,' he said. 'In particular, the Dee Foundation. She's become very pally with Mrs Saifre, you know.'

Ritchie stepped into the room, twirled a chair round from where it was tucked under the conference table, and sat down opposite him. Her face was serious, McLean noted, but she'd left his office door open. No secrets to be revealed then.

'Aye, I'd heard that. It's Saifre's doctors who've been treating her. Some kind of state-of-the-art experimental therapy's how it was explained to me. Gail's staying at her mansion out Loanhead way, too. Makes a sort of sense, I suppose, given her old place burned down. Seems a bit of a conflict of interests, mind you.'

'So you knew about this new scheme? Her precious Project Tantalus? She discussed it with you and Jayne?'

'Discussed is one way of describing the process, I suppose.

More like we've been given orders to make it work. Can't say I'm exactly thrilled at the prospect, but it comes with the chief constable's blessing.'

'I can't even work out why they want to do it. The Dee Foundation makes me uneasy, it's everywhere these days. But I can't deny it doesn't do some good, especially in the more deprived parts of town. I just can't see what's in it for them. We work with the charity sector when we can, but mostly they'd rather not be associated with the police at all. Makes the people they're trying to help suspicious.'

'All of which I've explained to Gail. As has Jayne. You've seen what she's like though, and apparently they did something similar on her old patch, although that was less plain-clothes involvement, more community policing.'

McLean scratched at his chin, feeling rough stubble where he'd missed a bit shaving in the pre-dawn light. 'Maybe I'm being negative because that woman's involved, and we know nothing good ever came of anything she touched. I'll play along for now. Not as if I've any choice in the matter. But only so I can work out what her angle is on all this.'

'That's more the Tony McLean I remember. Say yes, then go do what you were planning to do anyway.' Ritchie managed a weary smile, that faltered almost as soon as it appeared. 'On a different matter, any news about Em?'

McLean picked up his phone, the screen flicking into life bereft of any notifications. 'Not yet, no. And before you say it, yes I know the worry might impact my ability to do my job and I should seriously consider taking some time off to deal with it. But we can't spare any officers at the moment, Kirsty. And you know me. I'd rather have something to distract me than mope around waiting for a call.'

Ritchie arched a non-existent eyebrow at him. 'OK. So what are you throwing yourself into today?'

'This drug. Demon's Breath or Zombo or whatever it's called. We need a breakthrough on where it's coming from and who's distributing it before we have another overdose death on our hands. I'll be following up the investigation into Alistair Hamilton, but since our gallant leader wants us to work with the Dee Foundation I thought I'd ask them to talk to Simon McAllister. Maybe have DS Gregg liaise with them. She's much better at suffering fools than most of us.'

Ritchie nodded once. 'Yes, Sandy's probably best for that. Janie's picked up rather too many bad habits from you, I'm afraid.'

'She has?' McLean pretended to be surprised. Was thinking for yourself such a bad habit? 'It's no matter. I've something else I need her to look into anyway. If she hasn't done already.'

'Oh yes?'

'I had an interesting chat with Madame Rose last night. Some of it about Em, but mostly about the bones they found in that pit under the old Leith kirkyard. Apparently they belong to a woman called Izabell Kerr, and Rose claims to have been there when they buried her.'

'I knew she was old, but eight hundred years? That's pushing it a bit.'

'Aye, well. You know what she's like. And we've no way of telling whose those bones really are, only that they've been there a long time. No, it's why she was buried there, and the way she was buried that's more interesting. According to Rose, Izabell Kerr chose the time and place of her death, and for a specific reason.'

'Let me guess. Something mystical? Self-sacrifice, so a protection, perhaps?'

It was McLean's turn to raise an eyebrow, although his were altogether more bushy than the faint lines that were all that remained of Ritchie's. 'You been speaking to Rose behind my back?'

'Ha, no. Just a lucky guess. It sounds like the sort of mumbo jumbo she'd come up with.' Ritchie shook away the thought. 'But it happened far too long ago for us to be interested in it, so what do you want Janie to do?'

'I need her to speak to the builders in Straiton again. Find out who sold them the land, maybe even see the deeds. I'll get Lofty to do a bit of digging into the financials too.'

'Why is that important?' Ritchie asked, and then her brain caught up with her mouth. 'Oh. That's a bit of a leap, isn't it?'

'Call it a hunch if you like. I don't like the timing of the discoveries, and you know I'm no big fan of coincidences. There's similarities between the two burials, too.'

'So why not ask Rose if she knows about Emily Worstead?'

Because then he'd have to admit to giving her wild stories credence, and that opened up a whole can of worms he wasn't ready to deal with. 'Because then I'd have to bring her in for questioning, possibly arrest her as an accessory to a thirty-year-old crime. I'd rather establish a few more solid facts before I do that.'

27

The drive south to Straiton took them past the Cameron Toll shopping centre, which judging by the traffic and jam-packed car park was just as busy as ever despite having seen a gruesome death only a few days earlier. Janie had wanted to take DC Mitchell with her to visit the building site, but the detective constable had somehow managed to wangle a day off. Instead, she had DC Bryant in the passenger seat, bringing the unpleasant death of Alistair Hamilton to her attention.

'Why do you suppose he went there to do his drugs?' Bryant asked as they negotiated the roundabout and set off towards Liberton Brae.

'How do you mean?'

'Well, he lives in Newington, right? Far as I can tell he's basically squatting, sold off all the furniture to feed his habit. Why not snort at home? It's not a long walk here, I'll grant you. But it's not a quick stroll either. And he didn't have enough money on him to have been shopping for groceries.'

Janie instinctively reached for the gear lever as they began the climb up the steep hill, then remembered that the car was electric and had no gears. Out of the corner of her eye she saw Bryant glance down at her hand, and felt a slight flush creep up her neck at the thought the detective constable might have misunderstood the gesture. Or understood it perfectly and found it amusing.

'We don't even know if Hamilton was really living there. Hopefully Manda will turn something up to help us.'

'Manda? Oh, Dr Parsons. I keep forgetting you two live together.'

'We don't . . . We share a flat, OK?' Janie pressed down on the accelerator pedal, speeding a little above the legal limit in order to squeak through the traffic lights before they changed to red. 'And a word of advice, Jessica? Don't call her Dr Parsons, she really doesn't like it.'

'Why not? I'd have thought if she'd gone to all that trouble getting the damned thing in the first place, she'd want to flaunt it.'

'I guess she's not like that. I didn't even find out about it until we'd been sharing a flat for the best part of a year. Probably has something to do with the fact her PhD isn't in forensic science. I get the feeling she had a major falling out with her supervisors and only finished the thing to spite them.'

'Hell hath no fury . . .'

Janie couldn't stop herself smiling at that. It was a fairly accurate summation of her flatmate's character. 'Aye, well. You said it, not me. And if there's anything more weird than we already saw at that flat, she'll find it. Here's hoping there's a solid lead.'

'We could do with one, sure. So what are we doing coming back out here, then? Shouldn't we be in Newington helping out?' Bryant asked as they slowed to a halt several car lengths before the Burdiehouse roundabout. Traffic inched forward all the way to the Straiton junction, a steady stream of cars coming off the bypass that suggested there must have been an accident further east.

'Trust me, we'd only be getting in the way, and that's not something you want to do with Manda Parsons. This is something the boss asked me to look into, anyway.'

'The boss Kirsty, or the boss DI McLean? Only I sometimes get confused as to who's actually in charge. Weird how he used to be her DCI and now it's the other way round.'

'Know what you mean. It was DI McLean who asked me. He's still in charge of the CCU and this is technically part of their investigation now. He wants to know who used to own the land before the property developers bought it.'

'Couldn't it just have been a phone call?'

Janie chanced her luck with another set of lights. Well, it wasn't as if she didn't know anyone in traffic if it showed up on a camera. 'Sure, but the chances are we'd be fobbed off with a half-answer, or a promise that never gets carried out. And, besides, it's better to look someone in the eye as you ask them something. See the reaction the question brings, you know? Sometimes that's more useful than the actual answer.'

Bryant stared ahead, silent for a while as she considered what Janie had said. She waited until they had crossed the road and were pulling up in the car park of the housing development before speaking again.

'And it helps that the man in charge here's sweet on you, aye?'

Janie looked at her colleague to see if she was joking. 'You what?'

'Oh come on, Janie. Don't tell me you didn't notice? According to Cass, the last time we were here he was all over you. Helping you with your safety helmet, an arm into that wee buggy he drove us around in. Poor lad almost fainted when you gave him your number, the way I heard it.'

'I . . . But that was my business card. In case anything came up concerning the investigation.'

'Sure, you and I know that. But Johnny there? Like all his Christmases had come at once, apparently.'

'Ach, you're winding me up, Jessica. Careful I don't put you on report. And Cass too, if she's really been telling tales behind my back.' Janie climbed out of the car, then had to grab the door as a sudden gust of wind threatened to tear it right off. She struggled to close it, watching Bryant do the same on the other side. But even as they approached the steel stairs to the upper Portakabin and the site office, she could see the detective constable's wistful smile. Was it all some elaborate joke on Bryant's part? Or had Janie completely failed to notice Johnny Wendle's more than professional interest in her?

Janie couldn't quite make up her mind whether or not significant progress had been made on the building site since her last visit. Given that it had only been a few days, it was unlikely, but the central apartment block looked more substantial than before, casting longer shadows over the Portakabin offices. She and DC Bryant clanged up the metal stairs and into the reception area, where a different receptionist to the last time greeted them with a suspicious eye.

'Can I help youse?' she asked in an accent more west coast than Edinburgh. Before anyone could say more, the office door at the back swung swiftly open and Johnny Wendle strode out.

'Detective Sergeant Harrison, what a pleasant surprise.' He beamed at her with perfect white teeth, one massive hand held out to shake, barely even noticing DC Bryant. When Janie introduced her colleague, she was sure the detective constable was stifling a grin. No doubt she enjoyed not being the centre of attention for a change.

'I hope your build is back on schedule now,' Janie said as she and Bryant followed Wendle into his office, the Glaswegian receptionist sent in search of coffee. There wasn't much room to spare, most of the space taken up with the more expensive building site tools and two large desks covered in archaeological layers of paperwork that would have made even DI McLean anxious. The building developer cleared boxes from a couple of chairs, bade them sit and then squeezed in behind one of the desks. Janie stopped herself from leaning down to pick up the sheets of paper that drifted to the floor as he sat.

'So, what is it Police Scotland want this time?' he asked. 'I'm too cynical to believe this is merely a social visit.'

'You're right,' Janie said. 'It would be nice if we had the time and manpower to visit people who've helped us in the past, say thanks, that kind of thing. Sadly everyone's budgets are tight these days, ours perhaps more so than most. Which is why I've come to ask a favour, Mr Wendle.'

'A favour is it? Well then, you'll have to call me Johnny. Mr Wendle sounds suspiciously like my father.' Wendle smiled that toothy grin of his again, too bright surely to be natural.

'Johnny.' Janie tried the name, but it felt wrong. On the other hand, if it got them what they needed she'd make the sacrifice, and deal with Bryant later. 'What we're trying to track down is the previous owner of the land where you dug up those bones. For some reason the Land Registry records are incomplete, so we wondered if you'd be able to tell us who you bought it from. Maybe even see a copy of the deeds. They usually list all the previous owners, after all.'

If he hadn't been such a smiley, friendly person to begin with, Janie might have missed the change in Wendle's demeanour. As it was, she could see the thought processes her request brought about written across his changing face. He was about to say something, but a knock at the door interrupted them. Before anyone could answer, it was pushed open and the receptionist came in with the coffee on a tray.

'Oh. Thank you Eileen. Just stick it on the other desk will you?' Wendle put off answering Janie's question a while longer by fussing with a cafetière that looked like it should have been in a show home. Rather than leaving, Eileen the receptionist hung around by the door, making the already small room feel smaller still. Only once mugs had been filled and passed around did the property developer seem to notice her.

'I'll bring the tray out when we're finished here,' he said by way of dismissal. The receptionist took longer to leave than was polite, Janie felt, and she left the door open a crack when she was gone. Almost certainly listening in on the conversation.

'Sorry about that,' Wendle said once they were all settled again. 'She only started here yesterday. Poor old Kate, our normal secretary. Had a nasty fall at home, apparently. Eileen's come from an agency and we're still breaking her in.' He gave a little laugh to assure them he meant it only figuratively, but it was a pale shade of his previous enthusiasm. Janie said nothing, leaving the silence for him to fill. It didn't take him long.

'So, your question. It's . . . How can I put this? A bit complicated. We, that is, Wendle Stevens the company. We don't actually own this land. We've a contract with the actual owner that is quite . . .' He paused again, and looked so uncomfortable Janie decided to help.

'Complicated?'

'Exactly so.' Wendle smiled again. 'There are covenants, restrictions, what's the term? Non-disclosure agreements that mean I can't even tell you who the owner is.' His eyes widened as another thought occurred to him. 'I probably shouldn't even be telling you that much, truth be told.'

Janie took a sip of her coffee, surprised at how good it tasted. 'Can you tell me anything? I take it you've borrowed money to build the place?'

Wendle squirmed in his seat like the shy kid being asked a question in front of the whole classroom. 'Again, non-disclosure. It's all above board, I can assure you. There's nothing illegal going on here. We're not laundering money for Russian oligarchs or anything. But the kind of people who invest in these projects . . . they're not your high street bank or building society.'

'I see,' Janie said, although in truth she didn't. 'The found-ations where you uncovered the bones. Have you got that all sorted now? I hope it didn't muck up your plans too much.'

Wendle smiled more broadly now, the difficult subject dealt with and on to things he was clearly more comfortable discussing. 'We lost a few days, but a development as big as this you can always find something else for the men to do. Would you like to see how we're getting on? I mean, only if you have time?'

Janie glanced briefly at Bryant, caught the detective constable's eye and saw the slightest nod in her direction. When she turned back to Wendle, she gave him a smile as broad as his own, although she was painfully aware that her teeth were nowhere near as white.

'I think we could probably spare a few minutes, Johnny. I'd love another look round.'

'He's going to call you. I'd lay odds on it. Sometime in the next day or two. He's totally going to call.'

Janie eased the pool car into the traffic flow heading north back towards the city, hoping that no one would question her or DC Bryant too hard about why their visit to Straiton had taken the best part of an hour longer than necessary. Away from the Portakabin office, paperwork and over-watchful eye of Eileen the temporary receptionist, Johnny Wendle had relaxed considerably, falling into his natural role of enthusiastic salesman. He hadn't relaxed enough to tell them who owned the site or who was supplying the finance for the development, but he might just possibly have let slip that they were the same person or organ-isation. And even Janie, whose attitude to such things was generally uninterested, couldn't deny he'd been trying his best to flirt with her.

'I gave him my number for contact regarding the investigation. Not so he could ask me out on a date.'

'He's going to though. Mark my words. Could be your lucky break, Janie. He's rich and he's kind of cute too.'

'Aye, well. We'll see. Not sure he's my type.'

'No?' Bryant leaned back in the passenger seat, staring forward rather than looking at her. 'What is your type then?'

Janie kept her silence. Partly because she was navigating a tricky stretch of busy road. Partly because the question was a little bit impertinent coming from a detective constable, even if she'd been working closely with Jessica for a while now. And partly because she didn't really have an answer. She'd had a few boyfriends over the years, but nothing had ever come of any of those relationships. They'd petered out rather than exploded. Nowadays she was too busy for such things. Or they weren't important enough for her to make the time. One of those, for sure.

'Sorry, I shouldn't have asked,' Bryant said, no doubt mistaking Janie's lack of response for annoyance at the question. 'None of my business.'

'No, you're fine. I don't mind. It's nice to have a bit of banter every now and then. Not always talking shop. It's just . . . I don't know. Can't seem to muster any great enthusiasm for relationships right now. Friends? Sure. But all that other stuff? Well, Johnny Wendle's fair enough on the eye, I'll grant you. I'm just no' sure I've the energy.'

'Men, eh?' Bryant rolled her eyes theatrically. 'Far more effort than they're worth.'

28

McLean stepped out of the station and pulled up the lapels of his coat against the cold wind. He'd wasted the morning trying to make sense out of the chief superintendent's plans for Edinburgh's Major Investigation Teams. He needed something to clear his head of all that nonsense, so the text from Manda Parsons telling him they'd found something of interest was a welcome distraction. And since Alistair Hamilton's Newington flat was only a short walk away, he reckoned a quick visit was in order.

A pair of forensic technicians sat in the front of their white van, eating lunch as he approached. He didn't recognise either of them, but one of them must have known him, dropping her sandwich into a tupperware box before clambering out to greet him.

'Manda's upstairs, sir. No need for the full suit, but you might want to put some overshoes on, and maybe some gloves?' The technician slid open the van's side door, guddled around for a moment before coming out with the goods.

'Thanks.' McLean shoved the gloves in his coat pocket, but held on to the overshoes. Not much point putting them on until he reached the flat. He looked up at the windows, glass reflecting only the grey clouds back at him. 'Second floor, wasn't it?'

'Aye sir. On the left.'

He stepped into the cool narrow passage that led to the stairs and felt an instant sense of recognition. The layout of this tenement was slightly different to the one where he'd lived for many years, only a few streets away, but they'd been built at much the same time, and designed to serve similar purposes. This one even had a lump of brick placed in a handy spot to prop open the front door, although the stairwell lacked the aroma of cooking fat and cat piss.

As it turned out, he needn't have asked the forensic technician what floor Hamilton's flat was on. The door was wide open when he reached it, a roll of plastic sheeting laid out across the floorboards in the hall. He paused a moment to slip on the overshoes and pull on the gloves, then knocked hard on the door.

'Anyone in?'

A sound suspiciously like the back of someone's head coming into contact with the underside of an old porcelain sink was followed by a muffled 'Ow, bugger it' and then a few moments later Manda Parsons shuffled into view. The thunderous anger on her face evaporated almost instantly when she saw who it was had caused her accident.

'Oh, hey, Tony. I wasn't expecting you to come right over.'

'You know me. Any excuse to get out of the office.' He waited at the threshold, knowing better than to come in uninvited. 'You OK? Sounded like a nasty bump.'

Parsons rubbed the back of her head, winced. 'Bloody stupid, really. Just don't tell Janie, aye? She'll never let me hear the last of it. Come on in and see what we've found. Don't think there's any crucial evidence you're going to trample on, anyway.'

McLean stepped into a flat considerably smaller than his old place, but still reasonably well proportioned compared to the modern blocks that were going up all over the city. Parsons led him through to the kitchen first, and he understood what DS

Harrison had meant when she'd said the place had been stripped.

'This has all been pulled out recently.' Parsons walked over to the window, where a sink might once have been judging by the pipes jutting from the wall. 'Professionals by the look of things, but working in a hurry.'

'How d'you reckon that?'

'Well, I don't know what units were in here, but you can see where the backs of them were screwed to the wall. Most of them have been carefully unscrewed, but there's one or two been forced. They turned off the water at the main stopcock before taking out the sink, too. That's what I was checking in the bathroom when you arrived.'

McLean stared at the points on the wall that Parsons indicated without really understanding what he was looking at. He could see the missing units by the different colour of the walls behind them, and yes there were some screw holes. The rest he'd have to take on faith. 'Why would someone do something like that?'

'Well, any other place and I'd say they were remodelling, but as far as I've been told there's no order for a new kitchen in here. There's a few wee clues as to what might have been going on, mind. See the floorboards here?' Parsons pointed to what had, a long time ago, been neatly sanded and sealed wood but which now bore the scratches and stains of a lifetime's hard use. It reminded McLean of his own tenement kitchen when he'd first moved into the place, although he'd spent days sanding and sealing to get it back to a pristine state years later. The thought brought an unhappy wave of nostalgia over him.

'What am I looking at?' he asked, as much to swallow away the lump in his throat as for an answer.

'Stains, mostly.' Parsons crouched down, inviting McLean to do the same. He complied with considerably less grace than her athletic movement, his hip protesting that he was too old for this shit.

'These are your usual, run-of-the-mill dropped teabags, beer possibly, a bit of boiling water from a kettle or the stove, stale vomit, that kind of thing.' Parsons jabbed a gloved finger at the marks and swirls in the old timber. 'This one, however, is both recent and made by some kind of industrial solvent.' She crouched down even further, adopting a yoga pose that made McLean's back ache just to look at, and sniffed at the mark she had pointed out. 'You can smell it. Not bleach, something else. I've got some scrapings to go off to the lab. Ironic really.'

'Ironic?' McLean asked as he shifted his weight then gave up and stood again. Parsons let out a little *oof* sound as she rose to join him at adult level, so maybe she wasn't quite as lithe as she made out.

'Well, if they hadn't ripped everything out, we'd probably have had all the kit we needed right here. This kitchen's been used as some kind of lab, Tony. Chances are this is where they've been cooking up that nasty stuff in the first place.'

Darkening skies through the window wall of his office had McLean glancing up at the clock. Still barely tea time and the light was already fading from the day. Apart from a few unhappy years at boarding school in England, he'd lived his entire life in Edinburgh and it still caught him out as the days began to shorten with winter's approach. He stood up, stretched as the muscles in his back and neck reminded him he'd been sitting still for too long, then shuffled across to the door and flipped the switch to turn on the lights. As he did so, he spotted Detective Sergeant Harrison approaching along the corridor, shadowed by Detective Constable Bryant.

'Hoping I might have caught you in, sir. That's us just back from the building site.'

McLean stood aside to let the two of them in, indicating with an arm that they should grab a seat at the conference table. He briefly considered offering tea, but there was only the coffee machine and it was getting a bit late for that.

'What's the score, then?' He pulled out a chair and sat down. 'Do we know who used to own the land?'

'Whoever used to still does,' Harrison said. 'And I get the distinct impression they're bankrolling the whole enterprise too.'

McLean listened as Harrison spelled out the situation, including the non-disclosure agreement keeping Wendle Stevens from discussing the project. He was no expert, but that didn't sound like normal business procedure to him. Then again, the last property developers he'd dealt with had turned out to be stealing high-end motors and bringing drugs into the country through the Western Isles, so what did he know?

'It might explain why the Land Registry's having difficulty with the records, sir,' DC Bryant said once Harrison had finished. 'If the land's been in the same ownership a long time, it'll be on the Register of Sasines, but won't necessarily have made it to the digital record yet. They're meant to be updating all the land ownership across the country, but the pandemic held everything up for a while.'

He'd gone through all the rigmarole when he'd inherited his grandmother's house a few years back, so McLean felt he really should have thought of that. 'Have we put in a request to see the paper register?'

'Lofty's on it, sir. There's some kind of problem though. Hopefully get it sorted soon.' Harrison made that face he'd learned meant she was psyching herself up to ask a difficult question. 'Can I ask why it's important? I mean, I know it's part of the investigation into Emily Worstead's disappearance, but that was thirty years ago. No disrespect, but Jessica an' me? We weren't even born then. I thought the Cold Case Unit were doing the legwork on that one.'

Way to make him feel old. McLean had known that neither

Harrison or Bryant had hit thirty yet, but only on an abstract level. 'The CCU are dealing with it, yes. Helps that Duguid was SIO on the original disappearance. I'm more interested in why the body has turned up now. It could have been coincidence, of course. You know I'm not a big fan of those, but they happen sometimes. But what you've found out today makes me more suspicious, not less.'

'You think someone knew she was there and orchestrated the whole thing to have her discovered?'

Put like that it was as fanciful as any of Madame Rose's more outlandish claims. Had he been wrong to read so much into the old medium's words the night before? McLean fell back on the excuse he'd given Ritchie that morning. 'Call it a hunch. And what you've found out so far is useful, I'm just not quite sure how yet.'

Harrison shrugged, and for a moment McLean thought Bryant was going to say something, but her gaze slid past him to the door. A moment later a knock on the frame had them all looking that way to see DS Gregg clutching a sheet of paper.

'This has just come in sir. Suspicious death over in Wester Hailes.' She held out the page as McLean crossed the room. 'From the sound of things it might be another drug overdose. Symptoms identical to Devlin and McAllister.'

29

'Wester Hailes . . . Full of Potential'. The sign greeted them as they inched along Murrayburn Road, following the satnav directions to the address DS Gregg had given them. McLean let Harrison drive, and stared out at the rows of seventies bungalows, eighties low-rise apartment blocks and more modern industrial units that sprawled up the gentle slope south of Sighthill. In the middle distance, the trees of Kingsknowe Golf Course had turned dark gold, their leaves beginning to fall. Where had the year gone?

'Not been out this way in a while.' Harrison indicated and turned the car up a narrow street.

'Hasn't changed much,' McLean said.

The semi-detached houses on either side were that all too common mix of part council-owned, part private, distinguishable only by their state of repair. A little further along, the street opened into an estate of brown-and-grey-painted four-storey housing blocks, too close together to let any meaningful light into the small lower-floor windows. The outer edges of the estate looked like they had been recently renovated, and the few cars parked outside in marked bays were new enough to suggest reasonably well-off people lived here. Deeper in, the mood turned downwards, harling cracked or missing altogether. The cars were older, some without wheels or other vital parts like windscreens and engines. It was doubtful they'd find anywhere to plug in the electric Nissan.

'Seeing that a lot these days. Wonder what it means.' Harrison pointed through the windscreen towards a brick wall dividing the housing from nearby open ground. The spray can warriors had been hard at work covering every inch with competing designs, but on top of all the other sigils the horned devil leered out at them in varying shades of red.

'You know what it's like. Someone comes up with a cool design and everyone else starts to copy it. There'll be something new along soon enough.'

'Aye, I guess,' Harrison said, but McLean could tell she wasn't convinced. He wasn't either, but it was a small problem overwhelmed by the many large ones he already had to deal with.

Up ahead, a cluster of squad cars were parked half on the pavement, and a brand-new but filthy British Racing Green Jaguar looked dangerously out of place. The pathologist had arrived ahead of them.

'Good to see you, sir, Janie.' Police Sergeant Kenny Stephen strode up as McLean and Harrison walked towards a narrow vennel that ran through one of the housing blocks. Yellow tape flapped in the entrance, as good a sign of where the body might be found as the numerous uniform officers wandering around. Above them, some of the windows were showing lights now, but there didn't seem to be much public interest in what was going on. Keeping your nose out of other people's business was the way around here.

'What's the story, Kenny?' McLean asked. The report sheet from control had been as short on detail as these things always were.

'Young woman in the ground floor flat by the name of Fiona McLeod. Neighbour heard noises that she described as sounding like someone having a violent fight. Called us in because apparently Ms McLeod had a history of abusive boyfriends. Luckily for us, the neighbour keeps a spare key. When there was no answer at the door, she let us in. Not a pretty sight what we found.'

'Someone with the neighbour now?'

'Aye, sir. Constable Porter's making her a cup of tea. Poor dear had quite a shock.'

'OK.' McLean turned to Harrison. 'Why don't you go and have a wee chat with the neighbour. Find out what you can about this Fiona McLeod from her. Meantime, I'd better have a look at her body.'

As he ducked under the yellow crime scene tape and headed into the vennel, it struck McLean that whoever had designed these housing blocks had been trying to re-create something of the feel of the Old Town, although without much success. The narrow closes leading off the Royal Mile were an accident of their geography and medieval history, the cramming of as much housing and industry as possible into too small a space. Out here in what must have been rolling parkland before the builders turned up, there was no need to build fortress-like monolithic four-storey blocks with tiny openings that wouldn't have looked out of place on an ancient Borders tower house. And yet that was how the entrances had been designed.

'A bit bleak isn't it?' Harrison said as a bored constable checked their warrant cards before letting them through. There was barely room to walk side by side as they went down a narrow corridor that smelled strongly of rotting garbage and dog shit. At the end, they found two doors facing one another and a concrete staircase climbing to the higher floors. One of the doors stood ajar, suggesting it was where the body lay. Beyond it, McLean could see a surprisingly clean, if tiny, apartment. There was barely room for the both of them in the hallway.

'Think your door's that way.' McLean pointed at the other side of the narrow entrance passage. 'I don't imagine this'll take long, so you can find me outside when you're done.'

Harrison nodded, and turned away as McLean stepped into the apartment. It was warmer inside despite the open door, and as he took in a breath he noticed the faintest scent of lemons. A strange effect of the stench outside? Or something else? When he took another sniff the smell was back to rotting garbage and dog mess, so maybe he'd imagined it.

There weren't many rooms to choose from, and only one had its door open. The compact living room looked as if someone had taken an axe to the cheap furniture, throwing broken pieces outwards as they did so. Two small armchairs lay on their backs, an occasional table that must have stood between them now smashed in half. And yet the television stood untouched on its stand up against the wall, the photographs arranged on a cheap 1950s sideboard were all still standing upright, there was even a narrow bookshelf in the corner, stacked mostly with DVD cases, but also a few books neatly arranged.

'Ah, Tony. Thought they might send you out to this one.'

Focusing his attention back on the centre of the room, McLean finally let himself consider the body. He'd seen straight away where it was, of course. The balding pate of the figure crouched on the other side of the small sofa was a dead giveaway. But a lifetime of viewing crime scenes had taught him to start at the edges and work in. Often the body itself had little to say about the nature of its death, at least to his eyes. That was the job of the pathologist to puzzle out.

'They said it was similar to the last two, Angus. Is that your professional opinion too?'

'See for yourself.' Cadwallader pushed himself upright to a chorus of creaking joints and light groans. McLean stepped around the sofa on which the deceased appeared to have been lying, and got his first proper look at the body.

Fiona McLeod lay on her back, half on the floor, half propped up against the sofa and wedged in place by the cushions that had been dislodged by her fitting. So violent had her seizure been, she had kicked both armchairs over, and shattered the table. At first McLean thought she was wearing white-spotted dark red socks, but then his eyes focused enough to see that she had been barefoot, and her feet hadn't fared well as she'd thrashed around. Her hands weren't much better, one flung wide, the other reaching up to her neck with claw-like, crooked fingers, as if she'd been trying to strangle herself. Or maybe scratch open her neck so that she could breathe. She wore loose-fitting sweatpants and a hoodie top, the kind of clothes a person puts on for slobbing around the house after work. Although at the moment McLean was aware that he didn't know much at all about this woman, let alone whether she had a job. It was the look of utter terror on her pale white face as she stared up at the ceiling that transfixed him. Hers had not been a quick death, and neither had it been peaceful.

'I take it this is how she was found?'

'I believe so, yes. The neighbour let the local constables in. Don't imagine they'd have tried to revive her.'

'And you think this damage is self-inflicted? She wasn't beaten up or strangled?'

Cadwallader eyed his old friend with a strange expression. 'Not going to ask me the time of death, Tony? You must have a lot on your mind.'

'You could say that, Angus. Emma's in the hospital. She had a stroke. Collapsed. She's unconscious now. I'm still waiting for a straight answer on how she's going to be.'

Silence descended on the room as Cadwallader digested this information, the both of them staring down at the dead body.

'There's two reasons why I think this isn't a murder, Tony,' he said after a while. 'First, there's very little external damage that hasn't been caused by her hands and feet coming into collision with the objects all around her. That's the sort of thing you'd expect from a violent, uncontrolled seizure. And second . . .' The pathologist crouched down and pointed at something on the carpet partially beneath the body that glistened in the light from the lamp overhead as McLean moved his head to get a better look. '. . . That's broken glass from a vial remarkably similar to the ones you've found by the other two bodies. I sent Tracy back to the car for a sample kit before we move her. Surprised you didn't see her on the way in.'

As if his words had summoned her, the pathologist's assistant appeared in the doorway, one hand clutching something sealed in a clear plastic bag. The look she gave McLean was friendly and yet somehow also managed to communicate the fact that he was in the way.

'I'll leave you to it then,' he said, stepping aside to let Dr Sharp get to her work. Cadwallader gave him a pained smile.

'I'm sorry to hear about Em, Tony. She's been through so much, it hardly seems fair. You let me know if there's anything I can do to help, OK?'

'Thanks, Angus. I will.'

'Good, now shoo off out of the way. I'll let you know all about this poor woman as soon as I can.'

30

It was dark as they left the housing estate and drove back across the city to the station. McLean said nothing for a while, his mind half trying to process the scene, half worrying about the lack of updates from the hospital. Telling the pathologist about it had brought everything back to him, along with an extra layer of guilt that he'd managed to completely put the situation out of his mind for most of the afternoon.

'How'd you get on with the neighbour?' he asked as they turned on to the Lanark road. At this time of the evening most of the traffic was going the other way, which was a small mercy.

'Pretty much like Kenny said. Edna Morris. Nice old lady, though I'd imagine she could be a bit nosey. Said she's been living there for twenty years, and the victim, Fiona, moved in about five years back. They got on OK enough to swap a set of keys. Used to pop in on each other for a cuppa and a blether every now an' then.'

'Sounds like an ideal person to have as a neighbour. Retired, I take it.'

'Aye. Said she used to work for the Water Board. Finished there round about the same time Ms McLeod moved in.'

'And what about McLeod? She working?'

'She was, up until a couple of months back. Lost her job but never told Edna why, just that it wasn't fair. Seemed to have a bit of a chip on her shoulder about it, if the old lady's got the truth of it.'

'Kenny said something about abusive relationships?'

Harrison gave a little snort that might have been laughter, might have been something more bitter. 'Aye, according to Edna she had a knack for choosing bad'uns. That's what she called them, bad'uns. Sounded like my gran. Reminded me of her a bit, too.'

McLean pictured his own gran, the way he'd found her slumped unconscious in her favourite armchair. And overlaid on top of the image, Emma falling to the floor like a discarded puppet. The wine glass tumbling, tumbling, smashing.

'. . . couple of weeks back. Right old barney, she said.'

'Say that again.' He shook his head, aware both that he'd let his mind drift and that he'd almost fallen asleep, too. Just as well he hadn't been driving.

'Said the last boyfriend only lasted a month. They had a massive argument, couple of weeks back. She threw him out, apparently. Edna was well chuffed.'

'She know his name, this boyfriend?'

'She thought it was Thomas or Tommy or something. Couldn't be sure. Only ever saw him in passing a couple of times. Said she never liked him, but I'd not put too much credence in that. You know what folk are like. Probably didn't even think about him at all until McLeod mouthed off to her about him.'

'Still something we might have to look into. Angus reckons it's an overdose though, same as Devlin and Hamilton. There's glass fragments in the carpet similar to the vials we found. Kenny's going to keep a couple of constables posted on the door until we can get forensics to give the place a once over. Too much to hope they might turn up the name and address of her dealer.'

'That'd be nice, aye.' Harrison smiled briefly, then her face turned serious again. 'I take it by the way you're fiddling with that you've not heard anything more about Em?'

McLean looked down, surprised to find his phone in his hands. He had no memory of taking it out of his pocket, couldn't have said whether he'd checked it or not.

'No, nothing. And the longer it goes on, the worse it feels. Never felt so bloody helpless in my life.'

Except that he had. Twice before. First with his gran, a slow death played out over eighteen months. Then again with Emma after John Needham had drugged her. That had been three months, and years for her to recover afterwards. 'And it could all be nothing. Just my tired brain scrambling for connections where there are none.' McLean let his head tilt back until it hit the headrest. How easy it would be to close his eyes and sleep. Except for the image that wouldn't stop playing over and over in his mind, the wine glass falling, falling, smashing.

'You sure you wouldn't be better taking some time off, sir?' Harrison asked, and somehow they were already driving across the Meadows, the station only minutes away.

'You know me, Janie. I'd only fret.'

Harrison's expression was lost in the darkness, her face mostly shadows cast by the illuminations from the dashboard instruments. Even so, McLean could sense the exasperation coming off her in waves. Maybe it was the set of her jaw, or perhaps the hunch of her shoulders. Most likely it was because he knew she was right, the same way DCI Ritchie was right and Detective Superintendent McIntyre too. He should stop pushing hard against the despair or something inside him would break.

'I'll go home,' he conceded. 'Let's just get all this squared away first, OK?'

★ ★ ★

There was no news from the hospital, and no sign of either Ritchie or McIntyre to bring up to speed with the day's progress. Or rather lack of progress. McLean had no doubt Harrison could do the job without him, so he made good on his promise and drove home.

The cats eyed him with deep suspicion when he stepped into the kitchen, which was fair enough. It might have been dark outside, but it was still some hours before he would normally disturb them. They hadn't even eaten all of the food he'd put out for them before leaving that morning.

Checking the fridge revealed little in the way of food. The carton of milk was still just about fresh, but given the use-by date on it wouldn't remain so for much longer. Feeling the most like a student he had in years, McLean filled a bowl with cornflakes and had cereal for his supper. He was tempted to pour himself a beer and retreat to the library, but in the end that was a step too far.

His phone rang as he was filling the kettle to make some tea, and he almost missed the call in his rush to put it on the hob and grab the handset from the table. Assuming it was the hospital, he didn't even check the number before thumbing the screen to accept the call.

'Thought you weren't gonnae answer for a moment there.' Not the hospital.

'Caught me at an awkward moment. I assume this isn't a social call, Dalgliesh.'

'Aw, an' you used to call me Jo. What's up, Tony? You sound tired.'

McLean tried to think when he'd last spoken to the reporter. Had that been before or after Emma's collapse? She didn't seem to know, so it must have been before.

'I am tired, Jo. And I'm waiting on an important call from the hospital where my partner is currently lying in a coma.

So if you don't mind getting to the point?'

A moment's silence, and for once McLean didn't imagine he could hear the sound of Dalgliesh inhaling a lungful of strange chemicals from her electronic cigarette.

'Shit, I'm sorry Tony. What happened? Is she going to be OK?'

'She had a stroke, and I don't know. As you can imagine, I've not had a lot of sleep since it happened so forgive me if I'm a little tetchy. I take it this is about the new drug we're trying to track down.'

'Aye, it is. Little birdy tells me someone else has died with very similar symptoms. Up in the schemes at Wester Hailes.'

Well they were never going to keep it a secret for long. 'You and your little birdies. Aye, I saw them this evening and it looks to be the same. We don't know yet for sure though. There'll be a press release in the morning when we've more information, spoken to next of kin, that sort of thing.'

'Well you know I've been holding off on making the connection. Trying to do a deeper dive into it, still waiting on some of my sources to come up with the goods. Thing is, I'm no' the only one seeing it now. I know at least one other paper looking to make a splash about it, an' the internet's already buzzing wi' gossip.'

A clattering of metal told McLean the kettle had reached the boil. He hefted it off the hob with one hand, then went through the cupboards to fetch a mug and a teabag the same way, phone pressed to his ear all the while.

'Our team are monitoring the usual sites, even hits on the dark web forums. Haven't seen any mentions of these deaths yet.'

'Do you even know what any of those words mean, Tony?' Dalgliesh let out a strangled chicken noise that was half cough, half laugh, followed up by the hollow sound of her thumping her own chest. 'No disrespect to your team, but they're no' up to snuff if they've not seen the feeds I've seen.'

McLean rubbed at his forehead with the heel of his free hand. It was possible the internet team had found out all manner of things regarding this new drug and the two, maybe three, deaths associated with it, but he'd come home without talking to anyone in the incident room. There'd be reports he could access if he had the energy, but right now he wasn't sure he did.

'What is it you're wanting to tell me, Jo? Or were you just fishing for more information about Wester Hailes?'

'I didn't really need anything from you about that. Just a friendly call to let you know tomorrow's *Tribune*'s going to be running a piece on it and making the connections. Can't sit on it any more.'

'Any chance I can get a peek at the copy?'

'Should be with you any moment. Don't say I'm no' good to you.'

As if by magic, McLean felt his phone buzz the arrival of an email. One more thing to worry about.

'You any idea where this stuff's coming from? Who's distributing it?' He couldn't help seeing the irony in his question, that he'd be forced to rely on a journalist for information where his team of trained detectives had met only a wall of silence. How was that any different to the chief superintendent's plan for them to work more closely with the charity sector? So many ways different. Mrs Saifre wasn't involved, for one thing.

'Nothing yet. I've a few folk asking questions, an' we'll see what tomorrow's paper shakes loose, aye?' Dalgliesh paused, and this time McLean could hear the buzz of her electronic cigarette as she sucked hard on it even though they were on opposite sides of the city. 'I'll be sure an' let you know anything that turns up, if I think it'll help.'

'Thanks, I think.' McLean picked up his mug and stared at

the dry teabag lying in the bottom of it for far too long before he realised he'd not yet poured the boiling water in.

'Aye, well. Maybe read the piece first. I'm no' trying to put the knife in, but you know what editors are like. You take care of yourself, Tony. And I hope Emma's on the mend soon. She deserves a break, poor wee lass.'

Before he could point out that Emma was in her forties, so not technically a lass any more, Dalgliesh had hung up. McLean fetched the kettle and filled his mug, then tapped open the email attachment with the report. How like the reporter to neglect to mention it was the front page, continued on pages 3 and 4 inside. He squinted at the screen, pinching and zooming the tiny text as he read through it all.

When he'd finished, he picked up his mug, tipped the tea into the sink and went through to the library, where the whisky lived. Time to put a couple of calls in to DCI Ritchie and Detective Superintendent McIntyre. Tomorrow was going to be a long day.

31

It was just as well he'd not managed to get much sleep, heading in to the station while it was still dark and only a few hardy souls had read their morning paper. McLean had called the hospital on his way in to be told in no uncertain terms that it was inappropriate to phone at such an hour and that if there was any change to Emma's condition he would be the first person outside the neurology unit to know about it. He'd beaten both DCI Ritchie and Jayne McIntyre in, but only by a few minutes. They'd convened a hasty strategy meeting, called in all the favours they could, and now he was as ready as he'd ever be to face the press.

There was something about the swarm of faces that unsettled McLean. The way they all stared up at him with bleary expressions or eager inquisitiveness. It wasn't public speaking that bothered him; he could do that when necessary although he'd far rather let someone higher up the tree make a fool of themselves. Once the press conference was underway he usually found he could relax into it, if relax was the right word. There was a sense of satisfaction to be had in being able to trade blows with reporters, and piecing together where the mood was going by the nature of the questions asked was often a useful addition to the whole investigation. No, it was the waiting for things to start that unsettled him, the sense of anticipation and the worry that everything might go horribly wrong.

'Good morning, ladies and gentlemen.' Detective Superintendent McIntyre began the proceedings. 'As I'm sure you're all aware, Lothian and Borders Police were called out to a residence in Wester Hailes late yesterday afternoon following reports of what sounded like a fight. We were able to gain access to the residence, where the body of a recently deceased woman was found. Family have been informed, so I can confirm the identity of that woman. As some of you have already speculated, her name is Fiona McLeod. Early suspicions were that she had been attacked, but forensic examination of the body and the room in which it was found led us to the preliminary conclusion that Ms McLeod in fact overdosed on a narcotic that caused her to have multiple, violent seizures.'

A number of hands shot up, some of the reporters waiting to be invited to ask their questions. McLean could only assume they were new to the job.

'Is this the same drug that did for the young lad at Cameron Toll?'

'Have you traced the supplier yet?'

'Do you know who's making this stuff?'

'How many more deaths will there be before you arrest someone?'

McLean winced at that last question, recognising the voice but not immediately being able to put the name to it.

'There will be plenty of time for questions once I've finished.' McIntyre spoke over the hubbub, expecting it to subside. 'We have identified a common factor in this latest death and that of Mr Alistair Hamilton in the Cameron Toll shopping centre.'

'What about Rory Devlin? You remember him, aye?'

This voice McLean did recognise. Jo Dalgliesh had sat herself at the back, presumably so that she could make a quick escape if things turned nasty. Either that or she wasn't one for early mornings and had only just arrived.

'If you'll let me continue, Ms Dalgliesh. Yes, we are linking the three incidents. We believe the same drug was involved in each one. We have secured a sample of the substance in question and early analysis shows us it's like nothing we've seen before. Apparently its street name is either Demon's Breath or Zombo, but then you already know that. You also know that nobody's talking about it. Not to you, and certainly not to us.'

A few more hands went up, but McIntyre ignored them, turning instead to McLean. 'Detective Inspector McLean here is leading the investigation into the three deaths, so I'll hand over to him.'

McLean surveyed the eager and expectant faces, knowing he was going to come up short of what they wanted. 'I know you've all got deadlines to meet, so I'll keep this brief. I've seen a few suggestions that because the first two victims were young, unemployed and from deprived backgrounds we're not taking this investigation seriously. Let me put the lie to that. From the moment we knew Rory Devlin's death was due to an overdose, we have been working around the clock to trace the supply of this drug and shut it down. Alistair Hamilton's death only made us work that much harder, and I want Fiona McLeod to be the last victim.'

'Do you have any leads, Detective Inspector?' The same voice that had made the jibe about Rory Devlin earlier. McLean scanned the crowd trying to pinpoint the face of his accuser, but there were half a dozen hands raised.

'We are pursuing several avenues at the moment, but that doesn't mean we're not open to any information our friends in the fourth estate might be able to provide. As Detective Superintendent McIntyre has already told you, this drug is new and different, and it's come out of nowhere.'

'Is there a danger to the public at large?' The same questioner again, and this time McLean managed to focus on him. It took a moment, but the name came to him shortly afterwards. Skelton McCallum had been Jo Dalgliesh's boss at her previous paper, and had something of a reputation for stirring up trouble. Just what they needed right now.

'Three people have had a violent and fatal reaction to a recreational drug they've taken. One, Mr Hamilton, was in a public place when it happened and nobody else close by was in any way affected. So no, I don't think there's a danger to the public at large. That doesn't mean we're not treating this situation very seriously indeed. Three people are dead. I don't want to be investigating any more.'

McLean stared straight at McCallum as he spoke, and he could see the man starting to form another question. Before he could get it out, someone else's voice cut through the general hubbub.

'Detective Inspector. Will you be working closely with the Dee Foundation on this investigation? Given they're on the front line when it comes to dealing with drug abuse and social deprivation in the city?'

Again, McLean found himself scanning the crowd to see who had asked the question. He hadn't recognised the voice, but the mention of the Dee Foundation specifically made him suspicious.

'We always work as closely as possible with charities and other organisations who come into contact with the public. They often have a much better idea of what's going on than we do, and the people they're helping trust them more than they trust us. You'll understand why we can't be too explicit about who we're talking to and when, though. No one's going to use a drug rehabilitation service if they think all their details are getting passed on to the police.'

'But is it not true that Police Scotland are forming close ties with the Dee Foundation? I believe there's a Project Tantalus that's about to go live?'

'I think the detective inspector has answered your question. Thank you.' McIntyre cut in so quickly, McLean hadn't even managed to fully register the question, let alone formulate an answer. He tried to work out who had spoken in the crowd, but the combination of a general hubbub of noise and his lack of sleep made it almost impossible to focus.

'Well, I think that just about covers everything. Please see Sergeant Hwei for your briefing notes, and if you have any further questions. Meantime we've a job to do. Thank you, ladies and gentlemen.' The detective superintendent stood up, tapped McLean on the shoulder to do the same. 'Come on, Tony. Let's get out of here.'

'Well, that could have been better.'

McLean stared through the little glass window in the door to the conference room, watching as the last few members of the press filed out through the double doors at the back. Beside him, Detective Superintendent McIntyre sorted through her papers, shoving the important ones in her case and the unimportant ones in the bin. DCI Ritchie had already made her excuses and gone.

'Truth be told, Tony, we're lucky we got away with it for as long as we did. A couple of dead junkies doesn't move the needle much these days, but this woman, Fiona McLeod? She seems to have struck a chord.'

'That's the thing though, Jayne. Rory Devlin wasn't a junkie, or at least only started doing drugs a few months ago. He comes from a decent enough background, too. He didn't grow up in the schemes, and he sure as hell didn't have any kind of juvenile record. They only don't care about him because he died of an overdose in a spot well known for drug taking.'

'You sound like you wish the press were making life more difficult for you.'

McLean turned away from the window, leaned against the table and faced the detective superintendent. 'Well, at least if they were we'd get more resources for the investigation. And a bit of public outcry might shake out some information about this drug. The usual sources have turned up a complete blank on Demon's Breath. Doesn't help that we've a team of fresh-faced constables and sergeants. Too few seasoned officers with decent contacts.'

McIntyre took off her spectacles and was in the process of putting them away when something behind McLean caught her attention. He stood up as the door from the conference room swung open, narrowly missing him. Gail Elmwood stood in the doorway, glaring at him as if he'd just thrown a ball through her conservatory window.

'Don't you think it would've looked better with the chief superintendent heading up this press conference?' Her anger was tempered by the fact that she looked almost as exhausted as McLean felt.

'I'm sorry, ma'am. I was told you were away at Gartcosh all day today.'

'You were, were you?' Elmwood stepped into the small anteroom like a woman twice her age, one hand reaching out towards the table for support. McLean went to help, but she waved him away irritably. 'I'm not a geriatric, Tony. I can walk on my own.'

Even so, she still sat heavily in the chair he pulled out for her, letting out a sigh of relief as she did so.

'You needing us both, Gail?' McIntyre asked. 'Only I've a report to finish for the chief constable and –'

Elmwood cut her off with a wave of the hand. 'No worries, Jayne. It was Tony I was looking for anyway.'

'OK then. Catch up with you later.' McIntyre gave him a little nod as she slipped past, the look on her face as guilty as a schoolgirl caught pulling one of her classmates' hair. McLean glowered, but he couldn't really blame her.

'So tell me how the press conference went then?' Elmwood's tone dragged his attention away from the departing detective superintendent.

'I think it was OK. No obvious leading questions. I didn't get a sense they were looking to take our words and twist them into a knife. Someone seemed well briefed about Project Tantalus.'

If he'd any suspicions about how that had happened, the chief superintendent's lack of surprise answered them eloquently.

'Never been a fan of reporters. Only interested in it when you fuck things up. What about that one you've got in your pocket? Dag . . . Dalg . . .'

'I don't think Jo Dalgliesh would consider that much of a fair appraisal. Chances are she reckons she's the one in charge.'

'She?' Elmwood looked up at him askance, and McLean remembered the last time they'd talked about the journalist. The chief superintendent had assumed 'Jo' was a man, and he'd been happy to let her keep on thinking that.

'She, aye. She's the one broke the story, but she also gave me twelve hours' warning. Otherwise we'd not have managed to cobble this press conference together. So I owe her that much.'

'Long as you keep it professional, eh?' Elmwood laughed, and then started to cough. One thing she had in common with the reporter, McLean supposed.

'Was that what you wanted to see me about? The press conference?' he asked. 'I'm sorry we didn't ask you to attend. If I'd known you were here . . .'

'Nah, that's fine.' Elmwood rasped out the words before pulling a white handkerchief from her jacket pocket and coughing into it some more. 'I'm not really at my best this morning anyway. No, what I'm really here for is to tell you about an invitation you'll be receiving later today that you're going to accept. I know you well enough now, Tony. And I know how much you don't like the woman, so consider it an order. You won't come up with some lame excuse or engineer some last-minute crisis, right?'

'The woman' could only mean one person, even if Elmwood hadn't specifically named her. 'And what manner of invitation would this be?' McLean asked.

'Don't worry. It's business, not social. And you won't be the only policeman there. I'll be going, and the chief constable too. Might be one or two Specialist Crime people you know as well. Just make sure you're there.' Elmwood struggled to her feet, shoving the handkerchief back in her pocket as she did so. McLean couldn't help but notice the spots of dark red on the previously white linen.

'Make sure I'm where?' he asked as she turned away from him.

'It's in the invitation, Tony. On your desk.' And without another word, she walked away.

McLean resisted the urge to go straight to his office and find the mysterious invitation. If it was for something urgent then the chief superintendent would have to do better than her rather strange attempt at being mysterious. Besides, he had more important things to be getting on with, one of which had occurred to him as a direct result of his conversation with McIntyre.

'Who fancies a trip across town?' he asked of the collected detectives as he stepped into the CID room. It was surprisingly full for a change, but no one immediately volunteered. DCs Blane and Stringer were head to head, peering closely at a large computer screen, so either they'd seen him coming and were pretending or they were indeed actually busy. DS Gregg was going through some paperwork with DCs Bryant and Mitchell, and none of them had reacted to his voice. A couple of the other new DCs looked up nervously from their desks. He didn't know them well. Mostly they seemed to work with Ritchie, and DCI Dexter over in Vice. He'd take one of them if necessary, but he wasn't sure he had the energy for stilted conversation.

He was beginning to contemplate going alone when he felt more than heard a presence in the corridor behind him. Turning, McLean saw DS Harrison, a couple of folders clutched in her hands like some votive offering.

'You looking for me, sir?' she asked.

'That depends on how busy you are. There's a few people I need to go and speak to. The sort of people it's best not to visit alone.'

'Ten minutes?' Harrison checked her watch as she spoke.

'Call it half an hour. I could do with a coffee first. See if you can't sort us a pool car too. Not sure I want to take Em's up to Muirhouse.'

Harrison hid her surprise well, but he saw her eyes widen slightly at the name. She nodded once, then slid past him into the room. McLean took one more look at the collected detectives, deciding it was best to leave the quiet activity well alone, and set off towards the stairs and his office on the third floor.

The invitation Elmwood had warned him about was impossible to miss. It had been placed in the centre of his desk, all the various important paperwork he'd been dealing with pushed to the sides to make room. He fetched himself a cup of coffee, considered going down to the canteen in search of a chocolate muffin, but he knew he was only avoiding the inevitable. Finally sitting down, he took up the envelope.

He'd seen similar before, a few years back. That had been handwritten in the same skilled script, the paper the same ostentatiously heavy, probably handmade, card. Not quite knowing why, he raised it to his nose and sniffed, getting a whiff of something unpleasant. Like the memory of bad hangovers and backed up drains. His fingers felt dirty from touching it. Or he was being stupid.

Pulling open a seldom used drawer, McLean took out a silver paper knife that had once belonged to his grandfather and used it to neatly slit open the envelope. Inside, the card was handwritten like the name on the front.

> Chief Superintendent Gail Elmwood requests your attendance at a reception to mark the official collaboration between Police Scotland and The Dee Foundation.

The date and time were predictably short notice, but it was the venue that raised McLean's eyebrow. He knew the place, had been there before, albeit against his will. Mrs Saifre's mansion house lay just outside the city limits, to the south east of the bypass near Dalkeith. It made a certain sense to hold an event there, he supposed. What didn't make sense was the event itself. A memorandum of understanding between the two organisations would have been enough, and if they wanted to make a song and dance about it, the chief constable could have come over for a photo opportunity outside one of the foundation's outreach centres. Or they could have done it in the conference room downstairs, where he'd been less than fifteen minutes ago. A reception, in a house miles away from anywhere, was a waste of both time and money. Absolutely Mrs Saifre's style.

With a weary sigh, he slid the card back into the envelope, took one last look at the neat script on the front, then leaned over and dropped it in the bin.

32

Low cloud and spattering rain crept in off the Forth as they headed north across the city towards Muirhouse. McLean let Harrison drive, even though the few pool cars at the station had all been booked out and they'd been forced to take Emma's little Renault Zoe. Better that than his old Alfa; that would have drawn all the wrong kind of attention. Sooner or later he'd have to get himself a new car, but there never seemed to be the time to look into it. Maybe he could get his own Zoe. Or maybe Emma wouldn't be needing hers any more.

'Who's this bloke we're going to see?' Harrison asked as they approached the roundabout at the end of Ferry Road. McLean had been staring at the grey bulk of the Western General Hospital, his thoughts very much not on the case in hand, so it took a while for him to register the question.

'Jimmy Laird. Unpleasant fellow, and not somebody I'd normally go looking for. He can be useful though.'

'One of your Chises?' Harrison made it sound like a nasty disease, which McLean supposed it was in a way. Covert Human Intelligence Source. Who the hell came up with these acronyms?

'I always preferred informer myself. Or snitch, snout. Source is good, I guess. The rest of it's all nonsense.' McLean heard himself babbling, did his best to stop. 'But yes, Wee Jimmy Laird is one of my sources. Or at least he was. Haven't had to use him in a few years now.'

'You sure he's still alive?'

'Trust me, Sergeant. I'd know if he wasn't.'

The high-rise tower of Martello Court was almost as ugly as the new hotel development in the city centre, only not clad in expensive bronze sheeting. Or shaped like an artfully laid dog turd. Twenty-three storeys high, each floor was encircled by a balcony that would have been a great feature had the building been on the seafront at Cannes, perhaps. Clinging to the south shore of the Firth of Forth was less congenial, especially as winter approached. Harrison parked as close to the entrance as she could, and the two of them hurried to the front entrance as a squall of rain blew in off the sea.

'Let me guess, top floor and the lift's out?'

'Third floor, and I'd suggest the stairs anyway.' McLean looked around, seeing a brighter space than he remembered. 'Although they seem to have done a bit of work on the place.'

The climb to the third floor wasn't too arduous, and the stairwell had seen a recent lick of paint like the entrance lobby. Even so, it still had a lingering smell of stale piss and other less pleasant things about it. McLean tried to remember the last time he had been here, with Grumpy Bob most likely, or maybe young DC MacBride. What had happened to him? Got out while the going was good, and best of luck to him.

'Here we go.' He knocked hard on a door that appeared to have missed out on the renovations, then listened for signs of movement within. Nothing after a generous minute, so he knocked hard again. This time it sounded like something might have shaken loose, and sure enough after a few more tens of seconds the locks clacked and the door opened a crack. The face that peered out was unshaven, lined and dirty, lanky yellow-grey hair falling from a high forehead in greasy curls.

'Sorry, Jimmy. Did I wake you up?' McLean asked.

'Fuck's sake, Inspector. Nearly gave me a heart attack there. Banging away like the wrath of God.' The door closed as the chain slid off, then opened again. 'Who's the girlfriend?'

'Detective Sergeant Harrison is not my girlfriend, Jimmy. Now, you going to let us in or am I going to introduce myself a bit more loudly?'

'No need for threats, Inspector. Come in then.' Jimmy Laird was wearing a tatty old dressing gown over what McLean hoped was pyjamas, his feet bare and as dirty as the floor. The reek of him battled with a deeper stench that filled the whole flat, a mix of fried foods, weed and body odour that made the piss in the stairwell seem like fresh blossom in comparison. They followed him through to a front room that might have featured on one of those daytime television programmes about impossible cleaning tasks. Laird strode across the room heedless of the empty pizza boxes and other detritus that tumbled to the litter-strewn floor in his wake, dropping himself into the armchair that was the only piece of furniture immediately available. No offer of a cuppa, which was a relief. He took up a crumpled pack of cigarettes from where they'd been balanced on the arm of the chair, fetched one out, then seemed to realise he had no lighter close by.

'So, what do I owe this unexpected pleasure to, Inspector?'

'Demon's Breath. Sometimes referred to as Zombo. What can you tell me about it?'

'No idea what you're talking about, Inspector. I'm clean now, in't I? Haven't done anything harder than tobacco in years.' Laird shoved the cigarette in his mouth, then patted his dressing gown as if it were a fine silk smoking jacket, still finding no lighter.

'Even if I believed you, Jimmy, I know you like to keep your ear to the ground. There's nothing happens in these parts you don't hear about. Knowledge is currency, after all.' McLean shoved his hand into his pocket. He'd put some twenty-pound notes in there earlier, but he wasn't ready to play that card just yet.

'I am shocked – no, insulted – that you should think so little of me, Inspector.' Laird turned his attention to Harrison. 'Dear lady, can you not see how shocked I am? Me, an honest and upstanding member of society.'

'I've not heard anyone accuse you of anything yet, Mr Laird.' Harrison already had her hands in her pockets, McLean noticed. Probably for the best. You'd want a thorough scrub down after touching anything in this squalid hovel.

'Broxburn girl are you?' Laird leaned forward in his seat, plucking the cigarette from his mouth. It looked like it might break in two at any moment. 'Used to do some work out that way, back in the day.'

'Your knowledge of Edinburgh accents is impressive, Jimmy, but you're avoiding the question.' Now McLean pulled out a handful of cash. 'Zombo. What is it, and who's dealing it?'

'I told you, Inspector –'

'This could be a nice home, you know? These apartments are a good size, too. If I remember right. What is it, three bedrooms? That's a bit big for a man all on his own.' McLean shoved the money back in his pocket, turned slowly on the spot, pretending to look at the room. 'Housing association might not like the way you've treated the place. Might be they decide to move you out. Fumigate. Let a family move in. You'd be out on the street then, Jimmy.'

'I . . . You wouldn't . . . I don't . . .'

'Demon's Breath. It's a yellow liquid in a glass capsule. I'm guessing you break the top off, like poppers, aye? The liquid turns to vapour and you sniff it in. Straight to your brain. Instant hit, no?' McLean leaned forward, getting closer to the grubby man than he really wanted to, and stared at him until he finally looked away.

'OK. OK. Just . . . You didn't hear it from me. You were never here. Fuck. I'm too old for this shit.' Laird shoved the cigarette back in his mouth, patted himself for a lighter again. Only this time his hands were shaking. McLean waited, the silence stretching between them. He'd like to hurry this up, get out of this stinking shithole of a flat. Maybe go down to the shore and let the gales blow the stench out of him, the rain wash him clean. But this was his best bet, so he stayed put.

Finally, Laird broke. 'They're no' selling it, right? You can get it for free, but only if you know the right folk, and they like the look of you. Word is they've not got the formulation right yet, see? Been a few batches passed around, but there's too many side effects. People having hallucinations for days after. Some folk, it's like they've gone and there's someone else living in their body. Swear I've never seen anything like it, and you know me, Inspector. I'll try anything once. But not this.'

'So nobody's dealing it at the moment then? Our three dead bodies are just unlucky experimental subjects, is that it?'

'Dead . . . ? I didn't know anything about . . . Jesus.'

'What do you know, Jimmy? Anyone offer it to you? You ask anyone for it?'

Laird shook his head. 'Not my scene. Not any more. But, well, what I've heard is it's popular with the kids, aye? Least, that's where it's being pushed.'

'I thought you said it was experimental,' Harrison said. 'Nobody's dealing it at the moment, you said. So how d'you know it's popular with the kids?'

Jimmy had been staring at McLean, but his gaze shifted nervously in the detective sergeant's direction. He had gripped the cigarette so tightly now it was bent, a small tear in the paper letting flakes of tobacco tumble onto his dressing gown.

'Well, it's like I said, nobody's selling it, right? You can't buy it. There's no dealers, no network, no gang out there pushing it.

Far as I can tell, it's just a word of mouth thing, y'know? An' word is that's coz it's not ready yet. They're testing it, testing the market too.'

'And just who are "they" then?'

Laird shook his head, almost a tremor of fear more than a denial of knowledge. 'I don't know. And I know not to ask, too.'

'Why's that?' McLean asked.

'Coz bad things happen to folk who ask. Thought you might've noticed that, aye?'

'How so? What's happened to who?'

Laird said nothing, the tremors increasing. Either he really needed his morning dose of nicotine or he was terrified of something. McLean didn't want to bet on it being the former.

'Names, Jimmy. Who's been asking questions, and what happened to them?'

'Teddy Graham stepped in front of a bus a month or two back. Know for a fact he was trying to muscle in on this stuff. Shug Peters told me he'd track down the place they was brewin' it. Died in his sleep that same day, an' he was as fit as they come. Fraser Murdoch, remember him? He was on the up in the local heroin trade till he tripped an' fell down the stairs in that block over there.' Laird waved his hand at the window and a low-rise building barely visible through the foul weather. 'Broke his neck, and it was only a few steps he fell.'

'You think they were all killed?' Harrison asked. When McLean looked round he saw she was writing down names in her notebook.

'No' just them. See why the inspector comes to me, hen? It's coz I see things, I know things. I don't get involved, but I watch what's happening. An' I'm telling you I've seen more dealers in this city die in the last six months, maybe a year, than in the ten years before that. No' gangland killings, nothin' like that. It's wee accidents, stupid mistakes, folk just going to sleep and no' waking up in the morning. Aye, there's always an explanation, but I see patterns, and there's a pattern here.'

McLean took the money back out of his pocket, counted out fifty pounds and held it out. 'So you think someone's taking over the local supply, or just getting paranoid in your old age, Jimmy?'

Laird leaned forward, reaching for the money, then he stopped, closed his hand into a fist and withdrew. 'I'm saying this ain't a good place to be a dealer or a snitch any more, Inspector. Weren't never the one, but I'm no gonnae be the other any more.'

'Charming man. Don't think I'll ever get that smell out of my nose.'

Driving away from Martello Court, Harrison lifted one arm to her face and sniffed the sleeve of her jacket. McLean knew what she meant. The lingering odour had followed them downstairs and even the driving rain between the front entrance and Emma's Renault Zoe hadn't been enough to completely get rid of it. Had the visit been worth the necessary hot shower and change of clothes? He thought so, on balance.

'Nobody ever said the job was going to be easy. And horrible excuse for a human being though he is, Jimmy at least gave us some information. Far as I can tell no one else has managed to find out anything about this stuff.'

'Not for want of asking. Been like a brick wall out there, you know? And if what your man said there's true, I can start to see why.'

'Take it with a bucketload of salt. At least until you've run those names through the system. One of the reasons I've not been to see wee Jimmy is he's quite the storyteller when he sets his mind to it. There's usually a nugget of truth in what he's saying, but you have to dig through a fair pile of shite before you can find it.'

Harrison said nothing to that, only taking another quick sniff at her sleeve as they waited for the lights to change. The rain had turned from intermittent squalls to a constant battering downpour now, the windscreen wipers swinging back and forth like they were on speed. McLean fetched out his phone and checked the screen for messages again. In the five minutes since he'd last done so there had been no news.

'You want to swing past the hospital, sir? Since it's on our way?'

'Am I that obvious?'

'Can't say as I blame you. I'd be going out of my mind if it was me.' Harrison edged the car forward, indicated and pulled into the right lane for the Western General even though he hadn't told her to.

'Not entirely sure I'm in my right mind as it is.' McLean shoved his phone away again. 'Should have shaken down Jimmy Laird for information days ago, but I let myself get distracted. That's no way to run an investigation.'

'Aye, well. We do what we can. I'll be sure and check out those names he gave us, although I think I remember hearing about Teddy Graham and the bus. Most folk thought he'd done it on purpose. Too many debts with the wrong kind of people. The bus driver wasn't so sure though. Thought maybe he got pushed.'

McLean braced his feet against the footwell as Harrison took the opportunity of a small gap in the traffic to cross the road. 'See if you can't dig up the report into that, then. And have a chat with the drugs boys about any other suspicious deaths in the past year or two. Think we'd have noticed a turf war, mind you.'

Harrison nodded as she indicated and turned towards the car park. McLean stopped her before she could go through the barrier.

'It's OK. I'll make my own way back to the station.' He

unclipped his seatbelt and checked over his shoulder before opening the door. 'Unless you like hanging around in hospitals, that is?'

The irony of having left DS Harrison to drive Emma's car across town while Emma herself was here in the hospital was not lost on McLean as he walked the familiar corridors to the neurology unit. Most of the day shift nurses seemed to recognise him, greeting him with a smile or a cheery hello, and by the time he reached the ward he was in a more upbeat mood than he'd managed for days. The look on the face of Jeanie Robertson as she saw him brought it all crashing back down to earth.

'Hi, Tony. Didn't know you were going to be here. There's still no real change, I'm afraid.'

'I was just passing. Had something to do in Muirhouse and thought I'd pop in on the way back to the station.' Even as he said it, he could hear how lame the excuse sounded.

'Well, you can go and sit with her for a while if you'd like. Not strictly visiting hours, but then . . .'

McLean looked across the reception hall towards the ward door. Did he really want to go in there and sit with her? Take her cold, still hand in his and do what? Time was he'd told his grandmother about his day, but did he really want to trouble Emma with all that nonsense? Then again, would anyone else even listen to him?

'Thank you, Jeanie. I'd quite like that if it's OK.'

The corridor leading to the neurology unit hadn't exactly been noisy, but when the door closed behind him as he stepped into the ward, it was as if the world had suddenly been turned off. There were three beds occupied, each patient hooked up to machines far quieter than the ones McLean remembered from years past. Emma lay motionless, her face turned to the ceiling, eyes closed. At least she was breathing on her own now, no tube down the throat. She was still hooked up to a drip, wires trailing from various monitors taped to her skin. She looked so pale and fragile, as if she was fashioned from finest porcelain, not flesh and blood. McLean pulled up his chair close, but kept his hands clasped together on his lap.

When he spoke, the words came far more easily than he'd thought they would. 'It's all gone a bit shit since you fell down. We've got three dead bodies and nobody seems to want to tell us about the drug they all took that did for them. Rose wants to put those bones you and Hattie found back in the ground where they came from. I'm dangerously close to having to pull her in for questioning about another dead body we found, too.'

Emma said nothing, did nothing. Only the gentle hum of the machinery and her slow, almost imperceptible breathing convinced him she was alive at all.

'And as if that wasn't bad enough, I've got that bloody Saifre woman sticking her nose in where it's not needed. She's up to something, her and her bloody Dee Foundation. I've no idea what it is, but she's got the chief superintendent in her pocket now. Christ, what a mess.'

Emma's intake of breath stopped as he finished speaking, and for a moment he thought maybe she had reacted to something he had said. For another moment he worried she might have died, the complex tumble of thoughts and emotions only just beginning to unfurl before she slowly let the breath out again. Was that any different from the last one? The one before that?

'Could really do with you coming back, Em.' He slumped forward, resting his head on his hands, talking to his knees for a while before looking up at her unmoving face again. 'It's selfish, I know, but I need to focus. Need to see the connections my brain's telling me are there. And I find that so very hard to do with you lying here, connected to all these bloody machines.'

As if mocking him, one of the monitors across the room

started to beep. Not an insistent alarm, but a slow, regular rhythm that meant sooner rather than later a nurse would be along to check the patient. Emma paid no heed whatsoever.

'I thought this might help. Maybe it has done.' He reached out and took her hand, feeling the slimness of her fingers, the cool dry touch of her. He gave them a little squeeze, then let go. 'I'll come back again tomorrow, OK?'

Standing, he put the chair back where he'd found it, and headed for the door. Before he got there, it swung open. Nurse Robertson gave him the most cursory of glances before striding across the room to the beeping machine. McLean took that as his cue, one last look back at Emma's unmoving form, and then he left.

33

'Teddy Graham? There's a name I've not heard in a while. Threw himself under a bus, didn't he?'

Janie Harrison was still the newest detective sergeant in the station, even though she'd been in the job over a year now. She was also the youngest. Not counting Grumpy Bob, who only worked on a consultancy basis for the Cold Case Unit, Detective Sergeant Billy Colquhoun was the oldest, and not long off retirement. He'd worked in both Vice and Drugs, or the Sexual Crimes Unit and Counter-Narcotics to give them their most recent official titles, for most of his career, and while Janie knew he had a reputation for laziness and cutting corners, he was also a font of information. If you plied him with free coffee and cake.

'That's what some people say, for sure. But I've heard maybe he was pushed. You know anything about that, Sarge?' Janie gave the old sergeant her best innocent look.

'Way I heard it, he was up to his neck in debt with all the wrong people, and he'd developed a fondness for the product he was selling too. So he had plenty of incentive to top himself. What's this all about then, Janie? Why the sudden interest? You heard something different?'

So much for innocence. 'Aye, something like that. What about Shug Peters?'

'Shuggie? Aye, he had a heart attack, din't he. Was the best part of a month before anyone noticed he wasn't about. Not a pretty sight I can tell you. Think the phrase used was he'd become one with his mattress. I wasn't going to hang around long to see. No' easy to breathe in his place it stank that bad. You'd think the neighbours would have noticed something sooner, only those housing blocks all reek anyways.'

'You saw him, then?'

'Aye, I was on the team. Don't remember much about it, 'cept his face was this deathly white an' something had been at his lips. They were all blistered, like.' Colquhoun shivered at the memory, took up his mug and drank down a large gulp of coffee to warm away the image.

'How about Fraser Murdoch? You remember him?'

'Who've you been talking too, Janie? Shug Peters, Teddy Graham and now Fraser Murdoch? If I didn't know better I'd think you were looking for a transfer to our team.'

'All due respect to your boss, I think I'll stick with DI McLean for now. Well, DCI Ritchie, I should say.'

Colquhoun raised a shaggy grey eyebrow at that. Most of the hair on the top of his head had long since retreated, but he made up for it with the great mass protruding from his ears and framing the tops of his eyes. 'Heard stories about you and McLean. Nonsense, of course, but you want to tread carefully, Janie. Get yourself a reputation if you're not careful.'

Janie felt the tips of her ears heat up, although whether it was from embarrassment or anger at the endless gossip of police officers she couldn't have said. Most likely both.

'Fraser Murdoch, though. He fell down a flight of stairs and broke his neck, right?'

'Aye, that was the story, best we could tell. Bastard unlucky though. I mean, it was only a short wee flight of steps at the back of the building. Most folk would jar a knee or stub their toe.

Poor old Fraser somehow managed to kill himself.'

'You think it was suspicious, then? Maybe someone pushed him? Broke his neck and left him there so it'd look like an accident?'

'Now I know you are up to something.' Colquhoun ran a greasy finger around the edge of his plate, smearing up the last few crumbs and chocolate icing. 'Who's been telling you what?'

'Can't tell you who, that's not my decision to make. But you've heard about this new drug going round? Demon's Breath or Zombo or whatever they're calling it?'

'Heard's not the right word. Nobody's saying anything about it. Only knew it was a thing when that young junkie lad turned up in Restalrig. No' really sure why your team ended up investigating that rather than ours.'

'Well, they reckoned he'd been beaten to death to start with, remember. The drugs connection came later. And we're not really teams any more either. Sergeants just go where they're told to, aye?'

'You're not wrong there, lass.'

'Which is probably why nobody really noticed a pattern of deaths in the city's drugs underworld or whatever name we've got for it these days. Those three I asked about aren't the only players who've fallen off the board lately, are they.'

Colquhoun frowned. He'd been sucking the chocolate and cake crumbs off his finger, and now he removed it with a 'pop' sound. 'What are you getting at?'

'I've been asking around, and in the last eighteen months more than a dozen people of interest have died. Sure, some of them were old, and none of the deaths were more suspicious than Murdoch falling down the stairs or Teddy Graham chucking himself under a bus. They were all folk nobody in this station would much miss either. But who gains from them being out of the picture? Who picked up the business they'd been doing after they were gone? That's what I'd like to know.'

'Ah, Janie. Glad I caught you. Have you got time for a quick word?'

Janie had been on her way to DI McLean's office, hoping he might have been back from the hospital by now and keen to pass on what she had found out about the city's drug dealers before shift end. Somehow the day had got away from her again, but DCI Ritchie caught her at the top of the stairs.

'Of course.' She followed the detective chief inspector along the corridor, noticing in passing that McLean's office was empty anyway. Ritchie led her into the next room along, then closed the door and pointed to the small conference table. Only once they were both seated did she speak again.

'You've been working closely with Tony recently.' She unconsciously glanced towards the partition wall between the two offices as she asked the question.

'If folk've been making up stories again, I'll –'

'That's not what this is about, Janie.' Ritchie held up a hand to stop her. 'And nobody's gossiping any more. Not about that. As rumours go, it never had legs anyway.'

'So, what then?' Janie knew almost as soon as the words were out. 'Oh.'

'Exactly.' Ritchie rested her elbows on the conference table and leaned forward as if they were just two women out for a drink and a blether. On balance, Janie would have much preferred that option for this conversation.

'How is he coping, do you think?' the DCI asked after a moment's silence.

'I don't really know. He doesn't exactly over-share, does he.'

Ritchie smiled briefly. 'That's one way of putting it. He's his own worst enemy the way he bottles things up. And this . . . well, it's the kind of pressure that would break most people.'

'He's not most people though, is he. I mean, he's dealt with this kind of trauma in the past, right?'

'And you think that makes it easier, Janie? Christ, I can't begin to imagine what it must be like, knowing this has happened to Em before. And his grandmother was in a coma for eighteen months before she died. She was at the Western General all that time. According to Grumpy Bob he used to visit her at least once a week. Every day if he could. You ever wonder how it is he knows so many of the nursing staff and doctors there?'

'I knew about Emma, and all that stuff with Sergeant Needham. Thought that was why he knew everyone there. That and the way he just . . . knows everyone, you know? I'd not heard about his grandmother though. Wasn't she the city pathologist or something? That's why he's so comfortable down in the mortuary, too?'

Ritchie nodded. 'Angus Cadwallader studied under her. As did Hattie Turner, come to mention it. I never knew her, but I'm told she was a formidable lady. Raised Tony on her own after his parents died in an aeroplane crash. As if there wasn't enough tragedy in his life already. And don't even ask about his fiancée.'

Janie shook her head. 'I know about that.'

'So you probably understand why we're all a bit concerned about him. He's been acting a bit erratically of late.'

'Has he? How so? I mean, apart from coming into work when he should be taking time off. And I can kind of understand that. I'd not want to be sitting in that big old house twiddling my thumbs and waiting for the doctors to call with bad news. I'd need something to distract me. You'd be hard pushed to keep me away from work.'

Ritchie leaned back again, glancing at the opposite partition wall, the one beyond which lay the chief superintendent's office.

'You know he walked out on Gail a few days back? Middle of a briefing and he just stood up and walked out. Took me and Jayne the best part of an hour to calm her down.'

'I'm sure he had good reason,' Janie said, even though she had her doubts. The detective inspector's dislike of the chief superintendent was no secret, but he understood well enough the importance of chain of command, the need for a certain amount of discipline in the ranks. You couldn't just walk out on a superior officer, surely?

'I've no doubt he thought he did,' Ritchie said. 'But we can't pretend it isn't a warning signal. We need to keep an eye on him, stop him from doing something he'll only regret later.'

'You . . . you want me to spy on him?' Janie felt a mixture of discomfort and anger at the thought, which must have shown in her voice and on her face, as Ritchie swiftly raised both hands, palms out in a gesture of appeasement.

'No. Not at all. That's not what I mean. If anyone's going to spy on him, as you put it, then that'll be me and Jayne McIntyre. No, I need you to be aware of the situation, make sure it doesn't affect the detective constables too much. I know how most of them look up to Tony, and I know how much stress the whole team's under. You need to be there for them if something happens to him.'

Janie said nothing to that, not sure there was anything she could say. The detective chief inspector was right, of course. As one of only two detective sergeants in their team, it was up to her to manage the detective constables and support staff, even if Sandy Gregg was both more experienced and better at that side of things than she would ever be. It was the 'if something happens' that gave her pause. Ritchie might have said 'if' but Janie could see clearly enough that she meant 'when'.

34

Rain was lashing down when the taxi he'd taken from the hospital dropped him outside the city mortuary. It clattered off the cobbles and pavement, reflecting the glow of the street lamps, and for a moment McLean looked up in surprise that they were lit. Where had the day gone?

Soaked from the short run between pavement and front door, he shook the worst of the wet from him like a dog before the receptionist clicked him through to the business end of the building. He found Dr Cadwallader already in his scrubs, standing at the steel table in the middle of the examination theatre, Dr Sharp as ever at his side. The pathologist had been staring at the cadaver in front of him, but he looked up at the sound of McLean entering.

'I was beginning to wonder if you were going to come or not.'

'I was across town when I got your message. Traffic's a bit of a nightmare with all this rain.' McLean ran a hand through his hair, then wiped the dampness on his already moist trousers. 'You started already?'

'Just my preliminary visual examination. We'll get to your favourite bit soon enough.'

McLean stepped a little closer, reassured that he wouldn't have to see a body already opened up. It was still a harrowing sight. The convulsions that had killed Fiona McLeod had left her body twisted in impossible ways, her arms bent at angles that made him wince just to look at them, legs broken like she'd been in a car crash, not sitting at home on her sofa.

'Not a pretty sight, is it.' Cadwallader must have caught his expression. 'I'm afraid the poor girl didn't have a quick and painless death. It looks like almost every muscle in her body's clenched at the same time. Can't think of the last time I saw anything like it. Well, apart from those two young lads, and they're nothing like as bad as this poor lass.'

'It's the same thing though. The drug, right?' McLean considered what they'd already told the press, and how complicated it might be to row back on that.

'You spoke to the neighbour, didn't you?' the pathologist asked.

'Harrison did, yes. She said something about thinking there was a fight.'

'Went on for long enough that she called the police. Several minutes at least, maybe tens of minutes. Long enough for her to smash her feet to pieces.' Cadwallader waved his hand in the direction of them, and McLean was forced to focus on something he didn't really want to. He'd seen the damage in situ, of course, but there it had been part of the chaos of the scene. Here, stripped of all context, it was impossible not to wince at the bloodied and mangled stumps that must once have been toes, the tears in the skin where shards of metatarsal had punched their way out. He looked away again swiftly.

'What is this drug, Angus? What could possibly have that kind of effect on a person?'

Cadwallader shrugged. 'That's one for the pharmacologists to work out, I think. From what little I recall of the subject though, sometimes a general muscle relaxant can have the exact opposite effect on people.'

'Any idea why she suffered more than the other two?'

The pathologist paused from where he had been gently lifting and inspecting the crook of the dead woman's elbow. 'Not really. I could speculate it was because they were male and she's female, but that's purely conjecture. I'll have a better idea of her general health compared to the other two once I've opened her up and had a look inside, but apart from the recent, self-inflicted damage she looks to be in quite good shape. Certainly not a habitual drug user, I'd say.'

'Neither was Devlin until very recently, or so I'm told. Hamilton seems to have been a bit more of a junkie.'

'Well his pathology was certainly different. He was malnourished for one thing, had been for a while by the state of his teeth. Much more your typical addict than the other two, and I'd say he handled chemicals a lot, judging by the state of his fingertips. It's all in the report I sent over.'

McLean tried to remember reading it, found that he couldn't. Too busy struggling with everything else, not the least of which was having to deal with the Dee Foundation. 'I think I must have missed that one.'

Cadwallader put the woman's arm back down with all the care of a new father placing his infant child in its crib, then he fixed McLean with the sort of stare that father might give their wayward son sixteen years later. 'You've a lot on your mind, Tony. It's hardly surprising some things slip through. Talking of which, any news?'

It felt like days since he'd sat by Emma's bedside, and yet it was barely an hour. McLean shook his head. 'Nothing's changed. She's unconscious, but not on life support beyond a drip. Scans show some brain activity, but it's minimal. She needs time to come back to us.' Or to slip away.

'I dare say others have already told you to take some time off and you've not listened to them either, so I'll not bother.'

The pathologist fixed him with a headmasterly stare. 'As to Mr Hamilton, well, apart from his general ill-health, there's not much difference between him and this unfortunate lady or the other young man. He was, as you say, an addict though. And there was one other thing I brought up in the post-mortem report you might like to see, since you're here.'

Without waiting to confirm it, Cadwallader strode over to the cadaver store, pausing a moment to check the register before selecting one of the doors. It clunked open like an industrial refrigerator, and he hauled out the sliding bench upon which the body of Alistair Hamilton lay. He was covered in a white sheet the pathologist rolled down only as far as his neck, which at least saved McLean the discomfort of having to see the Y-shaped incision across his upper torso.

'Scrawny fellow, isn't he.' The pathologist moved around to the far side of the drawer so that the body lay between the two of them. McLean looked down, barely recognising the young man he had seen in the food court area of the Cameron Toll shopping centre. His face had taken on that waxy complexion of death he was all too familiar with, the closed eyes sunken, cheeks hollow as if he was already well on the way to becoming no more than a skeleton. His skin had a slightly more yellow pallor to it than McLean was used to seeing, almost nicotine-stained. But it was the young man's lips that drew his attention the most.

'That happened between us bagging him up at the shopping centre and his arrival here. Remind you of anything?'

If he hadn't seen the body before, McLean might have thought Alistair Hamilton had been tortured to death. Maybe forced to drink some strong acid, or branded across the face with a hot iron. His lips were blistered and raw, some strange effect of rigor mortis pulling them back into a grimace that revealed stained, broken teeth and echoed the pain such an injury in life would surely have brought. Worse than that though was the fact that it did indeed remind McLean of something.

'I'm not even going to suggest you might have missed that before.' He waved a hand over the dead man's face both to indicate the damage and that the pathologist could put it away now.

'I've taken samples and sent them off for analysis.' Cadwallader rolled the white sheet back over Hamilton's face and then slid the body into the cold store. 'I'll let you know as soon as the results are back.'

'What about Devlin? Any marks on him?' McLean nodded his head back towards the examination table. 'Her?'

'Nothing, see.' Cadwallader pulled out another drawer, rolled back the sheet to reveal Rory Devlin's dead face. He looked less cadaverous than Hamilton, despite them both being actual cadavers. 'Family are anxious to have him back as soon as possible. I guess they want to bury him and try to get on with their lives.'

McLean leaned as close as he felt comfortable, but he could see no blemish on Devlin's lips. None on Fiona McLeod's either. 'I'll get Harrison to speak to the Devlins, but I've a feeling it'll be a while yet before we can release his body to them. Let me know soon as you get those test results back can you, Angus. I really don't like the way this is all starting to shape up.'

35

McLean let himself into an incident room quite lacking in the buzz he would have liked to have seen, even if shift end was fast approaching. The only area where there seemed to be any action at all was the bank of telephones. Half a dozen PCs and support officers were fielding calls from the public, a direct result of the newspaper and television coverage Fiona McLeod's death had been given. Even that would be mostly rubbish, he knew. There was nothing quite like an outrage-inducing headline to bring out the crazies, even if most of them would be fielded by the control centre long before they got to any of these operatives.

'Ah, you're back, sir.'

He turned to see DS Harrison approaching from a desk in the far corner, where Lofty Blane was staring at a screen like he was the one who needed reading specs, not McLean.

'I'm back, yes. Would have been sooner, but I had a text from Angus about Fiona McLeod's post-mortem, so I stopped off to see what he'd found.'

'Anything useful?'

McLean noticed Harrison said 'useful' rather than 'interesting', which showed she was at least developing the hard layer of cynicism necessary to be an effective sergeant. There was an odd look about her, too. The way she kept glancing away and then back to him as they talked. If she'd been a suspect under interrogation, he'd have said she was as guilty as a puppy sitting next to a pile of poo. Something was up, but he lacked both time and energy to find out what. No doubt it would come out in the fullness of time.

'She wasn't a habitual drug user. Even less so than Rory Devlin. Angus reckoned the dose that killed her might well have been her first. Some luck, eh?' He looked around the room again. 'Any sign of Kirsty?'

Harrison gave a tiny, involuntary twitch at the name. 'Saw her earlier, sir, but I think she went off with the chief super to Gartcosh. Is it something I can help with?'

McLean shook his head slowly. 'Just something that came up with Hamilton's post-mortem. I didn't see the report when it came in, so I've only just found out about the blisters on his lips.'

Judging by the look on her face, Harrison had only just found out too. 'Blisters? I don't . . . Is it important?'

'Well, Kirsty might remember a case we had a few years back where a couple of people turned up dead with similar injuries. Might be nothing, might be coincidence but you –'

'Know how you feel about those, aye, sir. I do. You want me to get the files on that case? Maybe speak to Grumpy Bob about it?'

'I'll have a wee chat with Bob myself. Something else I need to talk to him about anyway. You get anywhere with those names Jimmy Laird gave us?'

'Aye, sir. Had a chat with Billy Colquhoun and a couple of the old Counter-Narcotics team. Seems everyone was too happy seeing them all deid to think much about who might pop up to take their place.'

'Really? I thought they were more on top of things than that.'

'Well, you know what it's like with everything being

centralised, and the NCA taking over a lot of that stuff. Least, that's what Billy told me. He also said that nobody's really showing up on the radar right now. Not in any flashy way so's anyone would notice. Struck me as odd, given there's just as many folk taking drugs as ever.'

'And someone's got to be supplying them, yes.' But who? McLean had the beginnings of a thought about that.

'I guess Demon's Breath is very small scale at the moment. Has to be or we'd have heard of it before, right?'

'True enough, but a dozen or more major drug dealers disappearing and nobody stepping up to fill the void?' McLean shook his head. It was a puzzle, but one for Counter-Narcotics, not Major Investigations. 'Anything else come up while I was gone?'

'Not much. We've been digging up everything we can about McLeod. Putting together a profile and tracking her last known movements. Might be a bit of overkill for an OD, but with the way the press interest is going . . .'

'You'll hear no complaints from me for being thorough, Janie. What have you got so far?'

'Well, Lofty's running her bank and council tax details at the moment. She wasn't flush, but she wasn't broke either. According to her friendly neighbour she was working up until a month or so ago.'

'Do we know who she was working for? Why she stopped?'

'Still waiting on it. The neighbour said she was something in the charity sector, but the poor old dear wasn't in much of a fit state to interview. She'd seen the body, after all.'

McLean looked across the room, not buzzing but quietly getting on with the job. Nothing much he could add here.

'Give her a call, see if we can't go over and have a chat.'

Harrison shoved her hand in her pocket and pulled out the keys for Emma's car. 'Plugged it in to charge when I got back. You want to go see the old dear now?'

McLean took the keys, glanced up at the clock. 'Maybe tomorrow morning when she's had time to calm down a bit. You'll be wanting to get home soon anyway.'

Harrison looked at him like he'd grown a second head, then seemed to remember herself. 'Aye sir. Tomorrow morning it is. You heading home too?'

It was probably an innocent question, but McLean couldn't help see the guarded concern behind it. She was right, of course. He should go home, try to get some rest, but the thought of the cold, empty house was not a welcoming one. Better to keep moving, working away at the puzzles all around him. Distract himself from the dark thoughts that wanted to overwhelm him.

'Soon,' he said, knowing it was a lie. 'There's someone I need to talk to first.'

Lunch had been meagre and a long time ago, so McLean thought he might swing past the canteen and grab something to eat. One look at the unappetising offerings and he could almost convince himself that a Mars bar was an adequate substitute for supper, although they seemed to be getting both smaller and more expensive every time he bought one. He had finished the vending machine spoils before he reached the end of the basement corridor and the open door to the Cold Case Unit office. Even he couldn't convince himself it was enough to fill the gnawing hole in his stomach. Well, there was always the option of a kebab when he finally went home.

'Evening, Bob. Hoped I might catch you still here.' McLean had taken two strides into the room before he noticed that both desks were occupied. Ex-Detective Superintendent Duguid peered at him over the top of his half-moon spectacles for a moment, then went back to whatever it was he had been reading.

'Been trawling through a lot of old paper archives.' Grumpy Bob hefted a weighty handful of old report folders up, then let them drop back onto the pile, a cloud of dust billowing around them in the harsh light of his desk lamp. 'Would have been much quicker if someone had thought to digitise some of it. Maybe even index it.'

'I thought you were running down who owned the land where they found Emily Worstead,' McLean said.

'Still waiting on the Land Registry for definitive answers on that.' Grumpy Bob leaned back in his chair, pulled off his reading glasses. 'Lofty's been doing his best, but someone over at Meadowbank House is giving him the runaround. It's strange. They're usually helpful enough. Makes me wonder if some pressure isn't being brought to bear.'

'So what's with the dusty archives then?' McLean waved a hand at the stack of folders.

'Missing persons cases going back as far as I could find. We've been looking for comparables. Other women with known incurable diseases, people in hospices and the like who just upped and disappeared.'

'Why would you . . . ?' McLean began the question, then stopped as a the pieces slotted together. 'Madame Rose?'

Across the room, Duguid let out a noise that was unmistakable in its dismissal of the medium. Grumpy Bob ignored him. 'Aye, she called me a couple of days ago. You know what she's like, always comes at things sideways, but once you've worked out what she's trying to tell you, it's usually helpful.'

McLean wasn't sure he'd ever heard a better description of Rose. She was hints and suggestions all wrapped up in a meeting the ladies at Jenner's Tea Room outfit. 'What did she tell you?'

'That the body under Leith kirkyard was someone called Izabell Kerr. She claimed to have been there to watch her being buried too, but we'll take that with the usual pinch of salt where Rose is concerned.' Grumpy Bob fetched his spectacles back onto his nose, then picked up a cleaner, more modern folder than all the archives cluttering up the desk, flipped it open to reveal freshly printed sheets. 'Oddly enough, Izabell Kerr existed. She was a wealthy woman in her time. Wealthy enough to have records that have survived down the years. She was the only child of a Leith merchant, Jeremiah Kerr. Inherited his business when he died. Never married, saw off plenty of predatory male business rivals and passed on her sizeable fortune to a distant relative when she was the extremely advanced age of sixty-seven.'

'That's not a bad innings at all, for the fourteenth century,' McLean said. 'But surely that can't be her in that pit. She'd have made provision for a proper burial somewhere, wouldn't she?'

Grumpy Bob flipped the folder closed again. 'That's the thing though. There is no record of her death, no gravestone, nothing. The last document referring to her is the gifting of her entire estate to her second cousin, but that's not a will. It's a deed of transfer. Which means she gave away everything before she died, and then disappeared off the face of the earth. Or rather, several feet underneath it. If you want to believe that it was really her they found in that pit beneath the kirkyard.'

'How did you find all this out so quickly?' McLean asked. 'Did Rose tell you? Seems unlike her to be so . . . detailed.'

'She pointed me in the right direction. Turns out a couple of postgraduate historians have written theses on Izabell Kerr, so all the work had been done already. Of course, there's no real way of confirming the woman dug up in Leith is her. Could just be one of Rose's little mind games. She'll have read those papers too, after all. On the other hand, there are a few references to Izabell's great height, and the skeleton is of an unusually tall woman for those times.'

McLean considered it for a moment. 'It's not really important who she is though, is it?'

Grumpy Bob shrugged. 'Not who she is, particularly. More

that if it is her, then she's like Emily Worstead in that she disappeared, never to be seen again, having first put her affairs in order.'

'Almost like she knew she was dying and wanted to do it on her own terms.' McLean followed the logic through, not really liking much where it took him. 'So all these other missing persons cases then?'

'We've whittled it down to six. All women, either elderly or known to be unwell at the time of their disappearance. That's from the past seventy years. Anything older's not worth following up. Might make a thesis for a history postgrad, mind.'

'So what's your next move, then? Try to find out financials on these cases, whether they all gave everything away before they disappeared? I'm not sure how that helps us work out what happened to Emily Worstead.'

'Which is exactly what I said when he started doing it,' Duguid said. 'Waste of time and money, in my opinion.'

McLean had to agree, but he'd known Grumpy Bob long enough to trust the detective sergeant's judgement. 'Well don't waste too much effort on it, but if you can find any living beneficiaries it might be worth having a chat.' He turned to leave, then remembered why it was he'd come down to the basement in the first place. 'Almost forgot, Bob. You remember that case a few years back. When Rosskettle Hospital exploded?'

It was hard to tell in the poor light of the basement, but McLean was fairly sure the old detective sergeant turned pale, gave a little shudder at the memory. 'Aye, I do. No' sure I've ever looked at a bath the same way since. What of it?'

'It all started with that politician, right? Andrew Wetherly, that was his name. Killed his wife and children then turned the gun on himself. We thought it was because the secret about Rosskettle was going to come out and he couldn't face that. But there was a detail in his post-mortem that got overlooked. Easy enough to do given how the back of his head was missing, but his lips were badly blistered, remember?'

The room had turned very quiet, Duguid listening in. 'Aye, that's right. There were a few other bodies turned up with similar injuries then, too. Why?'

'It's probably nothing, but one of the drug deaths I'm looking into right now has very similar damage. Blisters on the lips, even though we think the drug was sniffed, not ingested. Only appeared after he'd been taken to the mortuary. Angus brought it to my attention.'

Grumpy Bob scratched at the side of his head, a sure sign that he was thinking. After a moment he stopped, placed his hands down flat on his desk in front of him. 'That was the first time we ran into that Dee woman, wasn't it.' A statement, not a question.

'It was indeed. She was up to her neck in the whole thing, but we couldn't lay a finger on her, remember?'

'That bloody woman again?' Duguid shifted uncomfortably in his seat, as if he had piles and had forgotten his inflatable cushion. 'You need to be careful what you say about her in public. Most people think she's something of a modern-day saint, the way her foundation sprays its cash around.'

'A modern-day saint?' McLean laughed. 'Aye, I can imagine she'd like that. But then isn't that how the Devil's always worked?'

36

There wasn't much sign of police activity when McLean and Harrison arrived at the scabbier end of the housing scheme in Wester Hailes where Fiona McLeod had lived and died. Only a few torn-off strips of police cordon tape flapping in the breeze and tyre marks in the muddy grass between tarmac walkway and road to show that anything untoward had happened. Even the front door to McLeod's flat looked unremarkable as they passed it on the way to see her neighbour.

'Good of you to see us, Mrs Morris,' McLean said to the old lady as she ushered them into a front room that mirrored the one he had seen the day before. Minus the knocked-over furniture and dead body, of course.

'Please, call me Edna. An' anything to help the polis. I was a wee bit beside meself before, but I'm OK now. Doctor gave me some pills, an' I had the best night's sleep in ages. Din't even hear them lads in their cars racing round the estate like they do most nights.'

McLean smiled, even though his heart sank at the old lady's words. Not that he didn't care, so much as he wasn't sure he had the time to learn the entire history of the housing estate, bad neighbour by bad neighbour.

'All the same, we'll try not to keep you long. Just a few

questions about your neighbour, Miss McLeod. You got on well, I understand.'

'Well enough. She was a quiet one.' Edna pointed at an immaculate sofa. 'But sit down, please. I'll fetch us all some tea.'

McLean was about to say it was unnecessary, but he wasn't given the option. The old lady was out of the room with remarkable swiftness. He looked at Harrison, who merely shrugged and sat herself down. Pacing the room took little time, and there wasn't much to see anyway. He peered briefly out of the living room door to the hall and kitchen beyond. The sounds of tea being made were almost drowned out by the unwelcome rumble of his stomach. Perhaps breakfast should have been more than a hurried mug of coffee, but he'd promised the cats the remains of his late night kebab.

'Maybe she'll bring biscuits,' Harrison said, which was toeing the line of insubordination as far as McLean was concerned.

It took another five minutes, feeling all the while like hours, before Edna Morris reappeared with a tray. McLean helped her with it, noting that there were indeed biscuits, although he'd never been such a fan of bourbons.

'You were telling us about your neighbour,' he said once tea had been poured and cups allocated. 'How long ago did she move in?'

'Oh, let me see now. It wasn't that long after my husband passed away. Poor old Jack. He had such plans for his retirement but he only lasted a few weeks after they gave him his clock.' Edna waved a hand at the mantelpiece above a cheap electric fire, where an exquisitely ugly carriage clock took pride of place. Alongside it McLean had already noticed the professional portrait photograph of a middle-aged man, all awkward smile and thinning hair.

'That was five years back now. Maybe five and a half? I lost so much time with that virus going round and everyone keeping to themselves. Fiona was a blessing then. She did a lot of my shopping for me, you know?'

'You mentioned she had a bit of a history with bad boyfriends,' Harrison said.

'Oh, aye, that. She certainly knew how to choose them. Poor girl.' Edna took a sip of her tea, then offered the plate of biscuits up. 'They never lasted, mind. Don't know if it was her or them, but there'd be a row and then the next day they were gone and she'd be round here for a chat.'

'You've seen the papers, I take it?' McLean asked after he'd swallowed down a mouthful of stale bourbon and washed away the taste with too tannic tea.

'Aye, what they're saying about her taking drugs an' stuff?' Edna shook her head slowly. 'I don't know where they get their ideas from, but wee Fiona? Taking drugs? She'd never do anything like that.'

'You seem very certain about that, Mrs Morris,' Harrison said.

'Edna, please. And of course I'm certain. Oh, I'm no' stupid, mind. I see the folk round the estate dealing their wee packets of this and that. Sometimes you get a headache from the smoke just walking in from the bus stop, an' sometimes it's worse littered around the old play park at the back there. But Fiona wouldn't have anything to do with any of that. No' as a user.'

'Why do you say that? Not as a user?' McLean asked.

'Because she worked with them. The addicts. That was her job. At the outreach centre. If anyone knew how bad that stuff was for you it was Fi.'

'Outreach centre?' McLean looked at Harrison as he asked the question, but she just shrugged so he turned to Edna Morris. 'What outreach centre is this? I thought she was unemployed.'

'Oh, she was. Terrible business. They let her go a month or so back? She wouldn't say why, but she was proper cut up about it. She'd worked so hard with some of the folk there, see? That was the real Fiona McLeod, always putting the needs of others above her own. And then those horrible papers go and print all that rubbish about her taking drugs. Nonsense.' The old lady almost spat out the last, the look on her face describing her disgust far more eloquently than any words. She took out a handkerchief and wiped at her mouth lightly, as if even talking about the subject had left a bad taste.

'I'm sorry. From what you tell me she must have been a very special person.' McLean waited while Edna put her handkerchief away and then took another sip of her tea. 'I don't suppose you know which outreach centre it was that she worked at?'

Edna looked at him as if he was mad for a moment, before shrugging the expression away as if maybe his not knowing wasn't quite as astonishing as she had at first thought. 'Far as I know there's only the one near here. That place on the Lanark road, run by the Dee Foundation.'

Heavy traffic hindered their progress as McLean let Harrison drive him from the housing estate down towards Lanark Road. The clock on the dashboard screen told him it wasn't yet midday, but you could be forgiven for thinking it was peak rush hour.

'Do you know anything about this outreach centre?' he asked as Harrison deftly slotted the little Renault into a gap between two cars without either of them sounding their horns at her.

'I didn't even know there was one out here, sir. Used to be a place in Sighthill, but this isn't really drug central, despite what Mrs Morris might have said about the local youth. Mind you, there's food banks opening up all across the city, so I guess people are suffering even in reasonably affluent areas.'

McLean knew what she meant. He'd seen the articles in the papers, the queues outside unlet shops pressed into this new and unexpected use. It didn't say much about a society that it could let so many people go hungry, rely on charity. And yet somehow it had become the new normal. There were cuts to services everywhere, not just the police. People forced to work longer hours for lower pay, jobs with no security, a welfare system stretched precariously thin, letting too many fall through its safety net. His own unearned wealth sat awkwardly on his conscience, but what could he do? He paid his taxes, gave more to charity than anyone but he and his accountant knew. Although not to the Dee Foundation, as far as he was aware.

'Makes me glad I went into policing and not politics,' he said, unsure whether he was responding to Harrison's statement or his own thoughts. Probably a bit of both. Harrison clearly knew a trap when she saw one and kept her response to herself as they negotiated the traffic heading away from the city and turned into a small mixed industrial and retail estate.

The outreach centre was at the far end of a narrow car park, according to the satnav. If it weren't for the electronic directions it would have been easily missed. Unlike most of the retail and industrial estates popping up along Edinburgh's arterial roads, with their vast modern steel-clad buildings split into separate units internally, this estate was from an earlier age. The fronts of most of the buildings were harled and painted white. Some had windows where once there had been large roller doors, and were pressed into use as wholesale outlets, plant store and offices for plumbers and electricians. There was even a firm of architects in one building, the expensive cars neatly parked in front of it looking rather out of place among the panel vans.

They parked outside the smallest and least tidy-looking of the units, more stained grey than white and with its rusting metal roller door still fitted. McLean might have thought they were in the wrong place were it not for the small sign with 'Outreach Centre' on the wall at the corner, and an arrow pointing to where a narrow path led around to a smaller side entrance.

'Looks a bit like Fort Knox,' Harrison said as they stood in front of the door. Solid metal, painted black; there was no obvious handle, only a heavy-duty steel intercom mounted on the wall beside it. Looking up, McLean saw a camera behind a thick wire mesh, just out of spray can reach of a tall vandal. The path ran the length of the building, and beyond that he could make out the housing blocks of another estate, grey under a low sky that promised rain.

'Probably where they get their customers from,' he said, reaching for the intercom button. Before he could even press it, there was a loud clunk and the door swung open silently to reveal a well-lit but spartan reception area beyond. Stepping into the building behind Harrison, McLean caught the faintest scent of synthetic lemon for a moment before a less pleasant institutional odour washed over him.

'Detective Inspector, how nice to see you again.'

He turned at the voice, seeing a door opposite the entrance swing open and a familiar figure step through. She smiled at him with expensive, perfect white teeth, completely ignoring Harrison as she crossed the room and held out her hand. McLean shook it, her name coming to him in the nick of time.

'Ms Llewellyn. This is a surprise.'

37

True to its original purpose as a warehouse, the central mass of the outreach centre was one large open space that reminded McLean of nothing so much as the assembly hall in his hated boarding school in England. Skylights in the roof filtered murky daylight through a layer of grime, but now over-bright fluorescent tubes dazzled anyone foolish enough to look up. Not that the few people in the centre were doing much at all.

A group of a half-dozen or so late-teenage boys eyed him and Harrison with the innate suspicion of youth. They were clustered around a closed serving hatch, presumably awaiting a meal if the clanking pot noises from beyond were any indication. At the other end of the hall, two men and a woman lounged on mismatched sofas, reading tabloid papers or at least pretending to. Glancing briefly up against the glare had revealed a balcony circling the entire hall, doors at regular intervals, each with an internal glass window alongside. Whether that was so that the staff could keep an eye on what was going on inside, or the people inside could gain some natural light, McLean had no idea. Nor was he given the opportunity to ask. It put him in mind of prison rather than outreach, all the same.

Llewellyn led him and Harrison on a tour of the facilities, giving them a well-rehearsed pitch about the aims and achievements of the place. She showed them showering facilities, a small health centre, a room that might have been a safe place for taking drugs, were that even legal. They stopped briefly in an admin office where ranks of flat-screen monitors showed CCTV footage of most of the centre, the door they had entered by taking up the central screen. McLean suspected that she was delaying them, buying time for someone to come and back her up. Which meant also that she knew exactly why he was there. Still, he played along. It would be interesting to see who arrived and how swiftly. And if nothing else he could tell the chief superintendent that he had been here, doing his bit for her precious Project Tantalus.

'Some of the local youth come here for hot meals,' Llewellyn said as they stepped back out into the main hall and the counter opened to reveal a professional kitchen behind it. A young woman in stained chef's whites glanced briefly at them before returning to her work, doling out the day's offerings. She wasn't much older than the teenage boys she was serving. McLean was surprised at how orderly and well behaved they were as they presented their trays and then took their food to a nearby table.

'Is it that bad at home?' Harrison asked.

'Worse, sometimes. You should see this place first thing. We do pre-school breakfasts. It's heartbreaking.'

'I guess you run a food bank out of here too?' McLean asked, recalling his and Harrison's earlier conversation.

'Not here, but the Dee Foundation runs fourteen across the greater Edinburgh City area.' Llewellyn shook her head just once, her gaze on the floor or her expensive leather boots. 'All that money pouring into the financial districts and the city centre. A billion on the St James Quarter, wasn't it? But come out here and some people are so poor they have to decide between a meal or heating. It's criminal.'

At first, McLean had found himself nodding in agreement with Llewellyn. It wasn't hard, everything she said was true. But after a few minutes of carefully tuned sales pitch he began to hear the insincerity behind the words. And once he'd heard that, he couldn't hear anything else.

'It's all very laudable,' he said, interrupting her mid-flow and politeness be damned. 'But we really came here to talk to you about Fiona McLeod.'

Llewellyn reacted like she'd been jabbed with an electric cattle prod. 'Fiona. Yes. Of course.'

'She worked here until a couple of months ago, I understand.'

Llewellyn glanced towards a door at the far end of the main hall. McLean hadn't been shown through there, but it must have been the main entrance. It didn't take a genius to work out she was hoping for the cavalry to come and rescue her.

'She did, yes, Inspector.' The doctor turned her full attention back on him, eyes wide, smile wider. Those teeth must have cost a lot of money. 'She was a valuable member of the team, or at least we thought so. Worked well with the youngsters. Helping the school leavers into jobs, that kind of thing.'

'Sounds like someone you'd be sorry to lose. How did that happen, exactly? Did she quit or was she fired?' McLean returned the smile with one of his own, although he was all too aware that his teeth were nothing like as pearly as Ms Llewellyn's.

'Oh, we had to let her go. On reflection, we should probably have reported her to . . . the authorities.' Llewellyn put in a little theatrical pause that would have won a lesser actor a Bafta nomination. 'It was all a front, you see? Her good deeds hid a rotten core.'

'How so?' Harrison asked. Had McLean not been facing Llewellyn at the time he might have missed the look of pure hatred that flashed across the woman's face at the interruption, so swiftly was it morphed into a condescending smile.

'Where to start, really? She was using her contacts with the local youth to source and sell drugs, mostly. But there's also a sizeable hole in our accounts that might have been better used feeding those unfortunates who lost their jobs during the pandemic and haven't found work since.'

'So she was skimming off the top and dealing drugs? I'm surprised you didn't bring it to our attention.'

'Well, we're still conducting our internal investigation into the whole sorry affair. I dare say if she'd not . . . died in such a horrific fashion we might well have been presenting our findings to Police Scotland in due course.'

McLean bit back the retort he wanted to give, noticing that Llewellyn had glanced at her watch and at the door again. He changed his mind about wanting to see who came to her rescue. Now all he wanted was to be out of her presence, out of this place.

'I'm sure we'd be happy to review anything you sent us, although obviously we wouldn't be able to press charges now. If you can't learn from something like this, then you're doomed to have it happen again, eh?'

Llewellyn graced his sentiment with a smile, but not the full blinding white teeth this time.

'Anyway, we should probably be going. Don't want to waste any more of your precious time, Ms Llewellyn.'

'Please, call me Susan.'

McLean was fairly sure that he never would. He also noticed how her shoulders slumped ever so slightly in relief when he mentioned them leaving. Almost as useful to know as her lies about Fiona McLeod. He took one last look around the main hall of the outreach centre as she escorted him and Harrison back to the door they'd entered by. He couldn't work out what it was, but something about the place put him on edge, and stepping out into the damp grey outdoors was a welcome relief.

★ ★ ★

'Well that was all a bit strange.'

Building and roadworks at Haymarket meant progress was slow from Wester Hailes back towards the city centre. McLean had opted to drive this time, the meeting with Susan Llewellyn having left him restless and fidgety. He was still trying to put his finger on what exactly had unsettled him about the whole series of events.

'The outreach centre?' Harrison asked.

'Aye, that. But I was thinking more what Ms Llewellyn said about Fiona McLeod. You believe any of it?'

'I'm no' sure. It doesn't sound like the wifey old Mrs Morris had as a neighbour.'

'That was my thinking. Nothing points to her as a habitual user, so why suddenly start now? And why this new drug?'

'You think she didn't overdose, then?' Harrison reached for the dashboard in front of her as McLean was a little late with his braking.

'Oh, she overdosed. Angus is pretty sure of that. And the fragments of glass suggest the same delivery system as with Devlin and Hamilton. No, I was wondering whether she took the drug herself or it was forced on her. The neighbour said it sounded like a fight, so what if it was? Only by the time she'd called us in, her assailant was long gone, and she's smashed herself up so badly with the seizures there's no way to tell which bruises were self-inflicted and which weren't.'

Harrison said nothing for a moment, considering the hypothesis. 'Why would someone do that?'

'That's what I can't work out. Could just be that I'm overly suspicious in my old age, but whenever the Dee Foundation is involved I suspect foul play. This doesn't smell right. None of these drug deaths do.'

'You think she was killed to shut her up then? And now the

foundation's trying to paint her as some kind of evil corrupting influence? Why would they do that?'

To her credit, Harrison didn't call him an idiot to his face. McLean was grateful for that. Her patience and lack of criticism gave him the space he needed to try and mould his gut instincts into some kind of logical form. If he wasn't so dog-tired, so distracted, maybe he could have made easy sense of it all. As it was, he had to admit he was struggling.

'I don't know,' he said eventually. 'I don't even know if the Dee Foundation has anything to do with her death at all. I can see how they'll pitch it to cover themselves though. Working with the city's deprived underclass, doing their best to help folk up and out of the gutter. And along comes wee Fiona McLeod. Look at her, stealing from the petty cash to feed a drug habit that killed her. Just as well they caught her and chucked her out before she could do any real harm.'

'Seems like an awful lot of effort though. Why not just say she left and be done with it?'

'That's the bit I can't sort out in my head. My gut says she's been set up one way or the other. That's why the good Ms Llewellyn was lying to us. She needs a scapegoat for something that's going to come to light sooner or later.'

38

Janie stepped off the bus at Bruntsfield Links, glad that the rain had finally decided to call it a night. The day had been a frustrating one after she and the detective inspector had made it back to the station. He'd tried to motivate the team, asking for updates and setting them all new tasks, but she could see all he wanted to do was go back to the hospital and sit with Emma. Fair enough, she couldn't blame him for that, but neither could she forget DCI Ritchie's words. Or wonder at the stress he must be under. Something had to give, surely? She just hoped she had the strength to be there for him when it did.

It was late, well past shift end, but there was still plenty of the evening left. Manda wouldn't likely be home for an hour or so, which meant Janie could run a bath and relax with a book for a while. Maybe a glass of wine, too. No sooner had the thought popped into her head than she found herself stepping into the off licence that was so conveniently close to home. Like most of the shops in this part of town, it was tiny, owned and run by an enthusiastic young man called Paul who liked to dress as if he was a turn of the twentieth century Parisian, and had an immaculately groomed beard that would have frightened a backwoodsman. He knew his wine though, and his exotic spirits, and he smiled at her as she let the door close behind her, the little bell jangling away above her head. It was someone else who spoke her name, though.

'Detective Sergeant Harrison. This is a pleasant surprise.'

The voice was familiar, but even so it took Janie a little while to place it. As soon as she turned to see, it became obvious, of course.

'Mr Wendle. I didn't know you lived around here.'

'Please, call me Johnny.'

Through the corner of her eye, Janie saw Paul the shopkeeper had gone to deal with another customer. No rescue there, but then why did she need rescuing at all?

'Johnny it is.' She glanced down at his hands, holding a bottle of something white in one, something red in the other. 'Can't make up your mind?'

'Story of my life, I'm afraid. I'd buy both, but then I'd probably end up drinking both too, and that's not going to help with work tomorrow.' He reached up and put the red bottle back on the shelf, looked around for where he'd taken the white bottle down.

'Never a problem in my house,' she said. 'Manda's quite capable of polishing off two bottles of wine and never seems to show it the next morning.'

'Manda?' Wendle's frown made his face even more boyish.

'My flatmate. She's a forensic scientist. You might have seen her up at your building site the other day.'

'That? I did my best to keep out of the way while they were working. Last thing we needed was anything delaying them.'

'So, you live round here, or just can't get enough of Paul's wild selection of New Zealand Pinot Noirs?' Janie pointed at the bottle of red Wendle had put back. She was no great expert herself, but she could read a label.

'Paul?'

'The owner. Chap who serves you and takes your money? Beard you could build a nest in?'

Wendle looked over to the counter, now empty as the shop owner busied himself with the other customer. 'Oh, him. Is that his name? I've not really been in here that many times. Moved into a house on Napier Road about a month back. Still finding my way round the neighbourhood.'

'That would probably explain why I've not seen you around.' Well, that and the fact she hardly ever seemed to spend much time at home these days. Janie shifted her weight. She'd been standing awkwardly ever since Wendle had first spoken. 'It's a nice place to live, mind.'

Wendle shrugged. 'Aye, it is. Probably won't hang around long though. I never do. It's the curse of the property developer that we're always looking for the next project.'

'A bit like being a detective then. No sooner have we got our heads around something than it's time to start on the next case. I'm guessing the pay's no' as good, mind.'

Wendle gave a little half-laugh to that, but didn't exactly deny it. That the bottle of wine he'd put back was four or five times more expensive than anything she might buy had not gone unnoticed. Janie was a detective, after all.

'Look, this might sound a little forward, but do you fancy maybe getting a drink somewhere?' Wendle nodded towards the shop door, the irony that the two of them were in an off licence apparently lost on him. Janie followed his line of sight, then looked back at him. An hour in the bath with a book and a glass of wine was appealing, but she could do worse.

'Aye, why not.'

Janie couldn't remember the last time she'd sat in a pub with a man who wasn't a serving police officer. Truth be told, she wasn't entirely sure when the last time she'd done that had been either. There was a lot less of the whole team going out for a drink to celebrate success or drown their sorrows at failure these days. Maybe because the balance seemed to be forever tilted towards the latter. That and they were so overworked they were too tired to even think about it.

Johnny Wendle was easy enough company to keep, which was just as well since she was so out of practice. He talked a lot, and she found that she didn't mind that he barely asked any questions about her. If only suspects in the interview room would be so forthcoming. After a glass of wine, he suggested maybe they grab a bite to eat in the restaurant next door to the pub, and it seemed like a reasonable enough idea. Janie sent a quick text to Manda suggesting she might want to get her own supper tonight, and by the time they were being shown to a table for two in the corner by the fire, a single eye-roll emoji text had pinged back. No doubt her flatmate assumed she was working late. That would make for a fun conversation later.

'So how's the new development coming along, then?' she asked as they both stared at the menu. Of all the topics their chat had covered so far, work was surprisingly not one.

'We're back on schedule now. Can't say how much of a relief that is.' Wendle reached for his sparkly water and took a sip, placing the glass back down carefully before speaking again. 'The bigger the projects get, the tighter the margins, it seems. Something like that . . .' He paused, as if "digging up the bones of a woman who's been missing for thirty years" was too much detail for the comfortable setting. '. . . Well, it could have been worse, I guess.'

'Your backers must have been a bit anxious, though.'

'She was – they were – surprisingly good about it, actually. I could tell you some horror stories about finance people getting cold feet, mind.'

Janie noticed the slip, but pretended she hadn't. 'I can

imagine. You must have a lot of your own money tied up in a project like that. Last thing you need is the bank pulling the plug and leaving you with a hundred angry workmen to pay off.'

'Angry workmen are the least of the problem, believe me. It's the cost of building materials these days. And most places won't give you credit the way they used to either. Only takes a couple of late settled invoices and it's all cash up front.' Wendle went off on a long tirade about the woes of the building trade. Janie was happy to tune him out; their starters had arrived, and she hadn't realised until then just how hungry she was. The food was excellent too.

'How'd you get into it then, developing properties?' she asked when his monologue finally dried up as the pudding arrived.

'Oh, right place, right time. Or wrong place, wrong time, depending on your point of view. My partner – business partner, I should say – Bill Stevens, we were both students at the Uni must be what, ten years back now? Twelve? Where does the time go? Well, we were living in this shithole of a place out Burdie-house way. Five lads away from home for the first time, all of us in the rugby club so you can imagine what it was like. Then the landlord died and we were going to be chucked out, but Bill managed to persuade the estate to sell up. The other lads couldn't lay their hands on any cash for a deposit, but I had some money my gran had left me. We bought the place, Bill and me. Used the rent from our friends to pay the mortgage while we did it up. Sold it after we graduated for twice what we'd paid.'

'And you haven't looked back since?'

'Well, I'd not say that. There's been times we've almost gone under, but you learn from your mistakes. This housing development in Straiton's by far the biggest thing we've ever done. Don't think we'd have taken it on if the Foundation hadn't approached us directly.'

Janie almost asked, 'The Foundation?' but bit back the

question at the last moment. She grabbed her wine glass perhaps a little more forcefully than she meant to in an attempt to be nonchalant, spilling some on the white tablecloth where it stained like blood.

'You've met the boss before,' she said after almost choking down her mouthful of wine, her words coming out a little squeaky as she tried to steer the conversation away from what Wendle had just told her. She wanted to ask more about the mysterious 'Foundation', but she knew that asking directly wouldn't work.

'The boss?' Wendle asked, clearly oblivious to both her subterfuge and the clue he had inadvertently dropped.

'Detective Inspector McLean.'

'Oh, him. Aye. We met, what would it be, five, six years ago? Or was it more?' He picked up his half-full wine glass, looked at it as if the answer might be found in the murky red depths, then took a drink before continuing. 'We were trying to develop one of those big houses down on Leith Walk. You know the ones, with the wee shops in what would have been the front gardens back when they were first built? There was another property developer doing the same with another one, and that weird old tranny living in the one in the middle.'

Janie almost choked on her pudding, but Wendle seemed as oblivious to his gaffe as he was to everything else.

'We tried to buy him out, but he wouldn't budge. Then someone torched the place, or at least tried to. Still don't know how it wasn't gutted like our building.' Wendle took another drink, smiled at some happy memory. 'Still, the insurance paid out without a fuss, and after the fire we had a blank canvas to work with, more or less. Much cheaper to get the build done. We made good money on that project in the end.'

'And now you're working for Jane Louise Dee. That's quite a move up in the world.'

Janie had meant it as a gentle prod, looking for a wince or some other minor tell as Wendle tried to deny her allegation. With hindsight she probably should have waited until after he'd swallowed the mouthful of wine he'd taken at the end of his little speech. Sitting directly opposite him had been fine up until then.

'Oh my God, I'm so sorry.' He was on his feet so swiftly he almost knocked his plate to the floor, napkin dabbing at her in a manner that some might have taken as over-familiar. Janie had two older brothers and knew better, but she wasn't above using the moment to her advantage.

'It's OK. Really.' She took the napkin from him and wiped wine from her top. Then she checked her watch perhaps a little more ostentatiously than necessary. 'But it's getting late and I've an early start tomorrow. I should probably be going. Maybe stick this top in the wash, too.'

'It's . . . Oh God, Janie. I really didn't mean to. You just . . . I never said who . . .'

It was almost enough to make up for the tranny comment, seeing how desperate he was. 'Let's just forget about it all, OK?'

She looked around, aware that the rest of the restaurant had turned quiet, all eyes on the two of them. A waiter stood a little way off, unsure whether he should intervene or not. Janie ignored him, turning her attention back to Wendle. 'This was nice, but probably not such a good idea, aye? I'll go halfs on the meal.'

Wendle looked almost affronted at the suggestion. 'No, no. This was my invitation, my treat. But please, Janie. Don't go talking about who might or might not be behind the development, will you? It's not . . .'

She could see that he wanted to say it wasn't true, and at the same time that he couldn't bring himself to lie. Which in many ways made it even worse.

'I'm a detective, Johnny. It's not just what I do, it's who I am.

I'll not get you in any trouble. You don't deserve that. But she's bad news. The worst. Get out if you can is my advice.'

He stared at her with such a look of lost puppy about him, Janie couldn't help herself. She had to stand on tiptoes to do it, but she gave him a quick kiss on the cheek, a pat on the arm. And then she walked out of the restaurant leaving him to his fate.

39

McLean stopped by the incident room on his way up to his office, hoping to find someone he could talk to about all the disparate pieces of information, half-clues and lies that were starting to come together into something troubling. There was no sign of DCI Ritchie or Detective Superintendent McIntyre, and he knew Harrison had left for the day. Was he becoming too reliant on her? She'd fallen easily into the role vacated by Grumpy Bob when the old sergeant had retired, but in truth she didn't have his experience or much of a network of contacts she could tap for information. None of the newer detectives did, it seemed, not yet. Which was one reason they'd been struggling to shake out anything about this new drug.

'Working late as usual, Tony?'

Half in, half out of the room, he hadn't noticed the chief superintendent as she approached along the corridor. Now that she was close, he saw that she moved more freely than she had before, less like an invalid.

'Just tidying up a few loose ends before I head home. Well, the hospital then home.'

Elmwood tilted her head like a confused terrier, then appeared to remember. 'Oh, yes. Any news?'

'Nothing so far, but no news is good news, or so they say.'

The chief superintendent reached a hand out towards him, then stopped herself. A strange half-expression tried to form itself on her face, but whatever treatment she'd undergone to give her back her looks had left fine motor control behind. For a moment she looked almost frightened, but then the bland cartoon beauty reasserted itself.

'I'm sure it'll work out fine. She'll make a full recovery.'

McLean could think of nothing to say to that, but, fortunately for him, Elmwood merely nodded, slipped past him and then proceeded along the corridor towards the stairs. He watched her go, seeing the slight off-balance nature of her gait now. She was wearing flat shoes too, he noticed. No longer the heels that had been her hallmark. A part of him felt sorry for her, although only a bit. He was more concerned about her words. Far from being reassuring, he found it hard to believe anything she said, so telling him Emma would make a full recovery sounded like a curse.

He was being foolish, he knew. It was just that he really didn't like her. A visceral, base dislike, similar to how he felt about Jane Louise Dee. A psychiatrist might have something to say about that, probably involving a fear of powerful women or some such idiotic nonsense. He pulled out his phone, unsurprised to see no new messages apart from a reminder that he had a reception to attend tomorrow evening, and both those women would be there.

Shoving the phone away again, he walked to the stairs, lifted one foot onto the first step taking him up to the next floor and his office, then stopped. What was the point in going up there? What had been the point in going to the incident room? In coming back to the station at all? A better psychiatrist than the last one would tell him he was looking for displacement activities, avoiding doing the thing he had to do but really didn't want to. Checking the phone every five minutes was one thing, but driving across town, those all too familiar roads to the Western General, was another thing entirely. He had followed that same path, that same routine, so many times before with his gran. Day after day, month after month, of no change until one day she was gone. Could he face doing the same with Emma?

A twinge of protest from his hip as he turned a little too swiftly, and McLean set off down the weary stairs towards the car park. He could face it, when push came to shove. He had no other choice.

The hospital was never truly quiet, but at this late hour it didn't quite hum with the same activity he knew from daytime visits. McLean found himself slowing down as he paced the corridors towards the neurology unit and the coma ward. Like a dream where he was trying to run, but his legs ached and he could barely move them at all, each step was more effort than the last. He'd checked his phone, knew there was little point in coming here, and yet he had to do this, needed to.

The nurse at the administration desk wasn't one he'd been introduced to, although he thought he recognised her. She was working her way through a heap of folders that made the paper-work in his office seem light by comparison. When she looked up, her eyes were as tired as he felt, but she managed a flicker of a smile nonetheless.

'Detective Inspector. I thought we might see you here tonight.'

'I know there's no change, but I'd still like to sit with her. If that's OK.'

A little flicker of something like worry skirted across the nurse's face. Most people would have missed it, or put it down to general exhaustion. But he wasn't most people. He'd been trained to read faces, and he'd spent many years honing that skill.

'Yes, of course. It's not visiting hours, but then it's not as if the other patients are going to complain.'

McLean nodded his head once in agreement, thanked the nurse and turned away. He looked back briefly as he reached the ward door, unsurprised to see she was on the phone to someone. One hand held the handset, and the other hovered close to her mouth as if she was trying to keep her words unheard. He was too far away for that, and there was no one else in the unit as far as he could tell.

He'd barely sat down and taken Emma's hand in his own before he heard the door to the ward swish quietly open. Dr Wheeler stepped in, offered him another tired smile, then fetched a chair so that she could sit beside him.

'Katherine told me you were here,' she said by way of explanation, her voice low but audible above the quiet hum of life support machines. 'I'm glad, in a way. Didn't want to have to speak over the phone.'

'What is it?' McLean looked up at Emma's face, motionless in the soft pillow. Tried not to think of her as a lifeless corpse like Fióna McLeod.

'I'm concerned with Emma's lack of response to any stimuli, Tony. She's come off the medication we used to stabilise her after her collapse, but her brainwave activity hasn't changed the way I would have expected it to. It hasn't changed at all.'

McLean squeezed Emma's hand, hoping to prove the doctor wrong by getting some reaction back. There was none, and finally he dragged his gaze away from her. 'What does that mean?'

Dr Wheeler took in a deep breath, then let it out slowly. 'It means we're in similar territory to your grandmother, I'm afraid. It's still very early. She could improve, she should improve. She's got everything going for her in terms of her age, level of fitness, lifestyle.'

'But she might simply slip away without ever waking up again? In a month, a year, more?' McLean grasped Emma's hand tighter, squeezing it almost in desperation, but still there was no response. Even as in his head he heard her exasperated 'ow' and felt her playfully punch his arm in retaliation. Doctor Wheeler's words, soft so as to be almost inaudible, brought him crashing back to the here and now.

'That's a possibility you'll have to prepare for, Tony.'

The two cats stared up at him from the threadbare rug in front of the Aga when McLean let himself into the kitchen an hour or so later. He'd picked up a pizza on the way back from the hospital, unable to ignore the gurgling and churning of his stomach even though his brain told him he had no appetite.

'What are we going to do, eh?' he asked them as he opened the warming oven and slid the pizza box in. Neither of them gave much of an answer, although Mrs McCutcheon's cat sniffed the air as a waft of tomato, cheese and various meats settled over her.

'Later. Maybe.' He left them behind as he went through to the front of the house, but when he stooped to pick up the mail from the front door, they were both at his feet, tails high. They followed him through the hall, then up the stairs, but had the decency to stay out of the bedroom when he went in to shower and change. By the time he stepped into the kitchen again, they were back in front of the Aga, expectant whiskers twitching.

There were a couple of bottles of beer in the fridge, but, like his lack of appetite, he had no great desire for alcohol either. He managed a couple of slices of pizza before giving up the whole thing as a bad job and putting the kettle on. Dog-tired, but with too many thoughts to sleep, he drank his tea and stared sightlessly at the kitchen wall.

He might have been like that for five minutes or half an hour when a text pinged on his phone, the electronic 'ploing' noise finally breaking through where the gurgle of the Aga and tick tick tick of the clock had failed. He picked up the handset, thumbed the screen and stared blearily at the tiny, out-of-focus letters as he read the message DS Harrison had sent him.

Straiton Housing Project funded by JLD. Good chance she also owns land. Will check up tomorrow.

McLean stared at the screen for almost as long as he'd stared unseeing at the wall, the implications of what Harrison had discovered bouncing around in his skull like marbles in a pinball machine. His thumb hovered over the call button, and then he noticed the time in the corner of the screen. True enough, she was obviously awake otherwise she'd not have texted him. But it was very late and he couldn't remember the last time he'd slept properly. Maybe that was why nothing made sense any more. Time to go to bed, and if all he managed to do was stare at the ceiling, then so be it.

40

Low grey cloud hung over the pre-dawn city as McLean drew the curtains and peered out across the garden. He yawned, scratched at his stubbly cheek and let his eyes slowly find their focus. Against all expectations, he'd actually managed to sleep for a solid few hours. Only when he'd woken, rolled over and found the other side of the bed cold and empty had the memories come crashing in. There'd been no chance of sleep after that, so he'd reluctantly got up.

Movement in the garden below coalesced into one of the cats, Cecily Slater's, he thought. She stalked purposefully along the edge of one flowerbed towards a fat grey squirrel that was nibbling away on something, oblivious to the danger or wise to the lack of it. The garden looked neat, testament to Bill Bradford's hard work, but it was also showing the signs of rapidly approaching winter. Brown leaves tumbled to the shaggy grass, and there were very few flowers among the green.

A sudden explosion of noise had him taking an involuntary step back from the glass. For a moment he couldn't work out what had caused it. The cat had been nowhere near the squirrel. Then he saw a black cloud of clattering wings rise up out of the hollow that formed the Hermitage of Braid, beyond his garden boundary. A vast flock of crows climbed angrily into the sky, shrieking and cursing at one another like witches. No, not a flock, that was the wrong collective noun. A murder of crows, and that felt particularly apt.

He watched as they wheeled and dived in the air, no doubt disturbed by something down below that he couldn't see for the trees. Whatever it was could not have been all that serious, as within a few minutes of them taking off, they had all descended once more to their roosts. Glancing back down to the lawn, McLean saw the cat sitting in that nonchalant way cats have, licking one front paw. Of the squirrel there was no sign at all.

By the time he had showered, dressed and made it down to the kitchen, both cats were curled up in front of the Aga as if they hadn't moved all night. He set about making coffee, taking his time over breakfast for a change. Dr Wheeler's words still echoed in his head, mixing with all the others who had told him he needed a break, needed to stop trying to do everything himself, needed to slow down. Well, maybe he'd start paying attention, now that it was probably too late.

His phone didn't buzz until he was halfway down the second mug of coffee. Taking it out, he saw a familiar number on the screen, thumbed to accept the call. Detective Sergeant Gregg was at the other end of the line.

'Morning, sir. You still at home?'

'Morning, Sandy. Yes. Should be leaving in about five, ten minutes. Something up?'

'Aye, sir. Well, maybe. I'm in a wee bit early and I was going through the station briefings. Saw something that should've been brought to your attention yesterday by the look of it.'

'Oh aye?' McLean stopped himself asking why the detective sergeant had chosen to call now, early, rather than wait until he was at the station.

'They've dug up some more old bones, sir. Like the ones down in Leith and that cold case Grumpy Bob's looking into.'

McLean felt the mixture of cornflakes, toast and coffee turn sour in his stomach. 'What do mean by like?' he asked, the first of many questions that managed to squeeze out. 'And how old?'

'I've only the report from Control, but it's apparently a woman's bones. Likely been in the ground more than a century, so not our problem as such. Pathologist took one look and called in the archaeology team. I think they're at the site now.'

'Thanks for letting me know, I think.' McLean rubbed sleep out of the corner of his eye, picked up his coffee then decided it was probably too cold to be nice any more. 'But why phone? I'd have read the briefing myself soon as I got in to the station.' Well, he might have done. If he'd remembered, and not been distracted by a hundred and one other demands upon his time.

'It's where they found the body, sir. Down in the Hermitage. That's right by where you live, isn't it?'

By the time he'd driven round to the main gates, parked Emma's car and been directed along the Braid Burn to where the bones had been found, McLean realised he'd have been as well walking to the end of his garden and out through the gate there. Except that nobody had been that way since he'd been a boy, and the path down the steep side of the narrow glen had long since disappeared into thick rhododendron bushes. Even so, he fancied he could just about glimpse the chimney tops of his house through the trees now they had shed more than half of their leaves.

A couple of battered vans had been allowed onto the footpath along the edge of the burn, and when he approached them he found Professor Turner in conversation with two young students and a much older man he didn't recognise.

'Morning everyone,' McLean interrupted them. 'What's all this I hear about a body then?'

The professor turned a little too swiftly, almost falling over before the man steadied her with a practised hand. 'Oh, Tony. You gave me a bit of a shock there.' She took a little while to collect herself, then seemed to remember she was with company. 'This is my colleague, Professor Boyes.' She pointed to the old man. 'Harold, this is Tony McLean. Detective Inspector McLean, I should say. One of Edinburgh's finest.'

If Professor Boyes was impressed, he didn't show it. He had a face that seemed to hold itself in a perpetual sneer, as if the world around him was a constant source of disappointment. McLean's initial impression was only strengthened when his offer of a hand to shake was met with a disdainful glare.

'These bones are ancient, Detective Inspector. There's nothing for the police to get involved with.' Even Boyes's voice was unpleasant, a nasal whine that must have made his lectures excruciating. If he had any students to lecture.

'Nonsense, Harold. Tony's got a fine eye for detail. And besides, I expect his interest in this is beyond professional.'

Professor Boyes shrugged. 'On your own head be it.' He shoved his hands into his pockets and walked away in the direction of the car park.

'He seems nice,' McLean said. 'Surprised you put up with it.'

'He's my boss, technically. Head of the department, so I have to be nice to him. Sadly he doesn't seem to feel the same way about anyone else.'

'Why's he out here then? If this is just an old unmarked burial?'

Professor Turner looked past McLean at the disappearing back of the old man. 'I really have no idea. Perhaps he thinks I'm spending too much time digging around in the ground and not enough time sucking up to big business for sponsorship. Who knows?'

'Does that happen? I thought the university was government funded.'

'I forget how naive you can be sometimes, Tony. It's very refreshing.' The professor took a hold of his arm as if he was a child, despite her being several inches shorter than him, and guided him away from the vans towards the Braid Burn. 'I didn't want to ask while Harold was here, since it's none of his business really. But is there any news about poor Emma?'

McLean tried not to wince at the question, well intentioned though it was. He couldn't help remembering his conversation with Dr Wheeler the night before, and the utter lack of prognosis.

'She's doing OK,' was all he felt safe to say. Professor Turner looked at him with an expression she must have learned from his grandmother. Understanding both the lie and the need for it. She gave his arm a gently affectionate squeeze.

'Come on. I'll show you what all the fuss is about, shall I?'

McLean let himself be led along the footpath to where a narrow bridge crossed the burn. Beyond it, he remembered, the thick vegetation obscured an old walled garden. Or at least it had done the last time he'd been down this way. Now the bulk of the trees had been trimmed back or removed entirely, the old sandstone walls revealed. Where they hadn't collapsed entirely, they were being repointed, and where they had collapsed entirely pallets of new cut stone were waiting for the attention of a skilled mason.

'I'd no idea this place was being restored.' He let his gaze climb upwards, but this close to the steep side of the glen he could no longer see any sign of the houses. 'I used to have a den in here, when I was about six or seven.'

'Maybe that was some of your old toys we found in the upper soil layer then.'

'Or my father's maybe. McLeans have been living near here for generations.'

Professor Turner stopped walking, looked at him with a

curious expression. 'Yes, you have, haven't you. How strange.'

Without further explanation, she set off again, leading him across an area of ground that looked more like a battlefield than a garden. As they picked a careful route through the mud and broken stone, she filled him in on the details.

'They've been working on this place for a couple of weeks now. Used to be the Ladies' Garden, which sounds rather rude to me, but there you go. Day before yesterday, the diggers were supposed to be excavating down to the old stone drains. Un-blocking them before everything gets replanted, otherwise the whole thing'll just flood in the winter and the plants will all die. That's what the foreman said anyway.'

'What about these bones, then?' McLean asked.

'I'm getting to that, Tony.' Professor Turner stopped walking a few metres away from a large heap of dark black soil and a yellow mini-digger. The two students McLean had seen earlier were sifting the soil and picking out things of interest to archaeologists.

'According to the old plans dating back to the eighteenth century, the drains run from there to there.' The professor pointed in two directions, neither of them anywhere near the hole McLean could now see on the other side of the soil heap. 'Why the digger driver decided to dig here I've no idea. I can only guess the reason he went so deep is because he didn't find any drains. What he did find is far more interesting though. Come. Look.'

McLean followed the professor more slowly now as she squeezed past the digger to where an aluminium ladder poked up out of the hole. He was no expert, but the sides looked dangerously un-shored and the bottom of the hole a long way down. Nevertheless, the professor swung onto the ladder and clambered down with a casual ease. Once she was at the bottom, she pulled a torch from her coat pocket and switched it on, directing the beam towards the far end of the hole.

'You can come down if you want,' she said. 'Might get a better view.'

'It's OK. I can see just fine from here.' McLean stared at the pale shapes picked out in the light. Once white bone had turned ochre with years in the dark ground, but the contrast was still sufficient to make out a spine, ribs, arms and part of a skull. All too human.

'She's lying on her side, almost like she went to sleep, hands propping up her head like a pillow, see?' The professor crouched at the skull end, pointing at various things McLean had to admit he couldn't really see properly. It didn't matter, he got the gist of it.

'So this is much like your skeleton in Leith,' he said.

'Aye. She's not been in the ground as long. Need to do some tests to get a definitive answer there, but this one's likely a century old at least. Nothing you need to go looking for someone to arrest over.'

'Unlike Emily Worstead.'

'Emily . . . ?' The professor frowned, then realisation dawned. 'Oh, yes. Her. How's that coming along?'

'Slowly.' McLean recalled the text from DS Harrison he'd received the night before. A swift check of his watch showed him he'd missed the morning briefing. Hopefully he'd catch up with her soon enough. 'Might have had a bit of a clue fall into our laps though. Seems that land where she was buried belongs to Jane Louise Dee. Has done for a while, by all accounts.'

'That woman.' Professor Turner shook her head with obvious distaste, then flicked off her torch and began to climb back up the ladder. McLean helped her over the lip of the hole.

'You don't like her?' he asked.

'There's nothing to like and you know it. Sticking her nose in where it's not needed or wanted, greasing palms and promising favours. You'll have noticed the sign at the road end.' The professor waved a hand towards the distant car park.

McLean hadn't, but then he'd been preoccupied when he'd come in. 'No, why?'

'That bloody foundation of hers is funding this restoration. And the Gentlemen's Garden over the other side. Oh, she says it's because she used to love coming here as a child, but that's bollocks. Only reason she can possibly have for splashing her money around is to buy some local politicians. I'll bet you a meal at Kitchens there'll be a dubious planning application gone through on the nod soon.'

'I don't doubt it,' McLean said, even though bribing planning officials was too low rent for Mrs Saifre. Nevertheless, her connection to this place, this site, was too much of a coincidence for him to ignore.

'Perhaps when Em's better we can all go. Or I could see if I can use my influence to bag a table at Chez Innes.'

'Chez Innes? Really?' For all she tried to hide her surprise, Professor Turner couldn't mask the wonder in her voice. 'Meghan would kill just to try one of the starters.'

'Unfair, perhaps. I've known Bobby Innes a very long time.'

'Well, now you've raised the stakes I shall do all I can to hasten Emma's recovery. I shall go and visit. Talk to her some. I've heard that can help.'

'Sure she'd like that.' McLean stopped himself from saying it didn't matter as she wasn't really there. Instead, he turned his attention back to the pit. 'Tell her all about this place. These bones. You're going to dig them all up, I suppose.'

The professor looked at him as if he'd suddenly sprouted a second head. 'It's an unmarked grave, Tony. Unrecorded too. We kind of have to dig them up.'

'Aye,' he said. 'I suppose you do.'

★ ★ ★

As he left the professor to her digging and walked back to where he'd parked his car, McLean pulled out his phone and tapped an awkward text to Harrison. They needed to catch up, and since he'd missed the briefing it would mean dragging as many of the team up to his office as possible. He'd have to swing past the shops, pick up some biscuits and milk, or there'd be hell to pay.

Pausing as he slipped his phone into his pocket and juggled with the complicated key fob to get into the car, McLean looked around to see the large noticeboard placed right beside the entrance to the Hermitage. How he'd missed it coming in he had no idea, except that he'd been in a rush and trying to do too many things at once. From a distance, it wasn't easy to make out much of what it said, so he moved a little closer for a better look.

The Hermitage of Braid Walled Gardens Restoration Project didn't exactly roll off the tongue, and whoever had made the map and other graphics to show what the plans were had taken a few liberties. Nevertheless it was a sound project, and something that ordinarily he would have been happy to promote. Maybe even throw some money at it, if only to pay back for the lonely summers he'd spent in the Ladies' Garden as a boy. It had been a secret place, overgrown and forgotten, but it had been his secret place. A magical place for his pre-teen imagination, even knowing now that there had been bones buried deep under his den didn't bother him. Quite the opposite. McLean had felt only a sense of rest, of peace, as he'd seen the stained bones in their deep pit. Them being there felt natural, in a way. Them being dug up and taken to a cold laboratory for analysis was what felt wrong. He'd not known it at the time, but that feeling was what had prompted him to ask Professor Turner if she couldn't just leave the dead woman where she was. Where she was meant to be.

Shaking his head to dislodge the odd thought, something more in Madame Rose's repertoire than his own, McLean finally focused on the tiny script and logo in the bottom right-hand corner of the notice. Almost an afterthought, as if admitting to it was an embarrassment.

Project Funded by The Dee Foundation. In Association with Edinburgh City Council.

Turning away, he pressed the button to unlock the car, climbed in and pulled on his seatbelt, all the while wondering why the foundation, and its irritating, evil head, kept popping up all over the place, long-dead bodies not far behind. Maybe it was, as the professor said, a cynical attempt to bribe local politicians to let some other part of Mrs Saifre's empire build something ugly in an inappropriate place. And yet as he drove silently away from the Hermitage, McLean couldn't help thinking there was something far more sinister at play here.

41

Janie was in the Major Investigation Team room, checking her emails and trying to work out what to deal with first when the text came in. She'd wondered where the boss was when he didn't turn up for the morning briefing, but a quick chat with Sandy Gregg had put her in the picture about that. She didn't want to think too hard about what finding another body buried in the distant past meant, or what the information she'd wheedled out of Johnny Wendle the previous evening might mean in that new context.

She felt a little bad for Johnny. He'd meant well, and was clearly attracted to her. Although why he was attracted to her was another question. She'd never considered herself much of a prospect and thought even less about the few meagre specimens of manhood who had come sniffing around her like dogs. But then she remembered the casual way he'd referred to Madame Rose as a tranny, and her sympathy all but vanished. 'Dodged a bullet there, J,' was what Manda had said when she'd got home, still smelling like a vineyard. Her flatmate was probably right.

It took longer to gather together the team than she'd expected, given that none of them were meant to have any assignments out of the station that morning except Lofty Blane, who was off to the Land Registry to try and get a slightly better answer on the

281

ownership of the Straiton housing development land. The rest of the detective constables had managed to find places to hide that would have done Grumpy Bob proud, but she gathered them all together and up to DI McLean's office only forty minutes or so after he'd contacted her.

The man himself was standing by the coffee machine, staring at the slow drip of black liquid from the filter cone when she knocked on the the door frame, Stringer, Mitchell and Bryant all behind her in the corridor. He turned at the noise, managing a weak smile.

'Ah, come in, everyone. Coffee's on, there's fresh milk and I even bought biscuits.'

As they filed into the room, Janie had to admit the boss really didn't look well. He never ate properly, but since Emma's collapse he'd grown more gaunt by the day. Where normally he was well groomed, now his suit hung off him as if it had been tailored for a larger man, and he'd been running his hand through his hair by the disarrayed look of it. He'd been out to a crime scene already, of course. Or something close to a crime scene. That was some small excuse.

'Sandy Gregg told me about the body in the Hermitage, sir. Not something to worry us, I take it?' Janie found herself a seat at the conference table while the others jostled around the coffee machine.

'That depends,' McLean said. 'If what you texted me about last night is true, and the Dee Foundation or Saifre herself own the land where Emily Worstead's bones were found, then we've got a connection that's too much of a coincidence to ignore.'

'Lofty's digging as best he can, but I'm fairly sure my information's good.' She told him about Wendle and their impromptu meal, aware as she did that the rest of the team were now privy to her personal life. Judging by the way Mitchell and

Stringer had sat close together she was going to have to dig into their personal lives too, so it was only fair.

'I'm hearing the name Dee far too often,' McLean said once she was done. 'Rory Devlin found training and work through a Dee Foundation programme, Fiona McLeod worked in one of their outreach centres, dealing with drug addicts. Emily Worstead's body was buried on land belonging to Jane Louise Dee, who is also funding the building development work that led to those bones being uncovered. And now it seems that she's financing the work in the Hermitage that's led us to yet another body.'

'You don't think . . . these are all linked, sir?' DC Bryant asked. 'I mean, how?'

Janie waited for an answer. They all did. It wasn't unusual for the detective inspector to make wild leaps of logic that left everyone else scratching their heads or calling him mad. That he was almost always right was infuriating; that he often didn't even know himself how he came to his conclusions doubly so.

'None of you were in plain clothes when we first had a run in with Mrs Saifre, otherwise known as Jane Louise Dee,' he said after a while. 'DS Gregg was. You might want to ask her about the night her house exploded.'

Nobody said anything. Janie had heard the story, but only that it was a gas leak and that McLean himself had broken into the house, woken Sandy Gregg and dragged her unconscious husband out of the building in the nick of time.

'I still don't understand how it can all be connected, sir.' This time it was Stringer who spoke. 'We've two entirely separate cases here, surely? The buried bodies, I mean, one of them's over seven hundred years old. I heard the pathologist said the bones in the Hermitage had been there a century. I know Dee's old, but she's not that old.'

McLean rubbed at his face and Janie could almost feel the

exhaustion pulling at him. How did he even stay upright? There wasn't enough coffee in the world.

'You're right, Jay. I'm probably letting my prejudices get in the way of being objective here. I dislike Saifre. No, that's not nearly a strong enough word. If I never had to see her again in my life it would be too soon. She's tried to kill me, or have me killed, more than once. Oh, nothing I can prove, she's far too clever for that. But I can't see her move into charity, this omnipresent Dee Foundation, as anything more than a cynical attempt at remoulding her image. All the billionaires do it, I know. Philanthropy's the new drug for the ultra-rich. But here's the thing about Saifre. She never does anything by accident. Everything's meticulously planned, sometimes over years if not decades. If her foundation's restoring gardens in the Hermitage it's because she wants that done. If they're building houses in Straiton on her land, she's behind that too, right down to which house goes where. You all know I don't like coincidences, but as far as I'm concerned, where Mrs Saifre is involved nothing is a coincidence.'

The room fell silent after that, except for the quiet noise of DC Stringer munching on a chocolate hobnob. Janie wasn't surprised. She didn't think she'd ever heard the boss voice his feelings on anything before, at least not to such great length. Eventually someone would have to say something, she realised. Might as well be her.

'So, what are we going to do about it then? About her? Are we investigating this new body? The bones in the Hermitage?'

McLean shook his head. 'Can't. There's no justification, especially if Professor Turner confirms the bones are ancient, which I'm sure she will. Doesn't mean we can't ask a few discreet questions about the project to restore those walled gardens. Whose idea was it? Why now? What other unusual things are the Dee Foundation involved with?'

'Is that not going to be tricky to find out without raising suspicions, sir?' DC Mitchell asked.

'Anyone asks you why, you refer them to me.' McLean paused for a moment and Janie could almost see the thoughts piecing themselves together in his mind. 'But you're right. The bones aren't our priority. Even Emily Worstead's one for the Cold Case Unit, although I'm sure Grumpy Bob'll be glad of any new information, so keep him in the loop. The Dee Foundation connections with Devlin and McLeod on the other hand? That's an area of investigation I'd like to pursue further. Neither person was your typical addict before they overdosed on this new stuff. That's another coincidence I don't like.'

McLean watched the line of detectives as they filed out of his office, DS Harrison at the rear. For a moment he thought she was going to leave with them, but perhaps predictably she stopped at the door, checked everyone else was away down the corridor, and then turned back.

'I'll not ask, sir, but I've got everything crossed for Em. We all have. And if you need time, we're all ready to take up the slack.'

For a moment he couldn't think of anything to say. Despite a decent night's sleep he still felt dog-tired. The weariness made keeping the thoughts straight in his mind much more of a struggle than it should have been, and not for the first time he wondered whether he shouldn't have heeded Ritchie's advice and taken time off the moment Emma was hospitalised. The rational part of his mind knew that was the right thing to do, but it also knew he wouldn't be able to cope with sitting around the house.

'Thank you, Janie. I know you are, and I can't think of a team I'd trust more to get the job done without me. I need to be doing things though, otherwise I'll either go mad with worrying or drink myself to death. Neither option appeals particularly.'

She smiled at that, which cheered him up a bit.

'Well, I've a ton of stuff to be getting on with. You need anything, I'll be in the incident room.'

McLean nodded, thanked her again, then watched as she turned and left. He carried on staring at the open doorway for a long time afterwards, eyes not really seeing anything as his tired mind churned away at the mess of facts and suppositions piling up. Were they linked, all these horrific drug deaths and the bones popping up out of the ground everywhere? On the face of it, no. They couldn't be. Not beyond the name Dee popping up just as frequently, if not more so. But the Dee Foundation was every-where, providing outreach services, care homes, youth training and work experience, restoring the city's historic monuments, fingers in all the pies. Even doing its best to establish ties with Police Scotland far beyond anything that could be justified. It was hardly surprising then that it came onto their radar every time they looked into any crime in the city. Might as well say the thing linking all of this together was Edinburgh itself.

If anything, that bothered him the most. When had the Dee Foundation become such a fundamental part of the city? How long had it been growing, pushing tendrils into every crack of the establishment like fungus? Like a cancer metastasising in Edinburgh's flesh. And what was Saifre's purpose, what endgame did she have in mind? In admitting his irrational loathing of the woman to the team he had been admitting it to himself too. Voicing it out loud so that he could rationalise it, compart-mentalise it, put it to one side to stop it from distracting him. But the more he thought about it, the more he kept circling back to the thought that this was all part of some big plan.

Well, if he could work out what she was doing, he'd do his best to throw a spanner into it. And he'd be damned if he was going to waste time going to her little reception that evening, a reminder for which had lit up the screen of his phone as he let his thoughts run. He picked it up, swiped away the irritating notification and then flicked through the names in his contacts list. The call was answered on the second ring.

'I didn't know better I'd say youse were stalking me.'

'Very funny, Jo. This is my work phone and I'm calling from inside the station. Official as it gets, right?'

A moment of not quite silence while the reporter sucked in a breath that McLean could hear down the line. He could almost see the electronic cigarette glowing with its false light, smell the sickly sweet vapour.

'Depends what you want from me,' she said after a while.

McLean looked at his mug, the contents cold, then up at the clock showing the morning marching on but not yet finished. 'Let me buy you a coffee and I'll tell you all about it.'

42

The cafe was one of those soulless chains, predictable in its decor and the uninspiring range of cakes if Dalgliesh's constant complaining was anything to go by. Given that she'd suggested it and he was paying, McLean felt her moaning was a bit rich. He kept that to himself though; he wanted her to do him a favour after all.

'Well now, this is cosy.' Dalgliesh settled herself into a deep armchair in a quiet nook, leaving McLean to perch on a slightly less comfortable low stool. 'Can't say it isn't nice to meet up wi' old friends, but what say we get down to it, aye? What is it you want?'

'The Dee Foundation. I take it you've been keeping a beady eye on it?'

Dalgliesh's cake paused halfway between plate and face for a moment, then she shoved in a mouthful, chewed, swallowed and licked chocolate from the tips of her fingers before answering.

'It's never something simple with you, is it, Tony?'

'You've noticed though, haven't you? How it's running everything these days?'

'Oh, aye. I've noticed. Hard not to. Thing is, people like charity, especially when it's someone else who's giving away money.'

'Why is she doing it though? What's in it for Saifre? She's never struck me as someone who just wants to bask in the golden glow of public adulation.'

Dalgliesh snorted out a short laugh. 'Aye, that's right. You really don't like her do you.'

'Jo, she's tried to kill me. Why would I want to forgive and forget that? More to the point, why would she stop trying? Why would she change from the corrupt and evil business tycoon she used to be into this modern-day saviour? I don't buy it, and if you're half the journalist I take you for you don't buy it either.'

'Aww, you say the nicest things.' Dalgliesh took a smaller bite of cake, carried on speaking even though her mouth was full. 'But you're right. Well, part right. She's no modern-day saviour for sure. Way I hear it, the Foundation is one big influence machine. How better to buy politicians than with money people won't complain about? And the reach, too. Word is she's put a billion into it so far an' there's more to come. That's chickenfeed to the likes of her, but there's no' a person in this city hasn't heard of her now, and that's something you can't buy with ordinary advertising. Charity sector's a fine way to launder money, too. If you know how.'

'You think that's what she's doing?' McLean leaned forward on his stool, his voice low as if anyone might overhear them in this noisy, busy place. 'Is that something you're working on?'

'Do I look stupid to you?' Dalgliesh almost spat out the words. 'You said it yourself, Tony. She's tried to kill you. More'n once if what I've heard is true. You think she wouldn't do the same to me if she thought I was poking my nose where it wasn't supposed to be?'

'So you're –'

'For a smart man you can be remarkably dumb sometimes, you know? You've protection I can't even hope for, even if you won't see it. No, I listen, I look, but I'm no' going digging where that woman's involved. No' after the last time.'

McLean opened his mouth to say something, then closed it again as Dalgliesh's words sank in. He knew better than to push her, knew when she was playing him and when she was truly scared for her life.

'So apart from the Devil incarnate, what else did you want to ask me about?' Dalgliesh rubbed chocolate from the plate and licked it off her finger, gaze flicking over towards the serving counter as if she might ask for a second helping.

'You know we've been trying to track the source of this new drug, right? The one that killed the young lad out Restalrig way and those two others?'

'Rory Devlin, Alistair Hamilton and Fiona McLeod, you mean? Overdosed on Demon's Breath?' Dalgliesh narrowed her eyes at him. 'So you're confirming McLeod was another, aye?'

McLean shrugged. 'You didn't hear it from me, but yes, she's got all the same symptoms and we found fragments of glass from a vial underneath her and in her clothes. Same as the other two.'

'Well my editor's going to be a happy bunny tonight.'

'Don't get too excited yet, Jo. You gave us a name for the drug, but nobody else is talking about it at all. And here's a thing you might be more interested in. Teddy Graham, Shug Peters, Fraser Murdoch. Those names mean anything to you?'

'Aye, they're all deid. An' the world's a better place for it.'

'Them and pretty much every other local wannabe drug baron in the north of the city.'

'Teddy Graham threw himself under a bus. No' sure if it was an accident or deliberate, but it was all him. Nobody gave him a wee shove.' Dalgliesh stared off into the distance as if reading the information written in the air. 'Shug Peters died in his sleep. Heart gave out if I remember right. An' Fraser Murdoch was a clumsy drunk who tripped on the stairs. These were all accidents,

Tony. There's nobody muscling in on their action.'

McLean was impressed with the reporter's memory, although such details were her bread and butter of course. Like everyone else though, she was missing the point.

'That's the thing though, isn't it. Nobody's popped up to take their place. At least nobody loud enough to bring themselves to our attention. And yet drug use is still as high as it ever was. Higher, even. Where's it coming from? Who's dealing it? You ask around, people are either too scared to say anything at all, or they genuinely don't know. Doesn't that strike you as odd?'

Dalgliesh had leaned forward so that the two of them might have looked like an old couple staring into each other's eyes, but now she slumped back in her chair. She reached into her pocket and pulled out her electronic cigarette, shoved it in her mouth and sucked hard even though it was switched off.

'You thinking what I'm thinking?' she asked once she'd realised what she'd been doing and stopped.

'I hope not,' McLean said.

'Aye, funny. But you wouldn't have asked me your first question if you'd no' been thinking it already.' Dalgliesh tapped a bony finger against her temple. 'You tell me who's everywhere now, come from nothing and now running most of the care homes, the halfway houses and outreach centres, the young offender facilities. You want to know who's supplying the city's working classes with their drugs of choice, why not ask your new Foundation friends, aye?'

McLean almost slumped back in his seat as the realisation hit. Then he remembered that he was on a stool with no back. He should have seen it before. Deep down, his subconscious had been working up to it, aware that once voiced the idea would be impossible to ignore. Now the ramifications began to branch out in his mind like a time lapse film of fungi spreading through soil. 'Shit.'

'Aye, shit.' Dalgliesh drained her coffee and stood up swiftly. 'An' good luck proving any of it. Sorry, Tony. But you'll have to do it without me.'

The walk from the cafe back to the station should have given him time and space to think, but halfway up the Pleasance McLean found himself in the middle of a downpour with neither a hat or an umbrella to help. At least he'd worn his better coat, a long, heavy, dark camelhair that had once belonged to his grandfather. By the time he pushed through the back door and into the dry, it was twice the weight it had been before. He stood for a while, letting the worst of the drips fall on the floor in a circle around his feet, pondering whether to climb the stairs to his office or descend into the depths. It wasn't a hard decision.

Grumpy Bob looked up from his desk, the light from his lamp reflecting off his spectacles. A quick glance to either side confirmed to McLean that the rest of the Cold Case Unit were having the morning off.

'Heard they found some more bones. Not far from your place, I understand?'

'There's not much gets past you, is there, Bob? Aye, they dug up a body in the old walled Ladies' Garden. Professor Turner reckons she's been there a century or more, so no need to bother yourself about it just now.'

'Aye, right.' The ex-detective sergeant flipped closed the folder he'd been reading from and slid his glasses off his nose. 'So why're you down here then?'

'Well apart from not wanting to drip all over my own carpet, I was wondering if you still had your contacts at the Jobcentre.'

'Reckon so. Why?'

'I'm trying to find out something about Alistair Hamilton. The lad who had a fit in the Cameron Toll food court. We only identified him from a Jobseeker's Allowance card in his wallet, but apparently he's been off benefits for months. I can get all the information they've got on him eventually, but . . .'

'Sometimes it's quicker to ask the right person than wait for all the paperwork to be dealt with.' Grumpy Bob reached for the old-fashioned telephone on his desk and picked up the handset. 'Aye, I'll make a couple of calls. Should have something for you in an hour or two.'

'Cheers, Bob.' McLean made to leave, then stopped. 'Dagwood not in today?'

'He muttered something about a hospital appointment. Chest scan or something . . .' The ex-detective sergeant tailed off as his thoughts caught up with his mouth.

'Sure he'll let us know if it's anything serious. Same as I'll let you all know if there's any change with Em.'

'I wasn't going to ask. Know how irritating that can get.' Grumpy Bob stared at the handset as if he had no idea why he was holding it, then placed it back where it had come from. 'Probably better if I ask in person. Might borrow one of your new young detectives to give it the seal of authority, mind.'

43

'You got a minute to spare, Janie? Maybe an hour?'

Looking up from her desk and the neat stacks of files and folders arranged across it, Janie was surprised to see recently retired Detective Sergeant Grumpy Bob Laird at the CID room door. It was rare for the old DS to emerge from his new subterranean fiefdom, and she normally only bumped into him in the canteen these days.

'An hour? Sure.' She waved her hand at the endless paper-work. 'All afternoon?'

'You sound like Tony,' Grumpy Bob laughed before casting his gaze across the otherwise empty room. 'I'd have taken a constable, but they seem to be avoiding me.'

'All away running down actions, Bob. You know how it is. Send the constables out and then find yourself a nice quiet room to hide in while they do all the work.'

'That doesn't sound like Tony at all. Maybe there's hope for you yet lass.'

Janie bristled slightly at 'lass', but decided to let it pass. Closing up the folders she didn't want people looking at in passing, she stood up and grabbed her coat off the back of her chair. 'Where are we going? Do we need a car?'

Grumpy Bob glanced across at the window that took up most

of the far wall, smeared with spattering rain. 'Jobcentre on Nicolson Square. It's not far, but maybe we'll drive, aye?'

One of the benefits of the station having an electric vehicle for a pool car was that very few officers wanted to drive it. Janie couldn't quite understand the prejudice, but she wasn't going to complain if it meant she could always find a ride. Grumpy Bob climbed into the passenger seat and clipped his seatbelt on in what could only be described as an unconvinced manner, peering at the dashboard with its array of screens and buttons as if this newfangled technology would never catch on, don't you know.

'It's very quiet in here,' he said as Janie reversed out of the car park and into the street.

'Welcome to the future. Now which way do you reckon's quickest?'

The journey was short, shorter indeed than the time it took to find somewhere to park once they'd got there. Janie wondered why they weren't going to the central offices of the Department for Work and Pensions, down at Victoria Quay, but instead Grumpy Bob had said the Jobcentre on Nicolson Square so he must have had his reasons. They could have walked in half the time it had taken to drive, but they would have been soaked doing it. Even so, she had to shake out her coat in the doorway once they arrived.

'I'll need you to show your warrant card, Janie,' the retired detective sergeant said as they approached one of the counters. Then he turned to the young woman peering at him through the glass screen.

'Detective Sergeant Laird. This is my colleague Detective Sergeant Harrison,' he said in his most officious voice. 'We'd like to have a word with Katie Fellowes. Please.'

Janie held up her warrant card as instructed, and then passed it through to the young woman when requested. Only after it had been thoroughly inspected was it handed back.

'I'll see if she's available,' was all the response they got before the young woman picked up a phone, hit a single button and then turned away from them so they couldn't hear what she was saying.

'Friendly lot,' Janie said to Grumpy Bob.

'Oh, they're all right once you get to know them. Don't like us coming in too often, mind. It upsets the customers.'

Janie was going to ask what customers, since the place seemed to be empty, but a door nearby buzzed open and another woman stepped out. Older than the one on reception, she had straight grey hair that fell either side of an enormous pair of spectacles so thick it was difficult to make out the true shape of her face. Her magnified eyes stared at them both for a moment before focusing solely on Grumpy Bob.

'Detective Sergeant Laird. This is a surprise.' She was holding the door slightly ajar, presumably to stop herself from being locked out of the business side of the enterprise. Now she opened it wider and beckoned them both towards her. 'Come in, come in.'

'Right then. What is it you're after, Bob? I know there's no other reason you'd come knocking on my door. And anyway, didn't you retire a year back?'

Janie wasn't quite sure what to make of Katie Fellowes. She seemed friendly enough, had said all the right things when they were introduced, offered them coffee and found them seats in her tiny office. She obviously knew Grumpy Bob well, but there was something slightly off about the relationship. An ex-girlfriend maybe?

'You know me, Katie. Once a detective always a detective,' Grumpy Bob said as he settled into his chair. 'Retirement didn't really sit well, and there's a lot of old cases need reviewing every so often. We've a whole Cold Case team now to keep me busy.'

'Keep you out of the pub at lunchtime, more like,' Fellowes said, but there was a smile with it and only gentle chiding in the words.

'Well, there's that too,' Grumpy Bob conceded before pulling a sheet of A4 paper out of his pocket, unfolding it and sliding it across the table. 'And since it's very nearly lunchtime already, I wonder if you might be able to tell me something about this lad.'

Fellowes took the paper, stared at it a while, a frown on her face just about visible through the enormous spectacles and low fringe. 'Any reason why this can't go through the normal channels?' she asked as she turned to the computer on her desk.

'Time, mostly,' Janie said before Grumpy Bob could come up with an excuse that might get him in trouble. 'He's dead, if you're worried about complaints. We went through the normal channels already and got a bit of a runaround.'

'Let me guess, GDPR.' Fellowes leaned forward to better see her screen before Janie could answer that. She tapped in a few letters and numbers on the keyboard, lifted from the sheet of paper, then swirled and tapped her mouse for a moment, all the while making an oddly quiet clucking noise.

'Alistair Hamilton. Where are you my friend?' she asked the screen before finally breaking into a smile. 'Ah, yes. There.' She turned back to Janie. 'You want a printout?'

'Not if it'll land you in trouble. Just the basic details would be fine. We've got his address, but when he last signed on, how long for, were his benefits being paid into a bank account, did he do any retraining courses, that sort of thing. Even a date of birth would be useful.'

'You've got this one well trained, Bob. Good to see some traditions being passed on. OK, let me see.' Fellowes concentrated on the computer again, leaving Janie to take notes as she spoke. 'Born in '94, so that'd make him twenty-six, twenty-seven? He stopped claiming any benefits nine months ago, but we have no record of a new employer. If there is one, then you'll be needing his NI number and a favour from HMRC. Bank details I probably shouldn't divulge, but it's the Clydesdale branch in Newington.'

Janie jotted down all the details as Fellowes read them out. 'How long was he on Jobseeker's for, then?'

'That last time, three months. He's been on and off benefits since he turned eighteen, as far as I can tell. A few breaks here and there. Never seems to have held down a job for more than a few months though.'

'And training?'

'Oh yes.' Fellowes clicked the mouse, bringing up a screen that she had to scroll through for quite some time. 'Lots.' She scrolled down further still before coming to the last entry. 'Most recently three weeks at a place called Alba Fulfilment Solutions learning about warehousing.'

Janie paused, her pen hovering over the final 's' in 'Solutions'. 'How about any placements with the Dee Foundation?'

'That's one of theirs, yes,' Fellowes said. 'They take on a lot of the long-term unemployed. Generally speaking their success rate's high, too. Looks like they didn't do so well with this one.'

'What about education? Have you got his school details there? Qualifications?'

Fellowes looked up at Grumpy Bob, one eyebrow arched. 'She's thorough, this one. Good thing you're retired or she'd be after your job.' She tapped the keyboard a couple of times, then read from the screen. 'Local boy. Came out of James Gillespie's with a decent set of Highers. Went on to Edinburgh University to read Chemistry, but doesn't seem to have graduated.'

'Chemistry?' Janie asked, even though she had heard perfectly well.

'Aye, that's right. Is it important?'

'It might very well be.' She wrote down the word in her notebook and underlined it twice. 'It might very well be.'

'Before you ask, she's my sister-in-law. Well, ex-sister-in-law if I'm being correct.'

They'd said nothing on leaving the Jobcentre, too busy rushing the short distance to the car in rain so heavy it was bouncing as high as Janie's knees. She wiped the worst of the soaking from her face, brushed water from her hair, while Grumpy Bob stared through the rain-smeared windscreen at the blur outside, absentmindedly cleaning his spectacles with a handkerchief.

'I wasn't going to ask, honest.'

'Aye, you were. Me and Mrs Bob, we kind of drifted apart. It was all more or less amicable, as they say, even if she did up and go to Australia soon as the papers were all signed. I kept in touch with Katie though. Helps that she's local, too.'

'And a useful source of information is never to be wasted.' Janie finished wiping the drips from her nose and tapped the button that woke the car up. Setting the wipers to fast, she waited for a gap in the traffic before indicating and pulling out.

'Did we learn anything useful though. That's the question.' Grumpy Bob struggled to pull his seatbelt on.

'I reckon so. We've got Hamilton's employment history from when he left school, we've got his bank details so Lofty can do his magic with them. The chemistry angle is interesting, too.'

'How so?'

'I was looking into a possible link with the stuff Sergeant Needham used on Emma and his other victims. Chemical signature is very similar to this Demon's Breath drug.'

'Christ, no wonder Tony's so strung out if that's reared its ugly head again.' Grumpy Bob let out a low whistle. 'You know the story, right? About his fiancée and the original Christmas Killer?'

'Enough to know better than to ask. More to the point, whatever that chemical was, they sent a sample to the university chemistry department for analysis. The rest was destroyed.'

'So you reckon Hamilton might have been doing a little experimentation? Might even be the source of this stuff?' Grumpy Bob asked.

'Let's not leap to conclusions until we've spoken to the university. I already asked Lofty to look into that, anyway. Meantime we've got Hamilton tied to Alba Fulfilment Solutions, which is where Rory Devlin last worked before something turned him from a straight-up guy who wouldn't even smoke a joint passed round at a party into someone who'd hide out in a derelict warehouse to get his fix.'

'Thought that name sounded familiar,' Grumpy Bob said. 'And you definitely perked up a bit when Katie mentioned it. What was that about the Dee Foundation though?'

'Alba work closely with them, according to the boss. Wouldn't surprise me if it wasn't another arm of that woman's empire.'

'They seem to work closely with everyone. Soon be working closely with us too, if what I hear about the chief superintendent's little project is true.'

Janie eased the car to a stop as the lights changed to red. 'Oh, it's true. Apparently there's some official function this evening to celebrate the new alliance, or something like that. Three-line whip for everyone DI and above to attend, only I'd put good money on at least one absence.'

Grumpy Bob laughed, but the humour faded swiftly. 'Seriously though, Janie. Do you ever wonder if he's not getting a little bit obsessed with Dee and her foundation? I mean, don't get me wrong, I'd like to see the woman behind bars. She's evil, no two ways about it. But Tony . . . I don't know.'

'He's under a fair bit of pressure right now. You know, with Emma and everything.' Janie started to move forward as the lights changed, then slammed on the brakes as a car ran the red light straight across the junction. 'Jesus. What is wrong with people?'

'Woa. Nice reflexes. I never even saw him coming.' Grumpy Bob pulled out his notebook and scribbled something down. Old habits die hard, it would seem. 'I'll pass that on to traffic. With any luck the camera will have got him.'

'About the boss though.' Janie inched the car forward more slowly this time. 'Even with all the shit falling on him, I'd still trust his judgement more than most. Certainly more than the chief super. I worry about him, though.'

'Aye, me too, Janie. He's his own worst enemy. Always has been. Which isn't to say he's not got plenty of others out for him. He'll pull through though. He always does.'

'Until he doesn't,' Janie said, expecting the ex-detective sergeant to come up with another reassuring platitude. Instead, the silence grew, underscored by the rumble and swish of the car's tyres over tarmac turned into a stream by the downpour. He didn't say anything until they'd pulled into the station and parked up in one of the two spaces reserved for electric vehicles, which for a change didn't have a diesel squad car parked in it.

'He'll be fine as long as he's got us to look out for him, Janie. But if this . . .' Grumpy Bob gestured with both hands to indicate anything and everything. '. . . is to do with Saifre, then tread very carefully.'

44

The light of his phone screen broke McLean's concentration as he stared unseeing at the pathology report on Alastair Hamilton. Picking up the handset, he expected to see a text from the hospital informing him of the lack of change in Emma's condition, but instead it was a reminder from the chief superintendent about that evening's reception.

> 7pm. All senior CID officers to be in attendance, Tony. That includes you. Gail x

He stared at that final 'x' for far longer than should have been necessary. The whole message was highly unprofessional, even if he had no intention of attending the event anyway. That last little bit of overfamiliarity was distinctly out of character. Flicking back through her past texts, there was nothing similar at all. She never even signed off with her name. He shook his head and went back to the pathology report.

Unlike Rory Devlin or Fiona McLeod, it seemed Alastair Hamilton had been a habitual drug user. There were indications of injecting heroin, damage to his nasal passage that suggested cocaine on occasion, too. His general condition – thin and malnourished, poor teeth and dubious personal hygiene – was consistent with his being an addict, except that he appeared to have been clean at the time of his death according to the analysis of his blood. The Demon's Breath that had killed him left no trace in the bloodstream, apparently.

Which begged the question had he taken it at all? The pathology report mentioned the blisters on his lips, speculating that they might have been caused by some caustic agent, although again no traces were found. All in all it was a rather unhelpful summary, unusual for Angus.

McLean was reaching for his phone to call his old friend, see if they might meet up to discuss the findings, when it lit up and started to ring. He'd barely had time to register the name 'Dr Wheeler' on the screen before he'd snatched it up and thumbed to accept the call.

'Tony. Caroline Wheeler here,' she said, rather unnecessarily he felt.

'Caroline. Hi. Is this a call I really want?'

'No. I mean, no, it's not a call you don't want. Probably not one you do either. But I know what you're like so I thought I'd beat you to it. There's no change. Emma's stable, breathing on her own. Her brainwave activity is unchanged in the past twenty-four hours, so there's really no point in your dragging yourself across town and getting in the way of my nurses.'

Well that was blunt. He had to admire her for it.

'I had thought I might drop by later, but if you don't think it'll help.'

'Have an evening off, Tony. Get yourself a take out, watch some telly, I don't know. Do whatever it is you normally do when you're not working.'

McLean stared into the distance, through the window wall to the darkening evening outside. Low clouds obscured what little of the view wasn't tenement flats on the other side of the street, all smeared with rain that ran in rivulets down the glass. What did he do when he wasn't working? He had no good answer to that.

'I'll not come round then,' he said finally. 'But please, if there's any change –'

'Any time, day or night. Yes, the nurses know to call you. But understand we've got this, Tony. We'll look after Emma the best she can possibly be looked after. You go look after yourself.'

'I will. Thanks. For everything.'

Dr Wheeler hung up before he could say anything else, and for a while it was all McLean could do to stare at the window, the phone still held to his ear. Finally he pulled it away and slipped it in his pocket. He gathered up the reports he'd been trying to read and put them in his case. Wasn't that what he did when he wasn't working, after all? Work some more, only in a different place?

It was only as he went to disconnect Emma's Renault from its charge port and saw the cable snaking to a different electric car that McLean realised he'd forgotten to plug it in when he'd arrived at the station that morning. There was still plenty of juice to get him home, and the dire weather had managed to clear the roads of the worst of the traffic. He noticed the clock on the dashboard screen flick to seven o'clock as he turned off the quiet street and onto his driveway, a gentle snort not so much of laughter as amusement forcing its way out of his nose. Sure, he'd be in the shit tomorrow, but when was he ever not?

The two cats stared up at him from their usual spot in front of the Aga as he let himself into the kitchen. On instinct, he checked the feed and water bowls, topped up the one and refreshed the other. They had him well trained.

He heard the crunch of tyres on gravel, the low rumble of a car's engine as he went to the front door to collect the mail. Glancing out the hall window, he saw the security light come on and illuminate a shiny black Mercedes very much like the one in which the chief superintendent was ferried back and forth across the country.

By the time he'd taken the mail back to the kitchen and gone out the back door to see who was visiting unannounced, a uniformed officer McLean didn't recognise had climbed out of the driver's seat and was staring slack-jawed at the house.

'Can I help you, Sergeant?' he asked.

The man came to attention with almost military precision, and for a moment McLean thought he might snap off a salute.

'Detective Inspector McLean, sir. Orders from Chief Superintendent Elmwood. I'm here to take you to the Dee Foundation reception.'

McLean let out a weary sigh. Too much to hope that he could avoid it that easily. 'And if I wasn't here?' He shook his head. 'No, don't answer that. It's not your fault. Just let me grab my coat.'

He turned away from the car, seeing Emma's Renault Zoe sipping electricity from the charge point where he'd plugged it in only a few minutes earlier. How much range had there been left? Enough, surely. He hurried back into the kitchen, picked up his coat and grabbed the keys. The cats hadn't moved from their warm spot in front of the Aga, which was very sensible of them given the weather.

'I'll not be long,' he said to them.

Back outside, the rain that had eased a little earlier was now coming on strong again. McLean held up the keys for the sergeant to see. 'I'll drive myself, if it's all the same to you. Don't want to get stuck there any longer than necessary. I know the way, but you can follow me if you want.'

The house where Jane Louise Dee lived when she was conducting business in Scotland lay a few miles east of Dalkeith, outside the bypass and the city limits. When first they had met, she had been renting a house not all that far from McLean's own, formerly the residence of an old acquaintance of his grandmother. But, for whatever reason, Mrs Saifre had not bought that house when its previous owner had died, even though she clearly had the money to do so. Instead, she had found another lair from which to spin her webs. One tucked away out of sight of prying eyes.

As he drove up the long, straight driveway towards it, closely followed by the chief superintendent's Mercedes, McLean saw the Palladian mansion lit up by enough floodlights to paint the undersides of the rain clouds almost white. He'd been here before, in the depths of winter with the ground covered in deep snow, but somehow the dreich rain and wind buffeting in from the Firth of Forth suited the place better. A reminder of the dark era in Scotland's history that had built this and many other palatial houses across the nation, the wealth derived from transatlantic trade in sugar and slaves.

The wide circle of gravel in front of the main entrance was almost filled with cars, from the ridiculously expensive SUVs and 4x4s beloved of most senior police officers and politicians, right down to the twelve-year-old Ford Focus that DCI Ritchie still drove despite her recent promotion. There were a few squad cars too, but no charge point for an electric Renault Zoe. Not that McLean would have taken even that much from his host. He parked at the farthest point from the house, where it was unlikely anyone would block him in, even though that left him with a long walk through rain growing heavier by the minute.

The front doors hung wide open, the marble floor protected from the worst of the weather by a massive portico that sat uneasily with the rest of the architecture. Stepping over the threshold was like entering another world. Heat enveloped him, sweat mixing almost instantly with the rain on his forehead as he struggled out of his heavy coat before a suited flunky could reach him to help.

'Well, well, well. Look what the cat dragged in. And only what? An hour late?'

McLean shook his head, waved one hand to let another flunky know that he didn't want a drink before turning to face his accuser. Mrs Saifre, Jane Louise Dee, Lucifer Morningstar, whatever name she was going by these days, fixed him with a smile that was as full as it was insincere. She wore a low-cut black dress quite unsuitable for a woman of her age, but then she didn't look like a woman of her age. Without having done his research, McLean would have put her at around thirty-five, but the poor Edinburgh girl with a flair for tech and a head for business had been born at the tail end of the 1950s, if Wikipedia was to be believed.

'What can I say? You know I'm only here because my boss ordered it.' He cast his gaze across the open hallway, where a noisy host of people were mingling, warmed by large open fireplaces on either side of the room and a great measure of Saifre's hospitality. 'Talking of Chief Superintendent Elmwood, I don't see her mingling with the great and good.'

'She'll be down in a bit, don't you worry about that.' Saifre stepped in quickly, looped her arm inside McLean's before he could evade her. Her touch was like an electric shock, her grip impossible to break. This close, too close, he felt a heat boiling off her far greater than the crackling tree trunks in the fireplace. 'Come, Tony. Let me introduce you to your key liaison with our foundation going forward.'

Powerless to escape, McLean could do nothing but allow himself to be steered through the mess of people. Saifre seemed to have an invisible forcefield around her that gently pushed everyone out of the way as she approached. Soon enough they arrived at a small group listening intently to a tall woman dressed in a rather more sober black outfit than Saifre's. Even turned away from him as she was, McLean recognised her from the outreach centre, the day before.

'Ms Llewellyn,' he said, slightly stealing Saifre's thunder.

'Detective Inspector McLean. Good to see you again.' Llewellyn held out her hand almost as if she was expecting him to kiss it. McLean took the opportunity to extract himself from Saifre's firm hold.

'I wasn't aware that you were part of this project,' he said. 'I thought you were involved with the youth training schemes.'

Saifre laughed, a sound like the flaying of innocents. 'Susan is director of youth training and outreach, Tony. As such, she deals with exactly the parts of society you need help making contacts with. Didn't Gail explain it all?'

'I expect so. I've not really been paying attention. Too busy doing my real job.'

For a moment he thought he might have pushed it too far. Saifre's normally disturbing nonchalance slipped, a frown creeping across her perfect features that had a threat of anger behind it. McLean felt the heat of it like a flame across his skin, but it was Llewellyn who flinched like a dog used to being struck by its master for any perceived wrongdoing.

'That's exactly what we're trying to help with, Detective Inspector,' she said in hurried tones. 'Managing the connection between your teams and the communities you're trying to protect. Is that not right, Jane Louise?'

'Exactly so, Susan. Now if you'll excuse me Tony I've other guests to attend to, and the presentation's about to begin.' The burning rage disappeared almost as swiftly as it had appeared, Saifre's expression once more one of welcoming hospitality as she smiled like a shark and headed off through the crowd. McLean wasn't fooled. He'd seen the woman's true face too many times before.

'Ah, there's your boss now.' Llewellyn gestured towards the elegant marble staircase as a lone figure came slowly down. Elmwood had one hand on the balustrade for support, and she stopped on the last step, gazing out at the crowd as if summoning the courage to enter the fray. McLean almost felt sorry for her, but the moment was lost as she was joined by Saifre, whose embrace left no room for doubt about the nature of their relationship. What an odd couple they made, although there were obvious similarities between the two. After all, hadn't both come from nothing and fought ruthlessly to get to the top of their chosen professions, caring not one bit who they used, trampled or destroyed on the way?

45

Sitting at the back of a ridiculously large ballroom the better to make good his escape once it was all over, and perhaps the only person apart from the serving staff who was entirely sober, McLean didn't know whether to be baffled or angry about the presentation. It didn't help that he thought Project Tantalus was as ill-conceived as its name, of course. And he couldn't deny his visceral dislike of Mrs Saifre, that mixture of policeman's instinct and plain old fact. She was as bent as a three-bob note, as his old mentor Guthrie McManus had been fond of saying, and he couldn't buy into the perfect utopia she was selling with her new charitable foundation either. Dirty money was still dirty, no matter what it was used to pay for.

At least nobody had suggested he be part of the evening's entertainment, that particular honour shared out between the chief constable, chief superintendent and a veritable who's who of Edinburgh politicians. In fact, as the list of honourable gentlemen and ladies involved in the enterprise grew, he realised that there weren't any members of Specialist Crime Division or the local Edinburgh Major Investigation Teams standing up and singing the praises of this new approach to community policing. Nobody from plain clothes at all. And as the presentations came to an end with a question and answer session,

McLean had to admit that he still didn't really know what the new initiative was meant to achieve or how it was meant to work. Granted he'd not really been paying attention, but even so he'd hoped to have gained something from the evening other than a numb bum.

'Surprised to see you here, Tony. That's a tenner I owe Jayne.' Detective Chief Inspector Ritchie caught up with him as everyone was filing out of the ballroom back into the hall, where yet more booze and canapés awaited the unwary.

'I'm almost as surprised to see you here, Kirsty. I know you have even less time for Saifre than I do. What an utter waste of time this whole charade is.'

'Couldn't agree more. And believe me, I tried every trick I know to get out of this. Even called in some favours from my old Aberdeen team. Thought they might be able to engineer a crisis up there I just had to attend.' Ritchie shrugged. 'Didn't work though.'

'Why is it so important? I don't understand what the point of any of this is. Least of all why it has to happen here, at night. Or why anyone DI or above has to attend. If the high heidyins want a press junket, that's fine, but there's no need for the likes of us to be here other than the chief superintendent showing off. Sooner I can get out of here and back home the better. There's far more important things than –'

'Oh dear me, Tony. You're not sneaking off without saying goodbye are you?'

McLean turned to see the chief superintendent had somehow managed to creep up on the both of them unawares. She had a glass of champagne in one hand, surely not the first of the evening given the flush to her face.

'I thought the presentation was over, ma'am.'

'The presentation, yes. But this is an important networking opportunity. You need to meet the key players in the Dee

311

Foundation, your liaisons, the people you're going to be working with going forward.'

'I've already met Ms Llewellyn. Three times now, actually. And, anyway, would that not be more appropriate at the station, during working hours?' McLean let his gaze slip past Elmwood to a bunch of people close by. None of them were familiar, but neither did any of them appear to be waiting for an introduction.

'The details of how you'll work together are still being ironed out. I imagine it will take a while to find the best ways to integrate your operations anyway. So much easier to do that when you know the person you're talking to, wouldn't you say?'

McLean preferred not to. 'Nevertheless, I've places I need to be.'

For a moment he thought the chief superintendent was going to argue the point with him, but they were interrupted by the arrival of one of the city's more colourful Members of Parliament. McLean took the opportunity to slip away, aware from the look that Ritchie gave him that he'd pay for it later. When had it all got so complicated, so political? Truth was, it had always been that way, he'd just been better at keeping out of it. The promotion to DCI and then the arrival of Elmwood had dragged him into the limelight, and Saifre's unhealthy obsession with him didn't help. Well, she could worry about him another day.

Once he had finally found it, the cloakroom was a welcome quiet after the boorish hubbub of the main hall. McLean didn't mind a crowd, particularly a crowd of his fellow officers in a pub celebrating a case cracked. He was less happy being the only sober person in a group of drunks, and with a few notable exceptions that seemed to be the way Mrs Saifre's guests were heading. Pity the poor buggers when they woke up in the morning, their heads aching and their souls in hock.

'I was hoping to get a chance to speak to you alone.'

The voice sent a chill to the pit of his stomach. McLean hadn't heard the cloakroom door open, and yet when he turned around Mrs Saifre stood so close she might have kissed him. Or stabbed him in the chest. And where before she had burned with a hellish heat, now she brought an iciness to the room that might have cracked the marble floor.

'I was just leaving.' He located his coat on the rack and unhooked it before draping it over one arm.

'So I see. You really are no fun you know, Tony. Why can't you just let your hair down once in a while? Enjoy yourself. Live a little.'

'I was invited . . . No, I was instructed to attend a symposium and reception. I've far better things to be doing than watching a bunch of politicians get drunk.'

'Like sitting in a hospital ward and staring at your girlfriend?'

McLean went very still. Mostly because that was the only way he could stop himself from grabbing Saifre by the throat, and he couldn't help thinking she would probably enjoy that. He said nothing, merely stared at her face and those horrible black bottomless pits that were her eyes.

'Gail told me about her stroke. I'm so very sorry. It must be devastating after what happened with your grandmother.'

He knew that she was goading him, but McLean couldn't work out what response she was looking for. So he kept silent, kept watching.

'Gail's a remarkable woman, don't you think? Such a fighter, such spirit. Anyone else faced with her injuries – with what that hideous little man did to her? – well, they'd be a wreck. But not Gail, no. She bounced back harder than ever. With a little help from some advanced medical research I was able to make available for her.'

Saifre inched a little closer as she spoke, and McLean had to stop himself from taking a step back. He knew this game, and while he had no great desire to play it, he needed to know what the woman was up to. He held his ground, and his tongue.

'She's very grateful, of course. And we've grown quite fond of one another, can you believe it?'

McLean couldn't imagine Saifre being fond of anyone other than herself, but he'd seen others fall for her charms. It only marginally surprised him that Elmwood might have been one of them.

'And she's responded very well to the treatment, too. Another couple of months and you wouldn't even know she'd been scarred at all. The doctors are delighted with how much she's improved. Me too. We've learned so much from working on her.' Saifre paused, one hand raised halfway to her own face as if she couldn't decide what to do with it. 'Imagine that, Tony. A world where horrific injuries like poor Gail's can be healed without scarring.'

On the face of it, that sounded like a wonderful world. Only at what cost? Nothing was ever free, particularly where Saifre was concerned. She dealt in favours owed for favours given. And she wanted adulation, for the masses to adore her. That was what gave her power, after all. There was no altruism in the Dee Foundation, only a cynical use of her ill-gotten billions to buy influence. McLean didn't say as much, even though he could tell from her expression that she knew what he was thinking. That she enjoyed the fact he knew and was still powerless to do anything about it.

'Of course, that's not the only area where we've advanced medical science. I think you'd be far more interested in what we can do for people with locked-in syndrome, stroke sufferers. People like your own dear Emma Baird, no?'

'What are you talking about?' McLean finally broke his wall of silence, the rage threatening to overwhelm him.

'Oh, I know all about her case, Tony. The collapse, the

persistent coma, the sluggish brainwave activity. Sounds very similar to something my team came across last year. That patient made a full recovery, you know. I could make the same thing happen for Emma.'

'And what would I owe you in return?'

'Oh, Tony. It's always so transactional with you.' Saifre turned away from him, but not before he caught the faintest ghost of a smile on her lips, as if she thought she had won somehow. 'I don't want anything from you. I know better than to ask.'

'Then why bring it up at all? Why haven't you set up the treatment already? Emma's not my property, you know. You don't need my permission. If you didn't want anything from me, you'd have healed her already, not dangled the possibility in front of me like I'm some kind of trophy to be hooked.'

The slump of her shoulders was so minuscule it might have gone unnoticed had he not been hyper-aware of the whole situation. McLean caught it all the same. And when Saifre turned to face him once more, that smile was nowhere to be seen. 'You wouldn't be grateful? To have her back?'

'Of course I'd be grateful, but I know what you are, Mrs Saifre. I know how you work. And I trust the doctors and nurses already looking after Emma far more than I'll ever trust you. So thank you for your kind offer, but you're making it to the wrong person. Good night.'

McLean shrugged into his overcoat, still damp from its soaking earlier in the day. He probably smelled like a wet dog wearing it, or perhaps a camel, but he didn't care. Saifre watched him the whole time, then moved just enough for him to get past her to the door. It was only once he'd reached it, pulled it open and felt the rising noise from the hall wash over him that he spoke again.

'There was one thing I wanted to ask though. Alastair Hamilton. Does that name mean anything to you?'

Again, her reaction was so small it might be missed, had he not been looking for something, anything, as he said the name. It was there though, the slightest narrowing of the eyes, and then moments later a tiny reptilian flick of the tongue over those too-perfect lips before she answered his question with one of her own.

'Should it? I hear a lot of names every day. That one doesn't strike any particular bell.'

'Just a passing thought. Nothing important.' McLean wished he had a hat he could have doffed, settling instead for a slow nod of the head. 'Thank you. For this evening. I won't be coming back. And when you see Gail, please let her know that, OK?'

46

McLean drove home slowly, partly because he needed most of his attention for thinking, and partly because the predicted range left in the little electric car was barely enough to make the distance. The climb up Fairmilehead was particularly worrisome, and by the time he glided slowly past the entrance to the Hermitage, the round zero on the dashboard screen almost screamed at him. What would he do if the Renault just stopped? He couldn't exactly go and get a little red can full of electricity, could he?

He could almost hear the sigh of relief as he parked alongside the charging port at home and plugged in the cable.

'Touch and go there.' He patted the car on the roof affectionately. 'Thanks for not letting me down.'

It wasn't until he reached the back door that it registered with him it had stopped raining. Looking up, he could see the cloud base had risen, the clouds themselves breaking apart to reveal occasional glimpses of star-speckled sky above. A thin wedge of moon briefly illuminated the path to the coach house and the metal gate that led through to the garden beyond. At the far side of the property there was another, identical gate that opened onto the Hermitage itself, only a short distance away from the Ladies' Garden. Was it really only this morning he'd been down there chatting to Hattie Turner about the bones she'd found? It felt more like a month, but then his encounters with Mrs Saifre always left him feeling drained.

Neither of the cats were in residence when he let himself into the kitchen, although the reports and other papers he'd brought home with him to work on were still strewn across the table. McLean considered taking them through to the library and reading them with the aid of a stiff dram, but a glance at the clock showed him it was later than he'd realised. Not too late for a cup of tea though. And maybe some toast if the rumble from his stomach was its way of giving him a hint.

He was halfway through his second slice, dripping in a melted mess of butter and Marmite, when the cat flap clattered and one of the cats stalked in. At a quick glance he couldn't tell whether it was Mrs McCutcheon's or Cecily Slater's, but it didn't much matter as soon enough the other one followed. They both sat down by the Aga and began to wash, eyeing him with suspicion every now and then.

'Well, I don't know when she'll be back either. Soon, I hope.' He picked up his phone, the motion lighting up the screen and a continued lack of messages from the hospital. He'd drop by again in the morning, no matter what Dr Wheeler said. Every moment with her was precious now, no way of knowing if it would be the last.

The thought brought an almost physical pain to his chest, a tension so hard he nearly smashed his hands down on the table. How dare Saifre use Emma as some kind of crude bargaining chip in her evil little plans? How dare she scheme with the chief superintendent to find new ways to make his job more difficult than it already was? How dare she flood the city with her tainted money, buying sainthood from an army of the easily fooled?

His anger must have spilled out in some way, as when he looked at them again both cats had stopped their washing and were staring straight at him, hackles raised. McLean drained his mug and stood up, leaving the last half-slice of toast behind as he strode out of the kitchen. He paused for long enough to pull on a stout pair of boots and an old waxed jacket that he suspected had once belonged to his grandfather, then stepped out into the night to cool off.

The clouds had broken further in the time he'd been indoors, and now the wedge of moon shone bright through the gaps, darkening only for short periods as the wind hurried them along. McLean pushed open the gate and went through into the garden, unsure exactly what he hoped to achieve, but knowing he couldn't be indoors with only his thoughts and two cats for company.

As if summoned by the idea, he felt something brush past his leg and looking down saw he had acquired two small shadows in the darkness. They ranged about his feet, scampering off into the long grass and then running back again like they were kittens rather than the elderly spinsters they must have been. McLean wandered the night-time garden for long minutes, marvelling at how different it looked under moonlight compared to during the day. Not that he came out here much in the day either. This was the domain of Bill Bradford the gardener and, on occasion, Emma.

That tightness clamped his chest again as he thought about her, lying alone and lost in her hospital ward. If she was there at all. They'd been through so much, together and apart, in those years since she'd climbed into his bed while he was asleep, and he couldn't help thinking that she'd had the worst of it by a country mile.

Perhaps inevitably, his footsteps took him to the gate at the far end of the garden, tucked behind overgrown rhododendron bushes and tall trees. He'd expected it to be more overgrown than it was, but it seemed the gardener had been hard at work on this area. Beyond the wall, the land dropped steeply to the Hermitage below, the babbling Braid Burn most likely in spate given the day's rain. Somewhere down there in the darkness lay the Ladies' Garden, and the buried bones of some long-forgotten woman. What was her story? And what of Emily Worstead, buried only a few miles away as the crow flies? Or the much older bones, Izabell Kerr if Madame Rose was to be believed, thrown in a pit on the outskirts of Leith at a time when it was a separate town from Edinburgh?

Without much hope of it working, McLean found himself trying the handle on the gate. To his surprise, it clicked open, lock and hinges both well oiled. He'd have to have words with Bill the gardener about that. Not that anyone would likely wander in from the glen, the undergrowth was too thick for that, the old path all but obscured.

Wind shook raindrops from the tree canopy overhead, showering him in a sudden deluge that soaked his hair in an instant. Should have worn a hat as well as the raincoat. Should probably have stayed indoors where it was warm and dry. Looking down, he saw no sign of the cats any more, so presumably they had more sense than him. Most living creatures did. Likely most dead ones too.

He heard the clink of metal as he was beginning to pull the gate closed. At first his brain told him it was just the latch, but then it occurred to him that the sound hadn't been right for that. And neither had he actually finished closing it. Pausing, he strained to hear over the swish of the wind in the trees, the background roar of the city and the more natural rumble of the water in the burn. Was it his imagination playing tricks on him?

Nothing, and then just as he was about to give up and put the whole thing down to too little sleep and too much to worry, it came again. A distance off, the noise was like metal against stone, only muted. As if someone had wrapped a hammer in cloth. Or shoved a spade through earth.

A third clink and McLean knew it wasn't his imagination. He could also pinpoint where the noise was coming from, more or less. The Ladies' Garden, where his childhood self had built dens and constructed elaborate lonely adventures, blissfully unaware of the bones mouldering a few feet beneath him.

He didn't really mean to go and have a look, just maybe get a bit closer. A line of sight might reveal whether whoever was down there had a light, perhaps even what the hell they thought they were doing. Even so, McLean used the moonlight from a break in the clouds to double-check the path before pushing his way through the bushes. The damp scents of loam and rot wafting up from the ground brought back memories from decades earlier, the steps exactly where he remembered them as he descended into the narrow glen. No need to worry too much about making a noise, as the wind in the treetops and the rush of water below drowned out everything else.

The closer he came to the walled garden, the less easy it was to see anything. Winter might be on its way, but the trees were still leafy enough to block the moonlight, only occasional beams lessening the overall gloom. He'd been out in the garden long enough for his eyes to adjust to the darkness as much as they were ever going to, and yet there was no soft glow of head torch, only the slow, rhythmic sound of what McLean knew now to be a spade working away at the earth.

He picked a careful route along the low wall, the pallets of stone and dumpy-bags of sand for the restoration work looming out of the dark like mute sentinels. The site was much as he remembered it from that morning, the original archway entrance half taken down to allow access for heavy machinery. As he edged towards it, he began to hear other sounds over the general noise, a low mumbling, moaning, a bit like plainsong or chanting, but with an edge to it that was too discordant for comfort. What was he doing down here? Alone in the dark? Best get away before someone found him, call it in.

Shoving his hands in his pockets, he had that sinking feeling when he couldn't find his phone. Not in the coat, and not in his jacket underneath it either. Then he could see it, in his mind's eye. Laid out on the kitchen table so he could see the screen light up with any news while he ate his toast and drank his tea. Idiot that he was, he'd come out without it. But then he'd never intended going further than the garden, and never meant to be out more than a few minutes.

He turned away from the entrance and picked a slow path home. It was much harder going up the steep slope than it had been coming down. Heavy rain had made the steps almost lethally slippy, their old railway sleeper edges half rotted away, and he had to grab at branches to steady himself. There was one horrible moment when McLean was convinced he was going to go arse over tit all the way back down again, but he managed to keep his balance until he reached the top.

With only the rhododendron bush that had overgrown the path still to negotiate, he paused a moment to catch his breath, leaning his hands on his knees for support. Up here at the head of the glen, the wind rattled the treetops more strongly, and the clouds scudding past the moon shifted the gloom between relative light and deep shadow with a befuddling speed. Even so, McLean as much felt as heard the presence of something, someone, behind him. He turned swiftly to face whoever it was, and in the same moment that he saw no one at all, his foot went from under him. He pitched forwards, too close to the drop, flailed like a lunatic, arms windmilling as he tried to grab something, anything to stop the inevitable.

And then he was falling, branches everywhere, slapping at his face and knocking the wind out of him. From this new angle, he saw for an impossible instant lights in a circle in the Ladies' Garden, arranged around the pit where the bones had been dug up. Then something heavy smashed into the side of his head and everything went black.

47

Janie checked her phone as she rode the bus across town to the station, surprised to find no message from the boss waiting for her. Normally there were half a dozen, usually timed in the wee small hours when any sane person would be asleep in their beds. Today was one of those rare days when he had presumably managed to find someone else to bother. Although he'd been at the launch for the chief superintendent's latest pet project the night before, so maybe that was the reason.

She still had the phone in her hand, the surprising silence of the detective inspector on her mind, when she stepped off the bus in Clerk Street and glanced nervously up at the leaden grey sky. So when it vibrated an incoming call she answered without checking the screen, expecting it to be him.

'Hello?'

'Detective Sergeant Harrison?' Not the DI. A female voice, young. It took Janie a moment to recognise.

'Maggie? Maggie Devlin?'

'Aye. Sorry for phoning, like.'

'No, it's no bother. Wouldn't have given you my number if I'd not meant for you to use it. How can I help you?'

'It's about Rore.' The young woman paused a moment. 'Any

chance we could meet up, aye? I'm no' all that comfortable talkin' on the phone.'

'Sure.' Janie checked her watch. Early for a teenager to be up, so Maggie was probably calling from home. 'When's good for you? We can meet at the cafe we went to the last time.'

'Aye, that'd be grand. Mebbe an hour?'

Janie checked her watch. She'd have to miss the morning briefing, but Sandy Gregg was always more organised about these things anyway.

'No problem, Maggie. I'll see you there.'

The phone went dead before Janie could end the call herself. Slipping the handset into her pocket, she carried on her short walk to the station, wondering what Maggie could have to say that she'd not done already.

The CID room was almost buzzing with activity when she let herself in a few minutes later, a cluster of detective constables standing around Lofty Blane's desk peering at his screen.

'What's up?' she asked as she approached, dumping her bag on her chair in passing.

'Oh, hi, Janie.' DC Blane looked up from his screen. 'Just found some interesting information about the building site. You know, where they found the bones?'

'Anything useful?' Janie joined the small group staring at the screen, leaned in a little closer to see a web page from an online newspaper.

'I'm not sure. But I went to see the Land Registry yesterday. Remember how they were having trouble tracking down the deeds and everything?'

'I thought it was all digitised these days anyway.'

'Aye, it is. Only there's a backlog on registering everything, and the lockdown stopped a lot of the work. That's not why they couldn't find the deeds though. Seems a whole stack of them went missing a while back. No one noticed until this happened.'

Lofty pointed at the screen, and Janie read the headline 'Dispute over ownership of family farm'. She scanned the page, looking for a date, finally finding it under the byline. The name raised an eyebrow too.

'Jo Dalgliesh? I guess she's old enough to have been writing this sort of thing back then.'

'Isn't she chums with the inspector?' DC Mitchell asked.

'Chums is probably a bit strong. Way I hear it he used to hate her. She wrote some book about the man who murdered his fiancée. You can imagine that wouldn't endear someone to you.'

'Murdered his . . .' Mitchell's eyes widened in surprise, but Janie shook her head.

'If you don't know the story, I'm sure someone will tell you. Was twenty years ago. Not important now.' Janie pointed at the screen, which she'd only managed to half read. 'This is though, I think. Have you followed it up at all, Ben?'

Lofty cocked his head, perhaps surprised by the use of his name rather than his nickname. 'Aye. Well, this is me following up what the Land Registry told me. Seems there was a farm there. Most of the land's still grazed though I'm sure they'll put more houses up on it soon as they can. The farmer didn't have any family except a nephew, who thought he was going to inherit it when the old boy died. Didn't quite end up that way though. The farmhouse caught fire, opinion's divided how, but the official report said it wasn't suspicious. They reckon the farmer probably fell asleep in his armchair with a fag in his hand. He was near enough eighty-five, so it's possible, I guess.'

Janie reached for the mouse, used its little wheel to scroll down the page until she found a photograph of a burned-out farmhouse, the familiar shape of the Pentland hills at Mile End in the background. She recognised it from her visits to the building site, although the trees were taller now than when the photograph had been taken, the farmhouse even more dilapidated.

'Problem was, there was no will. Or there may have been but it burned with the house if it existed. Apparently he was like that, the farmer. Didn't trust lawyers.'

'I'm liking him already,' Janie said. 'But surely if there was no will, it would all have gone to the only surviving relative eventually.'

'You'd think. But that's when a lawyer from MacFarlane and Dodds pops up claiming the land didn't actually belong to the farmer, it was only on a long-term let. It actually belonged to his client, and they were taking possession of it now that the original leaseholder was dead.'

'MacFarlane and Dodds. Another one of the boss's favourites. He in yet, by the way?' Janie looked around the room as if McLean might have been lurking unseen in a corner all the while.

'Not seen him, no. He's usually in for the morning briefing though. I'll bring everyone up to speed on this then.'

'Aye, I'm going to have to miss that. So fill me in. How'd it all go down with the nephew? Can't imagine he'd not put up a fight.'

'Well, that was the thing. He couldn't find any deeds, so figured they'd all gone up in the fire like the will. Went to the Land Registry for copies, and they didn't have them either. The only legal documents anyone could produce were with the lawyers, along with a copy of the original lease. According to the article Ms Dalgliesh wrote here' – Lofty leaned forward and tapped the screen, causing it to wobble in an alarming fashion – 'the nephew was going to fight it anyway, but then he died in a car accident before he could bring any kind of challenge.'

'Convenient.' Janie stared at the screen, not really taking in the words, just seeing that photograph of the burned-out farmhouse. 'I take it the lawyers were representing Dee, and the title was in her name on the deeds.'

'Apparently so. Belonged to a branch of the family for generations according to the paperwork they had. And since nobody else had any to countermand it, not even the Land Registry themselves, there wasn't really any way of contesting it. So it's hers.'

'And this all happened in the early noughts. Ten or more years after Emily Worstead ended up in that deep grave.'

'Aye.'

'So why'd they drag their feet telling us who owned the land?'

Lofty shrugged. 'Embarrassed, maybe? I mean, keeping hold of the records of land ownership is basically their whole job. Losing a bunch of files isn't something they'd want to own up to. It wasn't just that land register they'd lost, according to the lady I spoke to.'

Because that would be suspicious, Janie didn't say, even though the thought was uppermost in her mind. 'It's good work anyway. Shame there's nobody linked to the farm still alive though. Would have been good to talk to anyone who worked that land around the time the body was buried.'

'There might be, but I'd not know where to even start looking,' Lofty said.

'Well, mention it to the boss when you see him. He can give Dalgliesh a call and see if she's got any contacts.' Janie slapped the big detective constable lightly on the shoulder. 'Meantime I've another possible lead to chase down. Make my apologies at the briefing, will you?'

The same sour-faced old lady stood behind the serving counter as Janie pushed open the door to the cafe. The place was a bit busier than the last time she'd been there, but still not exactly heaving. She found Maggie sitting in the corner by the window, her back to the wall so that she could see everyone coming and going.

'Am I late?' Janie asked, checking her watch as she saw that the young woman was halfway down a mug of coffee already, an empty plate bearing the telltale hints of scone and jam.

'No. I was early.' Maggie shuffled in her seat as if unsure whether to get up or not.

Janie waved for her to stay where she was. 'You wanting anything else?'

When the young woman shook her head, Janie pulled out the spare seat and sat. There was a pause while the old lady shuffled over to take an order anyway, so she opted for a coffee and a bacon roll on the grounds that it might take a while before they were interrupted again.

'So, what is it got you up and out the house so early in the morning?' she asked once they were alone again.

'That obvious am I?' Maggie shrugged, reached up and felt the back of her head.

'Oh, I'm sorry Maggie. I should've asked how you were feeling. Still sore?'

'Aye, a bit. Doctor gave me some painkillers but they made me feel sick. Least this just hurts when I touch it.'

Janie resisted the urge to tell her to stop touching it then. She'd never listened to grown-ups when she was Maggie's age; why should it be any different now?

'You said you wanted to talk about Rory,' she said instead. 'Has something come up? You remember something?'

Maggie stared off into the middle distance for a little while before answering. 'Y'ken how I told youse he'd changed? Like, he used to be an annoying wee shite, but he was my brother. It was kind've what you'd expect a big brother to be like, ken?'

Janie did, even if Maggie's mangling of the language wasn't entirely clear. 'I've two older brothers myself. I know exactly what you mean. They can be cruel sometimes, tease you until you hate them for it. But it's never really cruel, never spiteful.

And see if someone else tries it on with you, then there's all hell to pay from them.'

'Aye, that's exactly it. Rore was always pokin' fun at me, but he'd no' stand for a'body else doin' the same.' Maggie nodded her agreement, then winced and stopped. 'But then he changed. Almost overnight. An' he was just mean an' cruel an' what was that word you used? Spiteful, aye. That was it. Spiteful an' nasty. All the time. Never opened his mouth but to call me something foul.'

'So what changed him? You said "almost overnight". How long did it take?'

'That's what I was tryin' tae remember. Only gettin' whacked on the head made it no' easy tae think straight. But I've had a few days now an' I reckon I know when it was. He was at that job, the warehouse, ken? An' they do all kinds've training an' stuff. An' every month or so some of them go off on a weekend trip. Boot camp or whatever. See he was right excited about it. No' everyone got picked, it was kind've a special treat for the trainees who'd done the best or somethin'. I think he was mebbe sweet on one o' the girls goin' too.'

Maggie stopped speaking, her gaze moving up and past Janie, who looked around to see the old lady standing there with a mug and a plate.

'Bacon roll and white coffee?' she asked, as if she hadn't taken the order just a minute earlier.

'Aye, thanks.' Janie leaned to one side so the old lady could put her breakfast down on the table, then waited for her to go away again before turning back to Maggie.

'So. Rory went on some kind of corporate retreat or boot camp or something.'

'Aye. I'm no' sure of the actual date, but Mam'll have it down in the diary. He went off on the Friday like he was a wee kid at Christmas. An' then he came back late on the Sunday, didnae say a word. Just walked in, dumped his bag in the hall an' went to his room. I heard Mam and Da both go to try an' talk tae him, but he locked the door and wouldnae say anything. Next morning he came down tae breakfast, but he didnae eat much, hardly said a word. Went off to work an' when he came home he got in a right shouting match wi Mam. That's when he started being mean to me, ken? An' a week later – maybe two? – that's when he lost the job. Sure he'd started smoking weed by then too. Youse could smell it on him.'

Janie wiped bacon grease from her chin with a paper napkin, chewed and swallowed the last of her roll. An indulgence, perhaps, but she reckoned she'd earned it.

'So you think something happened at this thing he went to, then. Something so . . .' She struggled for a suitable word. '. . . so horrific it completely changed him? Turned an irritating but OK big brother into a complete shit. Someone who went out of his way to help a mate quit drugs took them up himself?'

Maggie frowned at that, but then nodded carefully once. 'Aye.'

'Do you know where he went on this thing? It was organised by the work, Alba Fulfilment Solutions?'

'No, no' them. It was the other folk. You know, the charity?'

'The Dee Foundation?'

'Aye, that's them.' Maggie cocked her head to one side as if trying to shake loose a memory, then winced again as her wound gave her grief. 'It was south of the city somewhere, I think. No' as far out as Penicuik, but that ways, aye. Where they held the camp. No' exactly sure where.'

The mention of Penicuik brought uncomfortable memories of a previous summer, a secret society performing cannibalistic rituals in a cave in the hills. That kind of thing might turn a young man to drugs, but there couldn't be anything else as bad as that, surely?

'Everything OK at home?' Janie asked, aware that she probably should have done that first, along with asking Maggie how her injury was healing. Judging by the way the young woman's shoulders slumped, the answer wasn't going to be a resounding yes.

'It's no' easy. Da's just about holding it together, ken. But Ma? She always had a temper on her, and now she's lashing out if either of us put a foot wrong. They fixed the door, but it still feels like home's no' safe any more, ken?' The young woman reached up for the back of her head again, then seemed to realise what she was doing and shoved her hands into her lap.

'Aye, I do,' Janie said. 'Had our place broken into when I was not much younger'n you. Couple of addicts looking for anything they could sell. They didn't find much, but they turned the place upside down. The thought of them going through my stuff stopped me sleeping for weeks. I'd no' really thought about it in a while, but there was one police officer did her best to help us. Cathy Fleming, that was her name. PC Fleming, I guess I should say. She's probably the main reason I signed up for the service out of school.'

'Where is she now? D'you see her ever?'

'Och, no. She retired a while back. Moved to Orkney, I think. Or was it Shetland? Some place a long way from Edinburgh, for sure. I think she'd had enough.'

Maggie smiled, a much better look on her face than the drained frown she wore most of the time. 'Aye, I can understand that.'

Janie felt her phone buzz in her pocket. Probably the boss, but certainly a reminder that she had to get back to the station soon. 'Look, Maggie. You've got my number, and I mean it when I say phone me any time. I can't promise easy answers, but I'll help you wherever I can. And there's no pressure on you to join the police when you're old enough, trust me.'

48

Walking back from the cafe to the car, Janie remembered her phone had buzzed in her pocket as she'd been talking to Maggie. Poor girl was taking her brother's death hard, but she was tough. A bit of support and she'd pull through, just a shame that support wasn't coming from her family.

She pulled out the handset and swiped the screen to wake it, fully expecting a slew of messages from the boss. Instead there was only a text from Manda reminding her to pick up pizza on the way home. Given how early it was in the morning, and the bacon roll sitting greasily in her stomach, she wasn't sure that was what she wanted right now.

As she plugged her phone into the car, she hit the speed dial number for DI McLean. He'd want to know about this latest piece of the puzzle, even if like all of the other pieces it had 'Dee Foundation' and their irritating little logo stamped on it. The call went to voicemail almost instantly, so she left a quick message for him to call her back ASAP. Where was he? Probably whisked off to Gartcosh by the chief superintendent or something.

The drive across town didn't take long, but when she pulled into the reserved spot for the electric car, there was no sign of Emma's Renault Zoe anywhere. Inside, the earlier buzz in the CID room had calmed a bit. Most of the desks were empty, only

Lofty Blane still stooped to his screen and DC Mitchell on a call in the far corner.

'You seen DI McLean this morning, Lofty?' she asked as she went around the back of his desk to see what he was doing. Numbers, by the look of his screen.

'Not yet, no. He wasn't at the briefing.'

Janie pulled out her phone and swiped it awake. No answer to the message she'd left, and no texts from him either. 'Anyone know where he is?'

Lofty's shrug might have tilted the earth's axis, but it was also a simple answer to her question. 'The hospital maybe?'

That would be it, of course. How could she forget? And if he was in the coma ward then he'd have switched his phone off.

'Well, if you see him tell him I'd like a word.' She bent down the better to see the columns and figures on the screen. 'What you got there?'

'Bank records for Alistair Hamilton. Or at least I think they are. Thought he was a drug addict with no money. This suggests otherwise.'

Janie looked closer, but still couldn't make head nor tail of the numbers. Except that they were all quite large.

'What's the story then?' she asked.

'Well, this account has substantial sums paid in and taken out on a fairly regular basis. Money seems to come from a number of overseas clearing banks, so likely foreign payments. It's never quite enough to make someone take notice, but add it all together and there's hundreds of thousands moving through in the past year.'

'Hundreds of thousands?' Janie put her emphasis on the first word. 'Not hundreds, not thousands. Do the money-laundering boys know about this?'

'Aye, well, they do now. I've had a word with the team at the NCA. They're very interested.'

'What about withdrawals?'

'Some of it's going to the same few accounts. We'll trace them, see who they belong to. There's quite a bit being taken out as cash though, which is strange given that Hamilton didn't even have a bank card in his wallet when we found him.'

'Seem to recall he had very little money on him. Just enough to buy himself a coffee. State of him, you'd not think he had two beans to rub together. So who's using this account?'

'Nobody.' Lofty reached for the mouse, scrolled down to the end of the page where a line of zeroes filled the bottom cells. 'It was cleaned out and closed down the same day he died.'

'Shit. The boss is going to have to see this.' Janie took her phone out, still surprised at the lack of texts. She dialled the number, got the same voicemail, hung up without leaving another message. It took her a little longer to find the next number, and when she dialled it took a while to negotiate with the receptionist to be put through. Finally, after some toe-curling hold music, a tired voice came on the line.

'Neurology ward. Nurse Robertson speaking.'

'Oh, hello. It's Detective Sergeant Harrison here. I think we might have met before. I was wondering if I could speak to Detective Inspector McLean.'

The silence at the other end of the line was probably only a second, but it seemed to go on for a lot longer. Too long.

'I'm afraid Tony – the detective inspector's not here.'

'He's not?' Now a cold hand gripped Janie's stomach. 'Has he just left? When did you last see him?'

'I've not been long on shift. Hold on a moment.' The line went muffled as the handset was pressed against a nurse's uniform. Janie looked down at Lofty, who raised a questioning eyebrow, but before she could say anything to him, Nurse Robertson was back. 'Tony's not been in since the day before yesterday. Doctor Wheeler phoned him last night, told him there'd been no change and we'd let him know if there was. I'm afraid Emma's still much the same as she was yesterday.'

Janie thanked the nurse, grateful that she didn't seem too worried at the DI's unexplained disappearance, and then ended the call.

'He's not at the hospital?' Lofty asked.

'Hasn't been there for a while.'

'So where is he then?'

Janie looked around the room, quiet in the absence of most of the detectives. 'I really have no idea.'

It didn't take long to ascertain that DI McLean wasn't in the building. A quick call down to the duty sergeant confirmed he'd not signed in that morning, let alone out again. Janie checked his office, all the same, then carried on to DCI Ritchie's when she found it empty. The detective chief inspector was sitting at her conference table on the far side of the room, papers strewn around her like she was a general studying the battle plan for a doomed campaign. She looked up as Janie knocked lightly on the door frame.

'Hey, Janie, what's up? Didn't see you at the morning briefing.'

'I got a call. Had to go deal with it. Maggie Devlin. You know, Rory Devlin's wee sister? She remembered some more stuff about her brother, thought it might be useful.'

'And is it?'

'I don't know. We already knew a lot of it. Where he worked before he went off the rails. She reckoned she could pinpoint the actual event though. Some kind of training weekend organised by our old chums the Dee Foundation.'

Ritchie sat up a little straighter, a frown creasing the pale lines where her eyebrows had once been. Apparently she'd lost them in a fire and they'd never grown back, if the station gossip was to be believed.

'That sounds like something Tony would be interested in. Have you spoken to him about it?'

'That's what I was coming to see you about. I can't find him anywhere, and he's no' answering his phone.'

Ritchie's frown deepened. 'Maybe he's at the hospital? Not that he often remembers to turn off his phone when he's visiting the wards.'

'Tried them, and he's no' been there in a couple of days.'

'Strange.' The DCI picked up her phone and swiped it awake, stared at the screen for a moment before she put it back down again. 'He's not tried to contact me either. Last I saw him he was sneaking away from the Project Tantalus launch. Kind of wish I'd managed to escape too. I got cornered by the Cabinet Secretary, and not in a good way.'

Janie wasn't entirely sure there was a good way to be cornered, certainly not by a senior politician, but she kept that to herself. 'You think he's away doing something he shouldn't be?'

'Tony?' Ritchie gave out a half-hearted laugh. 'That's an almost racing certainty. But doesn't he usually drag you or one of the detective constables into those sorts of things?'

'Aye, he does. Or at least bangs off a text to tell us not to worry. That's when I usually start worrying.'

Ritchie looked at her phone again, drummed her fingers on the tabletop for a few seconds. 'I'm sure he's fine, but if he's not answered his phone by lunchtime it might be an idea to drop round his house and see if he's there. Sure it's nothing, but he's been in an odd mood recently, and all the stuff with Emma can't be helping.'

Janie nodded her agreement. 'I don't know how he keeps going at all. I'll pop round later if he's not shown up.'

'Meantime, what's your next move on the drugs case? Grumpy Bob tells me you dug up some useful information on Alistair Hamilton.'

'Aye, we did. And Lofty's found out some interesting stuff from his bank account. That and the lips makes me wonder if Hamilton's no' quite the same as the other two.'

'Lips?' Ritchie raised another invisible eyebrow.

'Did you no' see the report? From Ang— . . . the pathologist? Apparently Hamilton developed horrible blistering on his lips post-mortem. Like he'd drunk something caustic, you know?'

The detective chief inspector had gone very still, and now she brought one hand up to her own lips, touching them lightly with two fingers. 'When did you know about this? Why didn't he tell me?'

'Think it was yesterday? The day before? You were over at Gartcosh all day, but that's why the DI got me looking into Hamilton, asked Grumpy Bob to help too. Why is it important?'

'An old case, a few years back. I got sick, thought I was going to die but Tony . . . Did something. I'm not sure what, but it helped. Or I managed to kick whatever foul bug was killing me.' Ritchie shuddered slightly, as if reliving some horrible memory, her hand going up to her throat as if she was clutching a string of pearls. Like someone had walked over her grave, as Janie's mum would probably say.

'Would this be the same case where Sandy Gregg's house exploded? And Grumpy Bob . . . ?' Janie left the question hanging.

'If Detective Sergeant Laird wants to talk about it, I'm sure he will. But yes, it was the same case. And our old friend Mrs Saifre was right at the heart of it. Not that we could ever prove anything, mind you. People as rich as she is never seem to have difficulty finding alibis.'

'Or lawyers, I assume. MacFarlane and Dodds seem to be her preferred solicitors, and there's something very dodgy about the land she apparently owns in Straiton.'

'Yes, Lofty Blane brought us all up to speed on that at the briefing. Not quite sure what to make of it though. It all happened a good decade or so after the body was buried on that land, and at the end of the day it was only one man's word ranged against a lot of impressive title deeds and lease contracts. If you ask me, it's more likely something Dalgliesh distorted than Saifre, much as it pains me to say it.'

'Maybe I should ask her,' Janie said.

'Who, Saifre? Oh, you mean Dalgliesh. Good luck getting any help out of her.'

Janie checked her watch, the morning moving on too quickly for her liking. 'Well, I need to talk to someone at the Dee Foundation too, probably not the boss woman though. I'd like to know more about these training camps they run and who's involved.'

'You think it's relevant? I mean, it's not as if they're the ones making and distributing this new drug.'

'No. But it's possible Rory met someone there who was connected with it. If I can get some names I can see if any of them have come to our attention before.'

'Judging by the type of people the Foundation gives help to, a lot of them will have some form of record. Probably juvenile, and that's a pain getting them unsealed.' Ritchie tapped the table again. 'Do what you think's best, Janie. But keep an eye on the cost, OK?'

She couldn't quite decide whether the morning had been unproductive because people were unhelpful or because she was constantly checking her phone and the clock on the CID room wall. Janie had wasted the better part of an hour getting the runaround from the Dee Foundation while trying to find out more about the training courses. Eventually she'd given up and handed the job over to DC Stringer to deal with. So much for the spirit of co-operation between the Foundation and the police that Project Tantalus was supposed to be about.

There hadn't been much more progress on Alistair Hamilton either. The bank account had thrown up more questions than answers, although the consensus now was that Hamilton's name and address had only been used to give it legitimacy. There were occasional small cash withdrawals, mostly from a machine around the corner from the Newington flat, but the last one had been fifty pounds a week before the young man had died, and the account itself had been closed shortly after. It seemed fairly certain that Hamilton had been making Demon's Breath in his Newington tenement, but equally he was only a small cog in a much larger machine. He remained a cypher, and as Janie stared up at the clock again, Inspector McLean remained missing.

She almost didn't answer the call when it came in, the ring tone on her phone not one of the ones she'd programmed for people she knew. Picking up the handset, she didn't recognise the number either, but answered it just in case.

'Hello?'

'Would that be Detective Sergeant Harrison I'd be speaking to?' A vaguely familiar voice. Female, just about. Hoarse and croaky as if whoever was speaking had spent a lifetime shouting, smoking, or both.

'Yes. Who is this?'

'Ah, that's right. We've no' really spoken that much. It's Jo. Jo Dalgliesh.'

'How on earth did you get this number?'

'That's no' important, Sergeant Harrison. What is important is where your boss has got to.'

'I . . . You know where he is?'

'No. That's the whole point, isn't it. I've been trying to call him all morning but he's no' answering his phone. Seems you don't know where he is either, an' that's a worry.'

Janie looked around the CID room, its collection of desks largely empty as the detectives went about their business. There was no reason to feel guilty about talking to the reporter, and yet a part of her cringed all the same.

'Why did you want to speak to him?' she asked.

'Well, he asked me to do a little digging for him, an' I know I good as told him to fuck off, but I may have had a wee snoop all the same.'

'Digging? Into what?'

'Your man Hamilton. The one who had a fit in the shopping centre and put everyone off their food? Tony reckoned he'd fallen in with a bad crowd, an' he was no' far wrong.'

Janie leaned forward, grabbing a notebook and pen. 'How'd you mean?'

'Seems he got himself thrown out of the university chemistry department for using the lab facilities to brew up some interesting wee chemicals. That would be about four years ago now, mind. And I've no' managed to find out anything else about him.'

Janie put the pen back down again. Although the information was interesting, it wasn't perhaps all that useful after all. 'I'm surprised we never turned that up ourselves.'

'Aye, well. They hushed it all up, apparently. Didn't want to lose their Home Office licence or something. Seems they only found out what he'd been doing because he sold some dodgy stuff to another student and she ended up in hospital after she'd had a seizure. Sound familiar?'

Janie picked the pen up again and scribbled some notes this time. 'Horribly familiar, aye. Thanks for letting me know. Listen, Ms Dalgliesh –'

'Call me Jo, why don't you.'

'I . . . Well, Jo. While I've got you on the phone, I was wondering if I might ask you something. About a story you wrote a while back, maybe twenty years.'

A silence at the other end of the line made Janie think she'd said something wrong, but then there was a noise like a great exhalation of breath before the reporter spoke again, the timbre of her voice slightly different. 'Memory's no' what it used to be, but sure. Try me.'

'It was a piece about some farmland down near Loanhead. How the old –'

'Oh fuck. No' Glenside Farm? Old John Robson? Jesus, I've no' thought about that in a while. What d'you want to know about it?'

'I don't know, really. Anything. Everything. What happened to the farmer's nephew? Didn't he try to fight his corner?'

Another short silence and then that exhalation. Janie remembered now, the electronic cigarette always either in the corner of the reporter's mouth or fidgeting between her fingers.

'Andy, aye. Andy Robson. Poor bastard. He didn't have much to go on, really. His uncle'd told him the farm was his. Shown him some papers that might've been anything, really. End of the day, though, all that went up wi' the farmhouse and Old John. Oh, he tried to fight it, for a while.'

'Did you believe him, though? I mean, you wrote the piece like you believed him, but . . .'

'But I'm a tabloid hack wi' no conscience?' Dalgliesh laughed, the mirth turning into a gurgling cough that went on longer than was healthy. 'Aye, actually. I did believe him. An' it made no sense either. I mean, he was no farmer, Andy. He didn't want the land, no' even the house. He'd have sold up to the first person waving cash in his face, and we all know that woman's no' short of cash.'

'Sai—'

'Best you don't name the devil; she'll only come a-calling if you do.' Dalgliesh made it sound like a proverb, although not one Janie had ever heard before.

'So what happened to him then? The nephew, Andy, did you say?'

'Aye, Andy. Poor bugger got hit by a car. Drunk driver, if I remember it right. Why're you interested?' There was a pause, but before Janie could find a way to explain, Dalgliesh put the pieces together herself. 'Oh, right enough. That body you found on the building site. Of course. I should have thought about it. That land would have been part of the farm, most likely. An' old John Robson would've still been alive when the body was buried. Interesting.'

Janie didn't like the sound of that last word, but there wasn't much she could do about it, and before she could even get another word out, Dalgliesh was talking again.

'Well, it's been a nice wee chat, Detective Sergeant . . . Janie, isn't it? Aye, that's right. You tell Tony what I've told you. And maybe tell him to remember what happened the last time he ignored my calls.'

Janie was going to ask what that was, but she never got the chance. Without even so much as a 'bye bye' the reporter was gone.

49

The house looked no different to the last time she'd been there; still ostentatiously large, elegantly proportioned and ever so slightly forbidding. Growing up on a council estate many miles from this most upmarket part of the city, Janie couldn't easily imagine what it must be like to live here. She didn't want to even think about how much it was worth.

Stepping out of the car, the first thing she noticed was how quiet it was. Never entirely silent, still the city's background rumble was muted by the trees, the rustle of their leaves in the wind as effective at soundproofing as any expensive noise-cancelling headphones. Quite a few of those leaves had turned brown and begun to fall, scattered over the gravel drive and parking area like debris from an explosion in a cardboard factory.

Emma's Renault Zoe was parked up by the old coach house, a snaking cord connecting it to a charging point that looked quite out of place in this turn of a different century building. It gave Janie a little hope that the detective inspector was simply at home nursing a sore head, although deep down she knew it could never be anything so easy with him. The dead leaves on its roof suggested the car hadn't been anywhere in a while.

She went to the front door first, tugged the brass bell pull and heard the jangle of noise echo in the hall beyond. Nothing happened, no sound from within. Then she heard a clatter in the direction of the back door, turned in time to see one of the black cats appear around the corner. It stared at her, head bobbing up and down ever so slightly as if it couldn't quite make her out. Hadn't she read somewhere that cats had very bad detail vision, being better tuned to low light and movement? Stupid thought – she dismissed it with a shake of the head. The cat arched its back, more of a stretch than a threat, then walked around in an exaggerated circle before disappearing the way it had come. A moment later Janie heard the clatter again, recognised it as the cat flap.

An invitation, then. She followed the cat's footsteps. Should have gone straight to the back anyway; McLean never used the front entrance. She peered in through the small panes that formed the top half of the door, just about making out the utility room through the ancient, thick glass. Knocking elicited no response, so she tried the handle.

It wasn't locked.

The creeping sense of unease that Janie hadn't really noticed before began to grow as she pushed open the door.

'Hello? Anyone home? Detective Inspector McLean, sir?'

She felt a bit foolish using his title, but equally didn't feel 'Tony' was appropriate either. It didn't matter, as there was no response. The door through to the kitchen stood ajar, but Janie waited a moment, straining her ears for any sound, even the telltale beep of an alarm about to go off. All that came was the gurgle of the old range cooker.

'Hello?' she tried again, louder this time as she crossed the utility room and went into the kitchen. The first thing she noticed was teapot, milk jug, empty mug and plate with a half slice of toast on it. The top was off the butter dish, and judging by the mess one or both of the cats had been licking at the butter for some considerable time. They both looked up at her from the threadbare old rug that lay in front of the cooker, as innocent as anything that inky black could ever be. Neither of them seemed at all perturbed by her intrusion.

Dragging her attention away from them, Janie took in the rest of the room, trying to see it with detective's eyes rather than as a place she'd sat and joked with people before. McLean had eaten toast and drunk tea, both of which could have been breakfast or late supper knowing him. His briefcase sat on one of the chairs pulled slightly out from the table, but it was closed. His jacket wasn't on the back of the chair he'd been sitting in to eat, as she'd seen him hang it before. And then she saw what she should have noticed first off. His phone, face up beside the teapot. What possible reason could he have for leaving that behind?

Taking a step back, Janie considered the utility room once more. Something had caught her attention, but not enough to register as she entered the first time. Now she saw it almost immediately. A pair of smart leather brogues looked quite out of place among a line of old wellingtons and muddy walking boots underneath a row of coats. It was possible the detective inspector liked to take off his shoes in the utility room and had a comfy pair of slippers waiting there for him, but Janie didn't think it likely. Time to call it in.

'I think he must have gone out to do something. Left his phone on the table, so he probably wasn't planning on going far.'

It hadn't taken long for DCI Ritchie to arrive after Janie had called her, and she'd brought Grumpy Bob along with her. Janie hadn't got far; a quick check of the house to see if McLean had collapsed in a room somewhere. That had felt weird, even if it was necessary. Now they all stood together in the kitchen awkwardly, the cats continuing to ignore them.

'You've checked the whole house?' Ritchie asked. 'Even the attic?'

'I didn't even know there was an attic. Why would he be up there?'

The detective chief inspector didn't answer, already heading out through the kitchen door and into the front of the house. By the time Janie caught up with her, she was taking the stairs a couple at a time. On the landing, she pulled open what looked like a press cupboard to reveal narrow steps leading further up. Ritchie didn't stop, her shoes clumping on the bare wooden steps in her hurry.

'Well thank fuck for that,' the DCI said through heavy breathing as Janie joined her in a large but cluttered attic room.

'Umm . . . What's going on?' she asked.

'You know how Tony's always limping slightly, trying to pretend his hip doesn't give him grief?'

Janie had, but thought better than to mention it. She nodded, then looked around the attic room as Ritchie explained further.

'Well he broke his leg. Up here in this very room. Falling off a chair.' Ritchie leaned into a corner and pulled out a broken plain wooden wheelback chair. 'This very one, unless I'm mistaken. He'd slung a rope over that beam up there and tried to hang himself.'

Janie had been half staring at the window in the gable end wall, but she turned to face Ritchie now. 'He what?'

'He claimed he was under some kind of hypnosis, but there were rumours for a while. There'd been a spate of young folk hanging themselves, and, well . . . It wasn't an easy case on any of us. The way Tony's been lately, I was worried when you said you'd found the house unlocked and his phone on the table.' Ritchie glanced up at the beam and then down at the dusty floor beneath it. 'Seems I may have jumped to the wrong conclusion. Still doesn't help us find out where he is.'

Janie stared at the spot under the beam where the detective chief inspector stood, unsettled by the story about DI McLean.

He had always seemed so centred, solid and reliable. To think that he'd come so close to dying, here in his own home and maybe even by his own hand . . . Was it her imagination, or did the room feel colder? She dragged her attention away, moving to the window and the excellent view of the garden it afforded.

'That's the Hermitage down there, isn't it?'

'What?' Ritchie walked over to where she stood. 'Oh, yes. I think there's a gate in the back wall.'

'That gate standing open there?' Janie pointed through the trees, and Ritchie bent low the better to see. From the ground it would have been obscured by rhododendron bushes, but from here it was as plain as the day.

'Think we'd better go and have a look, don't you?'

The wind had picked up, whipping the tops of the trees as they stepped out into the garden, although at ground level it was calm and peaceful. Grumpy Bob hadn't followed Janie and the DCI up to the attic, no doubt reasoning that it was a lot of effort for little reward, but he came outside with them both.

'Bit parky isn't it?' He rubbed his hands together, blowing on them before shoving them deep into his pockets.

'You can stay inside and look after the cats if you want, Bob,' Ritchie said, but the ex detective sergeant merely shook his head and set off across the leaf-strewn grass. It was, Janie had to admit, an impressive garden full of mature shrubs and surrounded by tall trees. The kind of place that took many years, a great deal of effort and no small amount of money to create. But then, if she'd got her facts right, the house had been in McLean's family since it was built well over a hundred years earlier, maybe two hundred. Architecture had never been her strong suit.

'What on earth do you think he was doing coming out here?' Ritchie asked as they approached the iron gate, hanging open in the substantial wall that kept the general public out of this little piece of paradise in the city.

'There was a body dug up in one of the walled gardens down there,' Janie said. 'Ancient bones, according to the pathologist, so not our responsibility. I know the detective inspector went to the site yesterday morning, talked to that archaeology professor friend of his about it. Maybe he went to have another look?'

'There's got to be an easier way, surely?' Grumpy Bob stepped through the arch in the wall with an exaggerated leap to one side, avoiding stepping on the central path like someone well versed in negotiating potential crime scenes. Not that there was much of a path beyond the wall, only a small area of scrubby ground that swiftly gave way to thick bushes.

'Someone's been through here though.' Janie joined Grumpy Bob on the other side, crouching down to better see the muddy ground and a clear boot print. She followed the direction it seemed to be leading, but it was hard to tell if there might once have been a path or not.

'OK, I'm calling in a Crime Scene team. You two, back in here.' Ritchie had her phone out, but didn't make a call until they had both stepped carefully back into the garden. Janie looked up at the house, its windows blank eyes. If only they could speak of what they had seen.

In hindsight, Janie realised she'd heard the car coming for quite a while before it actually appeared. Checking the coach house and other outbuildings while waiting for the Crime Scene team to arrive, she'd noticed a low rumble growing steadily louder, but it wasn't until something large began to inch slowly up the drive that she finally paid attention.

It wasn't the Crime Scene team, that much was for certain. Janie knew her cars, perhaps better than even most of her male colleagues. Her uncle ran a successful garage business, one of her brothers working alongside him now, and she'd grown up around the smell of grease and old engine oil. Still, she'd never seen anything quite like the car that came to a halt beside the front door.

Pre-war, for certain, it looked like something from an Art Deco poster. Low and sleek with a long louvred body swooping up into a perfectly proportioned teardrop rear. Ticking over, the engine made only the slightest of low waffling noises, twin plumes of steamy exhaust billowing up into the cold air. When it fell silent, Janie could still hear the faint plink of metal as it cooled down. She slowly closed her mouth, fallen open in surprise, as the door opened and a familiar figure climbed out with Swiss finishing-school elegance.

'Detective Sergeant Harrison. Janie. I'm so very glad to see you here.'

Madame Rose wore a heavy coat, her hair tied up in a Paisley pattern headscarf, face as ever immaculately made up. She closed the car door, glanced once at the house.

'Rose. I wasn't expecting . . . The detective inspector's not –'

'Not here. No. I am well aware of that. As I am well aware that it shouldn't have been possible for him to disappear. Not from here, of all places.'

Janie opened her mouth to ask both how Madame Rose had known DI McLean was missing and what exactly she meant. Neither answer would have been of any help in the current situation though, so she closed it again.

'Do you know when he was last seen? Is anyone looking for him?' Rose took a step towards the front door, then seemed to remember herself and started towards the rear.

'DCI Ritchie saw him last night around nine. He was leaving a reception outside the city. Must have made it home as the car's here.' Janie pointed at the little Renault Zoe, looking rather outclassed by Madame Rose's extravagant carriage. 'It looks like he went for a walk into the Hermitage in the dead of night. Can't think why he'd do that, and it's not as if you can get far before it's impenetrable bushes anyway.'

Rose stopped walking when she reached the corner of the building, which at least saved Janie the awkwardness of having to tell her this was being treated as a potential crime scene and she really shouldn't be here. The medium looked around, head raised slightly as if she was sniffing the air.

'The Hermitage, you say?' she asked after a long moment.

'Aye. He was down there yesterday morning. Apparently they found more buried bones when they were digging up one of the walled gardens for restoration. At least they're ancient, like the ones in Leith. Something for the archaeologists to worry about rather than us. We're run ragged enough as it is, without another body . . . Is everything OK, Rose?'

Janie put out a hand to help the medium as she took a balancing step to one side. Madame Rose grabbed her like a woman fainting in some Victorian melodrama, her not inconsiderable bulk almost toppling both of them to the ground. Somehow they managed to stay upright, and in a few short seconds Rose regained her composure.

'I'm so sorry, my dear. That was most unbecoming of me. But the Ladies' Garden, you say? How could I have not known?'

'Why should you have known? I don't think it's been widely reported yet.'

Rose stood a little straighter, took her hand from Janie's shoulder. 'I should have sensed it the instant she was uncovered, like I did with poor old Izabell and dear Emily.'

'Umm. How did you know the bones were a woman's?'

The medium turned her full attention on Janie, a stare that whilst not withering was uncomfortable. 'Janie, there are things you are perhaps not ready to accept, let alone understand. Things Tony refuses to accept even if he does understand them, on some level. Suffice it to say that these buried bones as you call them, they are there for a reason. These women gave themselves as sacrifice to be sentinels, to protect the city from forces that would turn it into something evil and rotten. And I . . .' Rose let out a sigh, took in another breath like the finest of ham actors. '. . . I am supposed to be their guardian. And I've failed in that.'

Janie wasn't quite sure how to respond, but fortunately they were both interrupted by first one, then the other of McLean's two adopted cats clattering out through the cat flap to see what all the fuss was about. They approached Madame Rose like an old friend, tails high and rubbing cheeks against her wool-stockinged calves. Neither of them gave Janie much more than a second glance before both of them sauntered off to the parked car and sat down beside the door.

'Well, at least my visit won't be completely wasted then.' Madame Rose walked back to the car, opened the door and let the two cats jump inside. Janie caught a glimpse of leather seats the colour of oxblood.

'You might want to move anyway,' she said. 'There's a Crime Scene investigation team on its way, and they're never as careful parking the van as they are with the evidence.'

Rose smiled, albeit briefly. 'I will take these two miscreants away, then. And see if I can't delve deeper into this mystery. Someone is playing a nasty game here, Janie. Someone with a deep understanding of the ancient ways. Keep your wits about you or I fear we may fall.'

50

When her phone rang and she saw the name that popped up on the screen, Janie almost left it to her voicemail. It had been too strange a day for her to deal with personal matters on top of everything else. The last thing she needed was some awkward apology from Johnny Wendle. On the other hand, he had been part of an earlier investigation that was still ongoing. What if this was important? Reluctantly, she snatched up the handset.

'Detective Sergeant Harrison speaking.' Well, might as well start things off formal.

'Ah . . . Yes . . . Detective Sergeant. Hello. It's Johnny here. Johnny Wendle?'

He sounded so flustered, Janie could almost forgive him for the 'tranny' comment. After all, the rest of the evening had been fun, and spitting out a mouthful of wine all over her hadn't really been his fault.

'Mr Wendle,' she started, then relented. 'Johnny. How are you?'

'I . . . I'm fine, I think. Listen, I'm really sorry about the other night. I didn't –'

'Johnny, it's OK. No need to apologise, but if that's what you're calling about, I'm kind've busy right now.'

There was a moment's silence on the line, underscored by DC Bryant clattering into the CID room, seeing Janie on the phone and quieting down with an apologetic shrug of the shoulders.

'I'm sorry. No. I mean, yes, I was calling to apologise, but that wasn't the only reason. It's about the building site. Where we found those bones.'

That got Janie's attention. She sat up straighter and grabbed her notepad. 'What about it?'

'It's . . . Well, it's difficult to explain. But I was going over some of the work done, and you're going to think this sounds weird, but there's some odd anomalies in the foundation pour for the house that was delayed.'

'The one where the bones were actually dug up?' Janie asked.

'Yes. I wasn't on site when they backfilled the hole and poured the concrete, but . . .' Wendle paused again, much to Janie's frustration. Why couldn't people just get to the point?

'Look, don't take this the wrong way, Janie. Detective Sergeant. But it would be a lot easier if I could just show you?'

'What, now?' Well, it was an unusual chat-up line, she had to admit that.

'Best done in daylight, and we've only a few hours of that left. I wouldn't think twice about it, but after what you said about . . . our benefactor, well, I did a bit of due diligence. Probably should've done that before getting involved in the first place, only the deal was so perfect.'

Janie could hear the tone of his voice change as he spoke, and it occurred to her that Johnny Wendle, all six foot six of him or however unfeasibly tall he was, giant, rugby-playing Johnny Wendle, was scared. Maybe there was hope for him after all.

'Give me half an hour, aye? Maybe forty minutes for the traffic.'

* * *

Despite her best efforts, it took a good hour to get to the building site. The weather had turned, dark clouds leaching the last of the afternoon light from the sky and threatening a deluge at any moment. Janie was glad of her heavy coat and stout boots as she clumped up the metal staircase to the top Portakabin office and knocked before pushing open the door.

'Oh, it's you.' The secretary looked up from her desk as Janie stepped inside, her stare less friendly than a guilty suspect in an interview room. Before she could make any response, the door behind had opened and Johnny Wendle appeared. Almost as if he'd been waiting. Well, the walls in these cabins were paper thin, and he'd probably heard her boots on the steps.

'Traffic bad?' he asked, trying for a nervous smile even as he glanced at the secretary. Janie wasn't sure what was going on there, but it wasn't the normal boss–employee dynamic she was used to. Almost the other way around.

'I'd forgotten about the roadworks on the brae.'

Wendle nodded as if that was explanation enough, grabbed a hi-vis coat from a hook beside the door. 'Well then. Might as well give you the tour before the rain comes on.'

He swept past her, opening the door and ushering her out before she could ask what he meant. His last glance back at the secretary confirmed that something was going on, but she still had no idea what.

'The tour? I thought there was something specific you wanted to show me.'

'There is, but Eileen there is one of you-know-who's staff. I thought she was just an agency secretary when we started on the project, but either I'm getting paranoid in my old age or she's spying on us all and reporting back. Less she knows about this the better, so I told her you were interested in buying one of the flats.'

Janie looked around the building site. To the north, the

bypass was a constant motion of cars and trucks, a dull roar that would maybe quieten a bit at night, but start again well before anyone really wanted to get up. To the east, the big box warehouses of the shopping and industrial estates dominated the skyline, separated from the estate by yet more dual carriageway. At least there were green fields to the west, although for how much longer remained to be seen. And south stood the old farmyard with its collapsing barns and burned-out farmhouse. She'd not paid much attention to it the last time, but knowing it had stood like that for twenty years, knowing the old farmer had burned to death there, sent an involuntary shiver through her that had nothing to do with the strengthening wind.

'Think I prefer my tenement flat, to be honest.' She rubbed her hands together for warmth. 'Can we get this over with, aye? It's been quite the day already.'

Wendle nodded, leading her down the steps and over to a little two-seater buggy that looked a bit like a golf cart on steroids. 'Quicker if we take this.' He indicated for her to climb in, then settled himself behind the wheel. Prepared for a spluttering, noisy and smelly two-stroke engine, Janie was pleasantly surprised to find the machine was electric. Less pleasantly surprised when they drove off in the opposite direction to the building plot where the bones had been dug up.

'I thought –'

'We're being watched.' Wendle shook his head slightly. 'Probably shouldn't have done so much reading up on our benefactor. She seemed so charming when we first met her. You have to believe me, Janie. If I'd known . . .' But he didn't say what he would have done, and she couldn't help wondering if the lure of big money might have worked on him anyway.

'So we go round the long way, is that it? Maybe have a look in one of the flats in case anyone else is watching?' She'd meant it sarcastically, but Wendle grinned with relief all the same. He drove the little buggy right to the centre of the development, where a couple of four-storey apartment blocks were taking shape, then worked his way around the edge of the site until they finally arrived at the plot. A lot of work had gone on since Janie had last been here, the hole filled in and foundations poured. The house was still a long way behind all the others though, topsoil scraped back to the harder packed subsoil, but none of the infill rubble and sand or concrete slab yet.

'What am I looking for?' Janie asked as they both climbed out and approached the spot where Emily Worstead had lain undisturbed for thirty years. The foundations had been widened, presumably to compensate for the disturbed ground, but it was another spot a short way off that Wendle pointed out.

'You saw the site when it was all dug up, right? They had all manner of high-tech equipment. Ground-penetrating radar, that sort of thing. Surveyed the whole area, but only found anything worth digging up around the bones.'

'Aye, I remember well enough.'

'We had to make good the hole so the foundations would be safe. Engineers moaned at me for hours about it, and the accountant wasn't too happy about the added cost. So you can imagine my surprise when I found out someone had dug a wider hole further along the founds here.' Wendle jumped down into the shallow trench. Its base was a neat pour of concrete waiting for the blocks to be laid, but instead of showing the wider section, he walked a half-dozen paces south and held his hands out like a fisherman exaggerating his catch.

'So someone can't read a plan? Can't operate a digger properly?' Janie stepped down onto the concrete herself, half expecting it to suddenly be liquid and suck her down into the earth.

'It's possible, but I was here the afternoon before the pour. I supervised them filling up the hole and making good, and this area hadn't been dug over again. The only reason I wasn't here for the pour itself was because my car broke down. I didn't come to check this until after lunch. Soon as I did I could see someone had been mucking about. The only question is, why?'

Janie looked at the ground, trying to see the difference Wendle was referring to. It was a bit like those archaeology shows Manda made her watch, where they pointed to a bit of brown dirt and seemed to know immediately what was natural and what had been turned over by a spade. The light wasn't good, clouds so low overhead they hid the tops of the Pentland hills nearby, but even so she could make it out easily enough once she got her eye in. Someone had dug a hole and then very carefully filled it back in so that it looked just like the rest of the foundation trench. A hole about two metres long and maybe a little over a metre wide. Very much like a grave, in fact.

A horrible thought passed through her mind, bringing with it a chill that went to the pit of her stomach. 'Help me up out of here, will you?' She took out her phone and did a quick search through her contacts.

'Who are you calling?' Wendle asked as he lifted her almost bodily out of the trench.

'An old friend, to ask for a favour. And I'm afraid you're not going to like what I want her to do.'

51

'Lucky you caught me when you did, Janie. I was just on my way out for a training session.'

Janie had known Constable Susan Brewster since they first crossed paths at Police Training College, too many years ago now to think about. They weren't best friends, but they'd kept in touch, and bumped into each other often enough for Janie to have Susan's phone number. And to beg a favour from time to time.

'Well, I hope I've not given you a wasted trip, but there's something I'd really like your dogs to have a sniff at.'

The dog handler had parked at the secondary site entrance on Johnny Wendle's suggestion, a set of tall wire mesh gates locked shut with a thick chain and padlock bigger than Janie's fist. It was closer to the house plot than the main entrance, and had the added benefit of not being immediately visible from the Portakabin offices.

'You said cadaver, so I only brought Toby.' Brewster opened the back of her van, leaned in to fix a lead to a patiently waiting spaniel. 'He's the best, mind. So where's this disturbed ground you think might be suspicious?'

'This way.' Wendle indicated the direction, all the while looking nervously around as if he had no right to be here, rather than being the man in charge. Brewster picked up on his anxious behaviour instantly, no doubt used to watching her dogs for any signs something was wrong.

'We all OK to be here?' she asked as they walked around the edge of the building site towards the plot.

'Johnny's just worried we might shut his building site down again,' Janie said, then pitched her voice a little higher so Wendle could hear. 'Isn't that right, Johnny.'

He almost jumped out of his skin. 'Sorry. Just a bit nervous around dogs.'

Janie let him have the lie, or half-truth. He had called her in, so he must have had his suspicions and wanted to be on the right side of things this time despite what it might cost him. That was certainly to his credit, and his anxiety gave her a shield for her own. She was trained not to jump to conclusions, to deal in hard fact rather than supposition. But the truth of it was someone had dug and then covered up a grave-sized hole almost exactly where they had found bones buried before. And Detective Inspector McLean was still missing.

'This'll be where you're wanting us, I take it?' Brewster asked, and Janie saw both that they had reached the plot and that Toby the spaniel was almost quivering with excitement. That he wasn't straining on the lead was testament to how well trained he was.

'Aye. There were bones dug up here a while back, but they'd been in the ground thirty years. That won't confuse him will it?'

'No. Old bones aren't that interesting. Not like in the cartoons. They much prefer something with a bit of meat still on it.' The dog handler crouched beside her charge, stroked his ears a couple of times and whispered something to him before letting slip the lead. Like a bullet, Toby took off towards the foundation trench, nose stuck firmly to the ground, head swishing from side to side as he followed the scent. He passed over the area where Emily Worstead had lain with barely a pause, heading straight for the freshly dug patch, where he stopped so abruptly his back legs lifted off the ground for a moment. A bark, a scratch at the concrete, then he sat down, tail wagging furiously.

'I'd say that was a positive result,' Brewster said as she crossed the ground to where the dog sat. Toby waited for her, his entire body shaking in excitement as she slipped his lead back on and gave him a rewarding cuddle.

'What does that mean then?' Wendle asked Janie. He had his hands shoved deep into his trouser pockets and looked as dejected as a lovesick teenager.

'It means that there are human remains under your building again, I'm afraid.' Janie pulled out her phone, tapped the speed dial for the Control Centre, which was less than a kilometre away now she thought about it. 'This has just become an active crime scene.'

It was impressive to see how swiftly things happened once Janie had put in the call to Control. Perhaps she wasn't the only one with the disappearance of DI McLean at the back of her mind. No, front and centre of her mind, she couldn't deny it. Even if it was the least likely of many possibilities that it might be his dead body down there.

Within minutes a pair of squad cars had turned up, two old sergeants and three constables cordoning off the building plot. Johnny Wendle offered the services of a mechanical digger, no doubt deciding it was in his best interests to be as helpful as possible. By the time DCI Ritchie arrived, the poured concrete had been removed and a mound of dark soil was beginning to pile up to one side of a fresh hole.

'What on earth's going on, Janie?' were her first words when she reached the small group of people standing close enough to watch without being in any danger from heavy machinery. Quite a few builders had wandered up to see what was going on, and

Janie was fairly sure she'd spotted Eileen the secretary nosing about for a while, although she was nowhere to be seen now. Gone to report to her mistress, most likely.

'This is where Emily Worstead's bones were found,' she said, knowing as she did so that it wasn't much of an explanation. 'Johnny here called me when he found out someone had been doing a little extra excavation.' She nodded at the tall man, who seemed unable to take his eyes off the hole that was appearing in his building site, and quite possibly his profit margin too.

'And you thought it both prudent and a good use of our scarce resources to call in a cadaver dog?' Ritchie asked.

'Susan – Constable Brewster's an old friend. Figured this could be just a training exercise off the books if it didn't turn anything up.'

'But it did. So now I'm going to have to square everything with the chief superintendent and get yet another investigation up and running.'

For a moment Janie thought she was being shot as the messenger, but Ritchie squared her shoulders and tried to give her a smile. 'You did good work here, really. I just wish we could catch a –'

'Looks like we've got something here.' The words echoed up from the trench, suddenly loud as the digger's diesel engine cut out. Janie took a step forward, then another, until she was standing at the edge of the pit. Two of the Crime Scene team had clambered down into it with spades and were carefully clearing earth away from something. Then as if they were mind-linked, they both stood up, backed away, leaving a clear view to the bottom.

A face stared up from the earth like some kind of nightmare, eyes and mouth open but caked with fine, dark soil. Janie could just see the fingertips of one hand off to the side, and it was impossible not to imagine it clawing upwards, digging out of this unmarked grave like a zombie. Even so, despite knowing that this image would haunt her nightmares for years to come, she let out a low sigh of relief. Someone had died here, most probably been buried alive.

But it wasn't Detective Inspector McLean.

52

Nobody was going to get much sleep any time soon, of that Janie was sure. Even if she went home and climbed into bed, she'd still see that dead face staring at her, one hand clawing for the air as if the unnamed victim had fought as the earth dragged him down. Now she knew why so many detectives turned to drink. They'd left the immediate area as the light finally gave way, the scene floodlit and in the hands of the experts. Now they were in the process of setting up a temporary incident room in one of the nearly finished blocks at the centre of the site. Kickstarting a new investigation into life with some borrowed trestle tables and a moveable whiteboard that still had a rude drawing on the flip side. It was important to move fast with this one, before those responsible could cover their tracks.

And still there was no word from DI McLean.

'We need a list of all the people who've worked here in the past two weeks. I want to interview every single one of them. We've got everyone who was here when we discovered the body, right?'

DCI Ritchie had taken charge, putting together a small team that seemed to have been poached mainly from the Rory Devlin, Alistair Hamilton and Fiona McLeod investigations. As yet, they didn't even have an identification for the dead body, although they knew that it was male, probably late teens or early twenties.

'They're no' happy about it, but as best we can, aye.' Janie had seen the men and women clustered around the Portakabins, eying the closed and locked site gates and making angry noises. Johnny Wendle was doing his best to keep them calm. 'We'd better get them processed as quickly as possible. Longer we leave it, more chance there is some of them slipping away. Lots of casual labour on a site like this. Once they're gone they'll be a pain to track down.'

'OK. We'll get that done first. Split into teams of two. A sergeant and a constable in each. I'll take Jessica with me.' Ritchie flipped open her notebook and started to scribble things down. 'We need names and addresses, of course. What part of the site they were working on, what their shifts were. Pretty much guaranteed the gossip will have spread by now, so there's no point trying to cover up what we're looking into. Anyone gives you any lip, tell them they're welcome to continue the conversation at the station.'

'Any idea when we might get an ID?' someone asked. Janie thought it might have been DC Bryant, but she was having trouble distinguishing voices over the hubbub.

'We haven't even got the body out of the ground yet.' Ritchie looked at her watch. 'Pathologist was still at it when we left the scene. Should be finished there by now, and he's going to do an initial post-mortem examination as soon as he can. Until we get the body cleaned up, we can't go public with photographs. You've all seen them, so you'll understand why. Last thing we want is the press printing that and giving folk nightmares.'

Janie glanced up at the whiteboard, where a series of A4 prints had been stuck to the top. Like a time lapse horror movie, the body emerged from the mud face and hands first, then neck, chest and finally the rest. He'd been naked, skinny but not malnourished. Short-cropped ginger hair and the pasty complexion of a native. Nobody who'd seen his face so far had recognised it, even after the mud had been carefully cleaned away. Someone, somewhere had to be missing a son, a brother, a friend.

'Can we get an artist's impression?'

'Sandy Gregg's already on it. We're on to missing persons too, but our first priority has to be interviewing everyone here before they start slipping away. Establish a timeline, see what Angus has to say about cause of death. OK people, let's get moving.'

Darkness had fallen completely by the time the last of the site workers was allowed to leave. Of the ones Janie had spoken to, a few had been angry at being held back from going home for so long, but most had been muted, shell-shocked even. It didn't take her long to work out that someone had managed to snap a few photographs of the body as it emerged from the dark soil, and these had been passed around quite freely. No doubt they'd be all over the internet already. So much for waiting until the body had been cleaned up before releasing an image for the press to circulate.

At least it confirmed for them that whoever had been buried under the foundations of the final house had not been one of the workforce. Almost everyone who had clocked in that day had been interviewed, with a couple of notable exceptions. Eileen, the secretary who appeared to frighten Johnny Wendle so much, had managed to disappear. An officer sent to her house had reported back that it was locked, no one home. Nobody had spoken to Wendle himself either, although he was still on site. As far as she was concerned, he wasn't a suspect. Quite the opposite; she was considering whether he might need to be taken into protective custody given the stories he'd heard about people who upset the woman bankrolling this project.

That thought niggled away in the back of Janie's mind as she sat in the makeshift incident room, glad that the building they had commandeered was close enough to completion to have its power and water connected. She wasn't sure where the mug had come from, but she was grateful for its warmth and the caffeine hit as she stared dully at the Cookie Monster image painted onto it. She'd murder for a cookie right now, though maybe not try to dispose of the body on a building site afterwards.

'Reckon that's everybody interviewed.' DCI Ritchie strode into the room with far more energy than Janie felt. 'Going to have to check them all against our records, but it's a start. Not much else we can do now until the post-mortem's been carried out. An ID would be useful, cause of death too.'

'Nothing from Mis Per that fits the profile yet?' Janie tapped the screen of her phone, seeing a few notifications but none of them relevant.

'Not that I've heard. Still, if he's only been dead a short while it's possible nobody's noticed him gone yet.' Ritchie pulled out a chair and sat down. 'You should go home, Janie. You look all done in.'

'Waiting for my second wind. And it's not as if we're overstaffed right now.'

Ritchie rubbed at her eyes, her earlier energy seeping away. 'Aye. I'm starting to get worried too. Tony's never done anything like this before. I mean, sure, he pushes himself far more than is healthy, but he's always got his shit together.'

'That's not what Grumpy Bob tells me. Way I heard it when his fiancée died they had a bit of an unofficial suicide watch going on for a while.'

Ritchie looked at her as if this was something she'd never heard before. Maybe it was. For a moment she said nothing, then shook whatever thought she was having away. 'Emma's not dead. She's not the victim of a serial killer, and Tony's twenty years older now.'

'So where is he?'

'I wish I knew. There's no sign of him in the Hermitage. It's like he just got up and walked out, leaving everything behind.'

The silence stretched between the two of them for a while, both of them lost in their own thoughts on the matter. Perhaps inevitably, when Janie started to say something, Ritchie spoke at exactly the same time.

'Why –'

'What –'

They both stopped, then the DCI nodded. 'You go on.'

'Why would someone bury a body out there?' Janie waved one hand in the direction of the building plot. 'Why that particular spot when we'd dug up another body just a few days ago?'

'Could be they thought it was unlikely anyone would look there twice. The ground's already been disturbed, after all.'

'Oh, I know that. But why there? Why now? There's building work all over the place where you could hide a body if that's all you wanted to do. Whoever put that poor lad in the ground there has to be linked to this site in some way. Am I making too much of a connection to say they had to have chosen the site because of the other bones?'

'You mean, hearing about it on the news gave them the idea?'

Janie shook her head slowly. 'Not exactly, no. I told you Madame Rose dropped by Tony's house not long after you and Bob had left, aye?'

Ritchie's cocked head suggested that Janie might have overlooked that particular report. 'Rose? What's she got to do with all of this?'

'She was quite upset, actually. Don't think I've ever seen her . . . I don't know, baffled? Is that the right word? But she said something. I kind've dismissed it at the time. Just the way she speaks you know? Riddles and portents and omens.' Janie might have slipped ever so slightly into a mimicry of the medium's Morningside accent.

'The forces of evil are afoot tonight. That sort of thing?' Ritchie's attempt wasn't quite so effective, but then she was an Aberdonian so it was hardly fair.

Janie almost laughed, but couldn't quite bring herself to. 'Something like that. But it was what she said about the bones. I guess I was thinking that when Johnny called me about what he'd found here.'

'Johnny is it? Is there something I should know, Janie?'

'No. Not really. He's OK maybe. Bit too self-centred though. A few questionable views, too.' Janie shook the thought away, not quite sure why she was even discussing the man. 'Point is, Rose said the bones were here for a reason. That they were supposed to be sentinels, keeping watch over the city or something.'

'You don't think she's snuck out here in the dead of night and put that young lad in the ground, surely.'

'No. That's not it at all.' Janie squeezed the sides of her Cookie Monster mug as she struggled to find the right words for something she couldn't quite get her head around in the first place. 'What I mean is, what if the discovery of Emily Worstead's bones wasn't an accident? What if we were meant to find them, take them away. Then someone else comes and buries new bones right where they were. Not just getting rid of Rose's sentinel, but replacing her with something else.'

Ritchie stared at her for a long while, not unfriendly but not giving anything away either. When she spoke, it was almost as if she was the sergeant and Janie the chief inspector, her tone was so measured.

'You . . . You don't believe in all that stuff, do you?'

Janie looked at the bottom of her empty mug, hoping there might be an answer to that question there. She'd seen so much she couldn't explain in the past few years, but then she couldn't explain how her phone worked either.

'It doesn't really matter if I believe it or not, does it? If whoever's doing this believes it. That's what matters, aye?'

'You've been working with Tony McLean too long.' Ritchie shook her head. 'You sound just like him.'

Janie ignored that, unsure whether it was a compliment or an insult. 'It's true though. Rose believes the bones, the old bones, Emily Worstead, that wifey we just found in the Hermitage – oh shit.' She was on her feet, grabbing up her phone before the thought had finished forming in her head. The mug tumbled over, a small dribble of coffee staining the tabletop.

'What?' Ritchie asked, but Janie had already dialled the number and clamped the phone to her ear. It rang once, twice, then picked up.

'Susan? It's Janie again. Aye, I'm sorry, I know it's late. But do you think Toby's up for a wee bit more work?'

53

The gates to the Hermitage were closed, but a harassed-looking warden climbed out of her car to greet them as Janie piloted the electric Nissan into the car park, closely followed by Constable Brewster's dog van. It had been a fraught half-hour, the sense of urgency building even though an hour, a day, a week would make no difference. And there was always the possibility that she was embarrassingly wrong, too.

'You're here for the building works?' the warden said as she strode up towards them, working her way through a sizeable collection of keys until she found the right one.

'Detective Sergeant Harrison.' Janie held up her warrant card so the warden could see it under the street lights. 'There's something we need to check.'

'An' it can't wait till morning?' The warden shrugged a complaint, but unlocked the smaller of the gates anyway.

'We might be needing to get vehicles in,' DCI Ritchie said, earning another weary shrug from the warden.

'I'll come in with youse. Gonnae have tae lock up once yer done.'

'Fair enough. Maybe you can show us the way then.'

They brought torches, but even so the darkness seemed to close in on them as they moved further into the deep glen. The clouds overhead had an orange tint to them, silhouetting the treetops as they waved about in the wind. Janie was no great reader of weather, but it felt like rain was on its way. At this time of year that was a near racing certainty.

'Surprised to get your call, you know. There's already been a dog team in here today,' the warden said as they walked along the darkened path towards the Ladies' Garden. 'Something about a missing person? Didn't find anything, mind.'

'Aye, I know.' Janie didn't add that she'd been part of that search team, combing the thick undergrowth and steep slopes from McLean's house down to the Braid Burn in case he'd fallen in the dark and knocked himself out. 'This is something a wee bit different. Least, I hope it is.'

Nobody said much as they walked deeper into the gloom. When the signpost loomed out of the darkness, the first thing Janie saw was the familiar logo and the words 'Funded by the Dee Foundation' alongside. Someone had sprayed that horned-devil sigil next to it, the paint running down the board like tears. Bloody thing was everywhere in the city these days.

Toby the spaniel had his nose down, eagerly snuffling about even though he was still on the lead. The group made their way through machinery and piles of building materials until they came to the edge of the walled garden. Janie looked up at the trees again, trying to work out where the detective inspector's house was from here. Despite her having been here during the day, it was almost impossible to tell.

'Do we know where the body was found?' Constable Brewster asked, playing her torch across the interior of the walled garden. It wasn't a vast area, maybe a third the size of a football pitch, but in the near total darkness the mounds of earth from various works took on monstrous form and size.

'This way,' Ritchie said, pointing her torch beam at a path that led towards the far wall. Somewhere close to the middle, as best as Janie could judge, an area of earth lay cleared of all over-growth, tilled like the finest of beds in her grandad's allotment.

'I was surprised to find they'd filled it in so soon, but apparently the archaeology team said they were done. Took all the bones off to the lab for analysis. Nothing else to see.'

'Well, let's give Toby a chance, shall we?' Constable Brewster motioned for everyone to step away from the area of tilled ground, then crouched down beside the quivering dog. Janie watched as Toby sprang forward, quartering the small area in scant seconds and letting out excited little yelps all the while. It was all over in moments, as he scratched at the ground in the dead centre of the patch, barked, and then sat down.

'I think that's another positive,' Brewster said after she'd called the dog back to her and given him his reward. 'There's a body or body parts down there. Stake my reputation on it.'

'Dear God, what's going on in this city?'

Janie looked around from her cold seat on a pile of cut stones at the edge of the Ladies' Garden to see Detective Superintendent McIntyre approaching from the direction of the main entrance. She hopped down off her perch, wincing as her muscles pro-tested, and went to greet her superior officer.

'Looks like another body's been buried where we found ancient bones. Took them a while to get the lights set up properly, so they've only just started digging.'

'Could they not have just waited until morning? If there's someone dead down there they're not going anywhere are they?'

'Detective Inspector McLean's still missing, ma'am.'

Janie hadn't wanted to say it out loud, but there was no avoiding the subject any longer. He'd been gone more than twenty-four hours, and this fresh grave was only a few hundred metres from his last known position.

McIntyre's shoulders slumped. 'Aye, there's that I suppose.

Even so I don't think Gail's going to be too pleased about the cost of all this. And you've another site out Straiton way, I hear. Been busy, Detective Sergeant.'

From the detective superintendent's tone, Janie could tell that it wasn't an admonishment. But neither was it a congratulatory pat on the back. She was well aware that the workload was spiralling out of control, so it only followed the budgets would be creaking under the strain too.

'I wish I'd been wrong the first time, honest. And that was nerve-wracking enough.'

'Any update on that body? I don't suppose we've anything as useful as an ID yet.'

'It's at the mortuary now. PM's scheduled for first thing tomorrow.' Janie glanced at her watch to check that she didn't mean today. Not yet, but not by far.

'You should go home, Janie. Get some rest and come back at this sharp in the morning.'

'Aye, I know. But there's no way I'm going to get any sleep until I know who's down there.' Janie nodded her head in the direction of the digging. No heavy machinery here: a team of Crime Scene technicians were excavating carefully using spades. Judging by how little of one of them she could see, they'd got down a fair distance already. But then the ground had been recently dug over.

'And you think you'll get any sleep once you know?' McIntyre asked, dragging Janie's attention back to the conversation. That was a sure sign she was too tired, losing her concentration.

'I just don't want it to be him,' she said, and glanced up at the dark shapes of the treetops so high overhead.

McIntyre placed a hand on her shoulder, and Janie noticed for the first time that she was wearing soft black leather gloves. Sensible, given the chill in the air, although at least the rain had held off so far.

'None of us want that, Janie. Well, maybe PC Carter, but no.'

It was a poor joke in bad taste, but Janie smiled anyway. 'I spoke to Hattie Turner about the dig over in Leith. She says they're still excavating and nobody's buried anything yet. But we should get someone there, just to check, you know?'

'I . . . What?'

'You know, the old kirkyard? Where they were doing the archaeology for the tramline extension. That was the first body dug up, right? What if someone's put something back in that pit that shouldn't be there?'

McIntyre removed her hand from Janie's shoulder, turned to face her. 'What are you talking about?'

'The bones. The ancient bones. They had to have been put there for a reason. That woman in Leith, the woman here. Emily Worstead out at Straiton. What if they're all connected? What if this is meant to undo whatever it was that burying them did?' Janie wasn't quite sure where the words came from, or how she could let them tumble out of her like that. Perhaps she was more exhausted than she realised, her brain twisting logic to make sense out of the senseless, the mystic mumbo-jumbo ramblings of a self-styled medium and fortune teller.

'Janie, I really think –'

'We've got something here.'

The shout from the excavation site stopped McIntyre from whatever it was she had been going to say in response to Janie's outburst. The two of them looked over to where one of the men with spades was helping his colleague out of the trench. Without a word, they approached, stepping around a neat mound of piled earth for a better look into the bottom of the pit.

McIntyre let out a gasp, but Janie had seen something similar already that day and was a little better prepared. Her first thought, half guilty, was one of relief that the face emerging from the loam was not that of Detective Inspector McLean after all. Her second, as she took in the details, the closed eyes and full lips, soft, dirty cheeks, thin nose and wisps of blonde hair, was that this was a young woman taken far too early from life. And her third, almost instant, was a shock of recognition.

'I've seen her before. Recently, too.'

But where? Try as she might, stare at that lost, almost peaceful face, Janie couldn't quite make the connection.

54

The Major Investigations room was quiet, despite being surprisingly full for half past five in the morning. Janie had managed to grab a coffee on her way in, and guarded it with her life as she stumbled through the collected plain-clothes and uniform officers to the front. DCI Ritchie and Detective Superintendent McIntyre were already there, looking remarkably well rested for what could only have been about four hours' sleep.

'Morning, Janie.' Ritchie raised one missing eyebrow at the coffee. 'Brought enough for everyone?'

'There's no' enough coffee in the world just for me. Never mind anyone else.'

'Fair enough.' Ritchie reached around to the table behind her and picked up her own mug, little tendrils of steam rising off the milky surface. 'Shall we get this show on the road?'

It didn't take much to call the room to order, McIntyre addressing everyone first.

'As you'll all no doubt be aware, thanks to some unorthodox policing on the part of Detective Sergeant Harrison, we've uncovered two freshly buried bodies, both in deep graves where ancient bones were found only recently.'

Janie wanted to point out that Emily Worstead had only

disappeared thirty years ago, so technically her bones weren't ancient. Wisely, she kept her mouth shut. No point in drawing even more attention to herself than the detective superintendent already had.

'The first body is that of a young male, approximately twenty years of age. The second is female perhaps a little younger. Both are caucasian and buried naked. No obvious signs of how they died. Post-mortem examinations will be carried out soon, but we are treating both cases as murder until I hear otherwise. You don't dump a body like that if they've died of natural causes.

'Photos of both victims are for our use only at the moment. Sandy Gregg's sorted some artist's impressions and we've put them out to the newsrooms already. I'll be heading up a press conference at six.' McIntyre checked her watch. 'So I'll leave you to the tender mercies of DCI Ritchie. But one more thing, since I know you all want to ask. Yes, Detective Inspector McLean is missing. No, none of the senior officers know where he's gone or why. He was last seen at a function outside the city, around nine p.m. the night before last. We know he arrived home at some point after that. I can't make any further comment than that, but be on the lookout, OK?'

Murmurs rumbled around the room, the first positive sign of life in some of those present. Two dead bodies was nothing compared to a missing DI. The noise faded away swiftly as DCI Ritchie stood to address them all.

'Two bodies buried in the last twenty-four hours. We need IDs and cause of death, but we also need to know how they got to where they were buried. Neither place is particularly hidden, so someone must have seen something. I want teams out knocking on doors in Straiton and around the Hermitage. We've follow-up interviews with all the workers on the building site to do, and there's an all-ports notice on a Miss Eileen Kennethmont, who disappeared around the same time the first body was discovered. We've got good CCTV coverage for both sites, but there's a lot of it to go through. Overtime won't be a problem here, so get cracking everyone.'

'What's the connection, though? That's what I can't see.'

Janie sat at her desk in the CID room, trying not to fall asleep while she waited for the call from the mortuary to let her know when the post-mortems were going to be carried out. She had one of the crime scene photographs on her computer screen, the young woman buried in the Ladies' Garden. Cleaned up by the pathologist as he'd examined her in situ, her face was even more familiar than when she'd first seen it emerge from the soil. And yet for the life of her, Janie couldn't think where she'd seen her or when.

'What was that?' She looked up to see DC Mitchell standing on the other side of her desk.

'These two bodies, right? They've got to be connected. Can't be a coincidence they've both ended up buried like that in what? Twenty-four hours?'

Janie half looked at the detective constable, half looked at the dead woman's face. She was so tired it was hard to think straight, so she used one of DI McLean's tricks. 'Go on.'

'Well, I was wondering. Two bodies, right? Both buried in places where we found old bones not that long ago.'

'You been talking to Madame Rose?'

'Madame who?' Mitchell tilted her head a bit like Toby the spaniel.

'Never mind. I'll introduce you some day. She's an old friend of the boss with some very strange ideas. She reckons the old bones were sentinels or guardians or something whacky like that.' Janie realised she was babbling and stopped herself. 'But your point?'

'Well, first it's strange we found those bones at all. They were both uncovered by accident, weren't they? The building site and this renovation down in the Hermitage?'

'And the ancient bones under old Leith kirkyard, too.' Janie reached for her notepad and scribbled on a fresh sheet. 'I meant to ask Constable Brewster to take her cadaver dog over there. Clean forgot last night.'

Mitchell frowned at that. 'Would a cadaver dog not struggle in a kirkyard? Surely it's full of dead bodies anyway.'

Janie had to admit she had a point. 'I don't think they're particularly fresh though, are they? Not still burying people there. Certainly not in the bit that's under the road.'

'True.' Mitchell nodded. 'But the point is, we've found lots of old bones recently, and now someone's replacing them with new bones. Still very much part of their bodies, but you get my meaning, right?'

Janie gave a shrug, her concentration still half on the image of the dead woman on her computer screen.

'So what connects them all?' Mitchell asked. 'There has to be a connection, doesn't there?'

Something clicked in Janie's mind then. The dead face finally slotting into a time and place, still very much alive. 'The Dee Foundation,' she said, alarmed at how high-pitched and squeaky her voice sounded.

'The Dee Foundation?' Mitchell echoed. 'Isn't that a bit far-fetched? I mean, they're a charity. They look after people, not bury them in unmarked graves.'

'No, this.' Janie pointed at the screen so that Mitchell had to walk around the desk to look. 'This woman. I knew I'd seen her somewhere, and it was at the Dee Foundation's outreach centre in Wester Hailes. She was there when we went to talk to them about Fiona McLeod. Me and DI McLean. And . ...' Janie's voice trailed away as another image formed in her head. Late last night, walking through the Hermitage with DCI Ritchie, PC Brewster and the warden who'd unlocked the gates for them. The sign for the restoration work. Funded by the Dee Foundation. And then there was Johnny Wendle, accidentally spraying her with a mouthful of good red wine when she mentioned the name of his mysterious benefactor, Jane Louise Dee. The odd history of how she owned the land when someone else claimed it was theirs.

'Who paid for the archaeological dig for the tramline extension?' The question came out before she'd had time to follow the thought through. 'No, forget that. It's the city paying for it, but I'd put good money on one of Saifre's companies being involved somewhere along the line. Or she's had a hand in planning the exact route.'

'I'm afraid you've lost me, Janie.' Mitchell's words cut through the whirling thoughts in her head, and Janie looked up to see an expression of puzzled concern on the detective constable's face. Was that the same look she gave DI McLean when he came up with his mad hunches and illogical connections? The ones that so often turned out to be right? It probably was.

'Sorry, Cass. My brain's too tired and too wired on caffeine, but there's definitely something we have to follow up here.' Janie waved a finger at the screen. 'This woman was at the outreach centre. I'm sure of it. She was working in the kitchens. Serving a meal to a bunch of young lads.'

'You want to head over there and talk to them?' Mitchell asked, at the same time as Janie's phone screen lit up with a text. She picked up the handset and took in the message.

'Later. They'll be busy running their breakfast club right now. And besides, I've a hot date in the mortuary.'

Janie hadn't witnessed many post-mortem examinations in her career as a detective, something for which she was quite grateful. Seeing the two bodies laid out side by side, with just enough space between the tables for the pathologist to fit in between, brought home the horror of the situation far more forcefully than their discovery in separate graves.

'Two different bodies, two different sexes, but on the face of it these two are remarkably similar.' Angus Cadwallader stood between them both one hand hovering over each cadaver like he was some magician about to perform a particularly gruesome trick. Janie had kept her distance, but approached the nearer of the two, the young woman she was convinced she'd seen at the outreach centre.

'I'd put both of them in their late teens or early twenties. Generally in good health, although undernourished. Neither of them had eaten in the twenty-four hours before they died, either. X-rays don't show up any signs of past injury, no fractured bones or anything useful like that to help identify them, I'm afraid. And there's no sign of bruising or contusions where they might have been beaten or tied up.'

'Do we know what the cause of death is?' Janie asked.

'I was getting to that. It's not a pretty picture, I'm afraid.' Cadwallader stepped out from between the two bodies and went over to the screens hanging on the wall that took the place of the old light boxes. He tapped a keyboard with a gloved hand and brought up some images Janie took a while to recognise.

'Both had mouths and nasal passages full of dirt, as might be expected given how they were buried. However, I've found particles of soil deep in their tracheas and even their lungs. Coupled with the fact that they both died of asphyxiation, I can only conclude that they were buried alive.'

The mortuary was always cold, but in that instant Janie felt like it had dropped several degrees, and even the gentle whoosh of the air-conditioning system seemed to fade away to silence. The pathologist let it grow for a while before finally speaking again.

'Horrific, I know. Makes me shudder to think of it, and I've seen pretty much everything in my years here.'

'But you said they showed no signs of injury, no contusions from being tied up,' Janie said, her words earning her a bright smile.

'Top marks, Detective Sergeant.'

'So, what? They climbed into those graves, lay down of their own accord and let someone bury them?' Janie heard the edge of terror in her voice, the creeping claustrophobia that would likely haunt her for months. Longer even. And was it her imagination, or was she finding it harder to breathe all of a sudden?

'It looks very much like that was the case. So they must have been drugged. I've sent blood samples off for analysis, will let you know as soon as I've any results. But the best I can come up with is what you said. They lay down in those graves and let someone pile the earth on top of them. I can only hope they were so far out of their minds at the time they felt nothing.'

'Which begs a lot of questions, not least of which is who did this to them? And why?'

'Those, my dear, are questions better suited to Tony McLean.' Cadwallader frowned. 'I take it there's still no news of his whereabouts.'

Janie shook her head, glanced up at the clock above the main door of the examination theatre. 'Nothing, and it's been well over twenty-four hours now. I'm very worried, Angus. He's had a lot on his mind lately, what with Emma and –'

'Now let me stop you there, young lady.' The pathologist cut across Janie's words like the scalpel he wielded on his patients. 'There are a lot of things you can call the detective inspector. Stubborn, for sure. A bit of a loner, certainly. Not one for following the rules, I'm sure most of his colleagues and superiors would agree. But suicidal, even under intolerable pressure? No. Scrub that idea from your mind. If he's gone walkabout of his own volition, then he has a very good reason for not getting in touch with anyone to let them know. And if he's not gone of his own volition . . .' Cadwallader let out the last of his breath in a sigh.

'We have to hope that whoever's got him wants him alive?' Janie asked.

'That we do, Janie. That we do.'

55

'You got a moment, Janie? Think you might want to see this.'
Tired beyond reason, it took Janie a bit longer to respond than was polite. DC Stringer looked worse than she felt, but there was a spark in his eye that suggested something interesting might have come to light.

'Sure, what is it?'

'Well, you know how you asked me to track down some information about those training weekends the Dee Foundation was running for the Jobseeker kids?'

It took her a while to spool back through her memories, her brain apparently made of cold treacle, but eventually she did. 'Aye, right enough. Maggie Devlin said her brother'd been on one and went off the rails right after. You get anywhere?'

'Not with the Foundation, no. Best I could get out of them was an email telling me that, and I quote, the youth-training programme was closed some months ago following an incident at a weekend camp. No indication as to how many months or what the incident was, and no response to any follow-up emails either. Not exactly the spirit of cooperation the chief superintendent was harking on about, is it?'

'Aye, I've found that with them too. If there's anything we can do for them, we're supposed to bend over backwards.

See when we ask for something back, it's all "new phone, who dis?"'

Stringer smirked at the joke, then turned serious. 'Well, I'm not so easily fobbed off, as you know. I went and had a chat with the boss man, Mr Woolley, at Alba Fulfilment Solutions. You remember, the place where Devlin was getting his work experience?'

Janie nodded, wondering where this was going.

'I must have got him at a bad moment, or a good moment depending on your point of view. Think he'd just had a bit of an argument with the boss lady at the Foundation.'

'What, Jane Louise Dee?'

Stringer laughed. 'Christ, no. Not her. She'd never get her hands dirty. No, this was Ms Susan Llewellyn, I think. Met her when me 'n' the boss first went there to talk about Devlin. Right old battleaxe. No offence.'

Janie hadn't been about to take any, but Stringer bringing it up made her wonder if she should. On the other hand, she'd met Llewellyn too, unless there was more than one working for the Dee Foundation, and battleaxe was probably a fair description.

'So what did you find out?'

'Well, first thing, the boot camps used to take place on farmland between Straiton and Bilston. Old Pentland, I think it might be. Sound familiar?'

'Glenside Farm?'

'The same. He wasn't sure exactly what they got up to, but the weekends were popular up until about six months ago. Before that the youngsters would come back full of enthusiasm, work harder, get decent job placements. Something changed though, and a lot of them were dropping out of the programme. Those that stayed were more trouble than they were worth. Least, that's what he said. Soon after that they cancelled the whole thing.'

'So, around about the time Rory Devlin went off the rails. What the hell happened out there?'

'Your guess is as good as mine. But I've something that might be useful. Just came in so I've not had a chance to look at it properly, but Mr Woolley emailed me the dates and lists of names for the weekends. I've pinged it over to your email.' Stringer pointed a finger at Janie's computer, and when she brought up the mail program, sure enough, there it was.

'Let's see what we've got then.' She clicked on the email, saw a line of attachments along the bottom, not much text to explain what it all was. Janie knew she should run this all past Mike Simpson in the IT department before opening any of them, but they had firewalls and malware shields and all manner of other things beside. Just to be on the safe side, she made sure the attachments were downloaded, then disconnected her laptop from the local network. Only then did she double click the first icon.

It was the information that she had been trying to get out of the Dee Foundation ever since she'd spoken to Maggie Devlin. A series of dates, each with a list of names. She scrolled down the screen, not recognising any until Rory Devlin appeared. The date was spot on for when Maggie had said her brother changed, but it was the names of the Dee Foundation staff in attendance that caught Janie's attention. Llewellyn had been there, as she appeared to have been for all of the weekends. There were a couple of other names that appeared regularly, but that particular boot camp had seen another member of staff helping out. Fiona McLeod.

'Hang on a minute.' Janie brought up the report she'd prepared after she and DI McLean had talked to McLeod's neighbour, checked the dates. They matched perfectly. Fiona McLeod had lost her job at the outreach centre a couple of days after the same weekend trip that had affected Rory Devlin so badly he'd turned to drugs. And she had turned to drugs too, apparently. Or rather, the same very unusual drug.

'I think we need to get Ms Llewellyn in for a little interview session,' she said, not much relishing the prospect but hoping maybe DCI Ritchie or better yet Detective Superintendent McIntyre might be persuaded to do the actual questioning.

'What about that file there?' Stringer poked his finger at the screen and a pdf file whose name was what looked like a random string of digits and numbers. Ah well, in for a penny, in for a pound. Janie clicked it, and the document opened up.

'Your man Woolley must have been really pissed off with the Dee Foundation,' she said as she stared at the first page of a long document. It was a CV, of sorts. A young offender by the name of Tavish Kiernan. His glowering mugshot looked out at her as Janie took in the details: his date of birth, address, blood type, offence records that should have been sealed, given they were crimes committed before he came of age. Scrolling down, she found yet more details about Tavish, and then similar records for another one of the Dee Foundation's clients. And another, and another.

'Should we be looking at this?' Stringer asked, even as he leaned over Janie's shoulder and drank it all in while she slowly scrolled down through the pages. And then stopped.

'Shit, Jay. We need to see DCI Ritchie right away.'

Staring out from the screen, angry eyes challenging whoever might be looking at her for a fight, was the young woman whose body had been dug up from the Ladies' Garden in the Hermitage the night before. Sophie Dornan was barely eighteen, and had been in and out of care since she was eight. What a horrible way to end such a miserable, wasted life.

'What, exactly, are you trying to say, Detective Sergeant?'

Janie had gone to DCI Ritchie's office hoping for a quick

meeting and to hash out a plan of action given the new information they had received. She hadn't bargained on Chief Superintendent Elmwood being there, even less so on her taking a keen interest in this new development.

'It's about these bodies we found yesterday, ma'am. We've got pretty positive ID on one of them. The woman's name is Sophie Dornan. I'm sure I saw her at the outreach centre in Sighthill when I was there with DI McLean looking into the Fiona McLeod death.'

'Yes, I gathered that from when you burst in here unannounced, like some overexcited toddler. What I want to know is how you came about this . . .' Elmwood waved a hand at the printout Janie had made before coming to see the DCI. '. . . information.'

'Is that important?' The words were out before she could stop herself, the chief superintendent's 'toddler' jibe and general air of hostility putting her off kilter.

'I should think it's crucial, Detective Sergeant. Especially given what you seem to be implying.'

Keep calm, Janie. Count to ten in your head, just like DI McLean taught you.

'I'm not implying anything, ma'am. All I'm doing is pointing out that we have some useful information that needs following up.'

Elmwood sat at the conference table, her chair angled around so that she could face Janie. DCI Ritchie was on the other side, two cups of coffee and a large amount of paperwork spread between them. Contrary to the chief superintendent's word, Janie had knocked first on the open doorway before stepping into the room, and she hadn't delivered her news until it had been asked for. By Elmwood. Now the chief superintendent glared at her as if she were something unpleasant on the bottom of her shoe.

'You have an unidentified source supplying you with unverified information that implicates a prestigious city charity in . . . I really don't know what. Is this some feeble attempt to undermine the good work we've been doing? I know Detective Inspector McLean is no fan of Project Tantalus, but I hadn't realised the rot had spread so far within his team.'

'With respect, ma'am, that's –'

'I've no time for your "respect" Detective Sergeant.' Elmwood emphasised the inverted commas with her fingers. 'What is it you actually want to do with this . . . information?'

Another swift count to ten, although for the life of her Janie couldn't understand the chief superintendent's hostility. From the look on DCI Ritchie's face, she couldn't either, although as yet she had not come to the detective sergeant's rescue.

'I want to speak to someone at the outreach centre, ma'am. Confirm the woman we found is Sophie Dornan. I want to show the photos of the young man we found to as many people there as I can. See if they know who he is. I want to speak to someone who will tell me what it was Fiona McLeod did that got her fired, and what the incident was that made them stop running their youth-training programme weekends. All of these things should be a piece of cake, given our close working relationship with the Dee Foundation due to Project Tantalus. And yet every time I call them, I get the runaround. My emails go unanswered.'

The chief superintendent tried to raise an eyebrow, her plastic-like skin doing no more than twitch in a manner that put Janie in mind of a reanimated corpse. Now that she was close, studying Elmwood's face as she waited for an answer, she could see that the woman was not well. Makeup and plastic surgery hid the worst of it, but it could only go so far.

'Is that all?'

Janie opened her mouth to say 'I'd really like a look around the buildings at Glenside Farm, get a feel for the place where this mysterious incident is supposed to have taken place', but she managed to stop herself in time.

'Yes, ma'am,' she said instead.

'Then I'll phone Susan Llewellyn and set up a meeting. Just as soon as you tell me who's been leaking information to you in a deliberate attempt to paint the Foundation in a bad light.'

'I . . . What?'

'Gail, is that really necessary?' DCI Ritchie finally decided to chip in.

'I'd have thought of all people you'd understand the need for this cooperation, Kirsty. We can't very well go asking the Foundation for information and hold back on them at the same time now, can we?'

That sounded very much like what the Foundation had been doing to them so far, but Janie kept that to herself. 'I –' she started to speak, but a rap of knuckles on the door frame stopped her. All eyes turned to see DC Stringer clutching a thicker sheaf of printouts. Janie had left him working his way through the records he'd been sent, so it was more than likely he'd found something important. His eyes widened a little as he saw the chief superintendent.

'Sorry to disturb. But I think you need to see this.'

'More nonsense about the Dee Foundation?' Elmwood might have rolled her eyes, but the lack of animation in her face made it hard to tell.

Janie ignored her. 'What is it, Jay?'

'Well, I was going through that stuff like you said, and I found this.' Stringer walked only as far into the room as was necessary to hand a printed sheet to Janie, as if he didn't want to risk being savaged by the chief superintendent. She found she couldn't blame him.

'That's Daniel Ferguson.' The detective constable nodded at the page Janie was now holding. 'Twenty-one years old, lives in a halfway house up Joppa way. Lived, I should say. Nobody's seen him in a couple of days. Probably because he's in the cold store at the city mortuary.'

'The other victim?' DCI Ritchie moved swiftly around the conference table for a better look. Janie couldn't help noticing that Elmwood struggled to stand, unsteady on her feet. She leaned heavily against the back of her chair, and the hand she held out for the printed sheets trembled.

'There's more,' Stringer said. 'Both Ferguson and Dornan were on the Dee Foundation's youth-training programme, and both attended the same weekend training camp as Rory Devlin.'

'These are confidential papers, Detective Constable. How did you get hold of them?'

Stringer looked to Janie for support she felt ill positioned to give, but another piece of information caught her eye and gave her a little hope she might be able to face down her ultimate boss.

'See who was on the staff at that training camp, too.' She jabbed a finger at the page, angled it towards the chief superintendent. 'Your friend Susan Llewellyn, and a certain Fiona McLeod. Ma'am, I think we're past the coincidences stage here. This needs proper investigation.'

'I . . .' Elmwood forced herself to stand straight, and Janie prepared for the tirade. But even as she watched, something seemed to go out of the chief superintendent. As if there had been a light behind her piercing grey eyes and it had just been switched off. Her shoulders slumped and before she could collapse entirely, DCI Ritchie was at her side, one hand ready to catch her. She waved it off irritably, but it was a weak effort.

'Are you OK, Gail?' Ritchie asked.

'I'm fine. Just a bit disappointed in your team, Kirsty. First McLean goes AWOL, and then all this.' She waved her hand again, even more ineffectually. 'Go do what you think's best, then. But don't come moaning to me when it all blows up in our faces.'

And, without another word, she limped to the door and away.

'Is she . . . ?' Janie stared at the open doorway for a moment, then back at DCI Ritchie, who shrugged.

'I think she's been trying to pretend she's fine ever since she came back to work, and it's all catching up with her now. But she's the boss and we do what we're told. Right?'

Janie couldn't tell whether Ritchie was joking or not. Her humour had always been deadpan, but then again this didn't feel like the right time for it.

'We still need to follow this up.' She flapped the sheets of paper against her free hand, all too aware that Stringer had many more.

'You never did say where you got it from, but, aye, you're right. Something stinks here and it's coming from the chief super's beloved charity. Colour me surprised there.' Ritchie pointed to the conference table. 'Come, sit. Let's thrash out a plan of action. I've a feeling things are about to get a bit fraught here, so the more prepared we are the better.'

Janie did as she was told, DC Stringer pulling out a chair for himself too as DCI Ritchie cleared away whatever it was she and the chief superintendent had been discussing. In its place, she laid out the printed sheets showing the details of Daniel Ferguson, Sophie Dornan and Rory Devlin.

'I don't suppose Alistair Hamilton's in there, for a full house?' Ritchie asked.

'I wouldn't have expected him to be. I don't think he's part of this at all. Well, no' the way you're thinking. Just a distraction.'

'How do you figure that?'

Janie counted out the points on her fingers. 'He's a long-term user, where Devlin wasn't, and it doesn't look like either of our new bodies were either. He's so off the grid we've had a hell of a time tracking him down. His financials are well dodgy. Oh, and he got kicked out of university for using the chemistry labs to brew up illegal highs.'

'So he's one of the bad guys.' Ritchie paused a moment, clearly thinking. 'And he fucked up, so he had to be got rid of. That would explain the professional clean-up crew at his flat. Maybe the blisters on his lips, too.'

'Blisters?' Stringer asked.

'Not important now. Something more up Tony McLean's alley than mine. Dammit, where is he?' Ritchie picked up one of the sheets of paper and stared at it with unseeing eyes. Janie knew how she felt, but something on the back of the sheet caught her attention.

'Is that Sophie Dornan's records?' She reached for the paper, having to tug slightly to get the DCI to let go. Turning it swiftly over revealed the young woman's angry face, and when she turned it back again she was able to read the full paragraph that she'd noticed.

'Seems that Sophie spent a while doing job experience work down in the Hermitage.' Janie flicked through the other pages until she found Daniel Ferguson's records, scanned the columns on both sides until she found his work placements. 'Too much to hope this one had been out at the building site in Straiton. I guess someone might've recognised him if he had been.' She paused, running her finger over the small print. 'He was on the Ladies' Garden refurbishment team too, though. They must have known each other.'

56

The gates to the Straiton housing development were closed as Janie drove silently past, no sign of activity within. She made a mental note to call Johnny Wendle and check he was OK. Not that she was interested in forming any kind of relationship with him, of course. He wasn't her type, as she kept on telling herself. But he'd been kind, had meant well, and was now in something deeper and nastier than he could have known.

'You know how to get to this place?' she asked as the satnav told them they had reached their destination somewhere around the back of Bilston when clearly they hadn't. The light was fading from the day already, a heavy sky overhead promising rain within the hour.

'Think it's a bit further along here. Should be a driveway on the right.' DC Mitchell peered at a folded OS map she'd brought along. Not one to trust to the digital world, it would seem. Janie drove another couple of hundred yards, pulling in to let an angry white van overtake with a toot of the horn. Then they were at the entrance.

A half-broken sign declared it as Glenside Farm, but the track had been closed off with heavy concrete blocks and high metal hurdles. More-modern signs urged casual trespassers to keep out, and threatened security dogs and CCTV surveillance, none of which she actually believed. Janie parked in a field entrance on the other side of the road before approaching the gateway on foot. Even with the low light, she could see where vehicles had been in and out, and recently. Judging by the width between the tyre tracks, something the size of a Transit van had come this way.

'You're going in, aren't you?' Mitchell said as Janie walked up to the gates, inspected the padlock and chains holding them closed. She'd struggle to climb over, but there was a narrow gap between the hurdles and the prickly hawthorn hedge that she could probably scrape through without coming to too much harm.

'You can stay here if you want,' she said, but the detective constable only grinned.

'And miss out on all the fun?'

The gap was larger than she'd thought, signs of local miscreant youth using it as a regular route evident once they'd pushed through to the other side. Janie took a moment to get her bearings, then headed off towards an old metal-sided barn a hundred metres or so away. Even though she knew the city was close by, the field she walked across felt strangely remote. It put her in mind of family camping holidays in the Highlands more than somewhere within easy walking distance of IKEA.

The shed was perhaps thirty metres long by twenty wide, completely enclosed and with a large roller door at one end. A small door allowing personnel access was not locked. Janie stepped into an inky black, echoing empty space, surprisingly warm compared to outside. She caught a scent on the air that took a moment to register. Lemon toilet blocks, perhaps? And overtones of exhaust fumes. That vaguely nitrous oxide smell you got from the newest diesels with their catalytic converters and chemical additives.

There was a modern light switch panel beside the door, but

she used her torch to look around as best she could. Overhead, striplights hung from an insulated roof, and the internal walls had been lined, much more modern than the corrugated iron on the outside.

'Tidy,' Mitchell said. 'Surprised it wasn't locked.'

Janie had to agree. She took her torch over to the roller door, playing the light on the smooth concrete floor until she found what she was looking for. Twin lines of faint rubber marked where a van had come in here. Recently, if the smell she'd noticed on entering was any indication.

'Whatever was in here, it's all been cleared out now. Not long ago, either. Could be a coincidence.'

Or they might have been tipped off, she didn't add.

Back outside, the light was fading ever faster, the omnipresent roar of the bypass bouncing off the low cloudbase. Janie looked around at the other farm buildings, seeing a better-tended environment than she'd been expecting. The grass in the fields was short and mostly free of weeds, the fences well maintained, not at all like the rotting fenceposts and rusted barbed wire she'd seen on many working farms. Even the tracks leading to the buildings were in good order, not a pothole to be seen in the rough chipping surface. The only place where the order broke down was the old farmhouse right at the centre of it.

Surrounded by yet more of the high metal fencing, adorned with more warning signs than strictly necessary, the old building gave off enough of an air of foreboding to deter all but the most determined trespasser. Janie could feel her heart hammering in her chest as she approached it, as if this was some scene from a horror movie and not real life at all. True, a man had died here, burned to death as he lay asleep in his armchair if the reports were to be believed. But that had been decades ago, and, besides, Janie didn't believe in ghosts.

'What is it about this place?' Mitchell asked, and Janie almost jumped out of her skin. She'd been so caught up in her thoughts she'd almost completely forgotten about her companion.

'I don't know, but it fair creeps me out.'

'You reckon we should have a closer look? Since we're here?'

Janie didn't want to, and yet even as she had the thought she realised how irrational it was. The whole point of coming out here had been to see the farm, and the farmhouse in particular.

'Aye. Let's be careful though. No idea how unsafe it might be.'

Far safer than it looked from a distance, Janie discovered as they slipped through a gap in the fence where it hadn't been properly pulled back over the old driveway to the front door. The roof appeared to have collapsed, blackened beams sticking out at odd angles and some of the slates still attached to sarking boards, but there was no broken glass around the empty windows, no front door, and inside it was clear that a lot of work had gone into cleaning up and making the structure safe. Janie took her torch out again, the last of the late-afternoon light struggling to make it through the clouds, let alone the mature trees that surrounded the building like skeletal guards.

'You'd think there'd be a few empty tinnies, some dog-ends, maybe discarded condoms, wouldn't you?' She played the light around a space that looked more like the inside of a church than a house. 'Place like this so close to so many people? I'd have thought they'd no' be able to keep the kids out.'

'It's weird, right enough.' Mitchell stood in the doorway, her earlier enthusiasm apparently evaporated. Janie, on the other hand, found her initial fear had gone and now she had a sense that there was something important here she needed to find.

It hadn't been a big farmhouse to start with, and the lack of internal walls or roof only made it seem smaller. Janie walked to one end, where an old fireplace sat in the gable wall, and as she went her footsteps sounded hollow despite the flagstone floor.

'I think there must be a basement here.' She raised her boot and brought it down hard, listening for the echo. 'See if you can find a way in.'

Janie turned a slow circle, taking in what remained of the building, once again struck by how clean and tidy it was.

'What about this?' Cass Mitchell's voice came from over by the front door, where the remains of a stone staircase climbed up to a first floor that was no longer there. Tucked in underneath it was a narrow wooden door, painted black so that it looked like a shadow. A simple bolt held it closed, no padlock to keep prying eyes away. Janie could imagine the farm's owner relying on the sense of unease that oozed out of the place doing a far better job than any ironmongery. She reached out, slid the bolt and pulled the door open.

A short flight of steps led down to utter darkness, an odd, slightly sickly smell wafting up as Janie stood at the top. When she played the light of her torch over the floor, she saw smooth grey concrete rather than the hard-packed earth she might have expected. If she'd expected a basement at all.

'You think we should call this in?' Mitchell asked.

'Cass, we're no' even supposed to be here. An' besides, there's no law says you can't have a basement, right? It's what you do with it that matters.'

'You're going down there, aren't you. I've seen this movie, Janie.'

'Just a wee look. I'll no go further than the bottom of the steps. You stay up here in case that door wants to shut itself on me, aye?'

Mitchell looked unhappy about it, but nodded her agreement. Janie kept the torch ahead of her as she descended carefully into the basement, straining her ears for any sound that might warn of danger. None came, and soon enough she was in a small room that extended under the centre of the house. Maybe three metres square, and just high enough that she could stand without braining herself on the hefty beams that held up the floor above. There was no obvious light, and no switch either.

Crouching down, she brushed the floor with the tips of her fingers, then rubbed them together to feel for dust. The concrete surface was smooth and almost surgically clean. Shining her torchlight on the walls she saw that they were smooth too, some kind of shiny polished plaster. What kind of use could a room like this be put to? It had clearly been built after the farmhouse had burned down.

'Everything OK?' Mitchell's voice echoed from above.

'Aye. It's fine. Weird, but fine.' Janie stepped further into the room, and caught that strange scent again. Almost as if it was a memory of lemon rather than lemon itself. And something else she couldn't quite put her finger on. A feeling of sickness, but not so much fever as injury. Whatever it was, it sent a shudder through her. She was about to turn, leave and never come back, when she caught a glimpse of something in the shadows where the walls intersected with the floor in the far corner. A black mark that didn't move with the torch light.

Crossing to it, she found a small square drain with a grille over the top. It made sense, keeping a room this clean would mean washing it down, and the water had to go somewhere. Shining her torch at the grille, something glinted behind it. For a moment she thought it might just be the reflection of water in a U-bend, but it didn't look quite right.

Kneeling down, Janie stuck her fingers in the grille and pulled, surprised at how easily it came up. Beneath it, the object she'd seen gleamed in the projected light of her torch. Belatedly perhaps, she shoved the torch in her mouth and fished in her pockets for a pair of latex gloves before shoving her hand in the drain to fetch out her prize. Holding it up, she played the torch on the metal case and leather strap of a man's wristwatch. A very familiar man's wristwatch. She'd seen the man glance at it enough times to recognise that.

'Oh fuck.'

57

'You absolutely sure it's the detective inspector's?'

Sat beside her in the passenger seat of the Nissan Leaf, DC Mitchell stared at the wristwatch in its clear plastic evidence bag as Janie drove as swiftly as she could back towards the city. She'd thought about calling in the find to Control, getting a full forensics team out to the farmhouse. But then she'd have to explain what she and Mitchell had been doing out there in the first place. The detective constable's question was the other reason why she'd held off. Sure, it looked like DI McLean's watch, but could she be a hundred per cent sure?

'It has to be,' she said as much to reassure herself as in answer. 'Shame it hasn't got anything useful on it like an inscription, mind you. It's still running, right?'

Mitchell held the bag up again, then checked her own watch. 'Yes. Pretty much accurate, too.'

Janie glanced at the clock on the dashboard, even though the slow-moving traffic on the approach to the bypass told her it was rush hour. 'I don't suppose you know if it's one of those watches needs winding up every day. That'd give us some idea of how long it's been there.'

'Couldn't say. Sorry.' Mitchell put the evidence bag down in the space between the seats and took out her phone. 'I can look it up, but might be easier to ask an expert. If you know anyone.'

Janie didn't, but as she glanced over to tell the detective constable as much, she saw the building site slide past. Through the locked secondary gate, where Toby the spaniel and Constable Brewster had met her the day before, she got a good look at the unfinished plot and the mound of earth beside the pit they'd dug Daniel Ferguson out of.

'Erm, traffic,' Mitchell shouted, and Janie slammed on the brakes to avoid rear-ending the car in front, which had come to a halt.

'Sorry. Distracted.' She looked forward for a moment, seeing twin lines of cars and the occasional bus all the way to the Loanhead roundabout. Brilliant. It gave her time to look back at the house plot again, the thought that had almost caused an accident finally beginning to form itself into something coherent. If coherent was the right word.

'Did anyone get around to revisiting the Leith kirkyard site? You know, where they found those ancient bones underneath the new tramlines?'

Mitchell looked at her like she was mad for a moment. 'Aye, Jessica and Lofty went over this afternoon. Hole's still there, but they're getting ready to fill it back in. Site manager said there was going to be a big concrete pour tomorrow, I think. Pressure from the bean counters to get on with the job. Something about hoping the rain kept off.'

As if in ironic answer, a spatter of drops began to smear the windscreen.

It was fully dark and the rain had turned from a drizzle into a steady downpour by the time they arrived back at the station. Janie considered not bothering to plug the car into the charge point, given the inevitable soaking she'd get doing so, but in the end figured a bit of dampness was worth it if it meant she could use the car later. And she was fairly certain she was going to need it again soon.

Inside, she sent DC Mitchell off to begin organising a warrant for searching the farmhouse and buildings, even though she was fairly sure they'd not find anything incriminating there. Then she took herself down to the basement and the Cold Case Unit, wondering how she was going to frame the question she needed an answer to.

As luck would have it, Grumpy Bob was still in. As was ex-Detective Superintendent Duguid. Dagwood, the other plain clothes and most of uniform had called him, she'd heard. Nobody had much liked working under him, although he got results. Apparently he'd mellowed in retirement, but Janie was still wary of him. Possibly because he reminded her of one of her great-uncles, a man with a fearsome and unpredictable temper when drunk.

Grumpy Bob looked up as she entered the room, peering at her over his half-moon spectacles like a history teacher.

'Janie. This is becoming a bit of habit, is it not? You looking for a transfer to the ghost squad?'

'Is that what you're calling yourselves now?' Janie felt a chill go down her back at the words, or maybe the temperature in the basement. She walked up to his desk, pulled the evidence bag from her pocket as she did so, and laid it down in front of him. 'Recognise that?'

Grumpy Bob picked up the bag, took one close look and almost dropped it. 'Where'd you get this? It's Tony's.'

'That's what I thought. Only I needed to be sure. It was hidden, a clue to where he'd been held captive, I reckon. Cass . . . DC Mitchell's sorting out a proper search there, but I think he's been moved on. He must have left that because there was nothing else he could think of.'

'Back up a bit, Detective Sergeant.' Without her noticing,

Duguid had moved from his desk and was now standing just behind her. 'Where did you find this?'

'A basement room underneath the remains of Glenside Farm, out by Straiton.' Janie explained as best she could why she'd gone there, surprised that neither retired detective pushed her on that point. 'I have a question,' she said once she had finished and before either of them could get out any of their own.

'Go on,' Duguid said, although Janie had been meaning to ask it of Grumpy Bob.

'A few years back, when you first had a run-in with Mrs Saifre, Jane Louise Dee, whatever her name is. It all got a bit weird at the end, did it not? I know about Sandy Gregg's house, but there was other stuff, right?'

Grumpy Bob took in a deep breath. 'Aye, there was. I don't like to talk about it, but if the inspector hadn't showed up when he did, I'd no' be here talking to you.'

'And he did something to help DCI Ritchie too, didn't he. Something they don't teach at Tulliallan, right?'

'He went to his local church and persuaded the minister to give him some holy water from the font.'

Everybody turned to see DCI Ritchie in the doorway, except for Grumpy Bob who was facing it anyway.

'He brought it to the hospital and made me drink it. I was that delirious I'd have done anything anyone said, but I remember it well. Don't think I'll ever forget the taste of it. Like the sweetest honey. And it cleared my mind. Before then I was losing it, fraying away, forgetting who I even was.'

Ritchie walked up to the desk as she spoke, picked up the evidence bag and looked briefly at the watch.

'Cass told me what you found. I've applied for a warrant to search the farm, but from what I've heard, they've taken him somewhere else already. You have an idea, I think?'

Janie looked at the three of them in turn, aware that she was both the youngest and the most junior officer in the room. And yet it fell to her to make the illogical leap.

'I do, aye. And I don't think you're going to like it much. But I need to speak to Angus Cadwallader and Professor Turner first.'

As they approached the end of Constitution Street, Janie began to wonder if she wasn't going completely mad. The rain had eased to a damp mist, the low clouds orange overhead, and everything seemed exactly as she would have expected it to look on a typical midweek evening. People hurried along the pavements, some with umbrellas, some hunched into their coats against the wet. Cars hissed past, their tyres sending plumes of spray to join with the light haar wafting in from the Forth.

'I've put a call in to the construction company, but nobody's answering. Guess it's past knocking-off time.'

DC Mitchell sat in the front passenger seat, her phone in her hand. She'd spent most of the journey with it held to her ear as she either made calls or received them.

'Or they don't want us to tell them to stop what they're doing.'

Glancing in the rear-view mirror, Janie saw Grumpy Bob sprawled out on the back seat like he was some celebrity being chauffeur-driven to his next engagement. She wasn't quite sure why he'd insisted on coming along, but she couldn't deny his company was welcome. And, unlike her and Mitchell, he wasn't exactly putting his career on the line here.

'If they're doing anything at all.' Janie peered through the windscreen as she turned into the street, ignoring the big red 'road closed' sign. The excavation work had spilled out across the road, a plywood-clad barrier about ten feet high keeping the public out.

Grumpy Bob leaned through between the two front seats and

pointed to a space not far from the road end. 'Let's park here, aye? Reckon we'd be better approaching on foot. Even if this car doesn't make much noise.'

Janie did as she was told and the three of them climbed out into cold night air. Almost at the same instant as she gently clunked closed the car door, the street lights flared, then went dark. All around them, the tenement windows went black as well, and overhead the orange glow on the underside of the clouds disappeared as near total darkness swept over the city.

'Power cut?' Mitchell asked, a little unnecessarily.

'A big one, by the look of things.' Grumpy Bob pulled out his phone, tapped the screen, then held it close to his face to see the tiny icons. 'Phones are down too. That doesn't feel right.'

'Where are all the cars?' Janie pointed up the street the way they had come where the road had fallen eerily silent. And now she concentrated, she couldn't hear much noise from the city at all. She'd have expected a few lights to still be on, too. Didn't office blocks have backups? Shops too? And where were all the people coming out to see what was going on, or sticking their heads out of windows to shout at each other?

'Can't even get through on the Airwave,' Mitchell said. She was standing much closer than might normally be thought polite, but Janie wasn't about to complain. Something was very wrong here.

'Keep your wits about you.' Grumpy Bob pointed to a narrow alley that ran up the side of the kirk, presumably coming out on Leith Walk, although it was impossible to see more than a few metres in the dark and the fog. 'I'll go up and round the other side. You two see if this site entrance is open.'

Janie was about to say that splitting up probably wasn't such a good idea, but the old detective sergeant was away before she could get the words out, swallowed up by the unnatural darkness.

The site entrance was nothing more sophisticated than a part of the plywood barrier that had been fitted with hinges so that it could open wide enough for a concrete truck to get in. At first glance, it appeared to be locked up for the night, but when Janie checked more closely, the padlock had only been looped between two links in the chain and not cinched shut. She eased it away from one of the links, trusting the ever-thickening haar to muffle the clinking sound, then gently pushed the wooden panel until there was a gap wide enough for her and Mitchell to squeeze through. Neither of them said a word, understanding on some telepathic level the need for silence.

Directly behind the barrier, a white Transit van had been parked with its rear facing towards the kirkyard. Janie placed a hand lightly on the bonnet, but it was as cold and moist as the air all around them. It was possible this van had come from Glenside Farm, but equally it could have been one of the million or so other Transit vans trundling around the country.

Stepping past it, Janie almost fell into a narrow trench dug parallel to the street outside. Quick as a snake, DC Mitchell grabbed her arm and hauled her back.

'Careful.' Her voice was a low whisper, so close to Janie's ear she could almost feel the detective constable's breath. 'They've taken down all the safety netting. Someone's here, too. I . . . I can sense them.'

Janie wasn't quite sure what to make of that, but as her heart stopped thumping quite so loudly in her chest, so she began to sense something too. It wasn't a noise, exactly. Or if it was a noise it was such a deep tone that she couldn't make it out, only feel it as an unsettling vibration in her soul. The utter pitch-black darkness didn't help, and her eyes were taking their time to adjust. One reason why she'd almost stepped into the trench.

She put her hand into her pocket, feeling for the small torch she always carried around with her, but something stopped her pulling it out and switching it on. A light would be useful, but it would also be a beacon to anyone lurking in the night. And there was something out there that meant her harm, she was sure of it.

The sound, when it came, was not what she had been expecting at all. A soft *shoof* noise far closer than Janie liked, followed by an oddly hollow drumming. A pause, then she heard the sound of a voice, too quiet to make out words but intoning something nonetheless. It put her in mind of those monks and their chanting, only this was no praise to God she was hearing.

Another soft *shoof*, followed by yet more of that hollow drumming sound, and it all suddenly clicked in her mind.

'They're burying something,' she whispered to Mitchell. 'Burying someone.' That, after all, was what had given her the idea to come here in the first place.

'What are we going to do?' Mitchell asked, but Janie had already made up her mind. Standing up tall, she stepped carefully over the narrow trench she'd almost fallen into, pulled her torch out, pointed it in the direction of the noises and switched it on.

'This is the police. Put your weapons down. You're all under arrest.'

The torch light fell on a figure dressed in a long, black robe, a cowl drawn over its head. Caught frozen in the beam, it held a shovel in one pale hand, the other raised with fingers splayed as if the light from Janie's tiny pen torch hurt its eyes.

Then a voice boomed from the darkness in foghorn words so loud they felt like punches, no language she had ever heard before. And all hell broke loose.

58

Janie found herself lying on her back without quite knowing
how she'd got there. Somehow she'd managed to keep hold of
her torch, but the light shone only on a mound of damp earth.
Her head was ringing, as if she'd been punched in the face, or a
gun had gone off nearby. Had she been shot? What about DC
Mitchell?

'Cass?'

She rolled onto her side, head clearing enough to hear the
sound of a fight off to one side. She swung the torch around,
catching a glimpse of Mitchell and a cloaked figure. As she
watched, the figure swung a spade around as a weapon. Mitchell
swerved to avoid it, then stepped in as the figure overbalanced.
The grunt it let out as the detective constable punched into the
throat area exactly how you're taught not to at Police Training
College suggested the cloaked figure was a man. He went down
hard, gasping for air as Janie scrambled to her feet.

'Look out!'

The warning was all she could manage, and it was almost
enough. Another cloaked figure emerged from the darkness,
swinging the spade its colleague had dropped. Mitchell ducked,
but the blade clipped the side of her head and she fell backwards,
dazed. Janie ran without thinking and slammed bodily into the

figure before it could bring the spade around for a killing blow. They both fell, but Janie was on top, one hand on the spade, the other still clutching her torch. Another man, by the shape and size of his hands, the air whooshed out of him as he hit the ground. There was a dull clunk of skull on gravestone and then he fell limp.

Before she could even take a breath, bright pain flared in Janie's scalp as someone grabbed her hair and pulled her off the unconscious man. She twisted round, ignoring the agony and tried to land a blow on her attacker, but before she could even steady herself another hand had grabbed the front of her coat. At least they let go of her hair at the same time, but Janie tensed for the punch that should surely be coming. In the near total darkness she could just about make out the shape of yet another cloaked and hooded figure, and was it her imagination or were there two circles of darkest red glowing in the depths of that cowl, like coals beginning to cool at the edge of the fire?

Words erupted from the darkness where there should have been a face. Janie couldn't understand them, but they battered against her senses like a hurricane wind, scorched her flesh so that it felt like her cheeks were blistering. She tried to fight her way free, but whoever it was underneath that cloak and cowl, they were strong. Janie felt herself lifted from the ground, feet dangling as she was swung around towards the pit. She smashed her hand, still clutching the torch like the most ineffectual of clubs, against the fist that had grabbed the front of her coat into a tight bunch. Might as well headbutt a mountain for all the good it did.

Her collar pulled tight around her neck, she struggled to breathe. Her head was starting to swim from lack of air and whatever it was her attacker was doing to make those alien words so loud. And then she felt the buzz of her phone in her pocket. Working again. A text come through. The arm holding her aloft sagged a little, so that she felt her feet brush against the ground. Light flickered in her peripheral vision, and at first Janie thought she was imagining it, the last of the oxygen gone from her brain. But, no, she really could see more as the power cut ended and the city began to come alive.

Another buzz, another text. The figure in the hooded cape released its hold and Janie staggered backwards, teetering on the edge of the pit. Those words that had lanced through her brain now sounded like gibberish, all the power they had contained vanished away.

'What . . . ? What have you done?'

Janie understood that, same as she understood the threat of the knife that had appeared in the caped figure's hand. A part of her understood that it was a woman's voice that had spoken, a familiar one at that. Most of her was too focused on the blade and the horrible knowledge that she had no way to escape it. Her attacker raised her arm, ready to strike, her face still shadowed by the hood, eyes still gleaming that odd, dull red.

'You will die for this. You will all –'

The words were cut off by a loud clanging noise. The knife fell away from lifeless fingers to clatter on the ground, and the cloaked woman crumpled after it. Behind where she had been standing, Janie saw the grinning face of Grumpy Bob, a spade clasped in both hands.

'Thought we'd probably heard enough from her.'

She couldn't do anything but stand and breathe heavily for a long while. Her collar was still rucked tight around her neck, and she had to pull quite hard to loosen it. All around, the sounds of the city began to filter back into the kirkyard, along with the lights coming on in windows and along the street. Janie stared down at the cloaked figure who had almost killed her. Lying at her feet, the figure's cowl had fallen away to reveal a pale face surrounded by dark hair. Janie picked up her torch from where she'd dropped it in the fight, shook it until it came back on and played the light over the still body.

'Thought it sounded like a woman,' Grumpy Bob said. 'Anyone you know?'

Janie squinted, then crouched and flicked a strand of hair out of the way so that she could get a better look. A thin trickle of blood was oozing from the woman's temple where Grumpy Bob had hit her with the spade, but she was easy enough to recognise.

'Susan Llewellyn. She's one of the top executives of the Dee Foundation. Maybe the senior director? Something like that anyway.'

'What the hell's she doing here? And these others.' DC Mitchell staggered up, holding one hand to the side of her face. Janie hoped she was going to be OK, but at least she was standing.

'Well they've all got spades, see?' She moved the torch around again, picking out the four unconscious bodies. At least she hoped they were unconscious, otherwise there'd be a mountain of paperwork.

'Is that the pit where they found the bones?' Mitchell pointed to the hole that Janie had almost been thrown into. How had such a slight woman had so much strength? She moved over towards the edge, shining the light into the depths. Soft earth lay at the bottom, claggy with the recent rain, and as her eyes adjusted to the scene, she thought she saw something else too. Something that reminded her of the recent exhumations she'd witnessed, and the unacknowledged reason she'd come here in the first place.

'Quick, Bob. Lower me down. Cass, take the torch.' Janie held one hand out to the detective sergeant, while passing the torch over with the other. To his credit, Grumpy Bob didn't ask why, just knelt in the dirt at the top of the pit, grasping Janie's wrist firmly so that she could in turn grip his. Lit by the slightly wavering and rapidly fading torch, she half slid, half clambered down until she could feel her feet begin to sink into the soft loam.

'Going to have to let go,' she said as she released Grumpy Bob's wrist. 'Maybe see if you can find a ladder or a rope?'

Something moved as Grumpy Bob let go and Janie trusted her full weight to the soil. And was that a noise? Like a groan?

'Shine the torch here, Cass.' She shouted the instruction, pointing her hand at the ground a few feet ahead of her. The light barely made a difference down here, batteries no doubt needing a recharge after all the recent use she'd put them to. Muttering under her breath about technology being useless, she fished around in her pocket for her phone. The screen lit up with the motion, telling her that two texts had come in. Swiping the messages away, Janie brought up the torch function. It wasn't much better, as if the air down here sucked in the light before it could reach anything. Or maybe it was the soil absorbing everything that came into contact with it, rain, sound, light.

Shifting her weight to get a better balance on the loose surface, she stepped as carefully as she could to where she thought she'd seen something from up above. And there it was again. A sliver of something pale against the dark earth, resolving itself into what had to be a nose.

Janie wedged her feet either side of the pit, trying hard not to kneel on anything in the middle as she reached out with her free hand and began to gently scoop away the soil. She knew what she was going to find, but even so it was a shock as the face began to appear. Bruised, eyes swollen shut and caked in dirt, it was still unmistakably Detective Inspector McLean.

59

The pain woke him, a pounding in his head that matched the heavy rhythm of his heartbeat. His throat was dry and itchy and his whole body ached as if he'd been trampled by a herd of stampeding cows. At least he could move, a little. Dimly he recalled a time when he couldn't, when everything was locked tight against his command and he was powerless in his own body. Laid out in damp soil, the first few clods of it thumping onto his chest. A spray of it across his face, like being water-boarded with mud.

Gasping, McLean opened his eyes and tried to sit up, finding that he wasn't perhaps so free to move as he'd thought. The ache in his head grew into a hot jab of fire that brought a wave of nausea so intense he thought he might pass out again.

'Hey, take it slowly. You've been through the wars.'

He knew that voice, although it took his addled brain too long to find the name that went with it. Slowly, he tilted his head in the direction from which it had come, seeing the tired face of Dr Caroline Wheeler looking down at him.

'Wh—' was all he managed to squeeze out, and even he wasn't sure what actual question he'd hoped to ask. The dryness in his throat was like the finest of dust, tickling everything so that he coughed. And once he started he couldn't stop for a long while.

'Here. Sip this.'

He felt a straw between his lips, the sweetest tasting water dribbling slowly into his mouth. Swallowing hurt almost as badly as trying to talk, but after a couple of goes it started to get easier.

'You're lucky to be alive, Tony McLean. You know that?' Dr Wheeler took the straw away. 'Still not sure what drug they put in you. Something curare-based, I suspect. You were completely catatonic. Barely breathing.'

'I . . .' He tried to move, and this time had a little more success until another, different, bright pain erupted in his left arm. Looking down he almost didn't recognise the swollen and purple hand poking out of the end of a tight wrap of bandages.

'A nasty fracture that should have been treated straight away. We've done what we can with it. Well, I say we, but that was mostly my colleague Dr Chambers. My area of expertise is more brains than bones.'

McLean let his head sink back into the pillow, stared up at the ceiling and tried to remember . . . anything. There was a big black hole that would take time to fill, he knew, but there was one important thing he had to ask.

'Emma?'

The tiniest flicker of something in her eyes, almost not there, but McLean saw it despite his throbbing head and bone-deep weariness. Maybe because of it.

'She's sleeping.' Dr Wheeler looked like she'd been going to leave it at that, then saw that it wouldn't be enough for him. How well she knew him. 'By which I mean she's not in a coma any more. She was awake for a while yesterday, but not totally lucid.'

'That's better than I could have hoped for.' McLean whispered the words, even as he knew there was something the doctor was holding back.

'She needs the rest, and so do you, Tony. I've no doubt

your colleagues will be anxious to speak to you soon. I'll let them know you're awake, but that's all. No debriefs until the morning.'

'Morning?' McLean started to lift his wrist, the reflex action of a lifetime. Pain stopped him, but also a bright memory. Alone in a dark place, injured, desperate. Finding a grille in the floor and hiding his watch there in the mad hope that someone might find him, might rescue him. It was madness, of course. But then he'd not been in his right mind. And someone had rescued him, in the end. 'What time is it?'

'It's late, Tony. That's all you need to know. Get some sleep, get yourself better. Build up your strength. God only knows you're going to need it in the coming days.'

He must have slept, because the artificial light was gone, replaced by more natural daylight filtering in from a window to one side of the bed. McLean felt stronger, too, the jackhammer pounding of his headache reduced to a background throb that only flared up if he moved his head too quickly. Also Dr Wheeler appeared to have morphed into Detective Sergeant Harrison, which was another clue.

'Tried to visit earlier, but that doctor's not to be messed with. How're you feeling, sir?'

'Like someone who doesn't deserve the respect that title implies, Janie.' McLean struggled until he was a little more upright, ignoring the pain in his head. The swelling in his hand had gone down a lot, but it was still tender.

'I've got your watch, if you're worrying about it. Might be a while before you can wear it again, mind.'

'My watch?' McLean looked down at his arm again, felt the shock of it breaking as he tumbled down the steep slope of the Hermitage in the dead of night. What a stupid thing to do.

'Aye. Some daftie shoved it in a drain in a hidden basement.

Just as well he did, otherwise we'd've had no idea he'd been there.'

Slowly, piece by piece, the story came out as Harrison filled him in on what had happened since he disappeared. McLean kept his own explanations to a minimum, partly because his throat hurt to talk for more than a few words at a time, partly because he couldn't yet remember all of the details. Mostly because thinking about it all brought back the feeling of earth hitting his chest, spattering over his face, blocking his mouth and covering his eyes while he could only lie there paralysed.

'How did you know?' he asked eventually. Judging by the look on Harrison's face, she understood the question well enough but probably didn't have an answer that made sense to her. Not in any sane way, at least.

'We found bodies buried at the building site in Straiton and in the Ladies' Garden in the Hermitage. They'd only been in the ground a matter of hours, poor sods. But there was something Madame Rose said, about the old bones being there for a reason. Made me think maybe someone was deliberately uncovering them so they could put other bones in their place. And if that was the case then where else had old bones been dug up recently? And who else might they try to bury?'

'So how did you find my little basement prison?' McLean saw it more clearly now. He'd woken in the dark, arm broken, no idea where he was. They'd emptied his pockets, whoever had put him there, but they'd left him his watch. The pain of getting it off his swollen wrist had been excruciating, and he must have been delirious when he'd hidden it in the drain, the only feature of the room. 'Where was it?'

'Glenside Farm, out by the Straiton building site. Manda's got a whole team going over that place, digging up all sorts of interesting secrets. Susan – DC Brewster from the dog team – She's got her wee spaniel Toby working overtime on the place.

The Dee Foundation has some serious questions to answer about what it's been doing there.'

'The Dee Foundation?' Another memory swam up into McLean's mind. A presence in the darkness, gloating, triumphant. 'What's it got to do with them?'

'The farm belongs to Saifre, but her precious charity used some of the barns and fields for their youth-training boot camps. Apparently they've been doing it for years, but stopped about six months ago after some incident nobody wants to talk about. Seems odd that's the same time Rory Devlin went off the rails and Fiona McLeod got the sack, right?'

McLean's head whirled as he tried to make sense of it all. Too many pieces to fit together, his brain too damaged by whatever they'd drugged him with. 'How does that even work? How could they get away with it for so long?'

'I guess they'll have to ask Ms Llewellyn that. If they get the chance. She's not woken up since Grumpy Bob whacked her with a shovel, and he swears he didn't give her more than a light tap.'

'Llewellyn?' McLean struggled for a moment, a memory coming to him. A visitor in the darkened basement. A woman, at least in form, but not the director of the charity. 'Not Mrs Saifre then?'

Harrison laughed, a bright little noise just the right side of hysteria. 'No' a chance, sir. Even if we could find anything to implicate her, you think the chief super'd let us arrest her new girlfriend? No, that one's far too canny to let herself get caught. Always little people to take the fall for her, aye?'

McLean nodded, then wished he hadn't as a spike of pain lanced behind his eyes.

'Shit's going to hit the fan all the same,' Harrison continued. 'It's like there was a spell stopping everyone from seeing what the Dee Foundation was up to, and now it's been broken. All sorts of stuff coming out.'

McLean leaned his head back into the pillow and let his eyes find their focus on the ceiling tiles. Like a spell had been broken. Try as he might, he couldn't think of any better way to sum it all up.

He probably should have stayed in his nice, comfortable room for longer, but McLean wasn't overly fond of hospitals. He'd spent far too much of his time in them already, and since all he had to worry about was a broken arm and some bruises, he reckoned the nurses would be better employed looking after people in greater need than him. Once Harrison had gone, and he'd stared at the ceiling long enough for the thoughts in his head to stop tumbling and start coming together, he'd known it was time to go.

Dressing had been difficult, not least because he'd been stark naked when buried in the old Leith kirkyard. Apparently they'd found his clothes in the Transit van parked at the old kirkyard, but they'd been taken away for forensic examination and were unlikely to be worth having back. The clothes the detective sergeant had left him wouldn't have been his first choice, but a broken arm and useless hand somewhat limited his options. He could have called for a nurse to help him dress, he supposed. Better to get the hang of doing it alone though; he couldn't rely on others for everything.

It felt good to be walking again, even if his muscles were cramped and sore, his arm awkward in its sling, his head light and sense of balance a little off-kilter. He was weaker than he'd realised though, slightly out of breath by the time he made it to the neurology department. Nurse Robertson greeted him with her customary cheerful smile and then led him past the ward to a lighter, open plan area further along the corridor.

'Emma. You've a visitor.' The nurse stepped aside and let McLean past so that he could see her.

She was awake, that was the main thing. He hadn't realised until that moment how much he'd feared she might never come back. She sat in a wheelchair beside a window looking out onto the trees at the back of the building, right hand on the windowsill, left arm draped across her lap. It stayed there, unmoving, as she turned very slowly to face him.

McLean had known a few stroke victims over the years. Some showed barely any signs, others were almost unrecognisable from their earlier selves. Emma fell somewhere between the two extremes. Her eyelid and mouth drooped slightly on the left side, as if she were made of wax and had been stood too close to the fire. When she saw him, the expression on the right side of her face flickered through surprise to suspicion and settled on worry, but the left side remained still. She reached out her right hand, and he went over, clasping it in his own. He could see her gaze flick to the cast, the sling. She let go, reaching up with unsteady fingers to gently touch the bruises on his face.

'I'm fine. Just a bad fall. It'll mend soon enough.'

A scowl of concentration marred her forehead for a while, and then Emma managed to force out what sounded like two words.

'Oh . . . knee.'

He took her hand in his again, squeezed it gently and tried his best to smile. Emma's stare back at him was defiant, and he knew she was still in there, still fighting. The stroke might have robbed her of speech, but she could learn. She would learn, he was sure of it. And she'd walk again, too, if he was any judge of her character. And if she wasn't giving up, then he'd do everything he could to help her. She deserved nothing less.

60

They made an odd spectacle, this little group of people. McLean couldn't call them a funeral cortège, or even celebrants. He wasn't really sure what they were, if he was being honest with himself. Witnesses, maybe.

Madame Rose stood centre stage, of course, but he noticed that it was Detective Sergeant Harrison who was closest to her. Grumpy Bob had come along, probably to see what all the fuss was about and maybe hopeful for some celebratory drink afterwards, even if it was before six in the morning. Hattie Turner was there, with her wife, Meghan, and so was a young woman it took McLean a while to recognise as Maggie Devlin. Detective Constable Mitchell stood a few paces back, DC Stringer at her side in a manner that suggested conversations with their detective sergeant needed to be had, a shuffling of teams on the cards. Not his problem right now.

There were no words said, only a moment's silence before Harrison took a canvas sack that Professor Turner had given her and climbed down the ladder into the pit. McLean shuddered thinking about it, his memories of the night he'd almost been buried alive becoming more vivid with each passing day. He woke most mornings in a cold sweat, heart racing, and he knew it would be a long time before he came to terms with what had happened to him. How close he had come to the most horrific of deaths.

In what seemed mere moments after she had descended the ladder, Harrison reappeared without the sack. Madame Rose helped her out, and then Grumpy Bob pulled up the ladder. Another moment, and both he and DC Stringer had taken up spades. As they bit into the pile of earth heaped up beside the pit and began shovelling loads over the ancient bones, McLean found he couldn't take the noise and the memories it brought. He turned his back and walked away.

'Thank you for coming, Tony. I know it must be hard, after what happened to you here.'

Somehow Madame Rose was at his side by the time he reached the plywood barrier that surrounded the site. McLean turned to face her, seeing the rest of their odd little party still standing around the pit. Harrison had taken up a spade too, he noticed.

'I'll be OK.' He shook his head as he said it, knowing full well what that meant. 'It's just still a bit overwhelming. What they tried to do to me. What they actually did to those two poor kids. More, if what I'm hearing about the youth-training camps is true. That's some can of worms there.'

'Interesting turn of phrase.' Madame Rose's mouth twisted at the corners in an inappropriate grin, and McLean couldn't help himself from smiling too. Humour, however dark, was often the best way to deal with these things.

'Is this enough?' he asked, nodding his head in the direction of the pit.

'It's a start. And a stop to what that evil woman was trying to do.' Madame Rose paused a moment, inscrutable thoughts creasing her forehead. 'I know you don't believe in all this stuff, Tony. So I'm truly grateful to you for indulging me.'

'Let's just say being buried alive changes your perspective on things.' McLean massaged his left hand with his right, easing away the dull ache that was his constant companion, the cast on his arm itchy, the sling around his neck an awkward weight. 'You know me, Rose. I'm not one for blind faith, unquestioning belief. But I can't deny the evidence of my own eyes, and I'd be a fool if I ignored the fact that other people do believe. And they believe in all manner of stupid, mad and evil things. Do all manner of stupid, mad and evil things because of their beliefs.'

He took one more look at the group, seemingly done with their work now. Soon the tramline builders would arrive and finish the job. Concrete would be poured and tracks laid, and Izabell Kerr would be back where she belonged, her bones keeping watch over the city for ever more. Madness, he knew. But then was it any worse than the madness that had almost seen him in her place?

'They all gave themselves willingly, Tony,' Madame Rose said, perhaps mistaking his backward glance for reproach. 'Izabell and Emily and all the others. The bones in the Ladies' Garden? That is your great-great-grandmother, Margaret Constance McLean. She was almost eighty when she knew her time was up. Quite a formidable woman in her prime.'

'I really don't need to know, Rose. Bad enough young Janie there persuaded Angus and Hattie to break the law and put the bones back where they'd come from. And this . . .' He waved his one good arm at the mismatched group of people making their way over, shook his head even though he knew he was going to accept it, compartmentalise it, move on.

Like he always did.

'Where the hell have you been all morning? I've been trying to contact you since eight.'

He hadn't really expected much, but McLean had hoped maybe a 'Good to see you back, Tony,' or even a 'Shouldn't you be at home on leave?' from the chief superintendent. He'd only come to the station to return the paperwork he'd taken home that fateful evening almost a month ago now. That and to see the chief superintendent about something that had been weighing on his mind.

'I'm technically not back at work for another two weeks, ma'am.' He raised his left arm, still in a sling. 'Doctor's not given me the all-clear on this yet. Think you of all people would appreciate the importance of that.'

Elmwood narrowed her eyes at him suspiciously. She hadn't stood up when he'd stepped into her office, and she looked far more haggard than he remembered from the last time they'd spoken. Her cheekbones were more prominent, the skin stretched shiny over them by whatever expensive cosmetic surgery she'd undergone to hide her burn scars. It shouldn't have been all that surprising, given the way the news had unfolded since the night a massive solar flare had knocked out the power along almost the entire east coast of Scotland. At least, that was the explanation electricity companies had come up with, and the spectacular auroras that had graced the night sky for a week afterwards seemed to back it up. McLean had missed them all, of course. Cooped up in hospital and then at home getting it ready for Emma's return.

'I suppose you're pleased with yourself.' Elmwood sounded very much like a woman who's spent a month fighting for her job in the light of uncomfortable allegations. McLean was surprised she'd not been quietly pensioned off already. Perhaps the high heidyins were looking for a scapegoat.

'Ma'am?' he asked, unable to help himself, knowing how much the title annoyed her.

'You've never been enthusiastic about any of my ideas to reform this backwater operation, but you really hated Project Tantalus, didn't you. Just couldn't bear the idea of working with

Jane Louise. So you went out and destroyed one of the best things happening to this city simply to prove a point, right?'

From anyone else, in any other circumstances, McLean might have felt the need to count a silent ten against the rising anger at such an accusation. Instead, he found himself strangely unmoved by Elmwood's words. Perhaps because they were so woefully misguided. Perhaps because they didn't really matter. Not any more.

'I was never a fan of that project, no. Specialist Crime needs to have contacts with the charity sector, it's true. But not formal like you were proposing. That just puts the people who need charity off asking for it. And embedding charity workers in a Major Investigation Team is just daft. We're trained specialists dealing with sensitive information.'

'Always the negative. Never looking for a way to do a thing, only an excuse as to why it can't be done. No wonder policing is so woeful in this city.'

That was unfair, but McLean let it go. Nothing the chief superintendent said really bothered him now.

'It might surprise you to know I take little joy from what's happened,' he said. 'True, I don't like the source of its money, but the Dee Foundation did . . . still does a lot of very good work with people who really need the services they provide. You can't expect me to overlook the fact one of their senior executives has been running some kind of satanic death cult though, can you? Drugging people and burying them alive? Not to mention using their outreach centres to muscle in on the city's drug trade.'

'Nothing's been proven –'

'Spare me the excuses, ma'am. We all know it's true.' McLean took little delight in the way Elmwood recoiled from his words. He'd watched the rapid unravelling of the Dee Foundation's youth-training and community outreach efforts after Jo Dalgliesh had come to visit him and Emma as they convalesced. All he'd given her was a name, but Dalgliesh could rake muck better than anyone. Susan Llewellyn had quite a colourful past, it appeared. Including a couple of years spent in a secure psychiatric hospital after a drug-overdose-induced psychotic episode where she'd claimed to be an emissary of the devil. How apt that Mrs Saifre had found her, taken her under her leathery wing.

'Nothing can be proven, Tony. And you know it.'

That much was true, he had to concede. Llewellyn's previous history meant she could never be charged. She was in Bestingfield now, and likely would never come out again. And, of course, Mrs Saifre had known nothing about her most trusted charity director's extra-curricular activities, thought her acolyte cured of her delusions and thriving in her work with the city's needy poor. She had merely written the cheques, the official statement said. Left the day-to-day running of the foundation to others. And now she'd left the country, fled to the US to lick her wounds, leaving her most recent lover behind to pick up the pieces. McLean had no doubt she'd be back, vengeful as ever. And meanwhile there were endless enquiries as Police Scotland simultaneously patted itself on the back for breaking open such a strange case and cast around to see who within the organisation could take the blame for destroying such a large chunk of the local charity sector. Not Elmwood – at least not yet. And looking at her now, he almost felt sympathy for the chief superintendent.

'I did warn you. About getting close to Jane Louise Dee. If you sup with the Devil you need to use a long spoon. Not climb into bed with her.'

Elmwood flinched at the accusation as if she'd been slapped, some rare colour coming to her cheeks as she fought down the anger. McLean couldn't begin to imagine what she must be going through, knowing what she must surely have worked out for herself by now. What must it be like, fighting that constant battle between the part of your soul you'd sold and the part you'd kept?

When she finally mastered her emotions and spoke, her words were flat and cold.

'Nevertheless, Detective Inspector. There are procedures, and I'm disappointed at how little you or your team seem to feel bound by them. I've asked Kirs – Detective Chief Inspector Ritchie to conduct an in-depth review of the whole fiasco, and there are going to be some long overdue changes in the operation of your Major Investigation Team.'

McLean nodded his understanding, then reached into his pocket and pulled out the sheet of paper that was the real reason he'd come into the station that morning. One-handed, he couldn't easily unfold it, so he simply placed it on Elmwood's desk and slid it towards her. Then he took out his warrant card from the same pocket and placed it alongside the letter.

'You can save everyone a lot of trouble,' he said, then turned and walked out of the room.

61

The pit is deeper than she had imagined, the earth dark and damp. Small roots cling to the sheer sides, a few worms blindly testing the unexpected void. High above, the sky has turned slate grey, and she can hear the wind as it tears at the treetops, whistles between the buildings. It will rain later, she knows with unerring certainty, but she is too tired to care. And, besides, she won't be around to worry about the weather. Not any more.

This wasn't how she imagined the end would come. Although now she thinks about it, she's not sure that she ever gave such things much consideration. Life was for living, so much to do, so little time. And now it has all run out.

She should be scared, here at the end. But instead she feels nothing at all. Not regret, not anger at the hand she has been dealt. If there is anything, it is only a sadness for those few who will miss her, maybe even mourn her. She wouldn't want to be the cause of any unhappiness.

It is dark down here in the earth, shadows growing as the day fades. As she fades with it. She'd expected to be cold, and yet as she lies down she feels nothing but warmth suffusing her, easing the aches and pains as if this were a perfectly run bath, not a grave.

But then this isn't a grave. Not really. She knows that now. She understands so much more of the world than her narrow Christian upbringing could ever have prepared her for. There are truths older than Christ, older than Adam and Eve. Older than God.

At the edge of the pit, she can see them. Her sisters. They glow with an inner fire as they wait patiently for the time to be right. She takes strength from their presence, the vigil they stand over her. Will she see them again, beyond this place and time? She hopes so.

And now the light is fading, her eyes grown cloudy as the sky overhead. Her breathing slows, but she feels no panic, no burning in her chest. She can no longer see, can scarcely hear anything but the slowing beat of her heart. And yet her senses are everywhere, spread out into the land, the hills and glens, rivers, lochs. The city and the endless sweep of the sea. She is the birds soaring overhead, the deer watching nervously from the tree line. She is the trees themselves, ancient and new, and she is the worms burrowing through the dark soil in which her mortal remains will lie for evermore.

With a last, almost inaudible sigh, she lets go of her body and joins with everything. There are others like her, she knows, and they come to greet her, to welcome her into their fold.

And as she drifts away, she feels the first few sprinkles of soil fall onto her cooling flesh, like fresh rain on a summer's day.

Acknowledgements

It never gets any easier, writing acknowledgements for a book. This is my twentieth published novel, and yet I still struggle. Naming and thanking people risks missing someone out by accident and all the terrible social embarrassment that entails.

Having said which, I will do my best. You might have picked this book up because it had my name on the cover, but a large team of professionals has worked on my words to make them better. I am hugely indebted to the team at Wildfire – Alex Clarke, Jack Butler, Serena Arthur, Jo Liddiard, Emily Patience and all the others toiling away to make mine and everyone else's books as good as they can be. A special thank you to Mark Handsley, whose copy-editing skills are always put to the test by my inability to manage timelines.

I doubt any of this would have happened without the earliest intervention of my agent, the indomitable Juliet Mushens. Thank you, Juliet, and thank you too, Liza DeBlock and Kiya Evans. Go Team Mushens!

This is the twelfth Inspector McLean novel, believe it or not, and every single one of them has been narrated by Ian Hanmore. I am a huge fan of audiobooks, and so lucky to have had such a skilled narrator for the whole series so far. I might write the words, but Ian really brings them to life.

I have stolen a fair few people's names over the years, so should probably apologise as much as thank them. Janie Harrison, Kirsty Ritchie, Kenneth Stephen, Stuart MacBride (remember him?), Alan Evans, Alastair Burns, Don Gatford, Susan Brewster, to name just a few. But most of all I want to thank the one who started it all, my long-suffering partner, whose surname I stole for my detective so many years ago. Thank you, Barbara, for that and everything else.

If you loved ALL THAT LIVES why not try
NOWHERE TO RUN, the latest book in James Oswald's
new Constance Fairchild series?

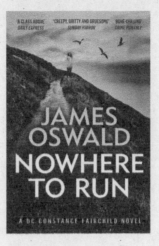

**The gripping new thriller in the brilliant Constance Fairchild
series, from one of Scotland's foremost crime writers.**

On compassionate leave following the death of her mother,
Detective Constable Constance Fairchild thought renting a cottage
near Aberystwyth, Wales would get her far enough from London
to finally relax. But trouble always seems to find Con, and it's not
long before she is cooling off in a police station cell after defending
herself from two would-be rapists.

In custody she meets a young Ukrainian woman, Lila, who confides
in Con that she's been forced by her manipulative boyfriend into
prostitution and running drugs. Fearing for her life, she has run
away from him, only to end up in the cells.

Con offers to help, but when her cottage is ransacked, and Lila
subsequently disappears, she realises she's stumbled into very dangerous
company. International drug smugglers and ruthless people traffickers –
those who will stop at nothing to protect their secrets. Out here at the
end of the line, will Con find that there's nowhere left to run?

Available now

WILDFIRE